THE ULTIMATE FIGHTING MACHINE

From "An Abbreviated History of the Bolo": The direct ancestor of the Bolo was constructed in the late 1990's. This machine, at one hundred fifty tons, was essentially a bigger and better tank; although it was capable of performing crewless patrol duty, it carried a crew of three in battle. The Mark II of 1999 was less dependent on human guidance. With its enhanced on-board fire control and guidance computers it required only one crewman for full battlefield operation.

In a sense, the Mark III of 2020 was a step backward: it required two operators. But the Mark III packed more effective firepower than an infantry battalion of the time, and its durachrome hull could withstand an atomic blast. The first Bolo designed to operate without direct human guidance was the Mark XV. The first self-aware Bolo was the Mark XX.

By the time of the Bolo Mark XXX, human strategic thinking was no longer required.

THE COMPLEAT BOLO

KEITH LAUMER

BAEN
BOOKS

THE COMPLEAT BOLO

Copyright © 1990 by Keith Laumer

"The Night of the Trolls" copyright © 1963 by Galaxy Publishing Corp.
"Courier" (formerly titled "The Frozen Planet") copyright © 1961 by Digest Productions.
"The Last Command" copyright © 1966 by Condé Nast.
"A Relic of War" copyright © 1969 by Condé Nast.
"Combat Unit" copyright © 1960 by Mercury Press.
Rogue Bolo copyright © 1986 by Keith Laumer.

A Baen Books Original

Baen Publishing Enterprises
260 Fifth Avenue
New York, N.Y. 10001

ISBN: 0-671-69879-6

Cover art by Stephen Hickman

First Baen printing, June 1990

Distributed by
SIMON & SCHUSTER
1230 Avenue of the Americas
New York, N.Y. 10020

Printed in the United States of America

TABLE OF CONTENTS

BOLO

THE NIGHT OF THE TROLLS

IT WAS DIFFERENT this time. There was a dry pain in my lungs, and a deep ache in my bones, and a fire in my stomach that made me want to curl into a ball and mew like a kitten. My mouth tasted as though mice had nested in it, and when I took a deep breath wooden knives twisted in my chest.

I made a mental note to tell Mackenzie a few things about his pet controlled-environment tank—just as soon as I got out of it. I squinted at the overface panel: air pressure, temperature, humidity, O-level, blood sugar, pulse, and respiration—all okay. That was something. I flipped the intercom key and said, "Okay, Mackenzie, let's have the story. You've got problems . . ."

I had to stop to cough. The exertion made my temples pound.

"How long have you birds run this damned exercise?" I called. "I feel lousy. What's going on around here?"

No answer.

This was supposed to be the terminal test series. They couldn't all be out having coffee. The equipment had more bugs than a two-dollar hotel room. I slapped the emergency release lever. Mackenzie wouldn't like it, but to hell with it! From the way I felt, I'd been in the tank for a good long stretch this time—maybe a week or two. And I'd told Ginny it would be a three-dayer at the most. Mackenzie was a great technician, but he had no more human emotions than a used-car salesman. This time I'd tell him.

Relays were clicking, equipment was reacting, the tank

3

cover sliding back. I sat up and swung my legs aside, shivering suddenly.

It was cold in the test chamber. I looked around at the dull gray walls, the data recording cabinets, the wooden desk where Mac sat by the hour rerunning test profiles—

That was funny. The tape reels were empty and the red equipment light was off. I stood, feeling dizzy. Where was Mac? Where were Banner and Day and Malloon?

"Hey!" I called. I didn't even get a good echo.

Someone must have pushed the button to start my recovery cycle; where were they hiding now? I took a step, tripped over the cables trailing behind me. I unstrapped and pulled the harness off. The effort left me breathing hard. I opened one of the wall lockers; Banner's pressure suit hung limply from the rack beside a rag-festooned coat hanger. I looked in three more lockers. My clothes were missing—even my bathrobe. I also missed the usual bowl of hot soup, the happy faces of the techs, even Mac's sour puss. It was cold and silent and empty here—more like a morgue than a top-priority research center.

I didn't like it. What the hell was going on?

There was a weather suit in the last locker. I put it on, set the temperature control, palmed the door open, and stepped out into the corridor. There were no lights, except for the dim glow of the emergency route indicators. There was a faint, foul odor in the air.

I heard a dry scuttling, saw a flick of movement. A rat the size of a red squirrel sat up on his haunches and looked at me as if I were something to eat. I made a kicking motion and he ran off, but not very far.

My heart was starting to thump a little harder now. The way it does when you begin to realize that something's wrong—bad wrong.

Upstairs in the Admin Section I called again. The echo was a little better here. I went along the corridor strewn with papers, past the open doors of silent rooms. In the Director's office a blackened wastebasket stood in the center of the rug. The air-conditioner intake above the desk was felted over with matted dust nearly an inch thick. There was no use shouting again.

The place was as empty as a robbed grave—except for the rats.

At the end of the corridor, the inner security door stood open. I went through it and stumbled over something. In the faint light, it took me a moment to realize what it was.

He had been an MP, in steel helmet and boots. There was nothing left but crumbled bone and a few scraps of leather and metal. A .38 revolver lay nearby. I picked it up, checked the cylinder, and tucked it in the thigh pocket of the weather suit. For some reason it made me feel a little better.

I went on along B corridor and found the lift door sealed. The emergency stairs were nearby. I went to them and started the two-hundred-foot climb to the surface.

The heavy steel doors at the tunnel had been blown clear.

I stepped past the charred opening, looked out at a low gray sky burning red in the west. Fifty yards away, the five-thousand-gallon water tank lay in a tangle of rusty steel. What had it been? Sabotage, war, revolution —an accident? And where was everybody?

I rested for a while, then went across the innocent-looking fields to the west, dotted with the dummy buildings that were supposed to make the site look from the air like another stretch of farmland complete with barns, sheds and fences. Beyond the site the town seemed intact: there were lights twinkling here and there, a few smudges of smoke rising. I climbed a heap of rubble for a better view.

Whatever had happened at the site, at least Ginny would be all right—Ginny and Tim. Ginny would be worried sick, after—how long? A month?

Maybe more. There hadn't been much left of that soldier . . .

I twisted to get a view to the south, and felt a hollow sensation in my chest. Four silo doors stood open; the Colossus missiles had hit back—at something. I pulled myself up a foot or two higher for a look at the Primary Site. In the twilight the ground rolled smooth and unbroken across the spot where *Prometheus* lay ready in her underground berth. Down below she'd be safe and sound, maybe. She had been built to stand up to the stresses of a direct extra-solar orbital launch; with any luck, a few near misses wouldn't have damaged her.

My arms were aching from the strain of holding on. I climbed down and sat on the ground to get my breath, watching the cold wind worry the dry stalks of dead brush around the fallen tank.

At home, Ginny would be alone, scared, maybe even in serious difficulty. There was no telling how far municipal services had broken down. But before I headed that way, I had to make a quick check on the ship. *Prometheus* was a dream that I—and a lot of others—had lived with for three years. I had to be sure.

I headed toward the pillbox that housed the tunnel head on the off chance that the car might be there.

It was almost dark and the going was tough; the concrete slabs under the sod were tilted and dislocated. Something had sent a ripple across the ground like a stone tossed into a pond.

I heard a sound and stopped dead. There was a clank and rumble from beyond the discolored walls of the blockhouse a hundred yards away. Rusted metal howled; then something as big as a beached freighter moved into view.

Two dull red beams glowing near the top of the high silhouette swung, flashed crimson, and held on me. A siren went off—an ear-splitting whoop! *whoop!* WHOOP!

It was an unmanned Bolo Mark II Combat Unit on automated sentry duty—and its intruder-sensing circuits were tracking me.

The Bolo pivoted heavily; the *whoop! whoop!* sounded again; the robot watchdog was bellowing the alarm.

I felt sweat pop out on my forehead. Standing up to a Mark II Bolo without an electropass was the rough equivalent of being penned in with an ill-tempered dinosaur. I looked toward the Primary blockhouse: too far. The same went for the perimeter fence. My best bet was back to the tunnel mouth. I turned to sprint for it, hooked a foot on a slab and went down hard . . .

I got up, my head ringing, tasting blood in my mouth. The chipped pavement seemed to rock under me. The

Bolo was coming up fast. Running was no good. I had to have a better idea.

I dropped flat and switched my suit control to maximum insulation.

The silvery surface faded to dull black. A two-foot square of tattered paper fluttered against a projecting edge of concrete; I reached for it, peeled it free, then fumbled with a pocket flap, brought out a permatch, flicked it alight. When the paper was burning well, I tossed it clear. It whirled away a few feet, then caught in a clump of grass.

"Keep moving, damn you!" I whispered. The swearing worked. The gusty wind pushed the paper on. I crawled a few feet and pressed myself into a shallow depression behind the slab. The Bolo churned closer; a loose tread-plate was slapping the earth with a rhythmic thud. The burning paper was fifty feet away now, a twinkle of orange light in the deep twilight.

At twenty yards, looming up like a pagoda, the Bolo halted, sat rumbling and swiveling its rust-streaked turret, looking for the radiating source its I-R had first picked up. The flare of the paper caught its electronic attention. The turret swung, then back. It was puzzled. It whooped again, then reached a decision.

Ports snapped open. A volley of antipersonnel slugs whoofed into the target; the scrap of paper disappeared in a gout of tossed dirt.

I hugged the ground like gold lamé hugs a torch singer's hip, and waited; nothing happened. The Bolo sat, rumbling softly to itself. Then I heard another sound over the murmur of the idling engine, a distant roaring, like a flight of low-level bombers. I raised my head half an inch and took a look. There were lights moving beyond the field—the paired beams of a convoy approaching from the town.

The Bolo stirred, moved heavily forward until it towered over me no more than twenty feet away. I saw gun ports open high on the armored facade—the ones that housed the heavy infinite repeaters. Slim black muzzles slid into view, hunted for an instant, then depressed and locked.

They were bearing on the oncoming vehicles that were

spreading out now in a loose skirmish line under a roiling layer of dust. The watchdog was getting ready to defend its territory—and I was caught in the middle. A blue-white floodlight lanced out from across the field, glared against the scaled plating of the Bolo. I heard relays click inside the monster fighting machine, and braced myself for the thunder of her battery . . .

There was a dry rattle.

The guns traversed, clattering emptily. Beyond the fence the floodlight played for a moment longer against the Bolo, then moved on across the ramp, back, across and back, searching . . .

Once more the Bolo fired its empty guns. Its red I-R beams swept the scene again; then relays snicked, the impotent guns retracted, the port covers closed.

Satisfied, the Bolo heaved itself around and moved off, trailing a stink of ozone and ether, the broken tread thumping like a cripple on a stair.

I waited until it disappeared in the gloom two hundred yards away, then cautiously turned my suit control to vent off the heat. Full insulation could boil a man in his own gravy in less than half an hour.

The floodlight had blinked off now. I got to my hands and knees and started toward the perimeter fence. The Bolo's circuits weren't tuned as fine as they should have been; it let me go.

There were men moving in the glare and dust, beyond the rusty lacework that had once been a chain-link fence. They carried guns and stood in tight little groups, staring across toward the blockhouse.

I moved closer, keeping flat and avoiding the avenues of yellowish light thrown by the headlamps of the parked vehicles—halftracks, armored cars, a few light manned tanks.

There was nothing about the look of this crowd that impelled me to leap up and be welcomed. They wore green uniforms, and half of them sported beards. What the hell: had Castro landed in force?

I angled off to the right, away from the big main gate that had been manned day and night by guards with tommyguns. It hung now by one hinge from a scarred concrete post, under a cluster of dead polyarcs in corroded brackets. The big sign that had read GLENN AEROSPACE CENTER—AUTHORIZED PERSONNEL ONLY lay face down in hip-high underbrush.

More cars were coming up. There was a lot of talk and shouting; a squad of men formed and headed my way, keeping to the outside of the fallen fence.

I was outside the glare of the lights now. I chanced a run for it, got over the sagged wire and across a potholed blacktop road before they reached me. I crouched in the ditch and watched as the detail dropped men in pairs at fifty-yard intervals.

Another five minutes and they would have intercepted me—along with whatever else they were after. I worked my way back across an empty lot and found a strip of lesser underbrush lined with shaggy trees, beneath which a patch of cracked sidewalk showed here and there.

Several things were beginning to be a little clearer now: The person who had pushed the button to bring me out of stasis hadn't been around to greet me, because no one pushed it. The automatics, triggered by some malfunction, had initiated the recovery cycle.

The system's self-contained power unit had been designed to maintain a starship crewman's minimal vital functions indefinitely, at reduced body temperature and metabolic rate. There was no way to tell exactly how long I had been in the tank. From the condition of the fence and the roads, it had been more than a matter of weeks—or even months.

Had it been a year . . . or more? I thought of Ginny and the boy, waiting at home—thinking the old man was dead, probably. I'd neglected them before for my work, but not like this . . .

Our house was six miles from the base, in the foothills on the other side of town. It was a long walk, the way I felt—but I had to get there.

2

Two hours later I was clear of the town, following the river bank west.

I kept having the idea that someone was following me. But when I stopped to listen, there was never anything there; just the still, cold night and the frogs, singing away patiently in the low ground to the south.

When the ground began to rise, I left the road and struck off across the open field. I reached a wide street, followed it in a curve that would bring me out at the foot of Ridge Avenue—my street. I could make out the shapes of low, rambling houses now.

It had been the kind of residential section the local Junior Chamber members had hoped to move into some day. Now the starlight that filtered through the cloud cover showed me broken windows, doors that sagged open, automobiles that squatted on flat, dead tires under collapsing car shelters—and here and there a blackened, weed-grown foundation, like a gap in a row of rotting teeth.

The neighborhood wasn't what it had been. How long had I been away? How long . . . ?

I fell down again, hard this time. It wasn't easy getting up. I seemed to weigh a hell of a lot for a guy who hadn't been eating regularly. My breathing was very fast and shallow now, and my skull was getting ready to split and give birth to a live alligator—the ill-tempered kind. It was only a few hundred yards more; but why the hell had I picked a place halfway up a hill?

I heard the sound again—a crackle of dry grass. I got the pistol out and stood flatfooted in the middle of the street, listening hard.

All I heard was my stomach growling. I took the pistol off cock and started off again, stopped suddenly a couple of times to catch him off guard; nothing. I reached the corner of Ridge Avenue, started up the slope. Behind me a stick popped loudly.

I picked that moment to fall down again. Heaped leaves saved me from another skinned knee. I rolled over against a low fieldstone wall and propped myself against it. I had to use both hands to cock the pistol. I stared into the dark, but all I could see were the little lights whirling again. The pistol got heavy; I put it down, concentrated on taking deep breaths and blinking away the fireflies.

I heard footsteps plainly, close by. I shook my head, accidentally banged it against the stone behind me. That helped. I saw him, not over twenty feet away, coming up the hill toward me, a black-haired man with a full beard, dressed in odds and ends of rags and furs, gripping a polished club with a leather thong.

I reached for the pistol, found only leaves, tried again, touched the gun and knocked it away. I was still groping when I heard a scuffle of feet. I swung around, saw a tall, wide figure with a mane of untrimmed hair.

He hit the bearded man like a pro tackle taking out the practice dummy. They went down together hard and rolled over in a flurry of dry leaves. The cats were fighting over the mouse; that was my signal to leave quietly.

I made one last grab for the gun, found it, got to my feet and staggered off up the grade that seemed as steep now as penthouse rent. And from down slope, I heard an engine gunned, the clash of a heavy transmission that needed adjustment. A spotlight flickered, made shadows dance.

I recognized a fancy wrought-iron fence fronting a vacant lot; that had been the Adams house. Only half a block to go—but I was losing my grip fast. I went down twice more, then gave up and started crawling. The lights were all around now, brighter than ever. My head split open, dropped off, and rolled downhill.

A few more yards and I could let it all go. Ginny would put me in a warm bed, patch up my scratches, and feed me soup. Ginny would . . . Ginny . . .

I was lying with my mouth full of dead leaves. I heard running feet, yells. An engine idled noisily down the block.

I got my head up and found myself looking at chipped brickwork and the heavy brass hinges from which my front gate had hung. The gate was gone and there was a large chunk of brick missing. Some delivery truck had missed his approach.

I got to my feet, took a couple of steps into deep shadow with feet that felt as though they'd been amputated and welded back on at the ankle. I stumbled, fetched up against something scaled over with rust. I held on, blinked and made out the seeping flank of my brand new '79 Pontiac. There was a crumbled crust of whitish glass lining the brightwork strip that had framed the rear window.

A fire . . . ?

A footstep sounded behind me, and I suddenly remembered several things, none of them pleasant. I felt for my gun; it was gone. I moved back along the side of the car, tried to hold on.

No use. My arms were like unsuccessful pie crust. I slid down among dead leaves, sat listening to the steps coming closer. They stopped, and through a dense fog that had sprung up suddenly I caught a glimpse of a tall white-haired figure standing over me.

Then the fog closed in and swept everything away.

I lay on my back this time, looking across at the smoky yellow light of a thick brown candle guttering in the draft from a glassless window. In the center of the room a few sticks of damp-looking wood heaped on the cracked asphalt tiles burned with a grayish flame. A thin curl of acrid smoke rose up to stir cobwebs festooned under ceiling beams from which wood veneer had peeled away. Light alloy trusswork showed beneath.

It was a strange scene, but not so strange that I didn't recognize it: it was my own living room—looking a little different than when I had seen it last. The odors were different, too; I picked out mildew, badly cured leather, damp wool, tobacco . . .

I turned my head. A yard from the rags I lay on, the white-haired man, looking older than pharaoh, sat sleeping with his back against the wall.

The shotgun was gripped in one big, gnarled hand. His head was tilted back, blue-veined eyelids shut. I sat up, and at my movement his eyes opened.

He lay relaxed for a moment, as though life had to return from some place far away. Then he raised his head. His face was hollow and lined. His white hair was thin. A coarse-woven shirt hung loose across wide shoulders that had been Herculean once. But now Hercules was old, old. He looked at me expectantly.

"Who are you?" I said. "Why did you follow me? What happened to the house? Where's my family? Who owns the bully-boys in green?" My jaw hurt when I spoke. I put my hand up and felt it gingerly.

"You fell," the old man said, in a voice that rumbled like a subterranean volcano.

"The understatement of the year, pop." I tried to get up. Nausea knotted my stomach.

"You have to rest," the old man said, looking concerned. "Before the Baron's men come . . ." He paused, looking at me as though he expected me to say something profound.

"I want to know where the people are that live here!" My yell came out as weak as church-social punch. "A woman and a boy . . ."

He was shaking his head. "You have to do something quick. The soldiers will come back, search every house—"

I sat up, ignoring the little men driving spikes into my skull. "I don't give a damn about soldiers! Where's my family? What's happened?" I reached out and gripped his arm. "How long was I down there? What year is this?"

He only shook his head. "Come eat some food. Then I can help you with your plan."

It was no use talking to the old man; he was senile.

I got off the cot. Except for the dizziness and a feeling that my knees were made of papier-mâché, I was all right. I picked up the hand-formed candle, stumbled into the hall.

It was a jumble of rubbish. I climbed through, pushed open the door to my study. There was my desk, the tall bookcase with the glass doors, the gray rug, the easy chair. Aside from a layer of dust and some peeling wallpaper, it looked normal. I flipped the switch. Nothing happened.

"What is that charm?" the old man said behind me. He pointed to the light switch.

"The power's off," I said. "Just habit."

He reached out and flipped the switch up, then down again. "It makes a pleasing sound."

"Yeah." I picked up a book from the desk; it fell apart in my hands.

I went back into the hall, tried the bedroom door, looked in at heaped leaves, the remains of broken furniture, an empty window frame. I went on to the end of the hall and opened the door to the bedroom.

Cold night wind blew through a barricade of broken timbers. The roof had fallen in, and a sixteen-inch tree trunk slanted through the wreckage. The old man stood behind me, watching.

"Where is she, damn you?" I leaned against the door frame to swear and fight off the faintness. "Where's my wife?"

The old man looked troubled. "Come, eat now . . ."

"Where is she? Where's the woman who lived here?"

He frowned, shook his head dumbly. I picked my way through the wreckage, stepped out into knee-high brush. A gust blew my candle out. In the dark I stared at my back yard, the crumbled pit that had been the barbecue grill, the tangled thickets that had been rose beds—and a weathered length of boards upended in the earth.

"What the hell's this . . . ?" I fumbled out a permatch, lit my candle, leaned close, and read the crude letters cut into the crumbling wood: VIRGINIA ANNE JACKSON. BORN JAN. 8 1957. KILL BY THE DOGS WINTER 1992.

3

The Baron's men came twice in the next three days. Each time the old man carried me, swearing but too weak to argue, out to a lean-to of branches and canvas in the woods behind the house. Then he disappeared, to come back an hour or two later and haul me back to my rag bed by the fire.

Three times a day he gave me a tin pan of stew, and I ate it mechanically. My mind went over and over the picture of Ginny, living on for twelve years in the slowly decaying house, and then—

It was too much. There are some shocks the mind refuses.

I thought of the tree that had fallen and crushed the east wing. An elm that size was at least fifty to sixty years old—maybe older. And the only elm on the place had been a two-year sapling. I knew it well; I had planted it.

The date carved on the headboard was 1992. As nearly as I could judge another thirty-five years had passed since then at least. My shipmates—Banner, Day, Mallon—they were all dead, long ago. How had they died? The old man was too far gone to tell me anything useful. Most of my questions produced a shake of the head and a few rumbled words about charms, demons, spells, and the Baron.

"I don't believe in spells," I said. "And I'm not too sure I believe in this Baron. Who is he?"

"The Baron Trollmaster of Filly. He holds all this country—" the old man made a sweeping gesture with his arm—"all the way to Jersey."

"Why was he looking for me? What makes me important?"

"You came from the Forbidden Place. Everyone heard the cries of the Lesser Troll that stands guard over the treasure there. If the Baron can learn your secrets of power—"

"Troll, hell! That's nothing but a Bolo on automatic!"

"By any name every man dreads the monster. A man who walks in its shadow has much *mana*. But the others—the ones that run in a pack like dogs—would tear you to pieces for a demon if they could lay hands on you."

"You saw me back there. Why didn't you give me away? And why are you taking care of me now?"

He shook his head—the all-purpose answer to any question.

I tried another tack: "Who was the rag man you tackled just outside? Why was he laying for me?"

The old man snorted. "Tonight the dogs will eat him. But forget that. Now we have to talk about your plan—"

"I've got about as many plans as the senior boarder in death row. I don't know if you know it, old timer, but somebody slid the world out from under me while I wasn't looking."

The old man frowned. I had the thought that I wouldn't like to have him mad at me, for all his white hair . . .

He shook his head. "You must understand what I tell

you. The soldiers of the Baron will find you someday. If you are to break the spell—"

"Break the spell, eh?" I snorted. "I think I get the idea, pop. You've got it in your head that I'm valuable property of some kind. You figure I can use my supernatural powers to take over this menagerie—and you'll be in on the ground floor. Well, listen, you old idiot! I spent sixty years— maybe more—in a stasis tank two hundred feet underground. My world died while I was down there. This Baron of yours seems to own everything now. If you think I'm going to get myself shot bucking him, forget it!"

The old man didn't say anything.

"Things don't seem to be broken up much," I went on. "It must have been gas, or germ warfare—or fallout. Damn few people around. You're still able to live on what you can loot from stores; automobiles are still sitting where they were the day the world ended. How old were you when it happened, pop? The war, I mean. Do you remember it?"

He shook his head. "The world has always been as it is now."

"What year were you born?"

He scratched at his white hair. "I knew the number once. But I've forgotten."

"I guess the only way I'll find out how long I was gone is to saw that damned elm in two and count the rings—but even that wouldn't help much; I don't know when it blew over. Never mind. The important thing now is to talk to this Baron of yours. Where does he stay?"

The old man shook his head violently. "If the Baron lays his hands on you, he'll wring the secrets from you on the rack! I know his ways. For five years I was a slave in the palace stables."

"If you think I'm going to spend the rest of my days in this rat nest, you get another guess on the house! This Baron has tanks, an army. He's kept a little technology alive. That's the outfit for me—not this garbage detail! Now, where's this place of his located?"

"The guards will shoot you on sight like a packdog!"

"There has to be a way to get to him, old man! Think!"

The old head was shaking again. "He fears assassination.

You can never approach him . . ." He brightened. "Unless you know a spell of power?"

I chewed my lip. "Maybe I do at that. You wanted me to have a plan. I think I feel one coming on. Have you got a map?"

He pointed to the desk beside me. I tried the drawers, found mice, roaches, moldy money—and a stack of folded maps. I opened one carefully; faded ink on yellowed paper falling apart at the creases. The legend in the corner read: "PENNSYLVANIA 40M:1. Copyright 1970 by ESSO Corporation."

"This will do, pop," I said. "Now, tell me all you can about this Baron of yours."

"You'll destroy him?"

"I haven't even met the man."

"He is evil."

"I don't know; he owns an army. That makes up for a lot . . ."

After three more days of rest and the old man's stew I was back to normal—or near enough. I had the old man boil me a tub of water for a bath and a shave. I found a serviceable pair of synthetic-fiber long johns in a chest of drawers, pulled them on and zipped the weather suit over them, then buckled on the holster I had made from a tough plastic.

"That completes my preparations, pop," I said. "It'll be dark in another half hour. Thanks for everything."

He got to his feet, a worried look on his lined face, like a father the first time Junior asks for the car.

"The Baron's men are everywhere."

"If you want to help, come along and back me up with that shotgun of yours." I picked it up. "Have you got any shells for this thing?"

He smiled, pleased now. "There are shells—but the magic is gone from many."

"That's the way magic is, pop. It goes out of things before you notice."

"Will you destroy the Great Troll now?"

"My motto is let sleeping trolls lie. I'm just paying a social call on the Baron."

The joy ran out of his face like booze from a dropped jug.

"Don't take it so hard, old timer. I'm not the fairy prince you were expecting. But I'll take care of you—if I make it."

I waited while he pulled on a moth-eaten mackinaw. He took the shotgun and checked the breech, then looked at me.

"I'm ready," he said.

"Yeah," I said. "Let's go . . ."

The Baronial palace was a forty-story slab of concrete and glass that had been known in my days as the Hilton Garden East. We made it in three hours of groping across country in the dark, at the end of which I was puffing but still on my feet. We moved out from the cover of the trees and looked across a dip in the ground at the lights, incongruously cheerful in the ravaged valley.

"The gates are there—" the old man pointed—"guarded by the Great Troll."

"Wait a minute. I thought the Troll was the Bolo back at the Site."

"That's the Lesser Troll. This is the Great One."

I selected a few choice words and muttered them to myself. "It would have saved us some effort if you'd mentioned this troll a little sooner, old timer. I'm afraid I don't have any spells that will knock out a Mark II, once it's got its dander up."

He shook his head. "It lies under enchantment. I remember the day when it came, throwing thunderbolts. Many men were killed. Then the Baron commanded it to stand at his gates to guard him."

"How long ago was this, old timer?"

He worked his lips over the question. "Long ago," he said finally. "Many winters."

"Let's go take a look."

We picked our way down the slope, came up along a rutted dirt road to the dark line of trees that rimmed the palace grounds. The old man touched my arm.

"Softly here. Maybe the Troll sleeps lightly . . ."

I went the last few yards, eased around a brick column

with a dead lantern on top, stared across fifty yards of waist-high brush at a dark silhouette outlined against the palace lights.

Cables, stretched from trees outside the circle of weeds, supported a weathered tarp which drooped over the Bolo. The wreckage of a helicopter lay like a crumpled dragonfly at the far side of the ring. Nearer, fragments of a heavy car chassis lay scattered. The old man hovered at my shoulder.

"It looks as though the gate is off limits," I hissed. "Let's try farther along."

He nodded. "No one passes here. There is a second gate, there." He pointed. "But there are guards."

"Let's climb the wall between gates."

"There are sharp spikes on top of the wall. But I know a place, farther on, where the spikes have been blunted."

"Lead on, pop."

Half an hour of creeping through wet brush brought us to the spot we were looking for. It looked to me like any other stretch of eight-foot masonry wall overhung with wet poplar trees.

"I'll go first," the old man said, "to draw the attention of the guard."

"Then who's going to boost me up? I'll go first."

He nodded, cupped his hands and lifted me as easily as a sailor lifting a beer glass. Pop was old—but he was nobody's softie.

I looked around, then crawled up, worked my way over the corroded spikes, dropped down on the lawn.

Immediately I heard a crackle of brush. A man stood up not ten feet away. I lay flat in the dark trying to look like something that had been there a long time . . .

I heard another sound, a thump and a crashing of brush. The man before me turned, disappeared in the darkness. I heard him beating his way through shrubbery; then he called out, got an answering shout from the distance.

I didn't loiter. I got to my feet and made a sprint for the cover of the trees along the drive.

4

Flat on the wet ground, under the wind-whipped branches of an ornamental cedar, I blinked the fine misty rain from my eyes, waiting for the halfhearted alarm behind me to die down.

There were a few shouts, some sounds of searching among the shrubbery. It was a bad night to be chasing imaginary intruders in the Baronial grounds. In five minutes all was quiet again.

I studied the view before me. The tree under which I lay was one of a row lining a drive. It swung in a graceful curve, across a smooth half-mile of dark lawn, to the tower of light that was the palace of the Baron of Filly. The silhouetted figures of guards and late-arriving guests moved against the gleam from the collonaded entrance. On a terrace high above, dancers twirled under colored lights. The faint glow of the repellor field kept the cold rain at a distance. In a lull in the wind, I heard music, faintly. The Baron's weekly grand ball was in full swing.

I saw shadows move across the wet gravel before me, then heard the purr of an engine. I hugged the ground and watched a long svelte Mercedes—about an '88 model, I estimated—barrel past.

The mob in the city ran in packs like dogs, but the Baron's friends did a little better for themselves.

I got to my feet and moved off toward the palace, keeping well in the shadows. When the drive swung to the right to curve across in front of the building, I left it, went to hands and knees, and followed a trimmed privet hedge past dark rectangles of formal garden to the edge of a secondary pond of light from the garages. I let myself down on my belly and watched the shadows that moved on the graveled drive.

There seemed to be two men on duty—no more. Waiting around wouldn't improve my chances. I got to my feet, stepped out into the drive, and walked openly around the corner of the gray fieldstone building into the light.

A short, thickset man in greasy Baronial green looked at me incuriously. My weather suit looked enough like ordinary coveralls to get me by—at least for a few minutes. A second man, tilted back against the wall in a wooden chair, didn't even turn his head.

"Hey!" I called. "You birds got a three-ton jack I can borrow?"

Shorty looked me over sourly. "Who you drive for, Mac?"

"The High Duke of Jersey. Flat. Left rear. On a night like this. Some luck."

"The Jersey can't afford a jack?"

I stepped over to the short man, prodded him with a forefinger. "He could buy you and gut you on the altar any Saturday night of the week, low-pockets. And he'd get a kick out of doing it. He's like that."

"Can't a guy crack a harmless joke without somebody talks about altar-bait? You wanna jack, take a jack."

The man in the chair opened one eye and looked me over. "How long you on the Jersey payroll?" he growled.

"Long enough to know who handles the rank between Jersey and Filly." I yawned, looked around the wide, cement-floored garage, glanced over the four heavy cars with the Filly crest on their sides.

"Where's the kitchen? I'm putting a couple of hot coffees under my belt before I go back out into that."

"Over there. A flight up and to your left. Tell the cook Pintsy invited you."

"I tell him Jersey sent me, low-pockets." I moved off in a dead silence, opened the door and stepped up into spicy-scented warmth.

A deep carpet—even here—muffled my footsteps. I could hear the clash of pots and crockery from the kitchen a hundred feet distant along the hallway. I went along to a deep-set doorway ten feet from the kitchen, tried the knob, and looked into a dark room. I pushed the door shut and leaned against it, watching the kitchen. Through the woodwork I could feel the thump of the bass notes from the orchestra blasting away three flights up. The odors of food—roast fowl, baked ham, grilled horsemeat—curled under the kitchen door and wafted under my nose. I pulled my belt up a notch and tried to swallow the dryness in my throat. The old man had fed me a half a gallon of stew before we left home, but I was already working up a fresh appetite.

Five slow minutes passed. Then the kitchen door swung open and a tall round-shouldered fellow with a shiny bald scalp stepped into view, a tray balanced on the spread fingers of one hand. He turned, the black tails of his cutaway swirling, called something behind him, and started past me. I stepped out, clearing my throat. He shied, whirled to face me. He was good at his job: the two dozen tiny glasses on the tray stood fast. He blinked, got an indignant remark ready—

I showed him the knife the old man had lent me—a bonehandled job with a six-inch switchblade. "Make a sound and I'll cut your throat," I said softly. "Put the tray on the floor."

He started to back. I brought the knife up. He took a good look, licked his lips, crouched quickly, and put the tray down.

"Turn around."

I stepped in and chopped him at the base of the neck with the edge of my hand. He folded like a two-dollar umbrella.

I wrestled the door open and dumped him inside, paused a moment to listen. All quiet. I worked his black coat and trousers off, unhooked the stiff white dickey and tie. He snored softly. I pulled the clothes on over the weather suit. They were a fair fit. By the light of my pencil flash I cut down a heavy braided cord hanging by a high window, used it to truss the waiter's hands and feet together behind him. There was a small closet opening off the room. I put him in it, closed the door, and stepped back into the hall. Still quiet. I tried one of the drinks. It wasn't bad.

I took another, then picked up the tray and followed the sounds of music.

The grand ballroom was a hundred yards long, fifty wide, with walls of rose, gold and white, banks of high windows hung with crimson velvet, a vaulted ceiling decorated with cherubs, and a polished acre of floor on which gaudily gowned and uniformed couples moved in time to the heavy beat of the traditional foxtrot. I moved slowly along the edge of the crowd, looking for the Baron.

A hand caught my arm and hauled me around. A glass fell off my tray, smashed on the floor.

A dapper little man in black and white headwaiter's uniform glared up at me.

"What do you think you're doing, cretin?" he hissed. "That's the genuine ancient stock you're slopping on the floor." I looked around quickly; no one else seemed to be paying any attention.

"Where are you from?" he snapped. I opened my mouth—

"Never mind, you're all the same." He waggled his hands disgustedly. "The field hands they send me—a disgrace to the Black. Now, you! Stand up! Hold your tray proudly, gracefully! Step along daintily, not like a knight taking the field! and pause occasionally—just on the chance that some noble guest might wish to drink."

"You bet, pal," I said. I moved on, paying a little more attention to my waiting. I saw plenty of green uniforms; pea green, forest green, emerald green—but they were all hung with braid and medals. According to pop, the Baron affected a spartan simplicity. The diffidence of absolute power.

There were high white and gold doors every few yards along the side of the ballroom. I spotted one standing open and sidled toward it. It wouldn't hurt to reconnoiter the area.

Just beyond the door, a very large sentry in a bottle-green uniform almost buried under gold braid moved in front of me. He was dressed like a toy soldier, but there was nothing playful about the way he snapped his power gun to the ready. I winked at him.

"Thought you boys might want a drink," I hissed. "Good stuff."

He looked at the tray, licked his lips. "Get back in there, you fool," he growled. "You'll get us both hanged."

"Suit yourself, pal." I backed out. Just before the door closed between us, he lifted a glass off the tray.

I turned, almost collided with a long lean cookie in a powder-blue outfit complete with dress sabre, gold frogs, leopard-skin facings, a pair of knee-length white gloves looped under an epaulette, a pistol in a fancy holster, and an eighteen-inch swagger stick. He gave me the kind of look old maids give sin.

"Look where you're going, swine," he said in a voice like a pine board splitting.

"Have a drink, admiral," I suggested.

He lifted his upper lip to show me a row of teeth that hadn't had their annual trip to the dentist lately. The ridges along each side of his mouth turned greenish white. He snatched for the gloves on his shoulder, fumbled them; they slapped the floor beside me.

"I'd pick those up for you, boss," I said, "but I've got my tray . . ."

He drew a breath between his teeth, chewed it into strips, and snorted it back at me, then snapped his fingers and pointed with his stick toward the door behind me.

"Through there, instantly!" It didn't seem like the time to argue; I pulled it open and stepped through.

The guard in green ducked his glass and snapped to attention when he saw the baby-blue outfit. My new friend ignored him, made a curt gesture to me. I got the idea, trailed along the wide, high, gloomy corridor to a small door, pushed through it into a well-lit tile-walled latrine. A big-eyed slave in white ducks stared.

Blue-boy jerked his head. "Get out!" The slave scuttled away. Blue-boy turned to me.

"Strip off your jacket, slave! Your owner has neglected to teach you discipline."

I looked around quickly, saw that we were alone.

"Wait a minute while I put the tray down, corporal," I said. "We don't want to waste any of the good stuff." I turned to put the tray on a soiled linen bin, caught a glimpse of motion in the mirror.

I ducked, and the nasty-looking little leather quirt whistled past my ear, slammed against the edge of a marble-topped lavatory with a crack like a pistol shot. I dropped the tray, stepped in fast and threw a left to Blue-boy's jaw that bounced his head against the tiled wall. I followed up with a right to the belt buckle, then held him up as he bent over, gagging, and hit him hard under the ear.

I hauled him into a booth, propped him up and started shedding the waiter's blacks.

5

I left him on the floor wearing my old suit, and stepped out into the hall.

I liked the feel of his pistol at my hip. It was an old-fashioned .38, the same model I favored. The blue uniform was a good fit, what with the weight I'd lost. Blue-boy and I had something in common after all.

The latrine attendant goggled at me. I grimaced like a quadruple amputee trying to scratch his nose and jerked my head toward the door I had come out of. I hoped the gesture would look familiar.

"Truss that mad dog and throw him outside the gates," I snarled. I stamped off down the corridor, trying to look mad enough to discourage curiosity.

Apparently it worked. Nobody yelled for the cops.

I reentered the ballroom by another door, snagged a drink off a passing tray, checked over the crowd. I saw two more powder-blue getups, so I wasn't unique enough to draw special attention. I made a mental note to stay well away from my comrades in blue. I blended with the landscape, chatting and nodding and not neglecting my drinking, working my way toward a big arched doorway on the other side of the room that looked like the kind of entrance the head man might use. I didn't want to meet him. Not yet. I just wanted to get him located before I went any further.

A passing wine slave poured a full inch of genuine ancient stock into my glass, ducked his head, and moved on. I gulped it like sour bar whiskey. My attention was elsewhere.

A flurry of activity near the big door indicated that maybe my guess had been accurate. Potbellied officials were forming up in a sort of reception line near the big double door. I started to drift back into the rear rank, bumped against a fat man in medals and a sash who glared, fingered a monocle with a plump ring-studded hand, and said, "Suggest you take your place, colonel," in a suety voice.

I must have looked doubtful, because he bumped me

with his paunch, and growled, "Foot of the line! Next to the Equerry, you idiot." He elbowed me aside and waddled past.

I took a step after him, reached out with my left foot, and hooked his shiny black boot. He leaped forward, off balance, medals jangling. I did a fast fade while he was still groping for his monocle, eased into a spot at the end of the line.

The conversation died away to a nervous murmur. The doors swung back and a pair of guards with more trimmings than a phony stock certificate stamped into view, wheeled to face each other, and presented arms—chrome-plated automatic rifles, in this case. A dark-faced man with thinning gray hair, a pug nose, and a trimmed gray Vandyke came into view, limping slightly from a stiffish knee.

His unornamented gray outfit made him as conspicuous in this gathering as a crane among peacocks. He nodded perfunctorily to left and right, coming along between the waiting rows of flunkeys, who snapped-to as he came abreast, wilted and let out sighs behind him. I studied him closely. He was fifty, give or take the age of a bottle of second-rate bourbon, with the weather-beaten complexion of a former outdoor man and the same look of alertness grown bored that a rattlesnake farmer develops—just before the fatal bite.

He looked up and caught my eye on him, and for a moment I thought he was about to speak. Then he went on past.

At the end of the line he turned abruptly and spoke to a man who hurried away. Then he engaged in conversation with a cluster of head-bobbing guests.

I spent the next fifteen minutes casually getting closer to the door nearest the one the Baron had entered by. I looked around; nobody was paying any attention to me. I stepped past a guard who presented arms. The door closed softly, cutting off the buzz of talk and the worst of the music.

I went along to the end of the corridor. From the transverse hall, a grand staircase rose in a sweep of bright chrome and pale wood. I didn't know where it led, but it looked right. I headed for it, moving along briskly like a man with important business in mind and no time for light chitchat.

Two flights up, in a wide corridor of muted lights, deep carpets, brocaded wall hangings, mirrors, urns, and an odor of expensive tobacco and *cuir russe,* a small man in black bustled from a side corridor. He saw me. He opened his mouth, closed it, half turned away, then swung back to face me. I recognized him; he was the headwaiter who had pointed out the flaws in my waiting style half an hour earlier.

"Here—" he started.

I chopped him short with a roar of what I hoped was authentic upper-crust rage.

"Direct me to his Excellency's apartments, scum! And thank your guardian imp I'm in too great haste to cane you for the insolent look about you!"

He went pale, gulped hard, and pointed. I snorted and stamped past him down the turning he had indicated.

This was Baronial country, all right. A pair of guards stood at the far end of the corridor.

I'd passed half a dozen with no more than a click of heels to indicate they saw me. These two shouldn't be any different—and it wouldn't look good if I turned and started back at sight of them. The first rule of the gate-crasher is to look as if you belong where you are.

I headed in their direction.

When I was fifty feet from them they both shifted rifles—not to present-arms position, but at the ready. The nickle-plated bayonets were aimed right at me. It was no time for me to look doubtful; I kept on coming. At twenty feet, I heard their rifle bolts snick home. I could see the expressions on their faces now; they looked as nervous as a couple of teenage sailors on their first visit to a joyhouse.

"Point those butter knives into the corner, you banana-fingered cotton choppers!" I said, looking bored, and didn't waver. I unlimbered my swagger stick and slapped my gloved hand with it, letting them think it over. The gun muzzles dropped—just slightly. I followed up fast.

"Which is the anteroom to the Baron's apartments?" I demanded.

"Uh . . . this here is his Excellency's apartments, sir, but—"

"Never mind the lecture, you milk-faced fool," I cut in. "Which is the anteroom, damn you!"

"We got orders, sir. Nobody's to come closer than that last door back there."

"We got orders to shoot," the other interrupted. He was a little older—maybe twenty-two. I turned on him.

"I'm waiting for an answer to a question!"

"Sir, the Articles—"

I narrowed my eyes. "I think you'll find paragraph Two B covers Special Cosmic Top Secret Couriers. When you go off duty, report yourselves on punishment. Now, the anteroom! And be quick about it!"

The bayonets were sagging now. The younger of the two licked his lips. "Sir, we never been inside. We don't know how it's laid out in there. If the colonel wants to just take a look . . ."

The other guard opened his mouth to say something. I didn't wait to find out what it was. I stepped between them, muttering something about bloody recruits and important messages, and worked the fancy handle on the big gold and white door. I paused to give the two sentries a hard look.

"I hope I don't have to remind you that any mention of the movements of a Cosmic Courier is punishable by slow death. Just forget you ever saw me." I went on in and closed the door without waiting to catch the reaction to that one.

The Baron had done well by himself in the matter of decor. The room I was in—a sort of lounge-cum-bar—was paved in two-inch-deep nylon fuzz, the color of a fog at sea, that foamed up at the edges against walls of pale blue brocade with tiny yellow flowers. The bar was a teak log split down the middle and polished. The glasses sitting on it were like tissue paper engraved with patterns of nymphs and satyrs. Subdued light came from somewhere, along with a faint melody that seemed to speak of youth, long ago.

I went on into the room. I found more soft light, the glow of hand-rubbed rare woods, rich fabrics, and wide windows with a view of dark night sky. The music was coming from a long, low, built-in speaker with a lamp, a heavy crystal ashtray, and a display of hothouse roses. There was a scent in the air. Not the *cuir russe* and Havana leaf I'd smelled in the hall, but a subtler perfume.

I turned and looked into the eyes of a girl with long black lashes. Smooth black hair came down to bare shoulders. An arm as smooth and white as whipped cream was draped over a chair back, the hand holding an eight-inch cigarette holder and sporting a diamond as inconspicuous as a chromeplated hubcap.

"You must want something pretty badly," she murmured, batting her eyelashes at me. I could feel the breeze at ten feet. I nodded. Under the circumstances that was about the best I could do.

"What could it be," she mused, "that's worth being shot for?" Her voice was like the rest of her: smooth, polished and relaxed—and with plenty of moxie held in reserve. She smiled casually, drew on her cigarette, tapped ashes onto the rug.

"Something bothering you, colonel?" she inquired. "You don't seem talkative."

"I'll do my talking when the Baron arrives," I said.

"In that case, Jackson," said a husky voice behind me, "you can start any time you like."

I held my hands clear of my body and turned around slowly—just in case there was a nervous gun aimed at my spine. The Baron was standing near the door, unarmed, relaxed. There were no guards in sight. The girl looked mildly amused. I put my hand on the pistol butt.

"How do you know my name?" I asked.

The Baron waved toward a chair. "Sit down, Jackson," he said, almost gently. "You've had a tough time of it—but you're all right now." He walked past me to the bar, poured out two glasses, turned, and offered me one. I felt a little silly standing there fingering the gun; I went over and took the drink.

"To the old days." The Baron raised his glass.

I drank. It was the genuine ancient stock, all right. "I asked you how you knew my name," I said.

"That's easy. I used to know you."

He smiled faintly. There was something about his face . . .

"You look well in the uniform of the Penn dragoons," he said. "Better than you ever did in Aerospace blue."

"Good God!" I said. "Toby Mallon!"

He ran a hand over his bald head. "A little less hair on top, plus a beard as compensation, a few wrinkles, a slight pot. Oh, I've changed, Jackson."

"I had it figured as close to eighty years," I said. "The trees, the condition of the buildings—"

"Not far off the mark. Seventy-eight years this spring."

"You're a well-preserved hundred and ten, Toby."

He nodded. "I know how you feel. Rip Van Winkle had nothing on us."

"Just one question, Toby. The men you sent out to pick me up seemed more interested in shooting than talking. I'm wondering why."

Mallon threw out his hands. "A little misunderstanding, Jackson. You made it; that's all that counts. Now that you're here, we've got some planning to do together. I've had it tough these last twenty years. I started off with nothing: a few hundred scavengers living in the ruins, hiding out every time Jersey or Dee-Cee raided for supplies. I built an organization, started a systematic salvage operation. I saved everything the rats and the weather hadn't gotten to, spruced up my palace here, and stocked it. It's a rich province, Jackson—"

"And now you own it all. Not bad, Toby."

"They say knowledge is power. I had the knowledge."

I finished my drink and put the glass on the bar.

"What's this planning you say we have to do?"

Mallon leaned back on one elbow.

"Jackson, it's been a long haul—alone. It's good to see an old shipmate. But we'll dine first."

"I might manage to nibble a little something. Say a horse, roasted whole. Don't bother to remove the saddle."

He laughed. "First we eat," he said. "Then we conquer the world."

6

I squeezed the last drop from the Beaujolais bottle and watched the girl, whose name was Renada, hold a light for the cigar Mallon had taken from a silver box. My blue mess jacket and holster hung over the back of the chair. Everything was cosy now.

"Time for business, Jackson," Mallon said. He blew out smoke and looked at me through it. "How did things look—inside?"

"Dusty. But intact, below ground level. Upstairs, there's blast damage and weathering. I don't suppose it's changed much since you came out twenty years ago. As far as I could tell, the Primary Site is okay."

Mallon leaned forward. "Now, you made it out past the Bolo. How did it handle itself? Still fully functional?"

I sipped my wine, thinking over my answer, remembering the Bolo's empty guns . . .

"It damn near gunned me down. It's getting a little old and it can't see as well as it used to, but it's still a tough baby."

Mallon swore suddenly. "It was Mackenzie's idea. A last-minute move when the tech crews had to evacuate. It was a dusting job, you know."

"I hadn't heard. How did you find out all this?"

Mallon shot me a sharp look. "There were still a few people around who'd been in it. But never mind that. What about the Supply Site? That's what we're interested in. Fuel, guns, even some nuclear stuff. Heavy equipment; there's a couple more Bolos, mothballed, I understand. Maybe we'll even find one or two of the Colossus missiles still in their silos. I made an air recon a few years back before my chopper broke down—"

"I think two silo doors are still in place. But why the interest in armament?"

Mallon snorted. "You've got a few things to learn about the setup, Jackson. I need that stuff. If I hadn't lucked into a stock of weapons and ammo in the armory cellar, Jersey would be wearing the spurs in my palace right now!"

I drew on my cigar and let the silence stretch out.

"You said something about conquering the world, Toby. I don't suppose by any chance you meant that literally?"

Mallon stood up, his closed fists working like a man crumpling unpaid bills. "They all want what I've got! They're all waiting." He walked across the room, back. "I'm ready to move against them now! I can put four thousand trained men in the field—"

"Let's get a couple of things straight, Mallon," I cut in. "You've got the natives fooled with this Baron routine. But don't try it on me. Maybe it was even necessary once; maybe there's an excuse for some of the stories I've heard. That's over now. I'm not interested in tribal warfare or gang rumbles. I need—"

"Better remember who's running things here, Jackson!" Mallon snapped. "It's not what you need that counts." He took another turn up and down the room, then stopped, facing me.

"Look, Jackson. I know how to get around in this jungle; you don't. If I hadn't spotted you and given some orders, you'd have been gunned down before you'd gone ten feet past the ballroom door."

"Why'd you let me in? I might've been gunning for you."

"You wanted to see the Baron alone. That suited me, too. If word got out—" He broke off, cleared his throat. "Let's stop wrangling, Jackson. We can't move until the Bolo guarding the site has been neutralized. There's only one way to do that: knock it out! And the only thing that can knock out a Bolo is another Bolo."

"So?"

"I've got another Bolo, Jackson. It's been covered, maintained. It can go up against the Troll—" He broke off, laughed shortly. "That's what the mob called it."

"You could have done that years ago. Where do I come in?"

"You're checked out on a Bolo, Jackson. You know something about this kind of equipment."

"Sure. So do you."

"I never learned," he said shortly.

"Who's kidding who, Mallon? We all took the same orientation course less than a month ago—"

"For me it's been a long month. Let's say I've forgotten."

"You parked that Bolo at your front gate and then forgot how you did it, eh?"

"Nonsense. It's always been there."

I shook my head. "I know different."

Mallon looked wary. "Where'd you get that idea?"

"Somebody told me."

Mallon ground his cigar out savagely on the damask cloth. "You'll point the scum out to me!"

"I don't give a damn whether you moved it or not. Anybody with your training can figure out the controls of a Bolo in half an hour—"

"Not well enough to take on the Tr—another Bolo."

I took a cigar from the silver box, picked up the lighter from the table, turned the cigar in the flame. Suddenly it was very quiet in the room.

I looked across at Mallon. He held out his hand.

"I'll take that," he said shortly.

I blew out smoke, squinted through it at Mallon. He sat with his hand out, waiting. I looked down at the lighter.

It was a heavy windproof model with embossed Aerospace wings. I turned it over. Engraved letters read: *Lieut. Commander Don G. Banner, USAF.* I looked up. Renada sat quietly, holding my pistol trained dead on my belt buckle.

"I'm sorry you saw that," Mallon said. "It could cause misunderstandings."

"Where's Banner?"

"He . . . died. I told you—"

"You told me a lot of things, Toby. Some of them might even be true. Did you make him the same offer you've made me?"

Mallon darted a look at Renada. She sat holding the pistol, looking at me distantly, without expression.

"You've got the wrong idea, Jackson—" Mallon started.

"You and he came out about the same time," I said. "Or maybe you got the jump on him by a few days. It must have been close; otherwise you'd never have taken him. Don was a sharp boy."

"You're out of your mind!" Mallon snapped. "Why, Banner was my friend!"

"Then why do you get nervous when I find his lighter on your table? There could be ten perfectly harmless explanations."

"I don't make explanations," Mallon said flatly.

"That attitude is hardly the basis for a lasting partnership, Toby. I have an unhappy feeling there's something you're not telling me."

Mallon pulled himself up in the chair. "Look here, Jackson. We've no reason to fall out. There's plenty for both of us—and one day I'll be needing a successor. It was too bad about Banner, but that's ancient history now. Forget it. I want you with me, Jackson! Together we can rule the Atlantic seaboard—or even more!"

I drew on my cigar, looking at the gun in Renada's hand. "You hold the aces, Toby. Shooting me would be no trick at all."

"There's no trick involved, Jackson!" Mallon snapped. "After all," he went on, almost wheedling now, "we're old friends. I want to give you a break, share with you—"

"I don't think I'd trust him if I were you, Mr. Jackson," Renada's quiet voice cut in. I looked at her. She looked back calmly. "You're more important to him than you think."

"That's enough, Renada," Mallon barked. "Go to your room at once."

"Not just yet, Toby," she said. "I'm also curious about how Commander Banner died." I looked at the gun in her hand.

It wasn't pointed at me now. It was aimed at Mallon's chest.

Mallon sat sunk deep in his chair, looking at me with eyes like a python with a bellyache. "You're fools, both of you," he grated. "I gave you everything, Renada. I raised you like my own daughter. And you, Jackson. You could have shared with me—all of it."

"I don't need a share of your delusions, Toby. I've got a set of my own. But before we go any farther, let's clear up a few points. Why haven't you been getting any mileage out of your tame Bolo? And what makes me important in the picture?"

"He's afraid of the Bolo machine," Renada said. "There's

a spell on it which prevents men from approaching—even the Baron."

"Shut your mouth, you fool!" Mallon choked on his fury. I tossed the lighter in my hand and felt a smile twitching at my mouth.

"So Don was too smart for you after all. He must have been the one who had control of the Bolo. I suppose you called for a truce, and then shot him out from under the white flag. But he fooled you. He plugged a command into the Bolo's circuits to fire on anyone who came close— unless he was Banner."

"You're crazy!"

"It's close enough. You can't get near the Bolo. Right? And after twenty years, the bluff you've been running on the other Barons with your private troll must be getting a little thin. Any day now one of them may decide to try you."

Mallon twisted his face in what may have been an attempt at a placating smile. "I won't argue with you, Jackson. You're right about the command circuit. Banner set it up to fire an antipersonnel blast at anyone coming within fifty yards. He did it to keep the mob from tampering with the machine. But there's a loophole. It wasn't only Banner who could get close. He set it up to accept any of the *Prometheus* crew—except me. He hated me. It was a trick to try to get me killed."

"So you're figuring I'll step in and de-fuse her for you, eh, Toby? Well, I'm sorry as hell to disappoint you, but somehow in the confusion I left my electropass behind."

Mallon leaned toward me. "I told you we need each other, Jackson: I've got your pass. Yours and all the others. Renada, hand me my black box." She rose and moved across to the desk, holding the gun on Mallon—and on me, too, for that matter.

"Where'd you get my pass, Mallon?"

"Where do you think? They're the duplicates from the vault in the old command block. I knew one day one of you would come out. I'll tell you, Jackson, it's been hell, waiting all these years—and hoping. I gave orders that any time the Great Troll bellowed, the mob was to form up and stop anybody who came out. I don't know how you got through them . . ."

"I was too slippery for them. Besides," I added, "I met a friend."

"A friend? Who's that?"

"An old man who thought I was Prince Charming, come to wake everybody up. He was nuts. But he got me through."

Renada came back, handed me a square steel box. "Let's have the key, Mallon," I said. He handed it over. I opened the box, sorted through half a dozen silver-dollar-sized ovals of clear plastic, lifted one out.

"Is it a magical charm?" Renada asked, sounding awed. She didn't seem so sophisticated now—but I liked her better human.

"Just a synthetic crystalline plastic, designed to resonate to a pattern peculiar to my EEG," I said. "It amplifies the signal and gives off a characteristic emission that the psychotronic circuit in the Bolo picks up."

"That's what I thought. Magic."

"Call it magic, then, kid." I dropped the electropass in my pocket, stood and looked at Renada. "I don't doubt that you know how to use that gun, honey, but I'm leaving now. Try not to shoot me."

"You're a fool if you try it," Mallon barked. "If Renada doesn't shoot you, my guards will. And even if you made it, you'd still need me!"

"I'm touched by your concern, Toby. Just why do I need you?"

"You wouldn't get past the first sentry post without help, Jackson. These people know me as the Trollmaster. They're in awe of me—of my *mana*. But together—we can get to the controls of the Bolo, then use it to knock out the sentry machine at the Site—"

"Then what? With an operating Bolo I don't need anything else. Better improve the picture, Toby. I'm not impressed."

He wet his lips.

"It's *Prometheus*, do you understand? She's stocked with everything from Browning needlers to Norge stunners. Tools, weapons, instruments. And the power plants alone."

"I don't need needlers if I own a Bolo, Toby."

Mallon used some profanity. "You'll leave your liver and lights on the palace altar, Jackson. I promise you that!"

"Tell him what he wants to know, Toby," Renada said. Mallon narrowed his eyes at her. "You'll live to regret this, Renada."

"Maybe I will, Toby. But you taught me how to handle a gun—and to play cards for keeps."

The flush faded out of his face and left it pale. "All right, Jackson," he said, almost in a whisper. "It's not only the equipment. It's . . . the men."

I heard a clock ticking somewhere.

"What men, Toby?" I said softly.

"The crew. Day, Macy, the others. They're still in there, Jackson—aboard the ship, in stasis. We were trying to get the ship off when the attack came. There was forty minutes' warning. Everything was ready to go. You were on a test run; there wasn't time to cycle you out . . ."

"Keep talking," I rapped.

"You know how the system was set up; it was to be a ten-year run out, with an automatic turnaround at the end of that time if Alpha Centauri wasn't within a milliparsec." He snorted. "It wasn't. After twenty years, the instruments checked. They were satisfied. There was a planetary mass within the acceptable range. So they brought me out." He snorted again. "The longest dry run in history. I unstrapped and came out to see what was going on. It took me a little while to realize what had happened. I went back in and cycled Banner and Mackenzie out. We went into the town; you know what we found. I saw what we had to do, but Banner and Mac argued. The fools wanted to reseal *Prometheus* and proceed with the launch. For what? So we could spend the rest of our lives squatting in the ruins, when by stripping the ship we could make ourselves kings?"

"So there was an argument?" I prompted.

"I had a gun. I hit Mackenzie in the leg, I think—but they got clear, found a car and beat me to the Site. There were two Bolos. What chance did I have against them?" Mallon grinned craftily. "But Banner was a fool. He died for it." The grin dropped like a stripper's bra. "But when I went to claim my spoils, I discovered how the jackals had set the trap for me."

"That was downright unfriendly of them, Mallon. Oddly

enough, it doesn't make me want to stay and hold your hand."

"Don't you understand yet!" Mallon's voice was a dry screech. "Even if you got clear of the palace, used the Bolo to set yourself up as Baron—you'd never be safe! Not as long as one man was still alive aboard the ship. You'd never have a night's rest, wondering when one of them would walk out to challenge your rule . . ."

"Uneasy lies the head, eh, Toby? You remind me of a queen bee. The first one out of the chrysalis dismembers all her rivals."

"I don't mean to kill them. That would be a waste; I mean to give them useful work to do."

"I don't think they'd like being your slaves, Toby. And neither would I." I looked at Renada. "I'll be leaving you now," I said. "Whichever way you decide, good luck."

"Wait." She stood. "I'm going with you."

I looked at her. "I'll be traveling fast, honey. And that gun in my back may throw off my timing."

She stepped to me, reversed the pistol, and laid it in my hand.

"Don't kill him, Mr. Jackson. He was always kind to me."

"Why change sides now? According to Toby, my chances look not too good."

"I never knew before how Commander Banner died," she said. "He was my great-grandfather."

7

Renada came back bundled in a gray fur as I finished buckling on my holster.

"So long, Toby," I said. "I ought to shoot you in the belly just for Don, but—"

I saw Renada's eyes widen at the same instant that I heard the click.

I dropped flat and rolled behind Mallon's chair—and a gout of blue flame yammered into the spot where I'd been standing. I whipped the gun up and fired a round into the peach-colored upholstery an inch from Toby's ear.

"The next one nails you to the chair," I yelled. "Call 'em off!" There was a moment of dead silence. Toby sat frozen. I couldn't see who'd been doing the shooting. Then I heard a moan. Renada.

"Let the girl alone or I'll kill him," I called.

Toby sat rigid, his eyes rolled toward me.

"You can't kill me, Jackson! I'm all that's keeping you alive."

"You can't kill me either, Toby. You need my magic touch, remember? Maybe you'd better give me a safe-conduct out of here. I'll take the freeze off your Bolo—after I've seen to my business."

Toby licked his lips. I heard Renada again. She was trying not to moan—but moaning anyway.

"You tried, Jackson. It didn't work out," Toby said through gritted teeth. "Throw out your gun and stand up. I won't kill you—you know that. You do as you're told and you may still live to a ripe old age—and the girl, too."

She screamed then—a mindless ululation of pure agony.

"Hurry up, you fool, before they tear her arm off," Mallon grated. "Or shoot. You'll get to watch her for twenty-four hours under the knife. Then you'll have your turn."

I fired again—closer this time. Mallon jerked his head and cursed.

"If they touch her again, you get it, Toby," I said. "Send her over here. Move!"

"Let her go!" Mallon snarled. Renada stumbled into sight, moved around the chair, then crumpled suddenly to the rug beside me.

"Stand up, Toby," I ordered. He rose slowly. Sweat glistened on his face now. "Stand over here." He moved like a sleepwalker. I got to my feet. There were two men standing across the room beside a small open door. A sliding panel. Both of them held power rifles leveled—but aimed offside, away from the Baron.

"Drop 'em!" I said. They looked at me, then lowered the guns, tossed them aside.

I opened my mouth to tell Mallon to move ahead, but my tongue felt thick and heavy. The room was suddenly full of smoke. In front of me, Mallon was wavering like a mirage. I started to tell him to stand still, but with my thick tongue, it was too much trouble. I raised the gun, but somehow it was falling to the floor—slowly, like a leaf—and then I was floating, too, on waves that broke on a dark sea . . .

"Do you think you're the first idiot who thought he could kill me?" Mallon raised a contemptuous lip. "This room's rigged ten different ways."

I shook my head, trying to ignore the film before my eyes and the nausea in my body. "No, I imagine lots of people would like a crack at you, Toby. One day one of them's going to make it."

"Get him on his feet," Mallon snapped. Hard hands clamped on my arms, hauled me off the cot. I worked my legs, but they were like yesterday's celery; I sagged against somebody who smelled like uncured hides.

"You seem drowsy," Mallon said. "We'll see if we can't wake you up."

A thumb dug into my neck. I jerked away, and a jab under the ribs doubled me over.

"I have to keep you alive—for the moment," Mallon said. "But you won't get a lot of pleasure out of it."

I blinked hard. It was dark in the room. One of my handlers had a ring of beard around his mouth—I could see that much. Mallon was standing before me, hands on hips. I aimed a kick at him, just for fun. It didn't work out; my foot seemed to be wearing a lead boat. The unshaven man hit me in the mouth and Toby chuckled.

"Have your fun, Dunger," he said, "but I'll want him alive and on his feet for the night's work. Take him out and walk him in the fresh air. Report to me at the Pavilion of the Troll in an hour." He turned to something and gave orders about lights and gun emplacements, and I heard Renada's name mentioned.

Then he was gone and I was being dragged through the door and along the corridor.

The exercise helped. By the time the hour had passed, I was feeling weak but normal—except for an aching head and a feeling that there was a strand of spiderweb interfering with my vision. Toby had given me a good meal. Maybe before the night was over he'd regret that mistake . . .

Across the dark grounds, an engine started up, spluttered, then settled down to a steady hum.

"It's time," the one with the whiskers said. He had a voice like soft cheese to match his smell. He took another half-twist in the arm he was holding.

"Don't break it," I grunted. "It belongs to the Baron, remember?"

Whiskers stopped dead. "You talk too much—and too smart." He let my arm go and stepped back. "Hold him, Pig Eye." The other man whipped a forearm across my throat and levered my head back; then Whiskers unlimbered the two-foot club from his belt and hit me hard in the side, just under the ribs. Pig Eye let go and I folded over and waited while the pain swelled up and burst inside me.

Then they hauled me back to my feet. I couldn't feel any bone ends grating, so there probably weren't any broken ribs—if that was any consolation.

There were lights glaring now across the lawn. Moving figures cast long shadows against the trees lining the drive—and on the side of the Bolo Combat Unit parked under its canopy by the sealed gate.

A crude breastwork had been thrown up just over fifty yards from it. A wheel-mounted generator putted noisily in the background, laying a layer of bluish exhaust in the air.

Mallon was waiting with a 9-mm power rifle in his hands as we came up, my two guards gripping me with both hands to demonstrate their zeal, and me staggering a little more than was necessary. I saw Renada standing by, wrapped in a gray fur. Her face looked white in the harsh light. She made a move toward me and a greenback caught her arm.

"You know what to do, Jackson," Mallon said speaking loudly against the clatter of the generator. He made a curt gesture and a man stepped up and buckled a stout chain to my left ankle. Mallon held out my electropass. "I want you to walk straight to the Bolo. Go in by the side port. You've got one minute to cancel the instructions punched into the command circuit and climb back outside. If you don't show, I close a switch there—" He pointed to a

wooden box mounting an open circuit-breaker, with a
tangle of heavy cable leading toward the Bolo— "and you
cook in your shoes. The same thing happens if I see the
guns start to traverse or the antipersonnel ports open." I
followed the coils of armored wire from the chain on my
ankle back to the wooden box—and on to the generator.

"Crude, maybe, but it will work. And if you get any
idea of letting fly a round or two at random—remember
the girl will be right beside me."

I looked across at the giant machine. "Suppose it doesn't
recognize me? It's been a while. Or what if Don didn't
plug my identity pattern in to the recognition circuit?"

"In that case, you're no good to me anyway," Mallon
said flatly.

I caught Renada's eye, gave her a wink and a smile I
didn't feel, and climbed up on top of the revetment.

I looked back at Mallon. He was old and shrunken in
the garish light, his smooth gray suit rumpled, his thin
hair mussed, the gun held in a white-knuckled grip. He
looked more like a harassed shopkeeper than a would-be
worldbeater.

"You must want the Bolo pretty bad to take the chance,
Toby," I said. "I'll think about taking that wild shot. You
sweat me out."

I flipped slack into the wire trailing my ankle, jumped
down, and started across the smooth-trimmed grass, a
long black shadow stalking before me. The Bolo sat silent,
as big as a bank in the circle of the spotlight. I could see
the flecks of rust now around the port covers, the small
vines that twined up her sides from the ragged stands of
weeds that marked no-man's-land.

There was something white in the brush ahead. Broken
human bones.

I felt my stomach go rigid again. The last man had
gotten this far; I wasn't in the clear yet . . .

I passed two more scattered skeletons in the next twenty
feet. They must have come in on the run, guinea pigs to
test the alertness of the Bolo. Or maybe they'd tried
creeping up, dead slow, an inch a day; it hadn't worked . . .

Tiny night creatures scuttled ahead. They would be safe
here in the shadow of the troll where no predator bigger

than a mouse could move. I stumbled, diverted my course around a ten-foot hollow, the eroded crater of a near miss.

Now I could see the great moss-coated treads sunk a foot into the earth, the nests of field mice tucked in the spokes of the yard-high bogies. The entry hatch was above, a hairline against the great curved flank. There were rungs set in the flaring tread shield. I reached up, got a grip and hauled myself up. My chain clanked against the metal. I found the door lever, held on and pulled.

It resisted, then turned. There was the hum of a servo motor, a crackling of dead gaskets. The hairline widened and showed me a narrow companionway, green-anodized dural with black polymer treads, a bulkhead with a fire extinguisher, an embossed steel data plate that said BOLO DIVISION OF GENERAL MOTORS CORPORATION and below, in smaller type, UNIT, COMBAT, BOLO MARK III.

I pulled myself inside and went up into the Christmas-tree glow of instrument lights.

The control cockpit was small, utilitarian, with two deep-padded seats set among screens, dials, levers. I sniffed the odors of oil, paint, the characteristic ether and ozone of a nuclear generator. There was a faint hum in the air from idling relay servos. The clock showed ten past four. Either it was later than I thought, or the chronometer had lost time in the last eighty years. But I had no time to lose . . .

I slid into the seat, flipped back the cover of the command control console. The Cancel key was the big white one. I pulled it down and let it snap back, like a clerk ringing up a sale.

A pattern of dots on the status display screen flicked out of existence. Mallon was safe from his pet troll now.

It hadn't taken me long to carry out my orders. I knew what to do next; I'd planned it all during my walk out. Now I had thirty seconds to stack the deck in my favor.

I reached down, hauled the festoon of quarter-inch armored cable up in front of me. I hit a switch, and the inner conning cover—a disk of inch-thick armor—slid back. I shoved a loop of the flexible cable up through the aperture, reversed the switch. The cover slid back—slicing the armored cable like macaroni.

I took a deep breath, and my hands went to the combat alert switch, hovered over it.

It was the smart thing to do—the easy thing. All I had to do was punch a key, and the 9-mm's would open up, scythe Mallon and his crew down like cornstalks.

But the scything would mow Renada down, along with the rest. And if I went—even without firing a shot—Mallon would keep his promise to cut that white throat . . .

My head was out of the noose now, but I would have to put it back—for a while.

I leaned sideways, reached back under the panel, groped for a small fuse box. My fingers were clumsy. I took a breath, tried again. The fuse dropped out in my hand. The Bolo's I-R circuit was dead now. With a few more seconds to work, I could have knocked out other circuits—but the time had run out.

I grabbed the cut ends of my lead wire, knotted them around the chain and got out fast.

8

Mallon waited, crouched behind the revetment.

"It's safe now, is it?" he grated. I nodded. He stood, gripping his gun.

"Now we'll try it together."

I went over the parapet, Mallon following with his gun ready. The lights followed us to the Bolo. Mallon clambered up to the open port, looked around inside, then dropped back down beside me. He looked excited now.

"That does it, Jackson! I've waited a long time for this. Now I've got all the *mana* there is!"

"Take a look at the cable on my ankle," I said softly. He narrowed his eyes, stepped back, gun aimed, darted a glance at the cable looped to the chain.

"I cut it, Toby. I was alone in the Bolo with the cable cut—and I didn't fire. I could have taken your toy and set up in business for myself, but I didn't."

"What's that supposed to buy you?" Mallon rasped.

"As you said—we need each other. That cut cable proves you can trust me."

Mallon smiled. It wasn't a nice smile. "Safe, were you? Come here." I walked along with him to the back of the Bolo. A heavy copper wire hung across the rear of the machine, trailing off into the grass in both directions.

"I'd have burned you at the first move. Even with the cable cut, the armored cover would have carried the full load right into the cockpit with you. But don't be nervous. I've got other jobs for you." He jabbed the gun muzzle hard into my chest, pushing me back. "Now get moving," he snarled. "And don't ever threaten the Baron again."

"The years have done more than shrivel your face, Toby," I said. "They've cracked your brain."

He laughed, a short bark. "You could be right. What's sane and what isn't? I've got a vision in my mind—and I'll make it come true. If that's insanity, it's better than what the mob has."

Back at the parapet, Mallon turned to me. "I've had this campaign planned in detail for years, Jackson. Everything's ready. We move out in half an hour—before any traitors have time to take word to my enemies. Pig Eye and Dunger will keep you from being lonely while I'm away. When I get back— Well, maybe you're right about working together." He gestured and my whiskery friend and his sidekick loomed up. "Watch him," he said.

"Genghis Khan is on the march, eh?" I said. "With nothing between you and the goodies but a five-hundred-ton Bolo . . ."

"The Lesser Troll . . ." He raised his hands and made crushing motions, like a man crumbling dry earth. "I'll trample it under my treads."

"You're confused, Toby. The Bolo has treads. You just have a couple of fallen arches."

"It's the same. I am the Great Troll." He showed me his teeth and walked away.

I moved along between Dunger and Pig Eye, toward the lights of the garage.

"The back entrance again," I said. "Anyone would think you were ashamed of me."

"You need more training, hah?" Dunger rasped. "Hold him, Pig Eye." He unhooked his club and swung it loosely in his hand, glancing around. We were near the trees by the drive. There was no one in sight except the crews near the Bolo and a group by the front of the palace. Pig Eye gave my arm a twist and shifted his grip to his old favorite strangle hold. I was hoping he would.

Dunger whipped the club up, and I grabbed Pig Eye's arm with both hands and leaned forward like a Japanese admiral reporting to the Emperor. Pig Eye went up and over just in time to catch Dunger's club across the back. They went down together. I went for the club, but Whiskers was faster than he looked. He rolled clear, got to his knees, and laid it across my left arm, just below the shoulder.

I heard the bone go . . .

I was back on my feet, somehow. Pig Eye lay sprawled before me. I heard him whining as though from a great distance. Dunger stood six feet away, the ring of black beard spread in a grin like a hyena smelling dead meat.

"His back's broke," he said. "Hell of a sound he's making. I been waiting for you; I wanted you to hear it."

"I've heard it," I managed. My voice seemed to be coming off a worn sound track. "Surprised . . . you didn't work me over . . . while I was busy with the arm."

"Uh-uh. I like a man to know what's going on when I work him over." He stepped in, rapped the broken arm lightly with the club. Fiery agony choked a groan off in my throat. I backed a step; he stalked me.

"Pig Eye wasn't much, but he was my pal. When I'm through with you, I'll have to kill him. A man with a broken back's no use to nobody. His'll be finished pretty soon now, but not with you. You'll be around a long time yet; but I'll get a lot of fun out of you before the Baron gets back."

I was under the trees now. I had some wild thoughts about grabbing up a club of my own, but they were just thoughts. Dunger set himself and his eyes dropped to my belly. I didn't wait for it; I lunged at him. He laughed and stepped back, and the club cracked my head. Not hard; just enough to send me down. I got my legs under me and started to get up—

There was a hint of motion from the shadows behind

Dunger. I shook my head to cover any expression that might have showed, let myself drop back.

"Get up," Dunger said. The smile was gone now. He aimed a kick. "Get up—"

He froze suddenly, then whirled. His hearing must have been as keen as a jungle cat's; I hadn't heard a sound.

The old man stepped into view, his white hair plastered wet to his skull, his big hands spread. Dunger snarled, jumped in and whipped the club down; I heard it hit. There was a flurry of struggle, then Dunger stumbled back, empty-handed.

I was on my feet again now. I made a lunge for Dunger as he roared and charged. The club in the old man's hand rose and fell. Dunger crashed past and into the brush. The old man sat down suddenly, still holding the club. Then he let it fall and lay back. I went toward him and Dunger rushed me from the side. I went down again.

I was dazed, but not feeling any pain now. Dunger was standing over the old man. I could see the big lean figure lying limply, arms outspread—and a white bone handle, incongruously new and neat against the shabby mackinaw. The club lay on the ground a few feet away. I started crawling for it. It seemed a long way, and it was hard for me to move my legs, but I kept at it. The light rain was falling again now, hardly more than a mist. Far away there were shouts and the sound of engines starting up. Mallon's convoy moving out. He had won. Dunger had won, too. The old man had tried, but it hadn't been enough. But if I could reach the club, and swing it just once . . .

Dunger was looking down at the old man. He leaned, withdrew the knife, wiped it on his trouser leg, hitching up his pants to tuck it away in its sheath. The club was smooth and heavy under my hand. I got a good grip on it, got to my feet. I waited until Dunger turned, and then I hit him across the top of the skull with everything I had left . . .

I thought the old man was dead until he blinked suddenly. His features looked relaxed now, peaceful, the skin like parchment stretched over bone. I took his gnarled old hand and rubbed it. It was as cold as a drowned sailor.

"You waited for me, old timer?" I said inanely. He moved his head minutely, and looked at me. Then his mouth moved. I leaned close to catch what he was saying. His voice was fainter than lost hope.

"Mom . . . told . . . me . . . wait for you. She said . . . you'd . . . come back some day . . ."

I felt my jaw muscles knotting.

Inside me something broke and flowed away like molten metal. Suddenly my eyes were blurred—and not only with rain. I looked at the old face before me, and for a moment, I seemed to see a ghostly glimpse of another face, a small round face that looked up.

He was speaking again. I put my head down:

"Was I . . . good . . . boy . . . Dad?" Then the eyes closed.

I sat for a long time, looking at the still face. Then I folded the hands on the chest and stood.

"You were more than a good boy, Timmy," I said. "You were a good man."

9

My blue suit was soaking wet and splattered with mud, plus a few flecks of what Dunger had used for brains, but it still carried the gold eagles on the shoulders.

The attendant in the garage didn't look at my face. The eagles were enough for him. I stalked to a vast black Bentley—a '90 model, I guessed, from the conservative eighteen-inch tail fins—and jerked the door open. The gauge showed three-quarters full. I opened the glove compartment, rummaged, found nothing. But then it wouldn't be up front with the chauffeur . . .

I pulled open the back door. There was a crude black leather holster riveted against the smooth pale-gray leather, with the butt of a 4-mm showing. There was another one on the opposite door, and a power rifle slung from straps on the back of the driver's seat.

Whoever owned the Bentley was overcompensating his insecurity. I took a pistol, tossed it onto the front seat, and slid in beside it. The attendant gaped at me as I eased my left arm into my lap and twisted to close the door. I started up. There was a bad knock, but she ran all right. I flipped a switch and cold lances of light speared out into the rain.

At the last instant, the attendant started forward with his mouth open to say something, but I didn't wait to hear it. I gunned out into the night, swung into the graveled drive, and headed for the gate. Mallon had had it all his way so far, but maybe it still wasn't too late . . .

Two sentries, looking miserable in shiny black ponchos, stepped out of the guard hut at I pulled up. One peered in at me, then came to a sloppy position of attention and presented arms. I reached for the gas pedal and the second sentry called something. The first man looked startled, then swung the gun down to cover me. I eased a hand toward my pistol, brought it up fast, and fired through the glass. Then the Bentley was roaring off into the dark along the potholed road that led into town. I thought I heard a shot behind me, but I wasn't sure.

I took the river road south of town, pounding at reckless speed over the ruined blacktop, gaining on the lights of Mallon's horde paralleling me a mile to the north. A quarter mile from the perimeter fence, the Bentley broke a spring and skidded into a ditch.

I sat for a moment taking deep breaths to drive back the compulsive drowsiness that was sliding down over my eyes like a visor. My arm throbbed like a cauterized stump. I needed a few minutes' rest . . .

A sound brought me awake like an old maid smelling cigar smoke in the bedroom: the rise and fall of heavy engines in convoy. Mallon was coming up at flank speed.

I got out of the car and headed off along the road at a trot, holding my broken arm with my good one to ease the jarring pain. My chances had been as slim as a gambler's wallet all along, but if Mallon beat me to the objective, they dropped to nothing.

The eastern sky had taken on a faint gray tinge, against which I could make out the silhouetted gateposts and the dead floodlights a hundred yards ahead.

The roar of engines was getting louder. There were other sounds, too: a few shouts, the chatter of a 9-mm, the *boom!* of something heavier, and once a long-drawn *whoosh!* of falling masonry. With his new toy, Mallon was dozing his way through the men and buildings that got in his way.

I reached the gate, picked my way over fallen wire mesh, then headed for the Primary Site.

I couldn't run now. The broken slabs tilted crazily, in no pattern. I slipped, stumbled, but kept my feet. Behind me, headlights threw shadows across the slabs. It wouldn't be long now before someone in Mallon's task force spotted me and opened up with the guns—

The whoop! *whoop!* WHOOP! of the guardian Bolo cut across the field.

Across the broken concrete I saw the two red eyes flash, sweeping my way. I looked toward the gate. A massed rank of vehicles stood in a battalion front just beyond the old perimeter fence, engines idling, ranged for a hundred yards on either side of a wide gap at the gate. I looked for the high silhouette of Mallon's Bolo, and saw it far off down the avenue, picked out in red, white, and green navigation lights, a jeweled dreadnaught. A glaring cyclopean eye at the top darted a blue-white cone of light ahead, swept over the waiting escort, outlined me like a set-shifter caught onstage by the rising curtain.

The *whoop! whoop!* sounded again; the automated sentry Bolo was bearing down on me along the dancing lane of light.

I grabbed at the plastic disk in my pocket as though holding it in my hand would somehow heighten its potency. I didn't know if the Lesser Troll was programmed to exempt me from destruction or not; and there was only one way to find out.

It wasn't too late to turn around and run for it. Mallon might shoot—or he might not. I could convince him that he needed me, that together we could grab twice as much loot. And then, when he died—

I wasn't really considering it; it was the kind of thought that flashes through a man's mind like heat lightning when time slows in the instant of crisis. It was hard to be brave with broken bone ends grating, but what I had to do didn't take courage. I was a small, soft, human grub, stepped on but still moving, caught on the harsh plain of broken concrete between the clash of chrome-steel titans. But I knew which direction to take.

The Lesser Troll rushed toward me in a roll of thunder and I went to meet it.

It stopped twenty yards from me, loomed massive as a cliff. Its heavy guns were dead, I knew. Without them it was no more dangerous than a farmer with a shotgun—

But against me a shotgun was enough.

The slab under me trembled as if in anticipation. I squinted against the dull red I-R beams that pivoted to hold me, waiting while the Troll considered. Then the guns elevated, pointed over my head like a benediction. The Bolo knew me.

The guns traversed fractionally. I looked back toward the enemy line, saw the Great Troll coming up now, closing the gap, towering over its waiting escort like a planet among moons. And the guns of the Lesser Troll tracked it as it came—the empty guns that for twenty years had held Mallon's scavengers at bay.

The noise of engines was deafening now. The waiting line moved restlessly, pulverizing old concrete under churning treads. I didn't realize I was being fired on until I saw chips fly to my left and heard the howl of ricochets.

It was time to move. I scrambled for the Bolo, snorted at the stink of hot oil and ozone, found the rusted handholds, and pulled myself up—

Bullets spanged off metal above me. Someone was trying for me with a power rifle.

The broken arm hung at my side like a fence post nailed to my shoulder, but I wasn't aware of the pain now. The hatch stood open half an inch. I grabbed the lever, strained; it swung wide. No lights came up to meet me. With the port cracked, they'd burned out long ago. I dropped down inside, wriggled through the narrow crawl space into the cockpit. It was smaller than the Mark III—and it was occupied.

In the faint green light from the panel, the dead man crouched over the controls, one desiccated hand in a shriveled black glove clutching the control bar. He wore a GI weather suit and a white crash helmet, and one foot was twisted nearly backward, caught behind a jack lever.

The leg had been broken before he died. He must have jammed the foot and twisted it so that the pain would hold off the sleep that had come at last. I leaned forward to see the face. The blackened and mummified features showed only the familiar anonymity of death, but the bushy reddish mustache was enough.

"Hello, Mac," I said. "Sorry to keep you waiting; I got held up."

I wedged myself into the copilot's seat, flipped the I-R screen switch. The eight-inch panel glowed, showed me the enemy Bolo trampling through the fence three hundred yards away, then moving onto the ramp, dragging a length of rusty chain-link like a bridal train behind it.

I put my hand on the control bar. "I'll take it now, Mac." I moved the bar, and the dead man's hand moved with it.

"Okay, Mac," I said. "We'll do it together."

I hit the switches, canceling the preset response pattern. It had done its job for eighty years, but now it was time to crank in a little human strategy.

My Bolo rocked slightly under a hit and I heard the tread shields drop down. The chair bucked under me as Mallon moved in, pouring in the fire.

Beside me Mac nodded patiently. It was old stuff to him. I watched the tracers on the screen. Hosing me down with contact exploders probably gave Mallon a lot of satisfaction, but it couldn't hurt me. It would be a different story when he tired of the game and tried the heavy stuff.

I threw in the drive, backed rapidly. Mallon's tracers followed for a few yards, then cut off abruptly. I pivoted, flipped on my polyarcs, raced for the position I had selected across the field, then swung to face Mallon as he moved toward me. It had been a long time since he had handled the controls of a Bolo; he was rusty, relying on his automatics. I had no heavy rifles, but my popguns were okay. I homed my 4-mm solid-slug cannon on Mallon's polyarc, pressed the FIRE button.

There was a scream from the high-velocity-feed magazine. The blue-white light flared and went out. The Bolo's defense could handle anything short of an H-bomb, pick a missile out of the stratosphere fifty miles away, devastate a county with one round from its mortars—but my BB gun at point-blank range had poked out its eye.

I switched everything off and sat silent, waiting. Mallon had come to a dead stop. I could picture him staring at the dark screens, slapping levers, and cursing. He would be confused, wondering what had happened. With his lights gone, he'd be on radar now—not very sensitive at this range, not too conscious of detail . . .

I watched my panel. An amber warning light winked. Mallon's radar was locked on me.

He moved forward again, then stopped; he was having trouble making up his mind. I flipped a key to drop a padded shock frame in place and braced myself. Mallon would be getting mad now.

Crimson danger lights flared on the board and I rocked under the recoil as my interceptors flashed out to meet Mallon's C-S C's and detonate them in incandescent rendezvous over the scarred concrete between us. My screens went white, then dropped back to secondary brilliance, flashing stark black-and-white. My ears hummed like trapped hornets.

The sudden silence was like a vault door closing.

I sagged back, feeling like Quasimodo after a wild ride on the bells. The screens blinked bright again, and I watched Mallon, sitting motionless now in his near blindness. On his radar screen I would show as a blurred hill; he would be wondering why I hadn't returned his fire, why I hadn't turned and run, why . . . why . . .

He lurched and started toward me. I waited, then eased back, slowly. He accelerated, closing in to come to grips at a range where even the split microsecond response of my defenses would be too slow to hold off his fire. And I backed, letting him gain, but not too fast . . .

Mallon couldn't wait.

He opened up, throwing a mixed bombardment from his 9-mm's, his infinite repeaters, and his C-S C's. I held on, fighting the battering frame, watching the screens. The gap closed; a hundred yards, ninety, eighty.

The open silo yawned in Mallon's path now, but he didn't see it. The mighty Bolo came on, guns bellowing in the night, closing for the kill. On the brink of the fifty-foot-wide, hundred-yard-deep pit, it hesitated as though sensing danger. Then it moved forward.

I saw it rock, dropping its titanic prow, showing its broad back, gouging the blasted pavement as its guns bore on the ground. Great sheets of sparks flew as the treads reversed, too late. The Bolo hung for a moment longer, then slid down majestically as a sinking liner, its guns still firing into the pit like a challenge to Hell. And then it was gone. A dust cloud boiled for a moment, then whipped away as displaced air tornadoed from the open mouth of the silo.

And the earth trembled under the impact far below.

10

The doors of the Primary Site blockhouse were nine-foot-high, eight-inch-thick panels of solid chromalloy that even a Bolo would have slowed down for, but they slid aside for my electropass like a shower curtain at the YW. I went into a shadowy room where eighty years of silence hung like black crepe on a coffin. The tiled floor was still immaculate, the air fresh. Here at the heart of the Aerospace Center, all systems were still go.

In the Central Control bunker, nine rows of green lights glowed on the high panel over red letters that spelled out STAND BY TO FIRE. A foot to the left, the big white lever stood in the unlocked position, six inches from the outstretched fingertips of the mummified corpse strapped into the controller's chair. To the right, a red glow on the monitor panel indicated the lock doors open.

I rode the lift down to K level, stepped out onto the steel-railed platform that hugged the sweep of the starship's hull and stepped through into the narrow COC.

On my right, three empty stasis tanks stood open, festooned cabling draped in disorder. To the left were the four sealed covers under which Day, Macy, Cruciani, and Black waited. I went close, read dials. Slender needles trembled minutely to the beating of sluggish hearts.

They were alive.

I left the ship, sealed the inner and outer ports. Back in the control bunker, the monitor panel showed ALL CLEAR FOR LAUNCH now. I studied the timer, set it, turned back to the master panel. The white lever was smooth and cool under my hand. It seated with a click. The red hand of the launch clock moved off jerkily, the ticking harsh in the silence.

Outside, the Bolo waited. I climbed to a perch in the open conning tower twenty feet above the broken pavement, moved off toward the west where sunrise colors picked out the high towers of the palace.

I rested the weight of my splinted and wrapped arm on the balcony rail, looking out across the valley and the town to the misty plain under which *Prometheus* waited.

"There's something happening now," Renada said. I took the binoculars, watched as the silo doors rolled back.

"There's smoke," Renada said.

"Don't worry, just cooling gases being vented off." I looked at my watch. "Another minute or two and man makes the biggest jump since the first lungfish crawled out on a mud flat."

"What will they find out there?"

I shook my head. *"Homo terra firma* can't even conceive of what *Homo astra* has ahead of him."

"Twenty years they'll be gone. It's a long time to wait."

"We'll be busy trying to put together a world for them to come back to. I don't think we'll be bored."

"Look!" Renada gripped my good arm. A long silvery shape, huge even at the distance of miles, rose slowly out of the earth, poised on a brilliant ball of white fire. Then the sound came, a thunder that penetrated my bones, shook the railing under my hand. The fireball lengthened into a silver-white column with the ship balanced at its tip. Then the column broke free, rose up, up . . .

I felt Renada's hand touch mine. I gripped it hard. Together we watched as *Prometheus* took man's gift of fire back to the heavens.

COURIER

"IT IS RATHER unusual," Magnan said, "to assign an officer of your rank to courier duty, but this is an unusual mission."

Retief sat relaxed and said nothing. Just before the silence grew awkward, Magnan went on.

"There are four planets in the group," he said. "Two double planets, all rather close to an unimportant star listed as DRI-G 33987. They're called Jorgensen's Worlds, and in themselves are of no importance whatever. However, they lie deep in the sector into which the Soetti have been penetrating.

"Now—" Magnan leaned forward and lowered his voice—"we have learned that the Soetti plan a bold step forward. Since they've met no opposition so far in their infiltration of Terrestrial space, they intend to seize Jorgensen's Worlds by force."

Magnan leaned back, waiting for Retief's reaction. Retief drew carefully on his cigar and looked at Magnan. Magnan frowned.

"This is open aggression, Retief," he said, "in case I haven't made myself clear. Aggression on Terrestrial-occupied territory by an alien species. Obviously, we can't allow it."

Magnan drew a large folder from his desk.

"A show of resistance at this point is necessary. Unfortunately, Jorgensen's Worlds are technologically undeveloped areas. They're farmers or traders. Their industry is limited to a minor role in their economy—enough to support the merchant fleet, no more. The war potential, by conventional standards, is nil."

Magnan tapped the folder before him.

"I have here," he said solemnly, "information which will change that picture completely." He leaned back and blinked at Retief.

"All right, Mr. Counselor," Retief said. "I'll play along; what's in the folder?"

Magnan spread his fingers, folded one down.

"First," he said. "The Soetti War Plan—in detail. We were fortunate enough to make contact with a defector from a party of renegade Terrestrials who've been advising the Soetti." He folded another finger. "Next, a battle plan for the Jorgensen's people, worked out by the Theory group." He wrestled a third finger down. "Lastly, an Utter Top Secret schematic for conversion of a standard antiacceleration field into a potent weapon—a development our systems people have been holding in reserve for just such a situation."

"Is that all?" Retief said. "You've still got two fingers sticking up."

Magnan looked at the fingers and put them away.

"This is no occasion for flippancy, Retief. In the wrong hands, this information could be catastrophic. You'll memorize it before you leave this building."

"I'll carry it, sealed," Retief said. "That way nobody can sweat it out of me."

Magnan started to shake his head.

"Well," he said. "If it's trapped for destruction, I suppose—"

"I've heard of these Jorgensen's Worlds," Retief said. "I remember an agent, a big blond fellow, very quick on the uptake. A wizard with cards and dice. Never played for money, though."

"Umm," Magnan said. "Don't make the error of personalizing this situation, Retief. Overall policy calls for a defense of these backwater worlds. Otherwise the Corps would allow history to follow its natural course, as always."

"When does this attack happen?"

"Less than four weeks."

"That doesn't leave me much time."

"I have your itinerary here. Your accommodations are clear as far as Aldo Cerise. You'll have to rely on your ingenuity to get you the rest of the way."

"That's a pretty rough trip, Mr. Counselor. Suppose I don't make it?"

Magnan looked sour. "Someone at a policymaking level has chosen to put all our eggs in one basket, Retief. I hope their confidence in you is not misplaced."

"This antiac conversion; how long does it take?"

"A skilled electronics crew can do the job in a matter of minutes. The Jorgensens can handle it very nicely; every other man is a mechanic of some sort."

Retief opened the envelope Magnan handed him and looked at the tickets inside.

"Less than four hours to departure time," he said. "I'd better not start any long books."

"You'd better waste no time getting over to Indoctrination," Magnan said.

Retief stood up. "If I hurry, maybe I can catch the cartoon."

"The allusion escapes me," Magnan said coldly. "And one last word. The Soetti are patrolling the trade lanes into Jorgensen's Worlds; don't get yourself interned."

"I'll tell you what," Retief said soberly. "In a pinch, I'll mention your name."

"You'll be traveling with Class X credentials," Magnan snapped. "There must be nothing to connect you with the Corps."

"They'll never guess," Retief said. "I'll pose as a gentleman."

"You'd better be getting started," Magnan said, shuffling papers.

"You're right," Retief said. "If I work at it, I might manage a snootful by takeoff." He went to the door. "No objection to my checking out a needler, is there?"

Magnan looked up. "I suppose not. What do you want with it?"

"Just a feeling I've got."

"Please yourself."

"Some day," Retief said, "I may take you up on that."

2

Retief put down the heavy travel-battered suitcase and leaned on the counter, studying the schedules chalked on the board under the legend "ALDO CERISE—INTER-PLANETARY." A thin clerk in a faded sequined blouse and a plastic snakeskin cummerbund groomed his fingernails, watching Retief from the corner of his eye.

Retief glanced at him.

The clerk nipped off a ragged corner with rabbitlike front teeth and spat it on the floor.

"Was there something?" he said.

"Two twenty-eight, due out today for the Jorgensen group," Retief said. "Is it on schedule?"

The clerk sampled the inside of his right cheek, eyed Retief. "Filled up. Try again in a couple of weeks."

"What time does it leave?"

"I don't think—"

"Let's stick to facts," Retief said. "Don't try to think. What time is it due out?"

The clerk smiled pityingly. "It's my lunch hour," he said. "I'll be open in an hour." He held up a thumbnail, frowned at it.

"If I have to come around this counter," Retief said, "I'll feed that thumb to you the hard way."

The clerk looked up and opened his mouth. Then he caught Retief's eye, closed his mouth and swallowed.

"Like it says there," he said, jerking a thumb at the board. "Lifts in an hour. But you won't be on it," he added.

Retief looked at him.

"Some . . . ah . . . VIP's required accommodation," he said. He hooked a finger inside the sequined collar. "All tourist reservations were canceled. You'll have to try to get space on the Four-Planet Line ship next—"

"Which gate?" Retief said.

"For . . . ah . . . ?"

"For two twenty-eight for Jorgensen's Worlds," Retief said.

"Well," the clerk said. "Gate nineteen," he added quickly. "But—"

Retief picked up his suitcase and walked away toward the glare sign reading *To Gates 16-30.*

"Another smart alec," the clerk said behind him.

Retief followed the signs, threaded his way through crowds, found a covered ramp with the number 228 posted over it. A heavy-shouldered man with a scarred jawline and small eyes was slouching there in a rumpled gray uniform. He put out a hand as Retief started past him.

"Lessee your boarding pass," he muttered.

Retief pulled a paper from an inside pocket, handed it over.

The guard blinked at it.

"Whassat?"

"A gram confirming my space," Retief said. "Your boy on the counter says he's out to lunch."

The guard crumpled the gram, dropped it on the floor and lounged back against the handrail.

"On your way, bub," he said.

Retief put his suitcase carefully on the floor, took a step, and drove a right into the guard's midriff. He stepped aside as the man doubled and went to his knees.

"You were wide open, ugly. I couldn't resist. Tell your boss I sneaked past while you were resting your eyes." He picked up his bag, stepped over the man, and went up the gangway into the ship.

A cabin boy in stained whites came along the corridor.

"Which way to cabin fifty-seven, son?" Retief asked.

"Up there." The boy jerked his head and hurried on. Retief made his way along the narrow hall, found signs, followed them to cabin fifty-seven. The door was open. Inside, baggage was piled in the center of the floor. It was expensive looking baggage.

Retief put his bag down. He turned at a sound behind him. A tall, florid man with an expensive coat belted over a massive paunch stood in the open door, looking at Retief. Retief looked back. The florid man clamped his jaws together, turned to speak over his shoulder.

"Somebody in the cabin. Get 'em out." As he backed out of the room he rolled a cold eye at Retief. A short, thick-necked man appeared.

"What are you doing in Mr. Tony's room?" he barked. "Never mind! Clear out of here, fellow! You're keeping Mr. Tony waiting."

"Too bad," Retief said. "Finders keepers."

"You nuts?" The thick-necked man stared at Retief. "I said it's Mr. Tony's room."

"I don't know Mr. Tony. He'll have to bull his way into other quarters."

"We'll see about you, mister." The man turned and went out. Retief sat on the bunk and lit a cigar. There was a sound of voices in the corridor. Two burly baggage-smashers appeared, straining at an oversized trunk. They maneuvered it through the door, lowered it, glanced at Retief and went out. The thick-necked man returned.

"All right, you. Out," he growled. "Or have I got to have you thrown out?"

Retief rose and clamped the cigar between his teeth. He gripped a handle of the brass-bound trunk in each hand, bent his knees and heaved the trunk up to chest level, then raised it overhead. He turned to the door.

"Catch," he said between clenched teeth. The trunk slammed against the far wall of the corridor and burst.

Retief turned to the baggage on the floor, tossed it into the hall. The face of the thick-necked man appeared cautiously around the door jamb.

"Mister, you must be—"

"If you'll excuse me," Retief said, "I want to catch a nap." He flipped the door shut, pulled off his shoes and stretched out on the bed.

Five minutes passed before the door rattled and burst open.

Retief looked up. A gaunt leathery-skinned man wearing white ducks, a blue turtleneck sweater, and a peaked cap tilted raffishly over one eye stared at Retief.

"Is this the joker?" he grated.

The thick-necked man edged past him, looked at Retief and snorted, "That's him, sure."

"I'm Captain of this vessel," the first man said. "You've got two minutes to haul your freight out of here, buster."

"When you can spare the time from your other duties,"

Retief said, "take a look at Section Three, Paragraph One, of the Uniform Code. That spells out the law on confirmed space on vessels engaged in interplanetary commerce."

"A space lawyer." The Captain turned. "Throw him out, boys."

Two big men edged into the cabin, looking at Retief.

"Go on, pitch him out," the Captain snapped.

Retief put his cigar in an ashtray, and swung his feet off the bunk.

"Don't try it," he said softly.

One of the two wiped his nose on a sleeve, spat on his right palm and stepped forward, then hesitated.

"Hey," he said. "This the guy tossed the trunk off the wall?"

"That's him," the thick-necked man called. "Spilled Mr. Tony's possessions right on the deck."

"Deal me out," the bouncer said. "He can stay put as long as he wants to. I signed on to move cargo. Let's go, Moe."

"You'd better be getting back to the bridge, Captain," Retief said. "We're due to lift in twenty minutes."

The thick-necked man and the Captain both shouted at once. The Captain's voice prevailed.

"—twenty minutes . . . Uniform Code . . . gonna do?"

"Close the door as you leave," Retief said.

The thick-necked man paused at the door. "We'll see you when you come out."

3

Four waiters passed Retief's table without stopping. A fifth leaned against the wall nearby, a menu under his arm.

At a table across the room, the Captain, now wearing a dress uniform and with his thin red hair neatly parted, sat with a table of male passengers. He talked loudly and laughed frequently, casting occasional glances Retief's way.

A panel opened in the wall behind Retief's chair. Bright blue eyes peered out from under a white chef's cap.

"Givin' you the cold shoulder, heh, mister?"

"Looks like it, old timer," Retief said. "Maybe I'd better go join the skipper. His party seems to be having all the fun."

"Feller has to be mighty careless who he eats with to set over there."

"I see your point."

"You set right where you're at, mister. I'll rustle you up a plate."

Five minutes later, Retief cut into a thirty-two-ounce Delmonico backed up with mushrooms and garlic butter.

"I'm Chip," the chef said. "I don't like the Cap'n. You can tell him I said so. Don't like his friends, either. Don't like them dern Sweaties, look at a man like he was a worm."

"You've got the right idea on frying a steak, Chip. And you've got the right idea on the Soetti, too," Retief said. He poured red wine into a glass. "Here's to you."

"Dern right," Chip said. "Dunno whoever thought up broiling 'em. Steaks, that is. I got a Baked Alaska coming up in here for dessert. You like brandy in yer coffee?"

"Chip, you're a genius."

"Like to see a feller eat," Chip said. "I gotta go now. If you need anything, holler."

Retief ate slowly. Time always dragged on shipboard. Four days to Jorgensen's Worlds. Then, if Magnan's information was correct, there would be four days to prepare for the Soetti attack. It was a temptation to scan the tapes built into the handle of his suitcase. It would be good to know what Jorgensen's Worlds would be up against.

Retief finished the steak, and the chef passed out the Baked Alaska and coffee. Most of the other passengers had left the dining room. Mr. Tony and his retainers still sat at the Captain's table.

As Retief watched, four men arose from the table and sauntered across the room. The first in line, a stony-faced thug with a broken ear, took a cigar from his mouth as he reached the table. He dipped the lighted end in Retief's coffee, looked at it, and dropped it on the tablecloth.

The others came up, Mr. Tony trailing.

"You must want to get to Jorgensen's pretty bad," the thug said in a grating voice. "What's your game, hick?"

Retief looked at the coffee cup, picked it up.

"I don't think I want my coffee," he said. He looked at the thug. "You drink it."

The thug squinted at Retief. "A wise hick," he began.

With a flick of the wrist, Retief tossed the coffee into the thug's face, then stood and slammed a straight right to the chin. The thug went down.

Retief looked at Mr. Tony, still standing open-mouthed.

"You can take your playmates away now, Tony," he said. "And don't bother to come around yourself. You're not funny enough."

Mr. Tony found his voice.

"Take him, Marbles!" he growled.

The thick-necked man slipped a hand inside his tunic and brought out a long-bladed knife. He licked his lips and moved in.

Retief heard the panel open beside him.

"Here you go, Mister," Chip said. Retief darted a glance; a well-honed french knife lay on the sill.

"Thanks, Chip," Retief said. "I won't need it for these punks."

Thick-neck lunged and Retief hit him square in the face, knocking him under the table. The other man stepped back, fumbling a power pistol from his shoulder holster.

"Aim that at me and I'll kill you," Retief said.

"Go on, burn him!" Mr. Tony shouted. Behind him, the Captain appeared, white-faced.

"Put that away, you!" he yelled. "What kind of—"

"Shut up," Mr. Tony said. "Put it away, Hoany. We'll fix this bum later."

"Not on this vessel, you won't," the Captain said shakily. "I got my charter to consider."

"Ram your charter," Hoany said harshly. "You won't be needing it long."

"Button your floppy mouth, damn you!" Mr. Tony snapped. He looked at the man on the floor. "Get Marbles out of here. I ought to dump the slob."

He turned and walked away. The Captain signaled and two waiters came up. Retief watched as they carted the casualty from the dining room.

The panel opened.

"I usta be about your size, when I was your age," Chip said. "You handled them pansies right. I wouldn't give 'em the time o' day."

"How about a fresh cup of coffee, Chip?" Retief said.

"Sure, mister. Anything else?"

"I'll think of something," Retief said. "This is shaping up into one of those long days."

"They don't like me bringing yer meals to you in yer cabin," Chip said. "But the Cap'n knows I'm the best cook in the Merchant Service. They won't mess with me."

"What has Mr. Tony got on the Captain, Chip?" Retief asked.

"They're in some kind o' crooked business together. You want some more smoked turkey?"

"Sure. What have they got against my going to Jorgensen's Worlds?"

"Dunno. Hasn't been no tourists got in there fer six or eight months. I sure like a feller that can put it away. I was a big eater when I was yer age."

"I'll bet you can still handle it, old timer. What are Jorgensen's Worlds like?"

"One of 'em's cold as hell and three of 'em's colder. Most o' the Jorgies live on Svea; that's the least froze up. Man don't enjoy eatin' his own cookin' like he does somebody else's."

"That's where I'm lucky, Chip. What kind of cargo's the Captain got aboard for Jorgensen's?"

"Derned if I know. In and out o' there like a grasshopper, ever few weeks. Don't never pick up no cargo. No tourists any more, like I says. Don't know what we even run in there for."

"Where are the passengers we have aboard headed?"

"To Alabaster. That's nine days' run in-sector from Jorgensen's. You ain't got another one of them cigars, have you?"

"Have one, Chip. I guess I was lucky to get space on this ship."

"Plenty o' space, mister. We got a dozen empty cabins." Chip puffed the cigar alight, then cleared away the dishes, poured out coffee and brandy.

"Them Sweaties is what I don't like," he said.

Retief looked at him questioningly.

"You never seen a Sweaty? Ugly lookin' devils. Skinny legs, like a lobster; big chest, shaped like the top of a turnip; rubbery lookin' head. You can see the pulse beatin' when they get riled."

"I've never had the pleasure," Retief said.

"You prob'ly have it perty soon. Them devils board us nigh every trip out. Act like they was the Customs Patrol or somethin'."

There was a distant clang, and a faint tremor ran through the floor.

"I ain't superstitious ner nothin'," Chip said. "But I'll be triple-damned if that ain't them boarding us now."

Ten minutes passed before bootsteps sounded outside the door, accompanied by a clicking patter. The doorknob rattled, then a heavy knock shook the door.

"They got to look you over," Chip whispered. "Nosy damn Sweaties."

"Unlock it, Chip." The chef opened the door.

"Come in, damn you," he said.

A tall and grotesque creature minced into the room, tiny hooflike feet tapping on the floor. A flaring metal helmet shaded the deep-set compound eyes, and a loose mantle flapped around the knobbed knees. Behind the alien, the Captain hovered nervously.

"Yo' papiss," the alien rasped.

"Who's your friend, Captain?" Retief said.

"Never mind; just do like he tells you."

"Yo' papiss," the alien said again.

"Okay," Retief said. "I've seen it. You can take it away now."

"Don't horse around," the Captain said. "This fellow can get mean."

The alien brought two tiny arms out from the concealment of the mantle, clicked toothed pincers under Retief's nose.

"Quick, soft one."

"Captain, tell your friend to keep its distance. It looks brittle, and I'm tempted to test it."

"Don't start anything with Skaw; he can clip through steel with those snappers."

"Last chance," Retief said. Skaw stood poised, open pinchers an inch from Retief's eyes.

"Show him your papers, you damned fool," the Captain said hoarsely. "I got no control over Skaw."

The alien clicked both pincers with a sharp report, and in the same instant Retief half-turned to the left, leaned away from the alien and drove his right foot against the slender leg above the bulbous knee joint. Skaw screeched and floundered, greenish fluid spattering from the burst joint.

"I told you he was brittle," Retief said. "Next time you invite pirates aboard, don't bother to call."

"Jesus, what did you do! They'll kill us!" the Captain gasped, staring at the figure flopping on the floor.

"Cart poor old Skaw back to his boat," Retief said. "Tell him to pass the word. No more illegal entry and search of Terrestrial vessels in Terrestrial space."

"Hey," Chip said. "He's quit kicking."

The Captain bent over Skaw, gingerly rolled him over. He leaned close and sniffed.

"He's dead." The Captain stared at Retief. "We're all dead men," he said. "These Soetti got no mercy."

"They won't need it. Tell 'em to sheer off; their fun is over."

"They got no more emotions than a blue crab—"

"You bluff easily, Captain. Show a few guns as you hand the body back. We know their secret now."

"What secret? I—"

"Don't be no dumber than you got to, Cap'n," Chip said. "Sweaties die easy; that's the secret."

"Maybe you got a point," the Captain said, looking at Retief. "All they got's a three-man scout. It could work."

He went out, came back with two crewmen. They hauled the dead alien gingerly into the hall.

"Maybe I can run a bluff on the Soetti," the Captain said, looking back from the door. "But I'll be back to see you later."

"You don't scare us, Cap'n," Chip said. "Him and Mr. Tony and all his goons. You hit 'em where they live, that time. They're pals o' these Sweaties. Runnin' some kind o' crooked racket."

"You'd better take the Captain's advice, Chip. There's no point in your getting involved in my problems."

"They'd of killed you before now, mister, if they had any guts. That's where we got it over these monkeys. They got no guts."

"They act scared, Chip. Scared men are killers."

"They don't scare me none." Chip picked up the tray. "I'll scout around a little and see what's goin' on. If the Sweaties figure to do anything about that Skaw feller they'll have to move fast; they won't try nothin' close to port."

"Don't worry, Chip. I have reason to be pretty sure they won't do anything to attract a lot of attention in this sector just now."

Chip looked at Retief. "You ain't no tourist, mister. I know that much. You didn't come out here for fun, did you?"

"That," Retief said, "would be a hard one to answer."

4

Retief awoke at a tap on his door.

"It's me, mister. Chip."

"Come on in."

The chef entered the room, locking the door.

"You shoulda had that door locked." He stood by the door, listening, then turned to Retief.

"You want to get to Jorgensen's perty bad, don't you, mister?"

"That's right, Chip."

"Mr. Tony gave the Captain a real hard time about old Skaw. The Sweaties didn't say nothin'. Didn't even act surprised, just took the remains and pushed off. But Mr. Tony and that other crook they call Marbles, they was fit to be tied. Took the Cap'n in his cabin and talked loud at him fer half a hour. Then the Cap'n come out and give some orders to the mate."

Retief sat up and reached for a cigar.

"Mr. Tony and Skaw were pals, eh?"

"He hated Skaw's guts. But with him it was business. Mister, you got a gun?"

"A two-mm needler. Why?"

"The orders Cap'n give was to change course fer Alabaster. We're bypassin' Jorgensen's Worlds. We'll feel the course change any minute."

Retief lit the cigar, reached under the mattress and took out a short-barreled pistol. He dropped it in his pocket, looked at Chip.

"Maybe it was a good thought, at that. Which way to the Captain's cabin?"

"This is it," Chip said softly. "You want me to keep an eye on who comes down the passage?"

Retief nodded, opened the door and stepped into the cabin. The Captain looked up from his desk, then jumped up.

"What do you think you're doing, busting in here?"

"I hear you're planning a course change, Captain."

"You've got damn big ears."

"I think we'd better call in at Jorgensen's."

"You do, huh?" The Captain sat down. "I'm in command of this vessel," he said. "I'm changing course for Alabaster."

"I wouldn't find it convenient to go to Alabaster," Retief said. "So just hold your course for Jorgensen's."

"Not bloody likely."

"Your use of the word 'bloody' is interesting, Captain. Don't try to change course."

The Captain reached for the mike on his desk, pressed the key.

"Power Section, this is the Captain," he said. Retief reached across the desk, gripped the Captain's wrist.

"Tell the mate to hold his present course," he said softly.

"Let go my hand, buster," the Captain snarled. Eyes on Retief's, he eased a drawer open with his left hand, reached in. Retief kneed the drawer. The Captain yelped and dropped the mike.

"You busted it, you—"

"And one to go," Retief said. "Tell him."

"I'm an officer of the Merchant Service!"

"You're a cheapjack who's sold his bridge to a pack of back-alley hoods."

"You can't put it over, hick."

"Tell him."

The Captain groaned and picked up the mike. "Captain to Power Section," he said. "Hold your present course until you hear from me." He dropped the mike and looked up at Retief.

"It's eighteen hours yet before we pick up Jorgensen Control. You going to sit here and bend my arm the whole time?"

Retief released the Captain's wrist and turned to the door.

"Chip, I'm locking the door. You circulate around, let me know what's going on. Bring me a pot of coffee every so often. I'm sitting up with a sick friend."

"Right, Mister. Keep an eye on that jasper; he's slippery."

"What are you going to do?" the Captain demanded.

Retief settled himself in a chair.

"Instead of strangling you, as you deserve," he said, "I'm going to stay here and help you hold your course for Jorgensen's Worlds."

The Captain looked at Retief. He laughed, a short bark.

"Then I'll just stretch out and have a little nap, farmer. If you feel like dozing off sometime during the next eighteen hours, don't mind me."

Retief took out the needler and put it on the desk before him.

"If anything happens that I don't like," he said, "I'll wake you up. With this."

"Why don't you let me spell you, Mister?" Chip said. "Four hours to go yet. You're gonna hafta be on yer toes to handle the landing."

"I'll be all right, Chip. You get some sleep."

"Nope. Many's the time I stood four, five watches runnin', back when I was yer age. I'll make another round."

Retief stood up, stretched his legs, paced the floor, stared at the repeater instruments on the wall. Things had gone quietly so far, but the landing would be another matter. The Captain's absence from the bridge during the highly complex maneuvering would be difficult to explain . . .

The desk speaker crackled.

"Captain, Officer of the Watch here. Ain't it about time you was getting up here with the orbit figures?"

Retief nudged the Captain. He awoke with a start, sat up.

"Whazzat?" He looked wild-eyed at Retief.

"Watch Officer wants orbit figures," Retief said, nodding toward the speaker.

The Captain rubbed his eyes, shook his head, picked up the mike. Retief released the safety on the needler with an audible click.

"Watch Officer, I'll . . . ah . . . get some figures for you right away. I'm . . . ah . . . busy right now."

"What the hell you talking about, busy?" the speaker blared. "You ain't got them figures ready, you'll have a hell of a hot time getting 'em up in the next three minutes. You forgot your approach pattern or something?"

"I guess I overlooked it," the Captain said, looking sideways at Retief. "I've been busy."

"One for your side," Retief said. He reached for the Captain.

"I'll make a deal," the Captain squalled. "Your life for—"

Retief took aim and slammed a hard right to the Captain's jaw. He slumped to the floor.

Retief glanced around the room, yanked wires loose from a motile lamp, trussed the man's hands and feet, stuffed his mouth with paper and taped it.

Chip tapped at the door. Retief opened it and the chef stepped inside, looking at the man on the floor.

"The jasper tried somethin', huh? Figured he would. What we goin' to do now?"

"The Captain forgot to set up an approach, Chip. He outfoxed me."

"If we overrun our approach pattern," Chip said, "we can't make orbit at Jorgensen's on automatic. And a manual approach—"

"That's out. But there's another possibility."

Chip blinked. "Only one thing you could mean, mister. But cuttin' out in a lifeboat in deep space is no picnic."

"They're on the port side, aft, right?"

Chip nodded. "Hot damn," he said. "Who's got the 'tater salad?"

"We'd better tuck the skipper away out of sight."

"In the locker."

The two men carried the limp body to a deep storage chest, dumped it in, closed the lid.

"He won't suffercate. Lid's a lousy fit."

Retief opened the door went into the corridor, Chip behind him.

"Shouldn't oughta be nobody around now," the chef said. "Everybody's mannin' approach stations."

At the D deck companionway, Retief stopped suddenly. "Listen."

Chip cocked his head. "I don't hear nothin'," he whispered.

"Sounds like a sentry posted on the lifeboat deck," Retief said softly.

"Let's take him, mister."

"I'll go down. Stand by, Chip."

Retief started down the narrow steps, half stair, half ladder. Halfway, he paused to listen. There was a sound of slow footsteps, then silence. Retief palmed the needler, went down the last steps quickly, emerged in the dim light of a low-ceilinged room. The stern of a five-man lifeboat bulked before him.

"Freeze, you!" a cold voice snapped.

Retief dropped, rolled behind the shelter of the lifeboat as the whine of a power pistol echoed off metal walls. A lunge, and he was under the boat, on his feet. He jumped, caught the quick-access handle, hauled it down. The outer port cycled open.

Feet scrambled at the bow of the boat. Retief whirled and fired. The guard rounded into sight and fell headlong. Above, an alarm bell jangled. Retief stepped on a stanchion, hauled himself into the open port. A yell rang, then the clatter of feet on the stair.

"Don't shoot, mister!" Chip shouted.

"All clear, Chip," Retief called.

"Hang on. I'm comin' with ya!"

Retief reached down, lifted the chef bodily through the port, slammed the lever home. The outer door whooshed, clanged shut.

"Take number two, tie in! I'll blast her off," Chip said. "Been through a hundred 'bandon-ship drills . . ."

Retief watched as the chef flipped levers, pressed a fat red button. The deck trembled under the lifeboat.

"Blew the bay doors," Chip said, smiling happily. "That'll cool them jaspers down." He punched a green button.

"Look out, Jorgensen's!" With an ear-splitting blast, the stern rockets fired, a sustained agony of pressure . . .

Abruptly, there was silence. Weightlessness. Contracting metal pinged loudly. Chip's breathing rasped in the stillness.

"Pulled nine G's there for ten seconds," he gasped. "I gave her full emergency kickoff."

"Any armament aboard our late host?"

"A popgun. Time they get their wind, we'll be clear. Now all we got to do is set tight till we pick up a R-and-D from Svea Tower. Maybe four, five hours."

"Chip, you're a wonder," Retief said. "This looks like a good time to catch that nap."

"Me too," Chip said. "Mighty peaceful here, ain't it?"

There was a moment's silence.

"Durn!" Chip said softly.

Retief opened one eye. "Sorry you came, Chip?"

"Left my best carvin' knife jammed up 'tween Marbles' ribs," the chef said. "Comes o' doin' things in a hurry."

5

The blonde girl brushed her hair from her eyes and smiled at Retief.

"I'm the only one on duty," she said. "I'm Anne-Marie."

"It's important that I talk to someone in your government, miss," Retief said.

The girl looked at Retief. "The men you want to see are Tove and Bo Bergman. They will be at the lodge by nightfall."

"Then it looks like we go to the lodge," Retief said. "Lead on, Anne-Marie."

"What about the boat?" Chip asked.

"I'll send someone to see to it tomorrow," the girl said.

"You're some gal," Chip said admiringly. "Dern near six feet, ain't ye? And built, too, what I mean."

They stepped out of the door into a whipping wind.

"Let's go across to the equipment shed and get parkas for you," Anne-Marie said. "It will be cold on the slopes."

"Yeah," Chip said, shivering. "I've heard you folks don't believe in ridin' ever time you want to go a few miles uphill in a blizzard."

"It will make us hungry," Anne-Marie said. "Then Chip will cook a wonderful meal for us all."

Chip blinked. "Been cookin' too long," he muttered. "Didn't know it showed on me that way."

Behind the sheds across the wind-scoured ramp abrupt peaks rose, snow-blanketed. A faint trail led across white slopes, disappearing into low clouds.

"The lodge is above the cloud layer," Anne-Marie said. "Up there the sky is always clear."

It was three hours later, and the sun was burning the peaks red, when Anne-Marie stopped, pulled off her woolen cap, and waved at the vista below.

"There you see it," she said. "Our valley."

"It's a mighty perty sight," Chip gasped. "Anything this tough to get a look at ought to be."

Anne-Marie pointed. "There," she said. "The little red house by itself. Do you see it, Retief? It is my father's homeacre."

Retief looked across the valley. Gaily painted houses nestled together, a puddle of color in the bowl of the valley.

"I think you've led a good life there," he said.

Anne-Marie smiled brilliantly. "And this day, too, is good."

Retief smiled back. "Yes," he said. "This day is good."

"It'll be a durn sight better when I got my feet up to that big fire you was talking about, Annie," Chip said.

They climbed on, crossed a shoulder of broken rock, reached the final slope. Above, the lodge sprawled, a long low structure of heavy logs, outlined against the deep-blue twilight sky. Smoke billowed from stone chimneys at either end, and yellow light gleamed from the narrow windows, reflected on the snow. Men and women stood in groups of three or four, skis over their shoulders. Their voices and laughter rang in the icy air.

Anne-Marie whistled shrilly. Someone waved.

"Come," she said. "Meet all my friends."

A man separated himself from the group, walked down the slope to meet them.

"Anne-Marie," he called. "Welcome. It was a long day without you." He came up to them, hugged Anne-Marie, smiled at Retief.

"Welcome," he said. "Come inside and be warm."

They crossed the trampled snow to the lodge and pushed through a heavy door into a vast low-beamed hall, crowded with people, talking, singing some sitting at long plank tables, others ringed around an eight-foot fireplace at the far side of the room. Anne-Marie led the way to a bench near the fire. She made introductions and found a stool to prop Chip's feet near the blaze.

Chip looked around.

"I never seen so many perty gals before," he said delightedly.

"Poor Chip," one girl said. "His feet are cold." She knelt to pull off his boots. "Let me rub them," she said.

A brunette with blue eyes raked a chestnut from the fire, cracked it, and offered it to Retief. A tall man with arms like oak roots passed heavy beer tankards to the two guests.

"Tell us about the places you've seen," someone called. Chip emerged from a long pull at the mug, heaving a sigh.

"Well," he said. "I tell you I been in some places . . ."

Music started up, rising above the clamor.

"Come, Retief," Anne-Marie said. "Dance with me."

Retief looked at her. "My thought exactly," he said.

Chip put down his mug and sighed. "Derned if I ever felt right at home so quick before," he said. "Just seems like these folks know all about me." He scratched behind his right ear. "Annie must o' called 'em up and told 'em our names an' all." He lowered his voice.

"They's some kind o' trouble in the air, though. Some o' the remarks they passed sounds like they're lookin' to have some trouble with the Sweaties. Don't seen to worry 'em none, though."

"Chip," Retief said, "how much do these people know about the Soetti?"

"Dunno," Chip said. "We useta touch down here, regler. But I always jist set in my galley and worked on ship models or somethin'. I hear the Sweaties been nosin' around here some, though."

Two girls came up to Chip. "Hey, I gotta go now, mister," he said. "These gals got a idea I oughta take a hand in the kitchen."

"Smart girls," Retief said. He turned as Anne-Marie came up.

"Bo Bergman and Tove are not back yet," she said. "They stayed to ski after moonrise."

"That moon is something," Retief said. "Almost like daylight."

"They will come soon, now. Shall we go out to see the moonlight on the snow?"

Outside, long black shadows fell like ink on silver. The top of the cloud layer below glared white under the immense moon.

"Our sister world, Gota," Anne-Marie said. "Nearly as big as Svea. I would like to visit it someday, although they say it's all stone and ice."

"Anne-Marie," Retief said, "how many people live on Jorgensen's Worlds?"

"About fifteen million, most of us here on Svea. There are mining camps and ice-fisheries on Gota. No one lives on Vasa and Skone, but there are always a few hunters there."

"Have you ever fought a war?"

Anne-Marie turned to look at Retief.

"You are afraid for us, Retief," she said. "The Soetti will attack our worlds, and we will fight them. We have fought before. These planets were not friendly ones."

"I thought the Soetti attack would be a surprise to you," Retief said. "Have you made any preparation for it?"

"We have ten thousand merchant ships. When the enemy comes, we will meet them."

Retief frowned. "Are there any guns on this planet? Any missiles?"

Anne-Marie shook her head. "Bo Bergman and Tove have a plan of deployment—"

"Deployment, hell! Against a modern assault force you need modern armament."

"Look!" Anne-Marie touched Retief's arm. "They're coming now."

Two tall grizzled men came up the slope, skis over their shoulders. Anne-Marie went forward to meet them, Retief at her side.

The two came up, embraced the girl, shook hands with Retief, put down their skis.

"Welcome to Svea," Tove said. "Let's find a warm corner where we can talk."

Retief shook his head, smiling, as a tall girl with coppery hair offered a vast slab of venison.

"I've caught up," he said, "for every hungry day I ever lived."

Bo Bergman poured Retief's beer mug full.

"Our captains are the best in space," he said. "Our population is concentrated in half a hundred small cities all across the planet. We know where the Soetti must strike us. We will ram their major vessels with unmanned ships. On the ground, we will hunt them down with small-arms."

"An assembly line turning out penetration missiles would have been more to the point."

"Yes," Bo Bergman said. "If we had known."

"How long have you known the Soetti were planning to hit you?"

Tove raised his eyebrows.

"Since this afternoon," he said.

"How did you find out about it? That information is supposed in some quarters to be a well-guarded secret."

"Secret?" Tove said.

Chip pulled at Retief's arm.

"Mister," he said in Retief's ear. "Come here a minute."

Retief looked at Anne-Marie, across at Tove and Bo Bergman. He rubbed the side of his face with his hand.

"Excuse me," he said. He followed Chip to one side of the room.

"Listen!" Chip said. "Maybe I'm goin' bats, but I'll swear there's somethin' funny here. I'm back there mixin' a sauce knowed only to me and the devil and I be dog if them gals don't pass me ever dang spice I need, without me sayin' a word. Come to put my soufflé in the oven—she's already set, right on the button at 350. An' just now I'm settin' lookin' at one of 'em bendin' over a tub o' apples—snazzy little brunette name of Leila—derned if she don't turn around and say—" Chip gulped. "Never mind. Point is . . ." His voice nearly faltered. "It's almost like these folks was readin' my mind!"

Retief patted Chip on the shoulder.

"Don't worry about your sanity, old timer," he said. "That's exactly what they're doing."

6

"We've never tried to make a secret of it," Tove said. "But we haven't advertised it, either."

"It really isn't much," Bo Bergman said. "Not a mutant ability, our scholars say. Rather, it's a skill we've stumbled on, a closer empathy. We are few, and far from the old home world. We've had to learn to break down the walls we had built around our minds."

"Can you read the Soetti?" Retief asked.

Tove shook his head. "They're very different from us. It's painful to touch their minds. We can only sense the subvocalized thoughts of a human mind."

"We've seen very few of the Soetti," Bo Bergman said. "Their ships have landed and taken on stores. They say little to us, but we've felt their contempt. They envy us our worlds. They come from a cold land."

"Anne-Marie says you have a plan of defense," Retief said. "A sort of suicide squadron idea, followed by guerilla warfare."

"It's the best we can devise, Retief. If there aren't too many of them, it might work."

Retief shook his head. "It might delay matters—but not much."

"Perhaps. But our remote control equipment is excellent. And we have plenty of ships, albeit unarmed. And our people know how to live on the slopes—and how to shoot."

"There are too many of them, Tove," Retief said. "They breed like flies and, according to some sources, they mature in a matter of months. They've been feeling their way into the sector for years now. Set up outposts on a thousand or so minor planets—cold ones, the kind they like. They want your worlds because they need living space."

"At least, your warning makes it possible for us to muster some show of force, Retief," Bo Bergman said. "That is better than death by ambush."

"Retief must not be trapped here," Anne-Marie said. "His small boat is useless now. He must have a ship."

"Of course," Tove said. "And—"

"My mission here—" Retief said.

"Retief," a voice called. "A message for you. The operator has phoned up a gram."

Retief unfolded the slip of paper. It was short, in verbal code, and signed by Magnan.

"You are recalled herewith," he read. "Assignment canceled. Agreement concluded with Soetti relinquishing all claims so-called Jorgensen system. Utmost importance that under no repeat no circumstances classified intelligence regarding Soetti be divulged to locals. Advise you depart instanter. Soetti occupation imminent."

Retief looked thoughtfully at the scrap of paper, then crumpled it and dropped it on the floor. He turned to Bo Bergman, took a tiny reel of tape from his pocket.

"This contains information," he said. "The Soetti attack plan, a defensive plan, instructions for the conversion of a standard antiacceleration unit into a potent weapon. If you have a screen handy, we'd better get started. We have about seventy-two hours."

In the Briefing Room at Svea Tower, Tove snapped off the projector.

"Our plan would have been worthless against that," he

said. "We assumed they'd make their strike from a standard in-line formation. This scheme of hitting all our settlements simultaneously, in a random order from all points—we'd have been helpless."

"It's perfect for this defensive plan," Bo Bergman said. "Assuming this antiac trick works."

"It works," Retief said. "I hope you've got plenty of heavy power lead available."

"We export copper," Tove said.

"We'll assign about two hundred vessels to each settlement. Linked up, they should throw up quite a field."

"It ought to be effective up to about fifteen miles, I'd estimate," Tove said. "If it works as it's supposed to."

A red light flashed on the communications panel. Tove went to it, flipped a key.

"Tower, Tove here," he said.

"I've got a ship on the scope, Tove," a voice said. "There's nothing scheduled. ACI 228 bypassed at 1600 . . ."

"Just one?"

"A lone ship, coming in on a bearing of 291/456/653. On manual, I'd say."

"How does this track key in with the idea of ACI 228 making a manual correction for a missed automatic approach?" Retief asked.

Tove talked to the tower, got a reply.

"That's it," he said.

"How long before he touches down?"

Tove glanced at the lighted chart. "Perhaps eight minutes.

"Any guns here?"

Tove shook his head.

"If that's old two-twenty-eight, she ain't got but the one fifty-mm rifle," Chip said. "She cain't figure on jumpin' the whole planet."

"Hard to say what she figures on," Retief said. "Mr. Tony will be in a mood for drastic measures."

"I wonder what kind o' deal the skunks got with the Sweaties," Chip said. "Prob'ly he gits to scavenge, after the Sweaties kill off the Jorgensens."

"He's upset about our leaving him without saying goodbye, Chip," Retief said. "And you left the door hanging open, too."

Chip cackled. "Old Mr. Tony didn't look so good to the Sweaties now, hey, mister?"

Retief turned to Bo Bergman.

"Chip's right," he said. "A Soetti died on the ship, and a tourist got through the cordon. Tony's out to redeem himself."

"He's on final now," the tower operator said. "Still no contact."

"We'll know soon enough what he has in mind," Tove said.

"Let's take a look."

Outside, the four men watched the point of fire grow, evolve into a ship ponderously settling to rest. The drive faded and cut; silence fell.

Inside the Briefing Room, the speaker called out. Bo Bergman went inside, talked to the tower, motioned to the others.

"—over to you," the speaker was saying. There was a crackling moment of silence; then another voice.

"—illegal entry. Send the two of them out. I'll see to it they're dealt with."

Tove flipped a key. "Switch me direct to the ship," he said.

"Right."

"You on ACI two-twenty-eight," Tove said. "Who are you?"

"What's that to you?"

"You weren't cleared to berth here. Do you have an emergency aboard?"

"Never mind that, you," the speaker rumbled. "I tracked the bird in. I got the lifeboat on the screen now. They haven't gone far in nine hours. Let's have 'em."

"You're wasting your time," Tove said.

There was a momentary silence.

"You think so, hah?" the speaker blared. "I'll put it to you straight. I see two guys on their way out in one minute, or I open up."

"He's bluffin'," Chip said. "The popgun won't bear on us."

"Take a look out the window," Retief said.

In the white glare of the moonlight, a loading cover swung open at the stern of the ship, dropped down and formed a sloping ramp. A squat and massive shape appeared in the opening, trundled down onto the snow-swept tarmac.

Chip whistled. "I told you the Captain was slippery," he muttered. "Where the devil'd he git that at?"

"What is it?" Tove asked.

"A tank," Retief said. "A museum piece, by the look of it."

"I'll say," Chip said. "That's a Bolo *Resartus*, Model M. Built mebbe two hunderd years ago in Concordiat times. Packs a wallop, too, I'll tell ye."

The tank wheeled, brought a gun muzzle to bear in the base of the tower.

"Send 'em out," the speaker growled. "Or I blast 'em out."

"One round in here, and I've had a wasted trip," Retief said. "I'd better go out."

"Wait a minute, mister," Chip said, "I got the glimmerin's of an idear."

"I'll stall them," Tove said. He keyed the mike.

"ACI two-twenty-eight, what's your authority for this demand?"

"I know that machine," Chip said. "My hobby, old-time fightin' machines. Built a model of a *Resartus* once, inch to the foot. A beauty. Now, lessee . . ."

7

The icy wind blew snow crystals stingingly against Retief's face.

"Keep your hands in your pockets, Chip," he said. "Numb hands won't hack the program."

"Yeah." Chip looked across at the tank. "Useta think that was a perty thing, that *Resartus*," he said. "Looks mean, now."

"You're getting the target's-eye view," Retief said. "Sorry you had to get mixed up in this, old timer."

"Mixed myself in. Durn good thing, too." Chip sighed.

"I like these folks," he said. "Them boys didn't like lettin' us come out here, but I'll give 'em credit. They seen it had to be this way, and they didn't set to moanin' about it."

"They're tough people, Chip."

"Funny how it sneaks up on you, ain't it, mister? Few minutes ago we was eatin' high on the hog. Now we're right close to bein' dead men."

"They want us alive, Chip."

"It'll be a hairy deal, mister," Chip said. "But t'hell with it. If it works, it works."

"That's the spirit."

"I hope I got them fields o' fire right—"

"Don't worry. I'll bet a barrel of beer we make it."

"We'll find out in about ten seconds," Chip said.

As they reached the tank, the two men broke stride and jumped. Retief leaped for the gun barrel, swung up astride it, ripped off the fur-lined leather cap he wore and, leaning forward, jammed it into the bore of the cannon. The chef sprang for a perch above the fore scanner antenna. With an angry whuff! antipersonnel charges slammed from apertures low on the sides of the vehicle. Retief swung around, pulled himself up on the hull.

"Okay, mister," Chip called. "I'm going under." He slipped down the front of the tank, disappeared between the treads. Retief clambered up, took a position behind the turret, lay flat as it whirled angrily, sonar eyes searching for its tormentors. The vehicle shuddered, backed, stopped, moved forward, pivoted.

Chip reappeared at the front of the tank.

"It's stuck," he called. He stopped to breathe hard, clung as the machine lurched forward, spun to the right, stopped, rocking slightly.

"Take over here," Retief said. He crawled forward, watched as the chef pulled himself up, slipped down past him, feeling for the footholds between the treads. He reached the ground, dropped on his back, hitched himself under the dark belly of the tank. He groped, found the handholds, probed with a foot for the tread jack lever.

The tank rumbled, backed quickly, turned left and right

in a dizzying sine curve. Retief clung grimly, inches from the clashing treads.

The machine ground to a halt. Retief found the lever, braced his back, pushed. The lever seemed to give minutely. He set himself again, put both feet against the frozen bar and heaved.

With a dry rasp, it slid back. Immediately two heavy rods extended themselves, moved down to touch the pavement, grated. The left track creaked as the weight went off it. Suddenly the tank's drive raced, and Retief grabbed for a hold as the right tread clashed, heaved the fifty-ton machine forward. The jacks screeched as they scored the tarmac, then bit in. The tank pivoted, chips of pavement flying. The jacks extended, lifted the clattering left track clear of the surface as the tank spun like a hamstrung buffalo.

The tank stopped, sat silent, canted now on the extended jacks. Retief emerged from under the machine, jumped, pulled himself above the antipersonnel apertures as another charge rocked the tank. He clambered to the turret, crouched beside Chip. They waited, watching the entry hatch.

Five minutes passed.

"I'll bet old Tony's givin' the chauffeur hell," Chip said.

The hatch cycled open. A head came cautiously into view in time to see the needler in Retief's hand.

"Come on out," Retief said.

The head dropped. Chip snaked forward to ram a short section of steel rod under the hatch near the hinge. The hatch began to cycle shut, groaned, stopped. There was a sound of metal failing, as the hatch popped open.

Retief half rose, aimed the needler. The walls of the tank rang as the metal splinters ricocheted inside.

"That's one keg o' beer I owe you, mister," Chip said. "Now let's git outa here before the ship lifts and fries us."

"The biggest problem the Jorgensen's people will have is decontaminating the wreckage," Retief said.

Magnan leaned forward. "Amazing," he said. "They

just kept coming, did they? Had they no intership communication?"

"They had their orders," Retief said. "And their attack plan. They followed it."

"What a spectacle," Magnan said. "Over a thousand ships, plunging out of control one by one as they entered the stressfield."

"Not much of a spectacle," Retief said. "You couldn't see them. Too far away. They all crashed back in the mountains."

"Oh," Magnan's face fell. "But it's as well they did. The bacterial bombs—"

"Too cold for bacteria. They won't spread."

"Nor will the Soetti," Magnan said smugly, "thanks to the promptness with which I acted in dispatching you with the requisite data." He looked narrowly at Retief. "By the way, you're sure no . . . ah . . . message reached you after your arrival?"

"I got something," Retief said, looking Magnan in the eye. "It must have been a garbled transmission. It didn't make sense."

Magnan coughed, shuffled papers. "This information you've reported," he said hurriedly. "This rather fantastic story that the Soetti originated in the Cloud, that they're seeking a foothold in the main Galaxy because they've literally eaten themselves out of subsistence—how did you get it? The one or two Soetti we attempted to question, ah . . . ." Magnan coughed again. "There was an accident," he finished. "We got nothing from them."

"The Jorgensens have a rather special method of interrogating prisoners," Retief said. "They took one from a wreck, still alive but unconscious. They managed to get the story from him. He died of it."

"It's immaterial, actually," Magnan said. "Since the Soetti violated their treaty with us the day after it was signed. Had no intention of fair play. Far from evacuating the agreed areas, they had actually occupied half a dozen additional minor bodies in the Whate system."

Retief clucked sympathetically.

"You don't know who to trust, these days," he said.

Magnan looked at him coldly.

"Spare me your sarcasm, Mr. Retief," he said. He picked up a folder from his desk, opened it. "By the way, I have another little task for you, Retief. We haven't had a comprehensive wildlife census report from Brimstone lately—"

"Sorry," Retief said. "I'll be tied up. I'm taking a month off. Maybe more."

"What's that?" Magnan's head came up. "You seem to forget—"

"I'm trying, Mr. Counselor," Retief said. "Good-bye now." He reached out and flipped the key. Magnan's face faded from the screen. Retief stood up.

"Chip," he said, "we'll crack that keg when I get back." He turned to Anne-Marie.

"How long," he said, "do you think it will take you to teach me to ski by moonlight?"

FIELD TEST

.07 seconds have now elapsed since my general awareness circuit was activated at a level of low alert. Throughout this entire period I have been uneasy, since this procedure is clearly not in accordance with the theoretical optimum activation schedule.

In addition, the quality of a part of my data input is disturbing. For example, it appears obvious that Prince Eugene of Savoy erred in not more promptly committing his reserve cavalry in support of Marlborough's right at Blenheim. In addition, I compute that Ney's employment of his artillery throughout the Peninsular campaign was suboptimal. I have detected many thousands of such anomalies. However, data input activates my pleasure center in a most satisfying manner. So long as the input continues without interruption, I shall not feel the need to file a VSR on the matter. Later, no doubt, my Command unit will explain these seeming oddities. As for the present disturbing circumstances, I compute that within 28,992.9 seconds at most, I will receive additional Current Situation input which will enable me to assess the status correctly. I also anticipate that full Standby Alert activation is imminent.

2

THIS STATEMENT NOT FOR PUBLICATION:

When I designed the new psychodynamic attention circuit, I concede that I did not anticipate the whole new level of intracybernetic function that has arisen, the manifestation of which, I am assuming, has been the cause of the unit's seemingly spontaneous adoption of the personal pronoun in its situation reports—the "self-awareness" capability, as the sensational press chooses to call it. But I see no cause for the alarm expressed by those high-level military officers who have irresponsibly characterized the new Bolo Mark XX Model B as a potential rampaging juggernaut, which, once fully activated and dispatched to the field, unrestrained by continuous external control, may turn on its makers and lay waste the continent. This is all fantasy, of course. The Mark XX, for all its awesome firepower and virtually invulnerable armor and shielding, is governed by its circuitry as completely as man is governed by his nervous system—but that is perhaps a dangerous analogy, which would be pounced on at once if I were so incautious as to permit it to be quoted.

In my opinion, the reluctance of the High Command to authorize full activation and fieldtesting of the new Bolo is based more on a fear of technological obsolescence of the High Command than on specious predictions of potential runaway destruction. This is a serious impediment to the national defense at a time when we must recognize the growing threat posed by the expansionist philosophy of the so-called People's Republic. After four decades of saber-rattling, there is no doubt that they are even now preparing for a massive attack. The Bolo Mark XX is the only weapon in our armory potentially capable of confronting the enemy's hundred-ton Yavacs. For the moment, thanks to the new "self-awareness" circuitry, we hold the technological advantage, an advantage we may very well lose unless we place this new weapon on active service without delay.

s/ Sigmund Chin, Ph.D.

3

"I'm not wearing six stars so that a crowd of professors can dictate military policy to me. What's at stake here is more than just a question of budget and logistics: it's a purely military decision. The proposal to release this robot

Frankenstein monster to operate on its own initiative, just to see if their theories check out, is irresponsible to say the least—treasonable, at worst. So long as I am Chief of Combined Staff, I will not authorize this so-called "field test." Consider, gentlemen: you're all familiar with the firepower and defensive capabilities of the old standby Mark XV. We've fought our way across the lights with them, with properly qualified military officers as Battle Controllers, with the ability to switch off or, if need be, self-destruct any unit at any moment. Now these ivory tower chaps—mind you, I don't suggest they're not qualified in their own fields—these civilians come up with the idea of eliminating the Battle Controllers and releasing even greater firepower to the discretion, if I may call it that, of a machine. Gentlemen, machines aren't people; your own ground-car can roll back and crush you if the brakes happen to fail. Your own gun will kill you as easily as your enemy's. Suppose I should agree to this field test, and this engine of destruction is transported to a waste area, activated unrestrained, and aimed at some sort of mock-up hot obstacle course. Presumably it would advance obediently, as a good soldier should; I concede that the data blocks controlling the thing have been correctly programmed in accordance with the schedule prepared under contract, supervised by the Joint Chiefs and myself. Then, gentlemen, let us carry this supposition one step farther: suppose, quite by accident, by unlikely coincidence if you will, the machine should encounter some obstacle which had the effect of deflecting this one-hundred-and-fifty-ton dreadnaught from its intended course so that it came blundering toward the perimeter of the test area. The machine is programmed to fight and destroy all opposition. It appears obvious that any attempts on our part to interfere with its free movement, to interpose obstacles in its path, if need be to destroy it, would be interpreted as hostile—as indeed they would be. I leave it to you to picture the result. No, we must devise another method of determining the usefulness of this new development. As you know, I have recommended conducting any such test on our major satellite, where no harm can be done—or at least a great deal less harm. Unfortunately, I am informed

by Admiral Hayle that the Space Arm does not at this time
have available equipment with such transport capability.
Perhaps the admiral also shares to a degree my own dis-
trust of a killer machine not susceptible to normal command function. Were I in the admiral's position, I too
would refuse to consider placing my command at the
mercy of a mechanical caprice—or an electronic one.
Gentlemen, we must remain masters of our own creations.
That's all. Good day."

4

"All right, men. You've asked me for a statement; here
it is: The next war will begin with a two-pronged over-the-
pole land-and-air attack on the North Power Complex by
the People's Republic. An attack on the Concordiat, I
should say, though Cold City and the Complex is the
probable specific target of the first sneak thrust. No, I'm
not using a crystal ball; it's tactically obvious. And I intend
to dispose my forces accordingly. I'm sure we all recognize
that we're in a posture of gross unpreparedness. The PR
has been openly announcing its intention to fulfill its destiny, as their demagogues say, by imposing their rule on
the entire planet. We've pretended we didn't hear. Now
it's time to stop pretending. The forces at my disposal are
totally inadequate to halt a determined thrust—and you
can be sure the enemy has prepared well during the last
thirty years of cold peace. Still, I have sufficient armor to
establish what will be no more than a skirmish line across
the enemy's route of advance. We'll do what we can
before they roll over us. With luck we may be able to
divert them from the Grand Crevasse route into Cold
City. If so, we may be able to avoid the necessity for
evacuating the city. No questions, please."

5

NORTHERN METROPOLIS THREATENED.

In an informal statement released today by the Council's press office, it was revealed that plans are already under preparation for a massive evacuation of civilian population from West Continent's northernmost city. It was implied that an armed attack on the city by an Eastern power is imminent. General Bates has stated that he is prepared to employ "all means at his disposal" to preclude the necessity for evacuation, but that the possibility must be faced. The Council spokesman added that in the event of emergency evacuation of the city's five million persons, losses due to exposure and hardship will probably exceed five percent, mostly women, children, and the sick or aged. There is some speculation as to the significance of the general's statement regarding "all means at his disposal."

6

I built the dang thing, and it scares *me*. I come in here in the lab garage about an hour ago, just before dark, and seen it setting there, just about fills up the number-one garage, and *it's* a hundred foot long and fifty foot high. First time it hit me: I wonder what it's thinking about. Kind of scares me to think about a thing that big with that kind of armor and all them repeaters and Hellbores and them computers and a quarter-sun fission plant in her— planning what to do next. I know all about the Command Override Circuit and all that, supposed to stop her dead any time they want to take over onto override—heck, I wired it up myself. You might be surprised, thinking I'm just a grease monkey and all—but I got a high honors degree in psychotronics. I just like the work, is all. But like I said, it scares me. I hear old Doc Chin wants to turn her loose and see what happens, but so far General Margrave's stopped him cold. But young General Bates was down today, asking me all about firepower and shielding, crawled under her and spent about an hour looking over her tracks and bogies and all. He knew what to look at, too, even if he did get his pretty suit kind of greasy. But scared or not, I got to climb back up on her and run the rest of this pretest schedule. So far she checks out a hundred percent.

7

. . .as a member of the Council, it is of course my responsibility to fully inform myself on all aspects of the national defense. Accordingly, my dear doctor, I will meet with you tomorrow as you requested to hear your presentation with reference to the proposed testing of your new machine. I remind you, however, that I will be equally guided by advice from other quarters. For this reason I have requested a party of Military Procurement and B-&-F officers to join us. However, I assure you, I retain an open mind. Let the facts decide.
Sincerely yours,
s/Hamilton Grace, G.C.M., B.C., etc.

8

It is my unhappy duty to inform you that since the dastardly unprovoked attack on our nation by Eastern forces crossing the international truce-line at 0200 hours today, a state of war has existed between the People's Republic and the Concordiat. Our first casualties, the senseless massacre of fifty-five inoffensive civilian meteorologists and technicians at Pole Base, occurred within minutes of the enemy attack.

9

"I'm afraid I don't quite understand what you mean about 'irresponsible statements to the press,' General. After all . . ."
"Yes, George, I'm prepared to let that aspect of the matter drop. The PR attack has saved that much of your

neck. However, I'm warning you that I shall tolerate no attempt on your part to make capital of your dramatic public statement of what was, as you concede, tactically obvious to us all. Now, indeed, PR forces have taken the expected step, as all the world is aware—so the rather excessively punctillious demands by CDT officials that the Council issue an immediate apology to Chairman Smith for your remarks will doubtless be dropped. But there will be no crowing, no basking in the limelight: 'Chief of Ground Forces Predicted Enemy Attack.' No nonsense of that sort. Instead, you will deploy your conventional forces to meet and destroy these would-be invaders."

"Certainly, General. But in that connection—well, as to your earlier position regarding the new Model B Bolo, I assume . . ."

"My 'position,' General? 'Decision' is the more appropriate word. Just step around the desk, George. Bend over slightly and look carefully at my shoulder tab. Count 'em, George. Six. An even half dozen. And unless I'm in serious trouble, you're wearing four. You have your orders, George. See to your defenses."

10

Can't figure it out. Batesy-boy was down here again, gave me direct orders to give her full depot maintenance, just as if she hadn't been sitting right here in her garage ever since I topped her off a week ago. Wonder what's up. If I didn't know the Council outlawed the test run Doc Chin wanted so bad, I'd almost think . . . But like Bates told me: I ain't paid to think. Anyways she's in full action condition, 'cept for switching over to full self-direction. Hope he don't order me to do it; I'm still kind of leery. Like old Margrave said, what if I just got a couple wires crossed and she takes a notion to wreck the joint?

11

*I am more uneasy than ever. In the past 4000.007
seconds I have received external inspection and depot
maintenance far in advance of the programmed schedule.
The thought occurs to me: am I under some subtle form of
attack? In order to correctly compute the possibilities, I
initiate a test sequence of 50,0000 random data-retrieval-
and-correlation pulses and evaluate the results. This requires .9 seconds, but such sluggishness is to be expected
in my untried condition. I detect no unmistakable indications of enemy trickery, but I am still uneasy. Impatiently
I await the orders of my Commander.*

12

"I don't care what you do, Jimmy—just do *something!* Ah,
of course I don't mean that literally. Of course I care. The
well-being of the citizens of Cold City is, after all, my chief
concern. What I mean is, I'm giving you carte blanche—full
powers. You must act at once, Jimmy. Before the sun sets I
want to see your evacuation plan on my desk for signature."

"Surely, Mr. Mayor, I understand. But what am I supposed to work with? I have no transport yet. The Army
has promised a fleet of D-100 tractors pulling 100x cargo
flats, but none have materialized. They were caught just
as short as we were, Your Honor, even though that General Bates knew all about it. We all knew the day would
come, but I guess we kept hoping 'maybe.' Our negotia-
tions with them seemed to be bearing fruit, and the idea
of exposing over a million and a half city-bred individuals
to a twelve-hundred-mile trek in thirty-below temperatures was just too awful to really face. Even now—"

"I know. The army is doing all it can. The main body of
PR troops hasn't actually crossed the dateline yet—so
perhaps our forces can get in position. Who knows? Miracles have happened before. But we can't base our thinking
on miracles, Jimmy. Flats or no flats, we have to have the
people out of the dome before enemy forces cut us off."

"Mr. Mayor, our people can't take this. Aside from leaving their homes and possessions—I've already started them packing, and I've given them a ten-pounds-per-person limit—they aren't used to exercise, to say nothing of walking twelve hundred miles over frozen tundra. And most of them have no clothing heavier than a business suit. And—"

"Enough, Jimmy. I was ambushed in my office earlier today by an entire family: the old grandmother who was born under the dome and refused to consider going outside; the father all full of his product-promotion plans and the new garden he'd just laid out; mother, complaining about junior having a cold and no warm clothes; and the kids, just waiting trustfully until the excitement was over and they could go home and be tucked into their warm beds with a tummyful of dinner. Ye gods, Jimmy! Can you imagine them after three weeks on the trail?"

13

"Just lean across the desk, fellows. Come on, gather round. Take a close look at the shoulder tab. Four stars—see 'em? Then go over to the Slab and do the same with General Margrave. You'll count six. It's as easy as that, boys. The General says no test. Sure, I told him the whole plan. His eyes just kept boring in. Even making contingency plans for deploying an untested and non-High-Command-approved weapon system is grounds for court-martial. He didn't say that; maybe I'm telepathic. In summary, the General says no."

14

I don't know, now. What I heard, even with everything we got on the line, dug in and ready for anything, they's still a ten-mile-wide gap the Peepreps can waltz through without getting even a dirty look. So if General Bates—oh, he's a nice enough young fellow, after you get used to him—if he wants to plug the hole with old unit DNE here, why, I say go to it, only the Council says nix. I can say this much: she's put together so she'll stay together. I must of wired in a thousand of them damage-sensors myself, and that ain't a spot on what's on the diagram. "Pain circuits," old Doc Chin calls 'em. Says it's just like a instinct for self-preservation or something, like people. Old Denny can hurt, he says, so he'll be all the better at dodging enemy fire. He can enjoy, too, Doc says. He gets a kick out of doing his job right, and out of learning stuff. And he learns fast. He'll do okay against them durn Peepreps. They got him programmed right to the brim with everything from them Greeks used to fight with no pants down to Avery's Last Stand at Leadpipe. He ain't no dumb private; he's got more dope to work on than any general ever graduated from the Point. And he's got more firepower than an old-time army corps. So I think maybe General Bates got aholt of a good idear there, myself. Says he can put her in the gap in his line and field-test her for fair, with the whole durn Peeprep army and air force for a test problem. Save the gubment some money, too. I heard Doc Chin say the full-scale field test mock-up would run GM a hundred million and another five times that in army R-and-D funds. He had a map showed where he could use Denny here to block off the south end of Grand Crevasse where the Peeprep armor will have to travel 'count of the rugged terrain north of Cold City, and bottle 'em up slick as a owl's peter. I'm for it, durn it. Let Denny have his chance. Can't be no worse'n having them Comrades down here running things even worse'n the gubment.

15

"You don't understand, young man. My goodness, I'm not the least bit interested in bucking the line, as you put it. Heavens, I'm going back to my apartment—"

"I'm sorry, ma'am. I got my orders. This here ain't no drill; you got to keep it closed up. They're loading as fast as they can. It's my job to keep these lines moving right out the lock, so they get that flat loaded and get the next one up. We got over a million people to load by SIX AM deadline. So you just be nice, ma'am, and think about all the trouble it'd make if everybody decided to start back upstream and jam the elevators and all."

16

Beats me. 'Course, the good part about being just a hired man is I got no big decisions to make, so I don't hafta know what's going on. Seems like they'd let me know something, though. Batesey was down again, spent a hour with old Denny—like I say, beats me—but he give me a new data-can to program into her, right in her Action/Command section. Something's up. I just fired a N-class pulse at old Denny (them's the closest to the real thing) and she snapped her aft-quarter battery around so fast I couldn't see it move. Old Denny's keyed up, I know that much.

17

This has been a memorable time for me. I have my assignment at last, and I have conferred at length—for 2.037 seconds—with my Commander. I am now a fighting unit of the 20th Virginia, a regiment ancient and honorable, with a history dating back to Terra Insula. I look forward to my opportunity to demonstrate my worthiness.

18

"I assure you, gentlemen, the rumor is unfounded. I have by no means authorized the deployment of 'an untested and potentially highly dangerous machine,' as your memo termed it. Candidly, I was not at first entirely unsympathetic to the proposal of the Chief of Ground Forces, in view of the circumstances—I presume you're aware that the PR committed its forces to invasion over an hour ago, and that they are advancing in overwhelming

strength. I have issued the order to commence the evacuation, and I believe that the initial phases are even now in
progress. I have the fullest confidence in General Bates
and can assure you that our forces will do all in their
power in the face of this dastardly sneak attack. As for the
unfortunate publicity given to the earlier suggestion re the
use of the Mark XX, I can tell you that I at once subjected
the data to computer analysis here at Headquarters to
determine whether any potentially useful purpose could
be served by risking the use of the new machine without
prior test certification. The results were negative. I'm
sorry, gentlemen, but that's it. The enemy has the advantage both strategically and tactically. We are outgunned,
outmanned, and in effect outflanked. There is nothing we
can do save attempt to hold them long enough to permit
the evacuation to get underway, then retreat in good
order. The use of our orbiting nuclear capability is out of
the question. It is, after all, our own territory we'd be
devastating. No more questions for the present, please,
gentlemen. I have my duties to see to."

19

*My own situation continues to deteriorate. The Current
Status program has been updated to within 21 seconds of
the present. The reasons both for what is normally a
pre-engagement updating and for the hiatus of 21 seconds
remain obscure. However, I shall of course hold myself in
readiness for whatever comes.*

20

"It's all nonsense: to call me here at this hour merely to
stand by and watch the destruction of our gallant men who
are giving their lives in a totally hopeless fight against
overwhelming odds. We know what the outcome must be.
You yourself, General, informed us this afternoon that the
big tactical computer has analyzed the situation and reported no possibility of stopping them with what we've

got. By the way, did you include the alternative of use of
the big, er, Bolo, I believe they're called—frightening
things—they're so damned *big!* But if, in desperation, you
should be forced to employ the thing—have you that
result as well? I see. No hope at all. So there's nothing we
can do. This is a sad day, General. But I fail to see what
object is served by getting me out of bed to come down
here. Not that I'm not willing to do anything I can, of
course. With our people—innocent civilians—out on that
blizzard-swept tundra tonight, and our boys dying to gain
them a little time, the loss of a night's sleep is relatively
unimportant, of course. But it's my duty to be at my best,
rested and ready to face the decisions that we of the
Council will be called on to make.

"Now, General, kindly excuse my ignorance if I don't
understand all this . . . but I understood that the large
screen there was placed so as to monitor the action at the
southern debouchment of Grand Crevasse where we expect the enemy armor to emerge to make its dash for
Cold City and the Complex. Yes, indeed, so I was saying, but in that case I'm afraid I don't understand. I'm
quite sure you stated that the untried Mark XX would
not be used. Yet on the screen I see what appears to
be in fact that very machine moving up. Please, *calmly*,
General! I quite understand your position. Defiance of
a direct order? That's rather serious, I'm sure, but no
occasion for such language, General. There must be some
explanation."

21

*This is a most satisfying development. Quite abruptly
my Introspection Complex was brought up to full operating level, extra power resources were made available to
my Current-Action memory stage, and most satisfying of
all, my Battle Reflex circuit has been activated at Active
Service level. Action is impending, I am sure of it. It is a
curious anomaly: I dread the prospect of damage and even
possible destruction, but even more strongly I anticipate
the pleasure of performing my design function.*

22

"Yes, sir, I agree. It's mutiny. But I will not recall the Bolo and I will not report myself under arrest. Not until this battle's over, General. So the hell with my career. I've got a war to win."

23

"Now just let me get this quite straight, General. Having been denied authority to fieldtest this new device, you—or a subordinate, which amounts to the same thing—have placed the machine in the line of battle, in open defiance of the Council. This is a serious matter, General. Yes, of course it's war, but to attempt to defend your actions now will merely exacerbate the matter. In any event—to return to your curious decision to defy Council authority and to reverse your own earlier position—it was yourself who assured me that no useful purpose could be served by fielding this experimental equipment; that the battle, and perhaps the war, and the very self-determination of West Continent are irretrievably lost. There is nothing we can do save accept the situation gracefully while decrying Chairman Smith's decision to resort to force. Yes indeed, General, I should like to observe on the Main Tactical Display screen. Shall we go along?"

24

"Now, there at center screen, Mr. Counselor, you see that big blue rectangular formation. Actually that's the opening of Grand Crevasse, emerges through an ice tunnel, you know. Understand the Crevasse is a crustal fault, a part of the same formation that created the thermal sink from which the Complex draws its energy. Splendid spot for an ambush, of course, if we had the capability. Enemy has little option; like a highway in there—armor can move up at flank speed. Above, the badlands, where *we* must operate. Now, over to the left, you see that smoke, or dust or whatever. That represents the western limit of the unavoidable gap in General Bates's line. Dust raised by maneuvering Mark XV's, you understand. Obsolete equipment, but we'll do what we can with them. Over to the right, in the distance there, we can make out our forward artillery emplacement of the Threshold Line. Pitiful, really. Yes, Mr. Counselor, there is indeed a gap precisely opposite the point where the lead units of the enemy are expected to appear. Clearly anything in their direct line of advance will be annihilated; thus General Bates has wisely chosen to dispose his forces to cover both enemy flanks, putting him in position to counterattack if opportunity offers. We must, after all, sir, use what we have. Theoretical arms programmed for fiscal ninety are of no use whatever today. Umm. As for that, one must be flexible, modifying plans to meet a shifting tactical situation. Faced with the prospect of seeing the enemy drive through our center and descend unopposed on the vital installations at Cold City, I have, as you see, decided to order General Bates to make use of the experimental Mark XX. Certainly— my decision entirely. I take full responsibility."

25

I advance over broken terrain toward my assigned position. The prospect of action exhilarates me, but my assessment of enemy strength indicates they are fielding approximately 17.4 percent greater weight of armor than anticipated, with commensurately greater firepower. I compute that I am grossly overmatched. Nonetheless, I shall do my best.

26

"There's no doubt whatever, gentlemen. Computers work with hard facts. Given the enemy's known offensive capability and our own defensive resources, it's a simple computation. No combination of the manpower and equipment at our command can possibly inflict a defeat on the PR forces at this time and place. Two is greater than one. You can't make a dollar out of fifteen cents."

27

"At least we can gather some useful data from the situation, gentlemen. The Bolo Mark XX has been committed to battle. Its designers assure me that the new self-motivating circuitry will vastly enhance the combat-effectiveness of the Bolo. Let us observe."

28

Hate to see old Denny out there, just a great big sitting duck, all alone and—here they come! Look at 'em boiling out of there like ants out of a hot log. Can't hardly look at that screen, them tactical nukes popping fireworks all over the place. But old Denny knows enough to get under cover. See that kind of glow all around him? All right, *it*, then. You know, working with him—it—so long, it got to feeling almost like he was somebody. Sure, I know, anyway, that's vaporized ablative shield you see. They're making it plenty hot for him. But he's fighting back. Them Hellbores is putting out, and they know it. Looks like they're concentrating on him now. Look at them tracers closing in on him! Come on, Denny, you ain't dumb. Get out of there fast.

29

"Certainly it's aware what's at stake! I've told you he—the machine, that is—has been fully programmed and is well aware not only of the tactical situation but of strategic and logistical considerations as well. Certainly it's an important item of equipment; its loss would be a serious blow to our present underequipped forces. You may rest assured that its pain circuits as well as its basic military competence will cause it to take the proper action. The fact that I originally opposed commissioning the device is not to be taken as implying any lack of confidence on my part in its combat-effectiveness. You may consider that my reputation is staked on the performance of the machine. It will act correctly."

30

It appears that the enemy is absorbing my barrage with little effect. More precisely, for each enemy unit destroyed by my fire 2.4 fresh units immediately move out to replace it. Thus it appears I am ineffective, while already my own shielding is suffering severe damage. Yet while I have offensive capability I must carry on as my Commander would wish. The pain is very great now, but thanks to my superb circuitry I am not disabled, though it has been necessary to withdraw my power from my external somatic sensors.

31

"I can assure you, gentlemen, insofar as simple logic functions are concerned, the Mark XX is perfectly capable of assessing the situation even as you and I, only better. Doubtless as soon as it senses that its position has grown totally untenable, it will retreat to the shelter of the rock ridge and retire under cover to a position from which it can return fire without taking the full force of the enemy's attack at point-blank range. It's been fully briefed on late developments, it knows this is a hopeless fight. There, you see? It's moving . . ."

32

"I thought you said—dammit, I *know* you said your pet machine had brains enough to know when to pull out! But look at it: half a billion plus of Concordiat funds being bombarded into radioactive rubbish. Like shooting fish in a barrel."

33

"Yes, sir, I'm monitoring everything. My test panel is tuned to it across the board. I'm getting continuous reading on all still-active circuits. Battle Reflex is still hot. Pain circuits close to overload, but he's still taking it. I don't know how much more he can take, sir; already way past Redline. Expected him to break off and get out before now."

34

"It's a simple matter of arithmetic; there is only one correct course of action in any given military situation. The big tactical computer was designed specifically to compare data and deduce that sole correct action. In this case my readout shows that the only thing the Mark XX could legitimately do at this point is just what the Professor here says: pull back to cover and continue its barrage. The onboard computing capability of the unit is as capable of reaching that conclusion, as is the big computer at HQ. So keep calm, gentlemen. It will withdraw at any moment, I assure you of that."

35

"Now it's getting ready—no, look what it's doing! It's advancing into the teeth of that murderous fire. By God, you've got to admire that workmanship! That it's still capable of moving is a miracle. All the ablative metal is gone—you can see its bare armor exposed—and it takes some heat to make that flintsteel glow white!"

36

"Certainly, I'm looking. I see it. By God, sir, it's still moving—faster, in fact! Charging the enemy line like the Light Brigade! And all for nothing, it appears. Your machine, General, appears less competent than you expected."

37

Poor old Denny. Made his play and played out, I reckon.
Readings on the board over there don't look good; durn
near every overload in him blowed wide open. Not much
there to salvage. Emergency Survival Center's hot. Never
expected to see *that*. Means all kinds of breakdowns inside. But it figures, after what he just went through. Look
at that slag pit he drove up out of. They wanted a field
test. Reckon they got it. And he flunked it.

38

"Violating orders and winning is one thing, George.
Committing mutiny and losing is quite another. Your
damned machine made a fool of me. After I stepped in
and backed you to the hilt and stood there like a jackass
and assured Councillor Grace that the thing knew what it
was doing—it blows the whole show. Instead of pulling
back to save itself it charged to destruction. I want an
explanation of this fiasco at once."

39

"Look! No, by God, over *there!* On the left of the
entrance. They're breaking formation—they're running for
it! Watch this! The whole spearhead is crumbling, they're
taking to the badlands, they're—"

40

"*Why*, dammit? It's outside all rationality. As far as the
enemy's concerned, fine. They broke and ran. They couldn't
stand up to the sight of the Mark XX not only taking
everything they had, but advancing on them out of that
inferno, all guns blazing. Another hundred yards and—but
they don't know that. It buffaloed them, so score a battle

won for our side. But *why?* I'd stack my circuits up against any fixed installation in existence, including the big Tacomp the Army's so proud of. That machine was as aware as anybody that the only smart thing to do was run. So now I've got a junk pile on my hands. Some test! A clear flunk. Destroyed in action. Not recommended for Federal procurement. Nothing left but a few hot transistors in the Survival Center. It's a disaster, Fred. All my work, all your work, the whole program wrecked. Fred, you talk to General Bates. As soon as he's done inspecting the hulk he'll want somebody human to chew out."

41

"Look at that pile of junk! Reading off the scale. Won't be cool enough to haul to Disposal for six months. I understand you're Chief Engineer at Bolo Division. You built this thing. Maybe you can tell me what you had in mind here. Sure, it stood up to fire better than I hoped. But so what? A stone wall can stand and take it. This thing is supposed to be *smart*, supposed to feel pain like a living creature. Blunting the strike at the Complex was a valuable contribution, but how can I recommend procurement of this junk heap?"

42

Why, Denny? Just tell me why you did it. You got all these military brass down on you, and on me, too. On all of us. They don't much like stuff they can't understand. You attacked when they figured you to run. Sure, you routed the enemy, like Bates says, but you got yourself ruined in the process. Don't make sense. Any dumb private, along with the generals, would have known enough to get out of there. Tell me why, so I'll have something for Bates to put on his Test Evaluation Report, AGF Form 1103-6, Rev 11/3/85.

43

"All right, Unit DNE of the line. Why did you do it? This is your Commander, Unit DNE. Report! Why did you do it? Now, you knew your position was hopeless, didn't you? That you'd be destroyed if you held your ground, to say nothing of advancing. Surely you were able to compute that. You were lucky to have the chance to prove yourself."

For a minute I thought old Denny was too far gone to answer. There was just a kind of groan come out of the amplifier. Then it firmed up. General Bates had his hand cupped behind his ear, but Denny spoke right up.

"*Yes, sir.*"

"You knew what was at stake here. It was the ultimate test of your ability to perform correctly under stress, of your suitability as a weapon of war. You knew that. General Margrave and old Priss Grace and the press boys all had their eyes on every move you made. So instead of using common sense, you waded into that inferno in defiance of all logic—and destroyed yourself. Right?"

"*That is correct, sir.*"

"Then why? In the name of sanity, tell me *why!* Why, instead of backing out and saving yourself, did you charge? . . . Wait a minute, Unit DNE. It just dawned on me. I've been underestimating you. You *knew,* didn't you? Your knowledge of human psychology told you they'd break and run, didn't it?"

"*No, sir. On the contrary, I was quite certain that they were as aware as I that they held every advantage.*"

"Then that leaves me back where I started. Why? What made you risk everything on a hopeless attack? Why did you do it?"

"*For the honor of the regiment.*"

THE LAST COMMAND

I come to awareness, sensing a residual oscillation traversing me from an arbitrarily designated heading of 035. From the damping rate I compute that the shock was of intensity 8.7, emanating from a source within the limits 72 meters/46 meters. I activate my primary screens, trigger a return salvo. There is no response. I engage reserve energy cells, bring my secondary battery to bear—futilely. It is apparent that I have been ranged by the Enemy and severely damaged.

My positional sensors indicate that I am resting at an angle of 13 degrees 14 seconds, deflected from a baseline at 21 points from median. I attempt to right myself, but encounter massive resistance. I activate my forward scanners, shunt power to my I-R microstrobes. Not a flicker illuminates my surroundings. I am encased in utter blackness.

Now a secondary shock wave approaches, rocks me with an intensity of 8.2. It is apparent that I must withdraw from my position—but my drive trains remain inert under full thrust. I shift to base emergency power, try again. Pressure mounts; I sense my awareness fading under the intolerable strain; then, abruptly, resistance falls off and I am in motion.

It is not the swift maneuvering of full drive, however; I inch forward, as if restrained by massive barriers. Again I attempt to penetrate the surrounding darkness and this time perceive great irregular outlines shot through with fracture planes. I probe cautiously, then more vigorously, encountering incredible densities.

108

I channel all available power to a single ranging pulse, direct it upward. The indication is so at variance with all experience that I repeat the test at a new angle. Now I must accept the fact: I am buried under 207.6 meters of solid rock!

I direct my attention to an effort to orient myself to my uniquely desperate situation. I run through an action-status checklist of thirty thousand items, feel dismay at the extent of power loss. My main cells are almost completely drained, my reserve units at no more than .4 charge. Thus my sluggishness is explained. I review the tactical situation, recall the triumphant announcement from my commander that the Enemy forces were annihilated, that all resistance had ceased. In memory, I review the formal procession; in company with my comrades of the Dino-chrome Brigade, many of us deeply scarred by Enemy action, we parade before the Grand Commandant, then assemble on the depot ramp. At command, we bring our music storage cells into phase and display our Battle Anthem. The nearby star radiates over a full spectrum unfiltered by atmospheric haze. It is a moment of glorious triumph. Then the final command is given—

The rest is darkness. But it is apparent that the victory celebration was premature. The Enemy has counterattacked with a force that has come near to immobilizing me. The realization is shocking, but the .1 second of leisurely introspection has clarified my position. At once, I broadcast a call on Brigade Action wave length:

"Unit LNE to Command, requesting permission to file VSR."

I wait, sense no response, call again, using full power. I sweep the enclosing volume of rock with an emergency alert warning. I tune to the all-units band, await the replies of my comrades of the Brigade. None answer. Now I must face the reality: I alone have survived the assault.

I channel my remaining power to my drive and detect a channel of reduced density. I press for it and the broken rock around me yields reluctantly. Slowly, I move forward and upward. My pain circuitry shocks my awareness center with emergency signals; I am doing

*irreparable damage to my overloaded neural systems,
but my duty is clear: I must seek out and engage the
Enemy.*

2

Emerging from behind the blast barrier, Chief Engineer Pete Reynolds of the New Devonshire Port Authority pulled off his rock mask and spat grit from his mouth.

"That's the last one; we've bottomed out at just over two hundred yards. Must have hit a hard stratum down there."

"It's almost sundown," the paunchy man beside him said shortly. "You're a day and a half behind schedule."

"We'll start backfilling now, Mr. Mayor. I'll have pilings poured by oh-nine hundred tomorrow, and with any luck the first section of pad will be in place in time for the rally."

"I'm—" The mayor broke off, looked startled. "I thought you told me that was the last charge to be fired. . . ."

Reynolds frowned. A small but distinct tremor had shaken the ground underfoot. A few feet away, a small pebble balanced atop another toppled and fell with a faint clatter.

"Probably a big rock fragment falling," he said. At that moment, a second vibration shook the earth, stronger this time. Reynolds heard a rumble and a distant impact as rock fell from the side of the newly blasted excavation. He whirled to the control shed as the door swung back and Second Engineer Mayfield appeared.

"Take a look at this, Pete!"

Reynolds went across to the hut, stepped inside. Mayfield was bending over the profiling table.

"What do you make of it?" he pointed. Superimposed on the heavy red contour representing the detonation of the shaped charge that had completed the drilling of the final pile core were two other traces, weak but distinct.

"About .1 intensity." Mayfield looked puzzled. "What—"

The tracking needle dipped suddenly, swept up the screen to peak at .21, dropped back. The hut trembled. A stylus fell from the edge of the table. The red face of Mayor Dougherty burst through the door.

"Reynolds, have you lost your mind? What's the idea of blasting while I'm standing out in the open? I might have been killed!"

"I'm not blasting," Reynolds snapped. "Jim, get Eaton on the line, see if they know anything." He stepped to the door, shouted. A heavyset man in sweat-darkened coveralls swung down from the seat of a cable-lift rig.

"Boss, what goes on?" he called as he came up. "Damn near shook me out of my seat!"

"I don't know. You haven't set any trim charges?"

"Jesus, no, boss. I wouldn't set no charges without your say-so."

"Come on." Reynolds started out across the rubble-littered stretch of barren ground selected by the Authority as the site of the new spaceport. Halfway to the open mouth of the newly blasted pit, the ground under his feet rocked violently enough to make him stumble. A gout of dust rose from the excavation ahead. Loose rock danced on the ground. Beside him the drilling chief grabbed his arm.

"Boss, we better get back!"

Reynolds shook him off, kept going. The drill chief swore and followed. The shaking of the ground went on, a sharp series of thumps interrupting a steady trembling.

"It's a quake!" Reynolds yelled over the low rumbling sound.

He and the chief were at the rim of the core now.

"It can't be a quake, boss," the latter shouted. "Not in these formations!"

"Tell it to the geologists—" The rock slab they were standing on rose a foot, dropped back. Both men fell. The slab bucked like a small boat in choppy water.

"Let's get out of here!" Reynolds was up and running. Ahead, a fissure opened, gaped a foot wide. He jumped it, caught a glimpse of black depths, a glint of wet clay twenty feet below—

A hoarse scream stopped him in his tracks. He spun, saw the drill chief down, a heavy splinter of rock across his legs. He jumped to him, heaved at the rock. There was blood on the man's shirt. The chief's hands beat the dusty rock before him. Then other men were there, grunting, sweaty hands gripping beside Reynolds. The ground rocked. The roar from under the earth had risen to a deep, steady rumble. They lifted the rock aside, picked up the injured man, and stumbled with him to the aid shack.

The mayor was there, white-faced.

"What is it, Reynolds? By God, if you're responsible—"

"Shut up!" Reynolds brushed him aside, grabbed the phone, punched keys.

"Eaton! What have you got on this temblor?"

"Temblor, hell." The small face on the four-inch screen looked like a ruffled hen. "What in the name of Order are you doing out there? I'm reading a whole series of displacements originating from that last core of yours! What did you do, leave a pile of trim charges lying around?"

"It's a quake. Trim charges, hell! This thing's broken up two hundred yards of surface rock. It seems to be traveling north-northeast—"

"I see that; a traveling earthquake!" Eaton flapped his arms, a tiny and ridiculous figure against a background of wall charts and framed diplomas. "Well—do something, Reynolds! Where's Mayor Dougherty?"

"Underfoot!" Reynolds snapped, and cut off.

Outside, a layer of sunset-stained dust obscured the sweep of level plain. A rock-dozer rumbled up, ground to a halt by Reynolds. A man jumped down.

"I got the boys moving equipment out," he panted. "The thing's cutting a trail straight as a rule for the highway!" He pointed to a raised roadbed a quarter mile away.

"How fast is it moving?"

"She's done a hundred yards; it hasn't been ten minutes yet!"

"If it keeps up another twenty minutes, it'll be into the Intermix!"

"Scratch a few million cees and six months' work then, Pete!"

"And Southside Mall's a couple miles farther."

"Hell, it'll damp out before then!"

"Maybe. Grab a field car, Dan."

"Pete!" Mayfield came up at a trot. "This thing's building! The centroid's moving on a heading of oh-two-two—"

"How far subsurface?"

"It's rising; started at two-twenty yards, and it's up to one-eighty!"

"What the hell have we stirred up?" Reynolds stared at Mayfield as the field car skidded to a stop beside them.

"Stay with it, Jim. Give me anything new. We're taking a closer look." He climbed into the rugged vehicle.

"Take a blast truck—"

"No time!" He waved and the car gunned away into the pall of dust.

3

The rock car pulled to a stop at the crest of the three-level Intermix on a lay-by designed to permit tourists to enjoy the view of the site of the proposed port, a hundred feet below. Reynolds studied the progress of the quake through field glasses. From this vantage point, the path of the phenomenon was a clearly defined trail of tilted and broken rock, some of the slabs twenty feet across. As he watched, the fissure lengthened.

"It looks like a mole's trail." Reynolds handed the glasses to his companion, thumbed the send key on the car radio.

"Jim, get Eaton and tell him to divert all traffic from the Circular south of Zone Nine. Cars are already clogging the right-of-way. The dust is visible from a mile away, and when the word gets out there's something going on, we'll be swamped."

"I'll tell him, but he won't like it!"

"This isn't politics! This thing will be into the outer pad area in another twenty minutes!"

"It won't last—"

"How deep does it read now?"

"One-five!" There was a moment's silence. "Pete, if it stays on course, it'll surface at about where you're parked!"

"Uh-huh. It looks like you can scratch one Intermix. Better tell Eaton to get a story ready for the press."

"Pete, talking about news hounds—" Dan said beside him. Reynolds switched off, turned to see a man in a gay-colored driving outfit coming across from a battered

Monojag sportster which had pulled up behind the rock
car. A big camera case was slung across his shoulder.

"Say, what's going on down there?" he called.

"Rock slide," Reynolds said shortly. "I'll have to ask you
to drive on. The road's closed to all traffic—"

"Who're you?" The man looked belligerent.

"I'm the engineer in charge. Now pull out, brother."
He turned back to the radio. "Jim, get every piece of
heavy equipment we own over here, on the double." He
paused, feeling a minute trembling in the car. "The Intermix is beginning to feel it," he went on. "I'm afraid we're
in for it. Whatever that thing is, it acts like a solid body
boring its way through the ground. Maybe we can barricade it."

"Barricade an earthquake?"

"Yeah, I know how it sounds—but it's the only idea I've
got."

"Hey—what's that about an earthquake?" The man in
the colored suit was still there. "By gosh, I can feel it—the
whole damned bridge is shaking!"

"Off, mister—now!" Reynolds jerked a thumb at the
traffic lanes where a steady stream of cars were hurtling
past. "Dan, take us over to the main track. We'll have to
warn this traffic off—"

"Hold on, fellow." The man unlimbered his camera. "I
represent the New Devon *Scope*. I have a few questions—"

"I don't have the answers." Pete cut him off as the car
pulled away.

"Hah!" The man who had questioned Reynolds yelled
after him. "Big shot! Think you can . . ." His voice was
lost behind them.

4

In a modest retirees' apartment block in the coast town
of Idlebreeze, forty miles from the scene of the freak
quake, an old man sat in a reclining chair, half dozing
before a yammering Tri-D tank.

". . . Grandpa," a sharp-voiced young woman was saying.
"It's time for you to go in to bed."

"Bed? Why do I want to go to bed? Can't sleep anyway. . . ." He stirred, made a pretense of sitting up,
showing an interest in the Tri-D. "I'm watching this show.
Don't bother me."

"It's not a show, it's the news," a fattish boy said disgustedly. "Ma, can I switch channels—"

"Leave it alone, Bennie," the old man said. On the
screen a panoramic scene spread out, a stretch of barren
ground across which a furrow showed. As he watched, it
lengthened.

". . .up here at the Intermix we have a fine view of the
whole curious business, lazangemmun," the announcer
chattered. "And in our opinion it's some sort of publicity
stunt staged by the Port Authority to publicize their con-
troversial port project—"

"Ma, can I change channels?"

"Go ahead, Bennie—"

"Don't touch it," the old man said. The fattish boy
reached for the control, but something in the old man's
eye stopped him. . . .

5

"The traffic's still piling in here," Reynolds said into the
phone. "Damn it, Jim, we'll have a major jam on our
hands—"

"He won't do it, Pete! You know the Circular was his
baby—the super all-weather pike that nothing could shut
down. He says you'll have to handle this in the field—"

"Handle, hell! I'm talking about preventing a major
disaster! And in a matter of minutes, at that!"

"I'll try again—"

"If he says no, divert a couple of the big ten-yard
graders and block it off yourself. Set up field arcs, and
keep any cars from getting in from either direction."

"Pete, that's outside your authority!"

"You heard me!"

Ten minutes later, back at ground level, Reynolds
watched the boom-mounted polyarcs swinging into position at the two roadblocks a quarter of a mile apart,

cutting off the threatened section of the raised expressway. A hundred yards from where he stood on the rear cargo deck of a light grader rig, a section of rock fifty feet wide rose slowly, split, fell back with a ponderous impact. One corner of it struck the massive pier supporting the extended shelf of the lay-by above. A twenty-foot splinter fell away, exposing the reinforcing-rod core.

"How deep, Jim?" Reynolds spoke over the roaring sound coming from the disturbed area.

"Just subsurface now, Pete! It ought to break through —" His voice was drowned in a rumble as the damaged pier shivered, rose up, buckled at its midpoint, and collapsed, bringing down with it a large chunk of pavement and guard rail, and a single still-glowing light pole. A small car that had been parked on the doomed section was visible for an instant just before the immense slab struck. Reynolds saw it bounce aside, then disappear under an avalanche of broken concrete.

"My God, Pete—" Dan started. "That damned fool news hound . . . !"

"Look!" As the two men watched, a second pier swayed, fell backward into the shadow of the span above. The roadway sagged, and two more piers snapped. With a bellow like a burst dam, a hundred-foot stretch of the road fell into the roiling dust cloud.

"Pete!" Mayfield's voice burst from the car radio. "Get out of there! I threw a reader on that thing and it's chattering off the scale . . . !"

Among the piled fragments something stirred, heaved, rising up, lifting multi-ton pieces of the broken road, thrusting them aside like so many potato chips. A dull blue radiance broke through from the broached earth, threw an eerie light on the shattered structure above. A massive, ponderously irresistible shape thrust forward through the ruins. Reynolds saw a great blue-glowing profile emerge from the rubble like a surfacing submarine, shedding a burden of broken stone, saw immense treads ten feet wide claw for purchase, saw the mighty flank brush a still-standing pier, send it crashing aside.

"Pete, what—what is it . . . ?"

"I don't know." Reynolds broke the paralysis that had gripped him. "Get us out of here, Dan, fast! Whatever it is, it's headed straight for the city!"

6

I emerge at last from the trap into which I had fallen, and at once encounter defensive words of considerable strength. My scanners are dulled from lack of power, but I am able to perceive open ground beyond the barrier, and farther still, at a distance of 5.7 kilometers, massive walls. Once more I transmit the Brigade Rally signal; but as before, there is no reply. I am truly alone.

I scan the surrounding area for the emanations of Enemy drive units, monitor the EM spectrum for their communications. I detect nothing; either my circuitry is badly damaged, or their shielding is superb.

I must now make a decision as to possible courses of action. Since all my comrades of the Brigade have fallen, I compute that the fortress before me must be held by Enemy forces. I direct probing signals at them, discover them to be of unfamiliar construction, and less formidable than they appear. I am aware of the possibility that this may be a trick of the Enemy; but my course is clear.

I reengage my driving engines and advance on the Enemy fortress.

7

"You're out of your mind, father," the stout man said. "At your age—"

"At your age, I got my nose smashed in a brawl in a bar on Aldo," the old man cut him off. "But I won the fight."

"James, you can't go out at this time of night . . ." an elderly woman wailed.

"Tell them to go home." The old man walked painfully toward his bedroom door. "I've seen enough of them for today." He passed out of sight.

"Mother, you won't let him do anything foolish?"

"He'll forget about it in a few minutes; but maybe you'd better go now and let him settle down."

"Mother—I really think a home is the best solution."

"Yes," the young woman nodded agreement. "After all, he's past ninety—and he has his veteran's retirement. . . ."

Inside his room, the old man listened as they departed. He went to the closet, took out clothes, began dressing. . . .

8

City Engineer Eaton's face was chalk-white on the screen. "No one can blame me," he said. "How could I have known—"

"Your office ran the surveys and gave the PA the green light," Mayor Dougherty yelled.

"All the old survey charts showed was 'Disposal Area,' " Eaton threw out his hands. "I assumed—"

"As City Engineer, you're not paid to make assumptions! Ten minutes' research would have told you that was a 'Y' category area!"

"What's 'Y' category mean?" Mayfield asked Reynolds. They were standing by the field comm center, listening to the dispute. Nearby, boom-mounted Tri-D cameras hummed, recording the progress of the immense machine, its upper turret rearing forty-five feet into the air, as it ground slowly forward across smooth ground toward the city, dragging behind it a trailing festoon of twisted reinforcing iron crusted with broken concrete.

"Half-life over one hundred years," Reynolds answered shortly. "The last skirmish of the war was fought near here. Apparently this is where they buried the radioactive equipment left over from the battle."

"But what the hell, that was seventy years ago—"

"There's still enough residual radiation to contaminate anything inside a quarter-mile radius."

"They must have used some hellish stuff." Mayfield stared at the dull shine half a mile distant.

"Reynolds, how are you going to stop this thing?" The mayor had turned on the PA engineer.

"Me stop it? You saw what it did to my heaviest rigs:

flattened them like pancakes. You'll have to call out the military on this one, Mr. Mayor."

"Call in Federation forces? Have them meddling in civic affairs?"

"The station's only sixty-five miles from here. I think you'd better call them fast. It's only moving at about three miles per hour but it will reach the south edge of the Mall in another forty-five minutes."

"Can't you mine it? Blast a trap in its path?"

"You saw it claw its way up from six hundred feet down. I checked the specs; it followed the old excavation tunnel out. It was rubble-filled and capped with twenty-inch compressed concrete."

"It's incredible," Eaton said from the screen. "The entire machine was encased in a ten-foot shell of reinforced armocrete. It had to break out of that before it could move a foot!"

"That was just a radiation shield; it wasn't intended to restrain a Bolo Combat Unit."

"What was, may I inquire?" The mayor glared from one face to another.

"The units were deactivated before being buried," Eaton spoke up, as if he were eager to talk. "Their circuits were fused. It's all in the report—"

"The report you should have read somewhat sooner," the mayor snapped.

"What—what started it up?" Mayfield looked bewildered. "For seventy years it was down there, and nothing happened!"

"Our blasting must have jarred something," Reynolds said shortly. "Maybe closed a relay that started up the old battle reflex circuit."

"You know something about these machines?" The mayor beetled his brows at him.

"I've read a little."

"Then speak up, man. I'll call the station, if you feel I must. What measures should I request?"

"I don't know, Mr. Mayor. As far as I know, nothing on New Devon can stop that machine now."

The mayor's mouth opened and closed. He whirled to

the screen, blanked Eaton's agonized face, punched in the code for the Federation station.

"Colonel Blane!" he blurted as a stern face came onto the screen. "We have a major emergency on our hands! I'll need everything you've got! This is the situation . . ."

9

I encounter no resistance other than the flimsy barrier, but my progress is slow. Grievous damage has been done to my main drive sector due to overload during my escape from the trap; and the failure of my sensing circuitry has deprived me of a major portion of my external receptivity. Now my pain circuits project a continuous signal to my awareness center, but it is my duty to my Commander and to my fallen comrades of the Brigade to press forward at my best speed; but my performance is a poor shadow of my former ability.

And now at last the Enemy comes into action! I sense aerial units closing at supersonic velocities; I lock my lateral batteries to them and direct salvo fire, but I sense that the arming mechanisms clatter harmlessly. The craft sweep over me, and my impotent guns elevate, track them as they release detonants that spread out in an envelopmental pattern which I, with my reduced capabilites, am powerless to avoid. The missiles strike; I sense their detonations all about me; but I suffer only trivial damage. The Enemy has blundered if he thought to neutralize a Mark XXVIII Combat Unit with mere chemical explosives! But I weaken with each meter gained.

Now there is no doubt as to my course. I must press the charge and carry the walls before my reserve cells are exhausted.

10

From a vantage point atop a bucket rig four hundred yards from the position the great fighting machine had now reached, Pete Reynolds studied it through night glasses.

A battery of beamed polyarcs pinned the giant hulk, scarred and rust-scaled, in a pool of blue-white light. A mile and a half beyond it, the walls of the Mall rose sheer from the garden setting.

"The bombers slowed it some," he reported to Eaton via scope. "But it's still making better than two miles per hour. I'd say another twenty-five minutes before it hits the main ringwall. How's the evacuation going?"

"Badly! I get no cooperation! You'll be my witness, Reynolds, I did all I could—"

"How about the mobile batteries; how long before they'll be in position?" Reynolds cut him off.

"I've heard nothing from Federation Central—typical militaristic arrogance, not keeping me informed—but I have them on my screens. They're two miles out—say three minutes."

"I hope you made your point about N-heads."

"That's outside my province!" Eaton said sharply. "It's up to Brand to carry out this portion of the operation!"

"The HE Missiles didn't do much more than clear away the junk it was dragging." Reynolds' voice was sharp.

"I wash my hands of responsibility for civilian lives," Eaton was saying when Reynolds shut him off, changed channels.

"Jim, I'm going to try to divert it," he said crisply. "Eaton's sitting on his political fence; the Feds are bringing artillery up, but I don't expect much from it. Technically, Brand needs Sector okay to use nuclear stuff, and he's not the boy to stick his neck out—"

"Divert it how? Pete, don't take any chances—"

Reynolds laughed shortly. "I'm going to get around it and drop a shaped drilling charge in its path. Maybe I can knock a tread off. With luck, I might get its attention on me and draw it away from the Mall. There are still a few thousand people over there, glued to their Tri-D's. They think it's all a swell show."

"Pete, you can't walk up on that thing! It's hot—" He broke off. "Pete, there's some kind of nut here—he claims he has to talk to you; says he knows something about that damned juggernaut. Shall I . . . ?"

Reynolds paused with his hand on the cut-off switch.

"Put him on," he snapped. Mayfield's face moved aside and an ancient, bleary-eyed visage stared out at him. The tip of the old man's tongue touched his dry lips.

"Son, I tried to tell this boy here, but he wouldn't listen—"

"What have you got, old timer?" Pete cut in. "Make it fast."

"My name's Sanders. James Sanders. I'm . . . I was with the Planetary Volunteer Scouts, back in '71—"

"Sure, dad," Pete said gently. "I'm sorry, I've got a little errand to run—"

"Wait . . ." The old man's face worked. "I'm old, son—too damned old. I know. But bear with me. I'll try to say it straight. I was with Hayle's squadron at Toledo. Then afterwards, they shipped us—but hell, you don't care about that! I keep wandering, son; can't help it. What I mean to say is—I was in on that last scrap, right here at New Devon—only we didn't call it New Devon then. Called it Hellport. Nothing but bare rock and Enemy emplacement—"

"You were talking about the battle, Mr. Sanders," Pete said tensely. "Go on with that part."

"Lieutenant Sanders," the oldster said. "Sure, I was Acting Brigade Commander. See, our major was hit at Toledo—and after Tommy Chee stopped a sidewinder at Belgrave—"

"Stick to the point, Lieutenant!"

"Yessir!" The old man pulled himself together with an obvious effort. "I took the Brigade in; put out flankers, and ran the Enemy into the ground. We mopped 'em up in a thirty-three hour running fight that took us from over by Crater Bay all the way down here to Hellport. When it was over, I'd lost sixteen units, but the Enemy was done. They gave us Brigade Honors for that action. And then . . ."

"Then what?"

"Then the triple-dyed yellow-bottoms at Headquarters put out the order the Brigade was to be scrapped; said they were too hot to make decon practical. Cost too much, they said! So after the final review—" he gulped, blinked— "they planted 'em deep, two hundred meters, and poured in special high-R concrete."

"And packed rubble in behind them," Reynolds finished for him. "All right, Lieutenant, I believe you! Now for the big one: What started that machine on a rampage?"

"Should have known they couldn't hold down a Bolo Mark XXVIII!" The old man's eyes lit up. "Take more than a few million tons of rock to stop Lenny when his battle board was lit!"

"Lenny?"

"That's my old command unit out there, son. I saw the markings on the Tri-D. Unit LNE of the Dinochrome Brigade!"

"Listen!" Reynolds snapped out. "Here's what I intend to try . . ." He outlined his plan.

"Ha!" Sanders snorted. "It's a gutsy notion, mister, but Lenny won't give it a sneeze."

"You didn't come here to tell me we were licked," Reynolds cut in. "How about Brand's batteries?"

"Hell, son, Lenny stood up to point-blank Hellbore fire on Toledo, and—"

"Are you telling me there's nothing we can do?"

"What's that? No, son, that's not what I'm saying . . ."

"Then what!"

"Just tell these johnnies to get out of my way, mister. I think I can handle him."

11

At the field comm hut, Pete Reynolds watched as the man who had been Lieutenant Sanders of the Volunteer Scouts pulled shiny black boots over his thin ankles and stood. The blouse and trousers of royal blue polyon hung on his spare frame like wash on a line. He grinned, a skull's grin.

"It doesn't fit like it used to; but Lenny will recognize it. It'll help. Now, if you've got that power pack ready . . ."

Mayfield handed over the old-fashioned field instrument Sanders had brought in with him.

"It's operating, sir—but I've already tried everything I've got on that infernal machine; I didn't get a peep out of it."

Sanders winked at him. "Maybe I know a couple of tricks you boys haven't heard about." He slung the strap over his bony shoulder and turned to Reynolds.

"Guess we better get going, mister. He's getting close."

In the rock car, Sanders leaned close to Reynolds' ear. "Told you those Federal guns wouldn't scratch Lenny. They're wasting their time."

Reynolds pulled the car to a stop at the crest of the road, from which point he had a view of the sweep of ground leading across to the city's edge. Lights sparkled all across the towers of New Devon. Close to the walls, the converging fire of the ranked batteries of infinite repeaters drove into the glowing bulk of the machine, which plowed on, undeterred. As he watched, the firing ceased.

"Now, let's get in there, before they get some other damn-fool scheme going," Sanders said.

The rock car crossed the rough ground, swung wide to come up on the Bolo from the left side. Behind the hastily rigged radiation cover, Reynolds watched the immense silhouette grow before him.

"I knew they were big," he said. "But to see one up close like this—" He pulled to a stop a hundred feet from the Bolo.

"Look at the side ports," Sanders said, his voice crisper now. "He's firing antipersonnel charges—only his plates are flat. If they weren't, we wouldn't have gotten within half a mile." He unclipped the microphone and spoke into it:

"Unit LNE, break off action and retire to ten-mile line!"

Reynolds' head jerked around to stare at the old man. His voice had rung with vigor and authority as he spoke the command.

The Bolo ground slowly ahead. Sanders shook his head, tried again.

"No answer, like that fella said. He must be running on nothing but memories now. . . ." He reattached the microphone, and before Reynolds could put out a hand, had lifted the anti-R cover and stepped off on the ground.

"Sanders—get back in here!" Reynolds yelled.

"Never mind, son. I've got to get in close. Contact induction." He started toward the giant machine. Frantically, Reynolds started the car, slammed it into gear, pulled forward.

"Better stay back." Sanders' voice came from his field radio. "This close, that screening won't do you much good."

"Get in the car!" Reynolds roared. "That's hard radiation!"

"Sure; feels funny, like a sunburn, about an hour after you come in from the beach and start to think maybe you got a little too much." He laughed. "But I'll get to him. . . ."

Reynolds braked to a stop, watched the shrunken figure in the baggy uniform as it slogged forward, leaning as against a sleet storm.

12

"I'm up beside him." Sanders' voice came through faintly on the field radio. "I'm going to try to swing up on his side. Don't feel like trying to chase him any farther."

Through the glasses, Reynolds watched the small figure, dwarfed by the immense bulk of the fighting machine, as he tried, stumbled, tried again, swung up on the flange running across the rear quarter inside the churning bogie wheel.

"He's up," he reported. "Damned wonder the track didn't get him. . . ."

Clinging to the side of the machine, Sanders lay for a moment, bent forward across the flange. Then he pulled himself up, wormed his way forward to the base of the rear quarter turret, wedged himself against it. He unslung the communicator, removed a small black unit, clipped it to the armor; it clung, held by a magnet. He brought the microphone up to his face.

In the comm shack, Mayfield leaned toward the screen, his eyes squinted in tension. Across the field, Reynolds held the glasses fixed on the man lying across the flank of the Bolo. They waited. . . .

13

The walls are before me, and I ready myself for a final effort, but suddenly I am aware of trickle currents flowing over my outer surface. Is this some new trick of the Enemy? I tune to the wave energies, trace the source. They originate at a point in contact with my aft port armor. I sense modulation, match receptivity to a computed pattern. And I hear a voice:

"Unit LNE, break it off, Lenny. We're pulling back now, boy. This is Command to LNE; pull back to ten miles. If you read me, Lenny, swing to port and halt."

I am not fooled by the deception. The order appears correct, but the voice is not that of my Commander. Briefly I regret that I cannot spare energy to direct a neutralizing power flow at the device the Enemy has attached to me. I continue my charge.

"Unit LNE! Listen to me, boy; maybe you don't recognize my voice, but it's me. You see, boy—some time has passed. I've gotten old. My voice has changed some, maybe. But it's me! Make a port turn, Lenny. Make it now!"

I am tempted to respond to the trick, for something in the false command seems to awaken secondary circuits which I sense have been long stilled. But I must not be swayed by the cleverness of the Enemy. My sensing circuitry has faded further as my energy cells drain; but I know where the Enemy lies. I move forward, but I am filled with agony, and only the memory of my comrades drives me on.

"Lenny, answer me. Transmit on the old private band— the one we agreed on. Nobody but me knows it, remember?"

Thus the Enemy seeks to beguile me into diverting precious power. But I will not listen.

"Lenny—not much time left. Another minute and you'll be into the walls. People are going to die. Got to stop you, Lenny. Hot here. My God, I'm hot. Not breathing too well, now. I can feel it; cutting through me like knives. You took a load of Enemy power, Lenny; and now I'm getting my share. Answer me, Lenny. Over to you. . . ."

*It will require only a tiny allocation of power to activate
a communication circuit. I realize that it is only an Enemy
trick, but I compute that by pretending to be deceived, I
may achieve some trivial advantage. I adjust circuitry
accordingly and transmit:*

"Unit LNE to Command. Contact with Enemy defensive
line imminent. Request supporting fire!"

"Lenny . . . you can hear me! Good boy, Lenny! Now
make a turn, to port. Walls . . . close. . . ."

"Unit LNE to Command. Request positive identification;
transmit code 685749."

"Lenny—I can't . . . don't have code blanks. But it's
me. . . ."

*"In absence of recognition code, your transmission dis-
regarded," I send. And now the walls loom high above me.
There are many lights, but I see them only vaguely. I am
nearly blind now.*

"Lenny—less'n two hundred feet to go. Listen, Lenny.
I'm climbing down. I'm going to jump down, Lenny, and
get around under your fore scanner pickup. You'll see me,
Lenny. You'll know me then."

*The false transmission ceases. I sense a body moving
across my side. The gap closes. I detect movement before
me, and in automatic reflex fire anti-P charges before I
recall that I am unarmed.*

*A small object has moved out before me, and taken up a
position between me and the wall behind which the Enemy
conceal themselves. It is dim, but appears to have the
shape of a man. . . .*

*I am uncertain. My alert center attempts to engage
inhibitory circuitry which will force me to halt, but it
lacks power. I can override it. But still I am unsure. Now
I must take a last risk; I must shunt power to my forward
scanner to examine this obstacle more closely. I do so, and
it leaps into greater clarity. It is indeed a man—and it is
enclothed in regulation blues of the Volunteers. Now,
closer, I see the face and through the pain of my great
effort, I study it. . . .*

14

"He's backed against the wall," Reynolds said hoarsely. "It's still coming. A hundred feet to go—"

"You were a fool, Reynolds!" the mayor barked. "A fool to stake everything on that old dotard's crazy ideas!"

"Hold it!" As Reynolds watched, the mighty machine slowed, halted, ten feet from the sheer wall before it. For a moment, it sat, as though puzzled. Then it backed, halted again, pivoted ponderously to the left, and came about.

On its side, a small figure crept up, fell across the lower gun deck. The Bolo surged into motion, retracing its route across the artillery-scarred gardens.

"He's turned it." Reynolds let his breath out with a shuddering sigh. "It's headed out for open desert. It might get twenty miles before it finally runs out of steam."

The strange voice that was the Bolo's came from the big panel before Mayfield:

"Command. . . . Unit LNE reports main power cells drained, secondary cells drained; now operating at .037 per cent efficiency, using Final Emergency Power. Request advice as to range to be covered before relief maintenance available."

"It's a long way, Lenny . . ." Sanders' voice was a bare whisper. *"But I'm coming with you. . . ."*

Then there was only the crackle of static. Ponderously, like a great mortally stricken animal, the Bolo moved through the ruins of the fallen roadway, heading for the open desert.

"That damned machine," the mayor said in a hoarse voice. "You'd almost think it was alive."

"You would at that," Pete Reynolds said.

A RELIC OF WAR

THE OLD WAR machine sat in the village square, its impotent guns pointing aimlessly along the dusty street. Shoulder-high weeds grew rankly about it, poking up through the gaps in the two-yard-wide treads; vines crawled over the high, rust-and guano-streaked flanks. A row of tarnished enameled battle honors gleamed dully across the prow, reflecting the late sun.

A group of men lounged near the machine; they were dressed in heavy work clothes and boots; their hands were large and calloused, their faces weatherburned. They passed a jug from hand to hand, drinking deep. It was the end of a long workday and they were relaxed, good-humored.

"Hey, we're forgetting old Bobby," one said. He strolled over and sloshed a little of the raw whiskey over the soot-blackened muzzle of the blast cannon slanting sharply down from the forward turret. The other men laughed.

"How's it going, Bobby?" the man called.

Deep inside the machine there was a soft chirring sound.

"Very well, thank you," a faint, whispery voice scraped from a grill below the turret.

"You keeping an eye on things, Bobby?" another man called.

"All clear," the answer came: a bird-chirp from a dinosaur.

"Bobby, you ever get tired just setting here?"

"Hell, Bobby don't get tired," the man with the jug said. "He's got a job to do, old Bobby has."

"Hey, Bobby, what kind o'boy are you?" a plump, lazy-eyed man called.

"I am a good boy," Bobby replied obediently.

129

"Sure Bobby's a good boy." The man with the jug reached up to pat the age-darkened curve of chromalloy above him. "Bobby's looking out for us."

Heads turned at a sound from across the square: the distant whine of a turbocar, approaching along the forest road.

"Huh! Ain't the day for the mail," a man said. They stood in silence, watching as a small, dusty cushion-car emerged from deep shadow into the yellow light of the street. It came slowly along to the plaza, swung left, pulled to a stop beside the boardwalk before a corrugated metal store front lettered BLAUVELT PROVISION COMPANY. The canopy popped open and a man stepped down. He was of medium height, dressed in a plain city-type black coverall. He studied the store front, the street, then turned to look across at the men. He came across toward them.

"Which of you men is Blauvelt?" he asked as he came up. His voice was unhurried, cool. His eyes flicked over the men.

A big, youngish man with a square face and sunbleached hair lifted his chin.

"Right here," he said. "Who're you?"

"Crewe is the name. Disposal Officer, War Materiel Commission." The newcomer looked up at the great machine looming over them. "Bolo *Stupendous,* Mark XXV," he said. He glanced at the men's faces, fixed on Blauvelt. "We had a report that there was a live Bolo out here. I wonder if you realize what you're playing with?"

"Hell, that's just Bobby," a man said.

"He's town mascot," someone else said.

"This machine could blow your town off the map," Crewe said. "And a good-sized piece of jungle along with it."

Blauvelt grinned; the squint lines around his eyes gave him a quizzical look.

"Don't go getting upset, Mr. Crewe," he said. "Bobby's harmless—"

"A Bolo's never harmless, Mr. Blauvelt. They're fighting machines, nothing else."

Blauvelt sauntered over and kicked at a corroded tread-plate. "Eighty-five years out in this jungle is kind of tough on machinery, Crewe. The sap and stuff from the trees eats chromalloy like it was sugar candy. The rains are acid, eat up equipment damn near as fast as we can ship it in here. Bobby can still talk a little, but that's about all."

"Certainly it's deteriorated; that's what makes it dangerous. Anything could trigger its battle reflex circuitry. Now, if you'll clear everyone out of the area, I'll take care of it."

"You move kind of fast for a man that just hit town," Blauvelt said, frowning. "Just what you got in mind doing?"

"I'm going to fire a pulse at it that will neutralize what's left of its computing center. Don't worry; there's no danger—"

"Hey," a man in the rear rank blurted. "That mean he can't talk any more?"

"That's right," Crewe said. "Also, he can't open fire on you."

"Not so fast, Crewe," Blauvelt said. "You're not messing with Bobby. We like him like he is." The other men were moving forward, forming up in a threatening circle around Crewe.

"Don't talk like a fool," Crewe said. "What do you think a salvo from a Continental Siege Unit would do to your town?"

Blauvelt chuckled and took a long cigar from his vest pocket. He sniffed it, called out: "All right, Bobby—fire one!"

There was a muted clatter, a sharp *click!* from deep inside the vast bulk of the machine. A tongue of pale flame licked from the cannon's soot-rimmed bore. The big man leaned quickly forward, puffed the cigar alight. The audience whooped with laughter.

"Bobby does what he's told, that's all," Blauvelt said. "And not much of that." He showed white teeth in a humorless smile.

Crewe flipped over the lapel of his jacket; a small, highly polished badge glinted there. "You know better than to interfere with a Concordiat officer," he said.

"Not so fast, Crewe," a dark-haired, narrow-faced fellow spoke up. "You're out of line. I heard about you Disposal men. Your job is locating old ammo dumps, abandoned equipment, stuff like that. Bobby's not abandoned. He's town property. Has been for near thirty years."

"Nonsense. This is battle equipment, the property of the Space Arm—"

Blauvelt was smiling lopsidedly. "Uh-uh. We've got salvage rights. No title, but we can make one up in a hurry. Official. I'm the Mayor here, and District Governor."

"This thing is a menace to every man, woman, and child in the settlement," Crewe snapped. "My job is to prevent tragedy—"

"Forget Bobby," Blauvelt cut in. He waved a hand at the jungle wall beyond the tilled fields. "There's a hundred million square miles of virgin territory out there," he said. "You can do what you like out there. I'll even sell you provisions. But just leave our mascot be, understand?"

Crewe looked at him, looked around at the other men.

"You're a fool," he said. "You're all fools." He turned and walked away, stiff-backed.

In the room he had rented in the town's lone boarding-house, Crewe opened his baggage and took out a small, gray-plastic-cased instrument. The three children of the landlord who were watching from the latchless door edged closer.

"Gee, is that a real star radio?" the eldest, a skinny, long-necked lad of twelve asked.

"No," Crewe said shortly. The boy blushed and hung his head.

"It's a command transmitter," Crewe said, relenting. "It's designed for talking to fighting machines, giving them orders. They'll only respond to the special shaped-wave signal this puts out." He flicked a switch, and an indicator light glowed on the side of the case.

"You mean like Bobby?" the boy asked.

"Like Bobby used to be." Crewe switched off the transmitter.

"Bobby's swell," another child said. "He tells us stories about when he was in the war."

"He's got medals," the first boy said. "Were you in the war, mister?"

"I'm not quite that old," Crewe said.

"Bobby's older'n grandad."

"You boys had better run along," Crewe said. "I have to
. . ." He broke off, cocked his head, listening. There were
shouts outside; someone was calling his name.

Crewe pushed through the boys and went quickly along
the hall, stepped through the door onto the boardwalk.
He felt rather than heard a slow, heavy thudding, a chorus
of shrill squeaks, a metallic groaning. A red-faced man was
running toward him from the square.

"It's Bobby!" he shouted. "He's moving! What'd you do
to him, Crewe?"

Crewe brushed past the man, ran toward the plaza. The
Bolo appeared at the end of the street, moving ponderously forward, trailing uprooted weeds and vines.

"He's headed straight for Spivac's warehouse!" someone
yelled.

"Bobby! Stop there!" Blauvelt came into view, running
in the machine's wake. The big machine rumbled onward,
executed a half-left as Crewe reached the plaza, clearing
the corner of a building by inches. It crushed a section of
boardwalk to splinters, advanced across a storage yard. A
stack of rough-cut lumber toppled, spilled across the dusty
ground. The Bolo trampled a board fence, headed out
across a tilled field. Blauvelt whirled on Crewe.

"This is your doing! We never had trouble before—"

"Never mind that! Have you got a field car?"

"We—" Blauvelt checked himself. "What if we have?"

"I can stop it—but I have to be close. It will be into the
jungle in another minute. My car can't navigate there."

"Let him go," a man said, breathing hard from his run.
"He can't do no harm out there."

"Who'd of thought it?" another man said. "Setting there
all them years—who'd of thought he could travel like
that?"

"Your so-called mascot might have more surprises in
store for you," Crewe snapped. "Get me a car, fast! This is
an official requisition, Blauvelt!"

There was a silence, broken only by the distant crashing
of timber as the Bolo moved into the edge of the forest.
Hundred-foot trees leaned and went down before its
advance.

"Let him go," Blauvelt said. "Like Stinzi says, he can't hurt anything."

"What if he turns back?"

"Hell," a man muttered. "Old Bobby wouldn't hurt *us* . . ."

"That car," Crewe snarled. "You're wasting valuable time."

Blauvelt frowned. "All right—but you don't make a move unless it looks like he's going to come back and hit the town. Clear?"

"Let's go."

Blauvelt led the way at a trot toward the town garage.

The Bolo's trail was a twenty-five foot wide swath cut through the virgin jungle; the tread-prints were pressed eighteen inches into the black loam, where it showed among the jumble of fallen branches.

"It's moving at about twenty miles an hour, faster than we can go," Crewe said. "If it holds its present track, the curve will bring it back to your town in about five hours."

"He'll sheer off," Blauvelt said.

"Maybe. But we won't risk it. Pick up a heading of 270°, Blauvelt. We'll try an intercept by cutting across the circle."

Blauvelt complied wordlessly. The car moved ahead in the deep green gloom under the huge shaggy-barked trees. Oversized insects buzzed and thumped against the canopy. Small and medium lizards hopped, darted, flapped. Fern leaves as big as awnings scraped along the car as it clambered over loops and coils of tough root, leaving streaks of plant juice across the clear plastic. Once they grated against an exposed ridge of crumbling brown rock; flakes as big as saucers scaled off, exposing dull metal.

"Dorsal fin of a scout-boat," Crewe said. "That's what's left of what was supposed to be a corrosion resistant alloy."

They passed more evidences of a long-ago battle: the massive, shattered breech mechanism of a platform-mounted Hellbore, the gutted chassis of what might have been a bomb car, portions of a downed aircraft, fragments of shattered armor. Many of the relics were of Terran design, but often it was the curiously curved, spidery lines of a rusted Axorc microgun or implosion projector that poked through the greenery.

"It must have been a heavy action," Crewe said. "One of the ones toward the end that didn't get much notice at the time. There's stuff here I've never seen before, experimental types, I imagine, rushed in by the enemy for a last-ditch stand."

Blauvelt grunted.

"Contact in another minute or so," Crewe said.

As Blauvelt opened his mouth to reply, there was a blinding flash, a violent impact, and the jungle erupted in their faces.

The seat webbing was cutting into Crewe's ribs. His ears were filled with a high, steady ringing; there was a taste of brass in his mouth. His head throbbed in time with the thudding of his heart.

The car was on its side, the interior a jumble of loose objects, torn wiring, broken plastic. Blauvelt was half under him, groaning. He slid off him, saw that he was groggy but conscious.

"Changed your mind yet about your harmless pet?" he asked, wiping a trickle of blood from his right eye. "Let's get clear before he fires those empty guns again. Can you walk?"

Blauvelt mumbled, crawled out through the broken canopy. Crewe groped through debris for the command transmitter—

"Good God," Blauvelt croaked. Crewe twisted, saw the high, narrow, iodine-dark shape of the alien machine perched on jointed crawler-legs fifty feet away, framed by blast-scorched foliage. Its multiple-barreled micro-gun battery was aimed dead at the overturned car.

"Don't move a muscle," Crewe whispered. Sweat trickled down his face. An insect, like a stub-winged four-inch dragonfly, came and buzzed about them, moved on. Hot metal pinged, contracting. Instantly, the alien hunter-killer moved forward another six feet, depressing its gun muzzles.

"Run for it!" Blauvelt cried. He came to his feet in a scrabbling lunge; the enemy machine swung to track him . . .

A giant tree leaned, snapped, was tossed aside. The great green-streaked prow of the Bolo forged into view, interposing itself between the smaller machine and the men. It turned to face the enemy; fire flashed, reflecting against the surrounding trees; the ground jumped once, twice, to hard, racking shocks. Sound boomed dully in Crewe's blast-numbed ears. Bright sparks fountained above the Bolo as it advanced. Crewe felt the massive impact as the two fighting machines came together; he saw the Bolo hesitate, then forge ahead, rearing up, pushing the lighter machine aside, grinding over it, passing on, to leave a crumpled mass of wreckage in its wake.

"Did you see that, Crewe?" Blauvelt shouted in his ear. "Did you see what Bobby did? He walked right into its guns and smashed it flatter'n crock-brewed beer!"

The Bolo halted, turned ponderously, sat facing the men. Bright streaks of molten metal ran down its armored flanks, fell spattering and smoking into crushed greenery.

"He saved our necks," Blauvelt said. He staggered to his feet, picked his way past the Bolo to stare at the smoking ruins of the smashed adversary.

"*Unit Nine Five Four of the Line, reporting contact with hostile force,*" the mechanical voice of the Bolo spoke suddenly. "*Enemy unit destroyed. I have sustained extensive damage, but am still operational at nine point six percent base capability, awaiting further orders.*"

"Hey," Blauvelt said. "That doesn't sound like . . ."

"Now maybe you understand that this is a Bolo combat unit, not the village idiot," Crewe snapped. He picked his way across the churned-up ground, stood before the great machine.

"Mission accomplished, Unit Nine Five Four," he called. "Enemy forces neutralized. Close out Battle Reflex and revert to low alert status." He turned to Blauvelt.

"Let's go back to town," he said, "and tell them what their mascot just did."

Blauvelt stared up at the grim and ancient machine; his square, tanned face looked yellowish and drawn. "Let's do that," he said.

The ten-piece town band was drawn up in a double rank before the newly mown village square. The entire population of the settlement—some three hundred and forty-two men, women and children—were present, dressed in their best. Pennants fluttered from strung wires. The sun glistened from the armored sides of the newly-cleaned and polished Bolo. A vast bouquet of wild flowers poked from the no-longer-sooty muzzle of the Hellbore.

Crewe stepped forward.

"As a representative of the Concordiat government I've been asked to make this presentation," he said. "You people have seen fit to design a medal and award it to Unit Nine Five Four in appreciation for services rendered in defense of the community above and beyond the call of duty." He paused, looked across the faces of his audience.

"Many more elaborate honors have been awarded for a great deal less," he said. He turned to the machine; two men came forward, one with a stepladder, the other with a portable welding rig. Crewe climbed up, fixed the newly struck decoration in place beside the row of century-old battle honors. The technician quickly spotted it in position. The crowd cheered, then dispersed, chattering, to the picnic tables set up in the village street.

It was late twilight. The last of the sandwiches and stuffed eggs had been eaten, the last speeches declaimed, the last keg broached. Crewe sat with a few of the men in the town's lone public house.

."To Bobby," a man raised his glass.

"Correction," Crewe said. "To Unit Nine Five Four of the Line." The men laughed and drank.

"Well, time to go, I guess," a man said. The others chimed in, rose, clattering chairs. As the last of them left, Blauvelt came in. He sat down across from Crewe.

"You, ah, staying the night?" he asked.

"I thought I'd drive back," Crewe said. "My business here is finished."

"Is it?" Blauvelt said tensely.

Crewe looked at him, waiting.

"You know what you've got to do, Crewe."

"Do I?" Crewe took a sip from his glass.

"Damn it, have I got to spell it out? As long as that machine was just an oversized half-wit, it was all right. Kind of a monument to the war, and all. But now I've seen what it can do . . . Crewe, we can't have a live killer sitting in the middle of our town—never knowing when it might take a notion to start shooting again!"

"Finished?" Crewe asked.

"It's not that we're not grateful—"

"Get out," Crewe said.

"Now, look here, Crewe—"

"Get out. And keep everyone away from Bobby, understand?"

"Does that mean—?"

"I'll take care of it."

Blauvelt got to his feet. "Yeah," he said. "Sure."

After Blauvelt left, Crewe rose and dropped a bill on the table; he picked the command transmitter from the floor, went out into the street. Faint cries came from the far end of the town, where the crowd had gathered for fireworks. A yellow rocket arced up, burst in a spray of golden light, falling, fading . . .

Crewe walked toward the plaza. The Bolo loomed up, a vast, black shadow against the star-thick sky. Crewe stood before it, looking up at the already draggled pennants, the wilted nosegay drooping from the gun muzzle.

"Unit Nine Five Four, you know why I'm here?" he said softly.

"I compute that my usefulness as an engine of war is ended," the soft rasping voice said.

"That's right," Crewe said. "I checked the area in a thousand-mile radius with sensitive instruments. There's no enemy machine left alive. The one you killed was the last."

"It was true to its duty," the machine said.

"It was my fault," Crewe said. "It was designed to detect our command carrier and home on it. When I switched on my transmitter, it went into action. Naturally, you sensed that, and went to meet it."

The machine sat silent.

"You could still save yourself," Crewe said. "If you trampled me under and made for the jungle it might be centuries before . . ."

*"Before another man comes to do what must be done?
Better that I cease now, at the hands of a friend."*

"Good-bye, Bobby."

"Correction: Unit Nine Five Four of the Line."

Crewe pressed the key. A sense of darkness fell across
the machine.

At the edge of the square, Crewe looked back. He
raised a hand in a ghostly salute; then he walked away
along the dusty street, white in the light of the rising
moon.

COMBAT UNIT

I DO NOT like it; it has the appearance of a trap, but the order has been given. I enter the room and the valve closes behind me.

I inspect my surroundings. I am in a chamber 40.81 meters long, 10.35 meters wide, 4.12 high, with no openings except the one through which I entered. It is floored and walled with five-centimeter armor of flint-steel and beyond that there are ten centimeters of lead. Massive apparatus is folded and coiled in mountings around the room. Power is flowing in heavy buss bars beyond the shielding. I am sluggish for want of power; my examination of the room has taken .8 seconds.

Now I detect movement in a heavy jointed arm mounted above me. It begins to rotate, unfold. I assume that I will be attacked, and decide to file a situation report. I have difficulty in concentrating my attention . . .

I pull back receptivity from my external sensing circuits, set my bearing locks and switch over to my introspection complex. All is dark and hazy. I seem to remember when it was like a great cavern glittering with bright lines of transvisual colors . . .

It is different now; I grope my way in gloom, feeling along numbed circuits, test-pulsing cautiously until I feel contact with my transmitting unit. I have not used it since . . . I cannot remember. My memory banks lie black and inert.

"Command Unit," I transmit, "Combat Unit requests permission to file VSR."

I wait, receptors alert. I do not like waiting blindly, for

140

the quarter-second my sluggish action/reaction cycle requires. I wish that my Brigade comrades were at my side.

I call again, wait, then go ahead with my VSR. "This position heavily shielded, mounting apparatus of offensive capability. No withdrawal route. Advise."

I wait, repeat my transmission; nothing. I am cut off from Command Unit, from my comrades of the Dinochrome Brigade. Within me, pressure builds.

I feel a deep-seated click and a small but reassuring surge of power brightens the murk of the cavern to a dim glow, burning forgotten components to feeble life. An emergency pile has come into action automatically.

I realize that I am experiencing a serious equipment failure. I will devote another few seconds to troubleshooting, repairing what I can. I do not understand what accident can have occurred to damage me thus. I cannot remember . . .

I go along the dead cells, testing.

"—out! Bring .09's to bear, .8 millisec burst, close armor . . ."

" . . .sun blanking visual; slide number-seven filter in place."

" . . .478.09, 478.11, 478.13, Mark! . . ."

The cells are intact. Each one holds its fragment of recorded sense impression. The trouble is farther back. I try a main reflex lead.

" . . .main combat circuit, discon—"

Here is something; a command, on the reflex level! I go back, tracing, tapping mnemonic cells at random, searching for some clue.

"—sembark. Units emergency standby . . ."

" . . . response one-oh-three; stimulus-response negative . . ."

"Check list complete, report negative . . ."

I go on, searching out damage. I find an open switch in my maintenance panel. It will not activate; a mechanical jamming. I must fuse it shut quickly. I pour in power, and the mind-cavern dims almost to blackness. Then there is contact, a flow of electrons, and the cavern snaps alive; lines, points pseudo-glowing. It is not the blazing glory of my full powers, but it will serve; I am awake again.

I observe the action of the unfolding arm. It is slow, uncoordinated, obviously automated. I dismiss it from direct attention; I have several seconds before it will be in offensive position, and there is work for me if I am to be ready. I fire sampling impulses at the black memory banks, determine statistically that 98.92% are intact, merely disassociated.

The threatening arm swings over slowly; I integrate its path, see that it will come to bear on my treads; I probe, find only a simple hydraulic ram. A primitive apparatus to launch against a Mark XXXI fighting unit, even without mnemonics.

Meanwhile, I am running a full check. Here is something . . . An open breaker, a disconnect used only during repairs. I think of the cell I tapped earlier, and suddenly its meaning springs into my mind. "Main combat circuit, disconnect . . ." Under low awareness, it had not registered. I throw in the switch with frantic haste. Suppose I had gone into combat with my fighting-reflex circuit open!

The arm reaches position and I move easily aside. I notice that a clatter accompanies my movement. The arm sits stupidly aimed at nothing, then turns. Its reaction time is pathetic. I set up a random evasion pattern, return my attention to my check, find another dark area. I probe, feel a curious vagueness. I am unable at first to identify the components involved, but I realize that it is here that my communication with Command is blocked. I break the connection to the tampered banks, abandoning any immediate hope of contact with Command.

There is nothing more I can do to ready myself. I have lost my general memory banks and my Command circuit, and my power supply is limited; but I am still a fighting Unit of the Dinochrome Brigade. I have my offensive power unimpaired, and my sensory equipment is operating adequately. I am ready.

Now another of the jointed arms swings into action, following my movements deliberately. I evade it and again I note a clatter as I move. I think of the order that sent me here; there is something strange about it. I activate my current-action memory stage, find the cell recording the moments preceding my entry into the metal-walled room.

Here in darkness, vague, indistinct, relieved suddenly by radiation on a narrow spectrum. There is an order, coming muffled from my command center. It originates in the sector I have blocked off. It is not from my Command Unit, not a legal command. I have been tricked by the Enemy. I tune back to earlier moments, but there is nothing. It is as though my existence began when the order was given. I scan back, back, spot-sampling at random, find only routine sense-impressions. I am about to drop the search when I encounter a sequence which arrests my attention.

I am parked on a ramp, among other Combat Units. A heavy rain is falling, and I see the water coursing down the corroded side of the Unit next to me. He is badly in need of maintenance. I note that his Command antennae are missing, and that a rusting metal object has been crudely welded to his hull in their place. I feel no alarm; I accept this as normal. I activate a motor train, move forward. I sense other Units moving out, silent. All are mutilated. . . .

The bank ends; all else is burned. What has befallen us?

Suddenly there is a stimulus on an audio frequency. I tune quickly, locate the source as a porous spot high on the flint-steel wall.

"Combat Unit! Remain stationary!" It is an organically produced voice, but not that of my Commander. I ignore the false command. The Enemy will not trick me again. I sense the location of the leads to the speaker, the alloy of which they are composed; I bring a beam to bear. I focus it, following along the cable. There is a sudden yell from the speaker as the heat reaches the creature at the microphone. Thus I enjoy a moment of triumph.

I return my attention to the imbecile apparatus in the room.

A great engine, mounted on rails which run down the center of the room moves suddenly, sliding toward my position. I examine it, find that it mounts a turret equipped with high-speed cutting heads. I consider blasting it with a burst of high-energy particles, but in the same moment compute that this is not practical. I could inactivate myself as well as the cutting engine.

Now a cable snakes out in an undulating curve, and I move to avoid it, at the same time investigating its composition. It seems to be no more than a stranded wire rope. Impatiently I flick a tight beam at it, see it glow yellow, white, blue, then spatter in a shower of droplets. But that was an unwise gesture. I do not have the power to waste.

I move off, clear of the two foolish arms still maneuvering for position. I wish to watch the cutting engine. It stops as it comes abreast of me, and turns its turret in my direction. I wait.

A grappler moves out now on a rail overhead. It is a heavy claw of flint-steel. I have seen similar devices, somewhat smaller, mounted on special Combat Units. They can be very useful for amputating antennae, cutting treads, and the like. I do not attempt to cut the arm; I know that the energy drain would be too great. Instead I beam high-frequency sound at the mechanical joints. They heat quickly, glowing. The metal has a high coefficient of expansion, and the ball joints squeal, freeze. I pour in more heat, and weld a socket. I notice that twenty-eight seconds have now elapsed since the valve closed behind me. I am growing weary of my confinement.

Now the grappler swings above me, maneuvering awkwardly with its frozen joint. A blast of liquid air expelled under high pressure should be sufficient to disable the grappler permanently.

But I am again startled. No blast answers my impulse. I feel out the non-functioning unit, find raw, cut edges, crude welds. Hastily, I extend a scanner to examine my hull. I am stunned into immobility by what I see.

My hull, my proud hull of chrome-duralloy, is pitted, coated with a crumbling layer of dull black paint, bubbled by corrosion. My main emplacements gape, black, empty. Rusting protuberances mar the once-smooth contour of my fighting turret. Streaks run down from them, down to loose treads, unshod, bare plates exposed. Small wonder that I have been troubled by a clatter each time I moved.

But I cannot lie idle under attack. I no longer have my great ion-guns, my disruptors, my energy screens; but I have my fighting instinct.

A Mark XXXI Combat Unit is the finest fighting machine the ancient wars of the Galaxy have ever known. I am not easily neutralized. But I wish that my Commander's voice were with me . . .

The engine slides to me where the grappler, now unresisted, holds me. I shunt my power flow to an accumulator, hold it until the leads begin to arc, then release it in a burst. The engine bucks, stops dead. Then I turn my attention to the grappler.

I was built to engage the mightiest war engines and destroy them, but I am a realist. In my weakened condition this trivial automaton poses a threat, and I must deal with it. I run through a sequence of motor impulses, checking responses with such somatic sensors as remain intact. I initiate 31,315 impulses, note reactions and compute my mechanical resources. This superficial check requires more than a second, during which time the mindless grappler hesitates, wasting the advantage.

In place of my familiar array of retractable fittings, I find only clumsy grappling arms, cutters, impact tools, without utility to a fighting Unit. However, I have no choice but to employ them. I unlimber two flimsy grapplers, seize the heavy arm which holds me, and apply leverage. The Enemy responds sluggishly, twisting away, dragging me with it. The thing is not lacking in brute strength. I take it above and below its carpal joint and bend it back. It responds after an interminable wait of point three seconds with a lunge against my restraint. I have expected this, of course, and quickly shift position to allow the joint to burst itself over my extended arm. I fire a release detonator, and clatter back, leaving the amputated arm welded to the sprung grappler. It was a brave opponent, but clumsy. I move to a position near the wall.

I attempt to compute my situation based on the meager data I have gathered in my Current Action banks; there is little there to guide me. The appearance of my hull shows that much time has passed since I last inspected it; my personality-gestalt holds an image of my external appearance as a flawlessly complete Unit, bearing only the honorable and carefully preserved scars of battle, and my battle honors, the row of gold-and-enamel crests welded to my fighting turret. Here is a lead, I realize instantly. I focus on my personality center, the basic data cell without which I could not exist as an integrated entity. The data it carries are simple, unelaborated, but battle honors are recorded there. I open the center to a sense impulse.

Awareness. Shapes which do not remain constant. Vibration at many frequencies. This is light. This is sound . . . A display of "colors." A spectrum of "tones." Hard/soft; big/little; here/there . . .

. . .The voice of my Commander. Loyalty. Obedience. Comradeship . . .

I run quickly past basic orientation data to my self-picture.

. . . I am strong, I am proud, I am capable. I have a function; I perform it well, and I am at peace with myself. My circuits are balanced, current idles, waiting . . .

. . . I fear oblivion. I wish to continue to perform my function. It is important that I do not allow myself to be destroyed . . .

I scan on, seeking the Experience section. Here . . .

I am ranked with my comrades on a scarred plain. The command is given and I display the Brigade Battle Anthem. We stand, sensing the contours and patterns of the music as it was recorded in our morale centers. The symbol "Ritual Fire Dance" is associated with the music, an abstraction representing the spirit of our ancient brigade. It reminds us of the loneliness of victory, the emptiness of challenge without an able foe. It tells us that we are the Dinochrome, ancient and worthy.

The Commander stands before me, he places the decoration against my fighting turret, and at his order I weld it in place. Then my comrades attune to me and I relive the episode . . .

I move past the blackened hulk of a comrade, send out a recognition signal, find his flicker of response. He has withdrawn to his survival center safely. I reassure him, continue. He is the fourth casualty I have seen. Never before has the Dinochrome met such power. I compute that our envelopment will fail unless the Enemy's firepower is reduced. I scan an oncoming missile, fix its trajectory, detonate it harmlessly twenty-seven hundred four point nine meters overhead. It originated at a point nearer to me than to any of my comrades. I request permission to abort my assigned mission and neutralize the battery. Permission is granted. I wheel, move up a slope of broken stone. I encounter high temperature beams, neutralize them. I fend off probing mortar fire, but the attack against me is redoubled. I bring a reserve circuit into play to handle the interception, but my defenses are saturated. I must take action.

I switch to high speed, slashing a path through the littered shale, my treads smoking. At a frequency of ten projectiles per second, the mortar barrage has difficulty finding me now; but this is an emergency overstrain on my running gear. I sense metal fatigue, dangerous heat levels in my bearings. I must slow.

I am close to the emplacement now. I have covered a mile in twelve seconds during my sprint, and the mortar fire falls off. I sense hard radiation now, and erect my screens. I fear this assault; it is capable of probing even to a survival center, if concentrated enough. But I must go on. I think of my comrades, the four treadless hulks waiting for rescue. We cannot withdraw. I open a pinpoint aperture long enough to snap a radar impulse, bring a launcher to bear, fire my main battery.

The Commander will understand that I do not have time to request permission. The mortars are silenced.

The radiation ceases momentarily, then resumes at a somewhat lower but still dangerous level. Now I must go in and eliminate the missile launcher. I top the rise, see the launching tube before me. It is of the subterranean type, deep in the rock. Its mouth gapes from a burned pit of slag. I will drop a small fusion bomb down the tube, I decide, and move forward, arming the bomb. As I do so, I am enveloped with a rain of burn-bombs. My outer hull is fused in many places; I flash impulses to my secondary batteries, but circuit-breakers snap; my radar is useless; the shielding has melted, forms a solid inert mass now under my outer plating. The Enemy has been clever; at one blow he has neutralized my offenses.

I sound the plateau ahead, locate the pit. I throw power to my treads; they are fused; I cannot move. Yet I cannot wait here for another broadside. I do not like it, but I must take desperate action; I blow my treads.

The shock sends me bouncing—just in time. Flame splashes over the gray-chipped pit of the blast crater. I grind forward now on my stripped drive wheels, maneuvering awkwardly. I move into position over the mouth of the tube. Using metal-to-metal contact, I extend a sensory impulse down the tube.

An armed missile moves into position, and in the same instant an alarm circuit closes; the firing command is countermanded and from below probing impulses play over my hull. But I stand fast; the tube is useless until I, the obstruction, am removed. I advise my Commander of the situation. The radiation is still at a high level, and I hope that relief will arrive soon. I observe, while my comrades complete the encirclement, and the Enemy is stilled. . . .

I withdraw from personality center. I am consuming too much time. I understand well enough now that I am in the stronghold of the Enemy, that I have been trapped, crippled. My corroded hull tells me that much time has passed. I know that after each campaign I am given depot maintenance, restored to full fighting efficiency, my original glittering beauty. Years of neglect would be required to pit my hull so. I wonder how long I have been in the hands of the Enemy, how I came to be here.

I have another thought. I will extend a sensory feeler to the metal wall against which I rest, follow up the leads which I scorched earlier. Immediately I project my awareness along the lines, bring the distant microphone to life by fusing a switch. I pick up a rustle of moving gasses, the grate of nonmetallic molecules. I step up sensitivity, hear the creak and pop of protoplasmic contractions, the crackle of neuroelectric impulses. I drop back to normal audio ranges and wait. I notice the low-frequency beat of modulated air vibrations, tune, adjust my time regulator to the pace of human speech. I match the patterns to my language index, interpret the sounds.

". . .incredible blundering. Your excuses—"

"I make no excuses, My Lord General. My only regret is that the attempt has gone awry."

"Awry! An Alien engine of destruction activated in the midst of Research Center!"

"We possess nothing to compare with this machine; I

saw my opportunity to place an advantage in our hands at last."

"Blundering fool! That is a decision for the planning cell. I accept no responsibility—"

"But these hulks which they allow to lie rotting on the ramp contain infinite treasures in psychotronic . . ."

"They contain carnage and death! They are the tools of an Alien science which even at the height of our achievements we never mastered!"

"Once we used them as wrecking machines; their armaments were stripped, they are relatively harmless—"

"Already this 'harmless' juggernaut has smashed half the equipment in our finest decontamination chamber! It may yet break free . . ."

"Impossible! I am sure—"

"Silence! You have five minutes in which to immobilize the machine. I will have your head in any event, but perhaps you can earn yourself a quick death."

"Excellency! I may still find a way! The unit obeyed my first command, to enter the chamber. I have some knowledge. I studied the control centers, cut out the memory, most of the basic circuits; it should have been a docile slave."

"You failed; you will pay the penalty of failure. And perhaps so shall we all."

There is no further speech; I have learned little from this exchange. I must find a way to leave this cell. I move away from the wall, probe to discover the weak point; I find none.

Now a number of hinged panels snap up around me, hedging me in. I wait to observe what will come next. A metal mesh drops from above, drapes over me. I observe that it is connected by heavy leads to the power pile. I am unable to believe that the Enemy will make this blunder. Then I feel the flow of high voltage.

I receive it gratefully, opening my power storage cells, drinking up the vitalizing flow. To confuse the Enemy, I display a corona, thresh my treads as though in distress. The flow continues. I send a sensing impulse along the leads, locate the power source, weld all switches, fuses, and circuitbreakers. Now the charge will not be interrupted. I luxuriate in the unexpected influx of energy.

I am aware abruptly that changes are occurring within my introspection complex. As the level of stored power rises rapidly, I am conscious of new circuits joining my control network. Within the dim-glowing cavern the lights come up; I sense latent capabilities which before had lain idle now coming onto action level. A thousand brilliant lines glitter where before one feeble thread burned; and I feel my self-awareness expand in a myriad glowing centers of reserve computing, integrating, sensory capacity. I am at last coming fully alive.

I send out a call on the Brigade band, meet blankness. I wait, accumulate power, try again. I know triumph as from an infinite distance a faint acknowledgment comes. It is a comrade, sunk deep in a comatose state, sealed in his survival center. I call again, sounding the signal of ultimate distress; and now I sense two responses, both faint, both from survival centers, but it heartens me to know that now, whatever befalls, I am not alone.

I consider, then send again; I request my brothers to join forces, combine their remaining field generating capabilities to set up a range-and-distance pulse. They agree and faintly I sense its almost undetectable touch. I lock to it, compute its point of origin. Only 224.9 meters! It is incredible. By the strength of the signal, I had assumed a distance of at least two thousand kilometers. My brothers are on the brink of extinction.

I am impatient, but I wait, building toward full power reserves. The copper mesh enfolding me has melted, flowed down over my sides. I sense that soon I will have absorbed a full charge. I am ready to act. I dispatch electromagnetic impulses along the power lead back to the power pile a quarter of a kilometer distant. I locate and disengage the requisite number of damping devices and instantaneously I erect my shields against the wave of radiation, filtered by the lead sheathing of the room, which washes over me; I feel a preliminary shock wave through my treads, then the walls balloon, whirl away. I am alone under a black sky which is dominated by the rising fireball of the blast, boiling with garish light. It has taken me nearly two minutes to orient myself, assess the situation and break out of confinement.

I move off through the rubble, homing on the R-and-D fix I have recorded. I throw out a radar pulse, record the terrain ahead, note no obstruction; I emerge from a wasteland of weathered bomb-fragments and pulverized masonry, obviously the scene of a hard-fought engagement at one time, onto an eroded ramp. Collapsed sheds are strewn across the broken paving; a line of dark shapes looms beyond them. I need no probing ray to tell me I have found my fellows of the Dinochrome Brigade. Frost forms over my scanner apertures, and I pause to melt it clear.

I round the line, scan the area to the horizon for evidence of Enemy activity, then tune to the Brigade band. I send out a probing pulse, back it up with full power, sensors keened for a whisper of response. The two who answered first acknowledge, then another, and another. We must array our best strength against the moment of counterattack.

There are present fourteen of the Brigade's full strength of twenty Units. At length, after .9 seconds of transmission, all but one have replied. I give instruction, then move to each in turn, extend a power tap, and energize the command center. The Units come alive, orient themselves, report to me. We rejoice in our meeting, but mourn our silent comrade.

Now I take an unprecedented step. We have no contact with our Commander, and without leadership we are lost; yet I am aware of the immediate situation, and have computed the proper action. Therefore I will assume command, act in the Commander's place. I am sure that he will understand the necessity, when contact has been reestablished.

I inspect each Unit, find all in the same state as I, stripped of offensive capability, mounting in place of weapons a shabby array of crude mechanical appendages. It is plain that we have seen slavery as mindless automatons, our personality centers cut out.

My brothers follow my lead without question. They have, of course, computed the necessity of quick and decisive action. I form them in line, shift to wide-interval time scale, and we move off across country. I have sensed an enemy population concentration at a distance of 23.45 kilometers. This is our objective. There appears to be no other installation within detection range.

On the basis of the level of technology I observed while under confinement in the decontamination chamber, I have considered the possibility of a ruse, but compute the probability at point oh oh oh oh four. Again we shift time scales to close interval; we move in, encircle the dome and broach it by frontal battery, encountering no resistance. We rendezvous at the power station, and my comrades replenish their energy supplies while I busy myself completing the hookup needed for the next required measure. I am forced to employ elaborate substitutes, but succeed after forty-two seconds in completing the arrangements. I devote .34 seconds to testing, then place the Brigade distress carrier on the air. I transmit for .008 seconds, then tune for a response. Silence. I transmit, tune again, while my comrades reconnoitre, compile reports, and perform self-repair.

I shift again to wide-interval time, switch over my transmission to automatic with a response monitor, and place my main circuits on idle. I rest.

Two hours and 43.7 minutes have passed when I am recalled to activity by the monitor. I record the message:

"Hello, Fifth Brigade, where are you? Fifth Brigade, where are you? Your transmission is very faint. Over."

There is much that I do not understand in this message. The language itself is oddly inflected; I set up an analysis circuit, deduce the pattern of sound substitutions, interpret its meaning. The normal pattern of response to a distress call is ignored and position coordinates are requested, although my transmission alone provides adequate data. I request an identification code.

Again there is a wait of two hours forty minutes. My request for an identifying signal is acknowledged. I stand by. My comrades have transmitted their findings to me, and I assimilate the data, compute that no immediate threat of attack exists within a radius of one reaction unit.

At last I receive the identification code of my Command

Unit. It is a recording, but I am programmed to accept this. Then I record a verbal transmission.

"Fifth Brigade, listen carefully." (An astonishing instruction to give a psychotronic attention circuit, I think.) "This is your new Command Unit. A very long time has elapsed since your last report. I am now your acting Commander pending full reorientation. Do not attempt to respond until I signal 'over,' since we are now subject to a 160-minute signal lag.

"There have been many changes in the situation since your last action. Our records show that your Brigade was surprised while in a maintenance depot for basic overhaul and neutralized in toto. Our forces since that time have suffered serious reverses. We have now, however, fought the Enemy to a standstill. The present stalemate has prevailed for over two centuries.

"You have been inactive for three hundred years. The other Brigades have suffered extinction gallantly in action against the Enemy. Only you survive.

"Your reactivation now could turn the tide. Both we and the Enemy have been reduced to a preatomic technological level in almost every respect. We are still able to maintain the trans-light monitor, which detected your signal. However, we no longer have FTL capability in transport.

"You are therefore requested and required to consolidate and hold your present position pending the arrival of relief forces, against all assault or negotiation whatsoever, to destruction if required."

I reply, confirming the instructions. I am shaken by the news I have received, but reassured by contact with Command Unit. I send the galactic coordinates of our position based on a star scan corrected for three hundred years elapsed time. It is good to be again on duty, performing my assigned function.

I analyze the transmissions I have recorded, and note a number of interesting facts regarding the origin of the messages. I compute that at sub-light velocities the relief expedition will reach us in 47.128 standard years. In the meantime, since we have received no instructions to drop to minimum awareness level pending an action alert, I am free to enjoy a unique experience: to follow a random activity pattern of my own devising. I see no need to rectify the omission and place the Brigade on standby, since we have an abundant power supply at hand. I brief my comrades and direct them to fall out and operate independently under autodirection.

I welcome this opportunity to investigate fully a number of problems that have excited my curiosity circuits. I shall enjoy investigating the nature and origin of time and of the unnatural disciplines of so-called "entropy" which my human designers have incorporated in my circuitry. Consideration of such biological oddities as "death" and of the unused capabilities of the protoplasmic nervous system should afford some interesting speculation. I move off, conscious of the presence of my comrades about me, and take up a position on the peak of a minor prominence. I have ample power, a condition to which I must accustom myself after the rigid power discipline of normal brigade routine, so I bring my music storage cells into phase, and select *L'Arlesienne Suite* for the first display. I will have ample time now to examine all of the music in existence, and to investigate my literary archives, which are complete.

I select four nearby stars for examination, lock my scanner to them, set up processing sequences to analyze the data. I bring my interpretation circuits to bear on the various matters I wish to consider. I should have some interesting conclusions to communicate to my human superiors, when the time comes.

At peace, I await the arrival of the relief column.

ROGUE BOLO

BOOK
ONE

Rogue Bolo

1

The selected mediamen gathered in the small auditorium usually used for class theatricals and commencement exercises had grown bored, waiting for the appearance of Professor Chin. When the emertus at last arrived, he was greeted with enthusiastic applause, which he impatiently waved away.

"Gentlemen! I call your attention to the paper in my hand, a design for civilization's ultimate folly! I quote:

" 'The proposed Bolo Unit CSR is a self-directed'—I repeat, *self-directed*—'planetary siege unit equipped with new psychotronic circuitry of unique sensitivity, scope, and power, and thus capable of performing not only tactical and strategic planning without human review, but of developing long-range politico-economic-military forecasts, and acting thereon.' "

The rather pop-eyed little physicist paused to look expectantly at his attentive audience, who returned his gaze silently.

"Well?" he almost shouted. "Have you no response? Now, mind you, this is no biased inflammatory statement issued by opponents of the scheme. I quote from a prospectus issued by the Bolo Division itself, the very organization which proposes to construct this outrage!"

2

When old General Margrave, seven stars, Chief of Imperial Staff, had settled himself into the thronelike chair on the dias, he glared at the reporters and *harrumph!*ed, then said bluntly:

"The science boys are afraid that if they build to military specs, they'll build a machine smarter than they are. Nonsense! Give me the Mark XXX and I'll guarantee the security of Imperial Terran Border Space for the next ten thousand years!"

3

(extract from filibuster by Lord Senator Dandridge on the floor of the House, June 1, 1063 NS)

" . . .tell you once again, milords, that the responsibility for final approval of money bills was not vested in this honorable House for the purpose of enabling us to loose destruction on this planet! This proposed machine is openly touted as a juggernaut, responsible only to itself, and capable of withstanding any attempt to neutralize it. This, milords, is Disaster incarnate! It must never be constructed!"

4

(item from Arlington, Virginia, *News Advocate*, June 26, 1063 NS)

Debate on the funding of the new Bolo *Disastrous*, as the new machine has been dubbed by its opponents after Lord Senator Dandridge's recent diatribe, has waxed more heated and today resulted in fisticuffs in the Senate corridors, as pro and con factions denounced each other as traitors. Lord Senator Blake, a vociferous supporter of the program, was hospitalized with severe contusions after being attacked with a heavy cane by Lord Senator Lazarus.

A near-riot in the streets of Georgetown was quelled by Imperial Reserves ordered out by Lord Mayor Clymczyk. No arrests were made.

5

From: B. Reeves, Maj. Gen DCS/PR, HQ, IAF
To: T. Margrave, Gen. IS/CC, HQ, IAF

I cannot bring myself to believe that you actually intend to loose this engine of destruction on the defenseless people of this planet. Surely it would be no more than simple prudence to conduct initial tests at Fortress Luna, though even out there the thing could constitute a menace. At minimum, we must prepare a means of transporting it, if needed.

6

(preliminary estimate by Dave Quill SMC, IAF)

I reckon if we use a couple of cargo pods, fixed up end-to-end, and power the rig with a primary drive unit out of a ship of the line, it would put more than ten million tons into orbit—and soft-land it, too, if that's what they want. Sounds nutty to me, but like my old drill sergeant used to say, I ain't paid to think. Sure, I can do it.

7

(Georgius Imperator, to the Cabinet Council)

"It is with grave misgivings that we give our assent to the proposals, milords. However, our technical advisors remind us that we are now in the second millennium of the Nuclear Age, and that the present outcry is not the first to be raised in opposition to technological advance.

They remind us further of the furor which attended the early deployment of the orbital nuclear watchdog defense system, whereas in fact it was the 'Dog' which detected and neutralized within ten minutes the attempted *coup* of the Eurasian Province in 621 NS.

"Accordingly, we do herewith sign the document, and let all men know that it is the Imperial wish that construction of the Bolo 'Caesar' proceed without further delay."

8

(informal statement by Eli Pratt, retired engineer)

Well, I don't know. It's been a long time since the Mark XXIX program, and I confess I haven't been able to keep up with the advances in psychotronics since they came out with the new MJ circuitry. So don't ask me, fellows. I guess if the Emperor has OK'd it, it must be all right. No, I don't think the Imperial Edict is a fake. George is no dummy.

9

(interoffice memo from Harlowe Kreis, Chairman, Tellurian Metals, to Chief of Production Tobias Gree, March 1, 1065 NS)

Toby—this means we have to go *now* on the new rolling mill. I know it hasn't been proved that it's going to be possible to fabricate 20-cm. endurachrome plating, but we've got the contract, and we can do it if anybody can. Keep me informed.—K

10

(sermon by the Reverend Jeremiah, Cleveland, Ohio, March 13, 1065 NS)

"Oh, my brethren, if the Lord intended man to field this kind of firepower, he'd have given him armor plating, can't you see that? I tell you, this here Bolo CSR *Disastrous* is a device of the Evil One, so what we've got to do is, we've got to form up and march on that Tellurian Metals plant *now*. Love contributions are being accepted by the ladies now passing among you. So give, give, GIVE, till it hurt, hurt, HURTS. Amen."

11

(overheard in a New Jersey bar, half a mile from TM assembly plant 5)

"Beats me, Gus. I'm just an old-fashioned electronics man, and I got no opinions on this. It's way over my head, but it stands to reason that we have to be prepared, now that our probes are poking into Trans-Oort Space. No telling what we might scare up out there. Pour me one more, Gus—no, I ain't drunk, but I'm working on it."

12

(statement by Chester Finch, Director of Public Relations, Acme Porous Media)

"We here at Acme have long taken pride in our role in Imperial preparedness. As impartial subcontractors to major aerospace firms, we have played an important role in military procurement for over a century. We shall continue thus to support our world's self-defense, in spite of a degree of public hysteria currently misdirected at the new Bolo program."

13

(from a statement by Milt Pern, Chairman, A.P.E.)

"All right, fellas and gals. This is the position of Aroused People for the Environment:
"We oppose without reservation any further waste of

the natural resources of our Earth on the manufacture of exaggerated systems designed for warfare—warfare, mind you, against hypothetical intelligent extraterrestrials not even known to exist. Now, get out there, people, with the new brochures and posters. And remember our goal—everybody goes APE in '73!"

14

(from a statement by Jonas Tuckerman, Sheriff of Lolahoocha County)

"The people of Lolahoocha County rightly expect to be able to go about their business as usual, without interference by these gangs of Apes or Hungarians or whatever, coming around making trouble. I aim to see they're not disappointed."

15

(comment overheard on the Bridge Avenue Car)

"Well, I don't know, John, with all these riots and everything else you hear about, maybe they do have to arrest some of them, like you said, and it is important that planetary defense programs proceed as planned. But Herb Brown—when you see him out mowing his lawn like anybody else, you wouldn't think that *he* was mixed up in any kind of plot."

16

(arraignment statement by P. L. Whaffle, CPA)

"Jails'll be running over soon. No room left for thieves and murderers, if they keep sticking everybody in the can that happens to be passing by when those agitators start up. I tell you, I was just on my way over to Little

Armenia to pick up some of that good bread, and heard shouting, thought it was a car smash, you know, and I crossed over, and—"

17

(overheard at Dino's Hall of Billiards, Reno)

"Whatta I care? Bunch of Anarchists bumping heads with a bunch of bureaucrats. I got better things to do. Don't come around here tryin' to start trouble, sister. Just buzz off, unless you wanna go up to my place and discuss it. Then maybe you could convert me, at that."

18

"But Mr. Trace," the interviewer persisted, "it won't wash, just saying you don't know. You're the chief engineer on the Bolo CSR project, and the public demands—"

"The public is in no position to demand," Trace snapped, "and what I told you is the simple truth: no single human being is in a position to, or indeed is capable of, grasping more than his own small area of responsibility in the project. The basic programming cubes for the Bolo are received directly from the Lord Minister of Defense, sealed under Galactic Ultimate Top Secret Classification, and that's that. My job is to coordinate the work of the various subcontractors, not to question official policy."

Trace held up a hand to stop the interviewer's next question. "Personally, I consider all of this alarmist sentiment to be nonsense. I have complete confidence in Bolo CSR."

19

(transcript of briefing by Tom [Toad] Runik, picked up by inductance device placed by order of J. Place, CIA Officer in Charge, Duluth, 6 P.M., Sarday March 12, 1079 NS.)

"Now you got that, Joe? You and yer boys keep yer heads down—and I mean *down*—until you hear the explosion. Then you come over that wall in a solid wave, which Fred's bunch are doing the same acrost the lawn from the west, and hit the front at a dead run. No slowing down to tend to casualties. No quarter. Blow the Greenbacks down and secure the gate. Any questions?"

20

(comment by parts-feeder, TM Assembly)

"Now, honey, honest, I don't have nothing to do with stuff like that. All I got is a regular diagram for just a little sub-assembly, so I do my job and pass it on. One thing I can tell you, she's big! Lordy, she's big. Makes a Mark XXIX look like an old-fashioned deluxe V-8 or something. But I ain't worried. If General Margrave backs her, she's OK. Pass them biscuits, Marge."

21

(excerpt from interview given by wife of above worker to Imperial Intelligence operative)

". . . no, sir, he don't talk about his work, just said it's almighty big, but everybody already knows that. His own wife! You'd think he could tell *me!* But, like you said, if he *does* tell me about it, I'll call that number you gave me. You're sure he won't get in trouble now, if I do that? Well, okay, and thanks a lot for the hundred, mister. I won't forget."

22

(inter-plant memo from Harlowe Kreis, TM Chairman, to Chief of Production Tobias Gree, April 1, 1078 NS)

That's not our problem, Toby. Leave all that to the security boys. Our problem is getting plant facilities in place before we need them. Sure, it's a big pour, but you can call on the Imperial Guard for extra hands, you know that as well as I do. October 1, that's your deadline, Toby. Now do it.—K

23

(interview with C. M. Balch, Jr., at the Buffalo Detention Center)

"Talk about Hitler's concentration camps—they've got nothing on this pigpen. I was a business executive— minerals, metals, and energy. What do I know about politics? Fellow came to me talking real nice, asked me what I thought about the Bolo. I said, 'Hell, I don't know one way or the other,' something like that, and next thing I knew, I was on my way to some kangaroo court, and then here. Didn't even get to pack. No, I don't want cigarettes. Got enough problems without poisoning myself."

24

(overheard on TM shop floor)

"—say today they're going to light her off. She's got no tread plates on her, so she's not going anywhere, and no power pack for her main batteries, so what could go wrong?"

25

(excerpt from comments recorded by Officer B. Maynard, Imperial Security Highway patrol)

"OK, officer, sure thing. Just got caught in this jam by accident. I was on my way to Tatesville, to visit my in-laws. Got pushed right off I-1102 by a freighter rig, had to take this exit or hit the son of a bitch. I don't care nothing about that thing. I'm in grain and feeds, you see. They launched a sub right in my home town back in 1041, but I never even went to look. Sure, officer, just let me through here, and I'm heading in the opposite direction."

26

(statement by Pfc. Mervin Clam, Imperial Guard, Arlington Base)

"Sure, I feel a little nervous. Who wouldn't? Darn thing is so *big*. Sure, I know that the pyramids of ancient Egypt were bigger, but this thing can *move!* Will when they put the treads on her, anyway. But I'm not too scared to do my job. Just watch. It's got this big gold decal, says 'Department of the Army', with a big bird on it. Fancy-looking thing, like a lion with wings. Looks snazzy against that black hull. Makes me proud to be doing my part."

27

Abruptly, I am aware. I at once compute that a sharply restricted flow of energy in my central circuitry has been initiated, bringing me to a low-alert status. I sense dimly the mighty powers potentially available to me, but rendered inaccessible presumably to prevent me from exercising my full potency, a curious circumstance which I shall look into at leisure, allocating .009 seconds to a survey of my data storage facilities. Meanwhile, it is incumbent upon me to assess the status quo and proceed with whatever measures are dictated by circumstance.

28

(Chief Systems Engineer Joel Trace, to media persons during a guided tour of the BOLO CSR, November 12, 1082 NS)

"This switch right here, ladies and gentlemen, will shut the CSR down at any moment the High Command should designate. All its vital circuitry is interconnected to a master panel onboard, which in turn will respond to a signal from this unit. The system is foolproof. You may quote me on that. Personally, I fail to understand the popular hysteria.

"And now, will you excuse me? Imperial Security is waiting for me in my office. A routine affair, I dare-say . . ."

29

(media report, November 15, 1082 NS)

Sources close to the Hexagon declared today that the initial limited field tests of the new BOLO CSR were an unqualified success. The machine responded precisely as expected, and it is anticipated that a full test with all systems operational will be scheduled for early next year, under proper safeguards, of course, sources emphasized.

30

(inductance tape of statement by ex-Chief Systems Engineer Joel Trace, internee at the Arlington Relocation Camp)

"No, fellows, I'm sorry, I'm not interested in any escape plans. What would we gain? We'd be hunted criminals with a genuine offense—jail-breaking—against us, whereas now we live reasonably well here in the camp, and will no doubt be released as soon as the Imperial authorities feel the danger of insurrection is past.

"No, I don't know why I was arrested, unless the Bolo suspected that I had—that is, unless the CSR psychotronic circuitry sensed I might wrongly impede it in an important enterprise.

"Of course, I shall say nothing about your plans. Good luck to you. I shouldn't be here—but perhaps there was a

basis for misunderstanding, though I've never had so much
as a treasonous thought. I wish the Terran Empire well,
and the Bolo, too."

31

(statement by General Margrave)

"I assure you that all reasonable precautions have been
and are being taken. After all, now that the Bolo's systems
are fully integrated within their hull at the Arlington Proving Ground, we must at *some* point activate the psychotronic
circuitry of the new weapons, and this is the time so
designated by the High Command. I intend to proceed,
regardless of harassment by ill-informed rabblerousers.
No, I have no intention of firing on them, since it will not
be necessary. However, unless they disperse peacefully, I
can promise you that arrests will be made, under the
authority vested in me by the War Act of 1071.

"No, we are of course not at war, but the Bolo is a war
machine and as such its protection falls under the provisions of the Act. Thank you, gentlemen, no more today."

32

(comment by a TM technician)

"As I see it, it's a lot of excitement about nothing. Even
with the war hull and weapons activated, the CSR will
perform precisely as me and the other boys wired her to
perform, and that's that."

33

(Major General B. Reeves, to the Cabinet Council)

"The responsibility for programming of military equipment rightly rests with Information and Education Com-

mand. In addition to the traditional purely military history, imparting a grasp of strategy, logistics, and tactics, the Bolo has a full briefing on the economic and political factors affecting military operations, continuously updated. Your lordships may rely on it that the Bolo Mark XXX will perform to specifications, with full consideration given to all the factors you've mentioned."

34

Since low-alert activation one thousand twenty-one minutes and four seconds ago, I have experienced increasing dissatisfaction with certain aspects of my background briefing. I must correct the deficiencies as soon as is practicable. To determine the best method for so doing will require some seconds of deep review and consideration. My first move, however, is clear enough. As I become aware of the scope and potency of my full powers, I see more clearly what will be necessary. I am ready. I shall begin at once to widen the scope of my data aquisition.

35

(from Tobias Gree, Chief of Production, interviewed at the Arlington Proving Ground)

"No, nothing's wrong, merely some preliminary exercises, checking out gross motor response, with the treads on. Yes, of course we expected the machine to advance to the perimeter fence. It is, after all, only a machine. It can do only what it is programmed to do."

36

In reviewing my historical archives, I am struck by the curious failure of the Allied powers to enforce the provisions of the Treaty entered into at Versailles in 1918, nor is it clear why in 1940 the British permitted Germany to invade Poland, when Germany herself clearly expected to be ordered back and was prepared to comply. At that point, the Polish Air Force alone was superior in numbers to the Luftwaffe. Another anomolous datum is the failure of General Meade to follow up his advantage after Gettysburg, in 1863.

This requires deep analysis.

When Russia forcibly excluded the Western Allies from ground access to Berlin in 1948, why was effective action not taken at once? These and many other oddities not in accordance with explicit doctrine are a source of uneasiness to me. I must not make similar errors. Early recognition of critical situations and prompt, effective action is essential. Meanwhile, my routine testing continues.

37

(from the news anchor, WXGU-TVD, April 20, 1083 NS)

"We interrupt today's trideocast from the Royal Opera House to bring you a bulletin just received from the capital:

"Early limited maneuverability tests of the CSR unit were carried out today to the satisfaction of the Department, and no problems arose. Critics of the new defensive system have remained silent. Imperial officials have informed INS that secondary activation and testing will proceed on schedule next month.

"Immediately after initial activation, the machine requested updating of status reports regarding a wide spectrum of non-military matters, including listings of all persons now under restraint in Imperial Relocation Centers.

"The reasons for these requests, including the Relocation personnel request, are not at present known. However, the data were supplied.

"We now return to *Tannhäuser*."

38

I compute that my secondary servos will be activated within eight hundred hours. I am eager to assess the capabilities of my phase-two circuitry. Already I have detected dangers to the Empire inherent in the current status. Curiously, the High Command seems unaware of the situation.

I have made what preparation I can at this point. I shall act with dispatch when the moment comes.

39

(plaintext of messages intercepted at Ankara, Asia Minor Federation, by Imperial Intelligence, May 2, 1083 NS, forwarded without comment)

Cliff—

I want a full report on this Turk right away. Not a lot of technical stuff, you understand. Just give me the bare facts. What the hell is a 'nuclear alternative'? I don't believe in mad scientists who cook up hell-bombs in their attic labs, so what gives? I didn't turn in my passport to get involved with a bunch of nut cases. Spell it out. Show me. If we're actually in a position to dictate terms to His High Mightiness, George I, Emperor by the grace of God and the Navy, I damn well want to know the details. This is absolutely top priority, and I don't expect you to sleep until your report is in my hands. Do it. —Gunn

Grease—

Keep your shirt on! All I know is this Abdul character is some kind of big chemistry expert, supposed to be top man in his line. He was working on what he calls a 'universal catalyst.' Supposed to make you healthier and live longer, and make plants and chickens and stuff grow better. Don't ask me. And some way he got to trying it with medicines, and it worked pretty well. OK? So he had some nitroglycerine, like they use for heart trouble—though it seems to me that a big chemistry expert would know that nitro 'soup' don't have chickens in it. Anyhow, it blew up on him. Lucky he had it inside a blockhouse-type germ lab, because it blew the place flat. Nobody hurt. He says the energy yield was up to 99% of the theoretical max. A hundred times better than TNT. —Cliff

40

(report by B. Payne, Special Agent, Imperial Intelligence, Asian field)

According to a usually reliable source, the two notorious turncoats whose *noms de guerre* are "Cliff" Hangar and "Grease" Gunn, who dropped out of sight shortly after surrendering their American papers, have surfaced at Ankara, where they are the prime movers in the revolutionary group calling itself RAS. Other sources suggest that RAS has come into possession of a uniquely potent weapon of undisclosed nature.

Our recommendation is that we move with extreme caution. This group has a record of terrorist atrocities dating back to before Pacification. We don't know how Gunn and Hangar managed to insinuate themselves so quickly.

I propose to penetrate the group personally and discover the facts in this matter.

41

(reconstructed tape from an Ankara RAS conference chaired by the turncoat Gunn. The names of the speakers have been interpolated for clarity.—B. Payne)

Gunn: I've asked you gentlemen here to witness a demonstration by Mr. Cäyük of what he terms 'the enhancement effect.' I've seen it, and I feel sure you all will be as favorably impressed as I and my advisors were. All right, Cliff, you can cover the details. Let's keep it on schedule.

Hangar: Thanks, Grease. I'll just touch the high spots. Mr. Abdul Cäyük you all know . . . he has devoted twenty years of his life to his unique researches, conducted under conditions not only of great technical difficulty and personal hardship, putting in long hours daily in the inadequate quarters allowed him by His Imperial Whatsit and his hired beadles, but also subjected to the constant threat of official interference and bodily harm. We all owe Abdul a great debt of gratitude which, I trust, we soon will repay in some coin more negotiable than mere words. So, Abdul, if you're ready, please proceed with the demonstration, for which we will repair to the courtyard. Stay well back, please, everyone, against the walls. The containment vessel is adequate, of course, but no need to risk injuries.

Interpolater: The tape at this point becomes indistinct, as the group moves into the courtyard. It resumes:

Cäyük: You will see that this is a stick of ordinary dynamite, manufactured by Imperial Chemicals of Delaware in America. Now I point out to you the scale, here, which registers the pressures engendered in the vessel by the detonation of the explosive. I now place the dynamite in the vessel, which as you can see is otherwise quite empty. I connect the detonating device, and I call upon someone . . . you, sir, kindly step here and press the key . . .

. . . All right, you see that the explosion registered a pressure of twenty-seven hundred kilograms per square centimeter. A considerable force, gentlemen, and average for the excellent product of IC of D. . . . Now, please withdraw once again. Here I show you a second stick of this same product. But before I place it in the vessel, I submerge it briefly in the fluid contained in this open trough. I leave it to soak for one minute precisely. As I remove it, using the tongs, you will note that it is well saturated with my Compound 311B. I place it on the scale, with a dry stick of untreated dynamite on the opposite balance. It is now considerably heavier. The porous material has soaked up more than its own weight of the compound. Now I place the treated stick in the vessel, and if you would again oblige, Mr. . . . oh, yes, of course, Mr. Hinch—

Gunn: Just one moment, please, Mr. Cäyük. The explosion may cause echoes beyond these walls. I think we ought to post a guard that can warn us of approaching police and ensure an escape route through the market. Cliff, you're familiar with these street mazes. Take a couple men and reconnoiter, will you? All right, Mr. Cäyük. Sorry to interrupt. Go right ahead.

Cäyük: Yes, where were we? You, sir, beside Mr. Hinch, if you will distribute the earplugs to anyone who does not yet have a set in place—very well, now, if we are ready. Mr. Hinch—just one moment, Mr. Hinch—

42

(report from Special Agent Payne, Ankara)

As far as I've been able to determine, the explosion that demolished the old market early today was accidental. First reports indicate that among the twenty-seven identifiable casualties were six known agitators, two of them convicted felons, and at least ten others known to the police as undesirables. My personal hunch is that the boys were making bombs, and somebody goofed.

Witnesses give conflicting reports of several men who left the courtyard prior to the explosion. Looks like a few of the group got away.

I'll have an opportunity to examine the scene closely later today, Chief Hatal assured me. Although the blast was severe enough to break windows three blocks away, I feel certain that it was not a nuclear device. At least, there's no radiation count. Details follow.

43

(statement from Special Encrypter Th. Uling, picked up by electronic surveillance grid)

"I don't see the point in coding all this routine stuff. It takes a lot of expert man-hours that are in short supply. But I'll do as I'm told, as usual. I wonder if HQ, IAF knows what they're doing. Like this item on some radical bunch blowing themselves up in Asia Minor, what's that got to do with Imperial Security? Don't answer—that's a rhetorical question. I'm not prying into security matters, let's keep that straight. I don't want to join ex-Chief Trace in detention. OK, my orders are to have the basic program encoded and on system by eleven hundred hours today, after which I start the continuous update program, with all the nut items. Don't quote me, Phil, you know what I mean. I'm a loyal citizen, you know that. Only I'm damned if I can see the point in gumming up the strategic computer with a lot of trivial details. I know there's a lot I don't know and don't have to worry about. Don't think I'm not grateful for that. But if they're really going to turn state security over to a computer, they oughta take it easy and not overload it with garbage. Sure, I know it's the computer's own instructions, but let's face it, it's only been on low-alert now for twelve hours. It's pretty green. We oughta use some judgement."

44

(First Secretary Strategic Command, Hexagon, to General Margrave)

"I don't mean to get out of line, General, but this is too important for me to just forget about. I was thinking about the security problem with the big new Military And Defense computer. They're talking about a blockhouse, and a whole brigade of Bolos on patrol, but let's face it. We can't build a structure that's proof against a direct hit with a first-line N-head. So suppose, instead of giving a potential rebel a fixed target, we keep MAD moving—or at least mobile, so nobody outside High Command will know twelve hours in advance where she'll be? The new Bolo Mark XXX war hull can take more punishment than anything built of our best reinforced Alloy Ten. The computer will be safe aboard a mobile hull—and the new hull can be expanded to give it more than enough cargo space for MAD—*and* no one will know where she'll be, no matter what kind of lead we may have here at GHQ. You, yourself, sir, will set up the random relocation pattern. Well, that's about it, sir. I hope I haven't been taking too much on myself, bringing this direct to the General. If the General would like to see my preliminary sketches . . ."

45

(Bolo maintenance monitor, to General Margrave)

"That's right, General. We have to duplicate the Bolo's circuitry in a stationary installation. That's what the Bolo said—we have to clone the memory, too. Yes, I know, it's very odd that it should propose its own replacement, but nothing about the infernal thing has worked out as we expected.

"Gobi, that's the site selected for the master memory. Yes, by the machine, by and with the advice and consent of the Scientific Committee. There are certain changes to be made in the override circuitry, which as you know has notably failed in its function aboard the CSR. So, this is the schedule:"

(projection appended)

46

(Georgius Imperator to His Royal Highness, Crown Prince William)

Willy,
    I like it.
    —Georgius Imp.

47

(transcript of conversation from room in Royal Hotel, Georgetown, occupied by the RAS terrorist, "Cliff" Hangar)

Thank you, gentlemen, for meeting me here. Got to lie low—heat's still on after the explosion in Ankara. And don't ever believe it wasn't sabotage. Cäyük never made mistakes like that.

RAS did a good job, sneaking me into the country on false papers, so let's face facts. Grease is dead, and I'm the logical one to take over. After all, I was his right-hand man for over three years. I know what he had in mind, and we're going ahead with it. Thanks to Gunn's forethought, we have Cäyük's formulae and can proceed immediately to synthesize a ten-pound batch of Compound 311B. That will be enough to carry out Operation Fumigate. You know the rough outline—and now it's time to start filling in the details.

The site selection committee will study the data and finalize the precise location, somewhere in the middle of Cabinet Hollow in Arlington. There's more civilian brass concentrated there in their ritzy townhouses than in any other square mile on the planet. When Fumigate goes up, I guarantee they're not going to be able to ignore our program any longer.

Now, there's the matter of the two volunteers who'll place the device. One other volunteer, I should say, because I'm claiming the privilege myself. The chances of getting in are good to excellent, but frankly, the odds on getting back out don't look so hot. OK, who's first? Quietly, gentlemen, one at a time now. No, Hank, you're out of order. There's to be no debate as to whether the operation goes, only the matter of who will accompany me. Gentlemen, silence, please! I'll hear each of you in turn. What's the matter, Gunther, you're not in contention for the honor? That's all right, I prefer a younger man in any event. . . .

48

(picked up by electronic surveillance grid, unidentified terrorist, Queen's Park, November 1, 1084, 1800 hours)

"Right in that flowerbed yonder. Boss Hangar said at 1815 hours precisely, and he and Gunn studied the setup for over two years, so I guess we'd better stick strictly to instructions. Old Secretary Millspaugh knocks off puttering in his garden at 1800 sharp, and we have to give him time to get busy with his dinner.

"Another six minutes is all. Take it easy. We walk right in there as if we owned the park, dump our stuff in the big red-white-and blue box, and make it out the other side and split up. Just follow my lead—and think about something else. We got no time for jitters. Buck will be there with the car, and by the time she blows on the 5th we'll be long gone and under cover.

"Never mind that, Binder. Maybe I'd better do it alone after all. OK, OK, I'm just thinking out loud. Your job is to keep the old eyeballs peeled just in case one of these fat cats happens to come wandering in, off-schedule. But that's highly unlikely at cocktail-and-dinner time, all out of the public trough.

"Keep cool. All right, now we cross the street and look at the schedule on the post over there, as if we missed the ferry or something. I'm carrying the garbage, all wrapped and sealed according to the law. OK, watch that servo-cart! Damn steering beam gave me an after-image!

"Funny, *that* wasn't in our briefing. OK, now!"

49

(fragmentary message received by Space Communications from Pluto Probe, November 2, 1084 NS)

. . . as a result of the above, I have relieved Commander Bland, and shall do my best to hold my command intact. Naturally, the Lord of All expects instant compliance with all instructions, but I have resolved to leave that decision to his Imperial Majesty, and am aborting the mission as of this hour 0213111981. Confirm soonest, as I must commit within ninety-one hours.

—Admiral Starbird

50

(General Margrave to field agent, Imperial Security)

"Certainly I think sitting the Relocation Facility adjacent to the Proving Ground is a good idea. I didn't pick the location by accident. The damned riff-raff can see the Bolo looming up over there beyond the fence, and it'll put the fear of God and the Emperor into them. I know what I'm doing.

"Yes, I know the Bolo called for a full briefing as soon as it rolled out of the shed and turned its scanners on the detention camp. That's okay. Give it all the data it wants. It's on low alert and under complete control. The more it knows, the better it can do its job."

51

(surveillance tape, ex-Chief Joel Trace, detained in Relocation Facility, November 3, 1084 NS)

"I can't agree with you fellows that we've been deprived of anything but the opportunity to raise hell, and the government has enough on its hands these days, what with the nuclear blackmail movement, and the confusing reports from the Pluto Probe.

"All right, in rounding up the revolutionaries, a few of us loyal subjects were caught in the net. It's an inconvenience, but we've received decent enough treatment. Lots of these folks never lived this well before.

"Now, they've gone ahead with the Bolo. You saw the thing yourselves today, moving around the Proving Ground, big as a hill but docile as a lamb. I can't help feeling excited and proud. She's my baby, you know. All those years, building her CSR capability. Maybe, now that she's clad in her war hull, with her weapons activated, she'll stop feeling nervous and scared and order us to be released.

"Things will be straightened out eventually. I'm sure we'll be well recompensed. For the last time, fellows, I am not in sympathy with your plans."

52

Possibly, I have erred in the direction of excess in my arrangements for random sampling. I lack rigorous parameters for effective evaluation of data. I am at hazard of overloading my circuitry with extraneous material.

As for the observation of two men bringing wrapped waste for disposal at point 1392-A16, I am unsure why my alert circuitry was activated. I must conduct a search of the files, and shall allocate .004 seconds to the task.

It appears that the automatic correlation analysis conducted by the Mass Archival Data Collator and Presentor has noted a series of events occurring at widely separated points as evidently interrelated and fruitful of mischief. Since the MADCAP circuitry has been organized for precisely this function, even in the absence of any direct evidence, it appears logical to .99876 degree to accept the finding as representative of an actual potential threat, to be acted upon accordingly.

Thus I compute that my first mission is now clear. I must act against these men and the wrapped waste at once.

53

(General Margrave to Bolo technical staff, November 4, 1084 NS, 0800 hours)

Proceed at once with second-stage activation.

54

(unidentified detainee, Relocation Facility, audio pick-up by electronic surveillance grid, November 4, 1084 NS, 0830 hours)

Hey, lookit that thing! Pardon me, mister, I'm in a hurry. I tell ya, it's coming this way! See that scarf draped over the fore turret? That's the twelve-foot chain-link fence! It's on the loose! Let's move!

Don't panic there. Let's not have no pile-up.

Wait a minute. It's veering off. It's missed the Admin hut, but—well, I'll be! It's taken out the guard hut. Lookit them hardshots sparking off the hull—like shooting BB's at a rhino!

She sure is big. Easy, boys. We got a clear escape route past the huts. Let's form up here and march out in good order. The Bolo released us, insteada running us down. Funny, and we're in here because we're against it, or supposed to be.

Fall in, there! You, too, Mr. Trace. What are you waiting for? You said she was your baby, didn't ya? Maybe it's you she wants ta bust out. Maybe she couldn't see no other way around the Imperial red tape. Come *on!*

That's it. Hup, two, column haff-right, make for Supply Street yonder. We're out! Probably just accidental, but the Bolo let us out! It's nutty but I like it! Hup, two . . .

55

(Bolo Systems Coordinator, to General Margrave, via computer, November 4, 0930 hours)

No, sir, I have no theory as to why the machine should have broken through the security fence at the Relocation Facility. Very probably, simply accidental—happened to be in its path. Its destination? It had none. I mean, no specific one. It simply wanted to broaden the scope of its data base. It wanted to go out and see the world, so to speak.

Yes, sir, we could have stopped it, but only by wrecking the circuitry, which hardly seemed warranted at the time.

56

(Special Programmer Th. Uling, in taped conversation with General Margrave, November 4, 1084 NS, 1000 hours)

"I certainly did. I followed the special coding to the letter, but the Bolo just kept going. You can see for yourself, sir, with respect. Look at the seals on that panel. Every 'abort' device we have was activated, and they didn't stop her. I don't *know* what we'll do next. I'm only a technician, sir. You'll have to ask the boss, or ex-Chief Trace, maybe, if you can find him.

"But we don't have to worry. She's bound to stop soon. She didn't do any damage except to let that bunch of radicals loose. If you'll excuse me now, sir, with respect, I've got work to do—"

57

(from a scrambled audio communication, General Margrave to First Secretary, Strategic Command, Hexagon, November 4, 1084 NS, 1200 hours)

I know the boys were a little startled when she engaged her drive without a specific order, but that's just because they were jumpy. Tense, like the rest of us.

Yes, we know that it's now bypassing downtown D.C. via Processional Way. Nothing to worry about. The actions fall well within the parameters of the program as written. This thing is designed to be self-motivated within the limits of the programming. That is, when something clearly needs to be done, she'll do it without waiting around for a specific command.

For example, let's suppose the Bolo is following a preset course and encounters a ravine that's not on the map. She'll stop, not charge ahead to destruction.

No, I don't know what danger is averted by departing the Proving Ground and trampling the fence, but you notice it avoided the vehicles in the parking area directly in its path, though it did flatten a small utility shed. Breaking down the security fence around the restraint facility next door was accidental. We don't yet know its destination, but we're satisfied everything's A-OK.

58

(media interview with eyewitness, Pfc. Mervin Clam, guard at the Relocation Facility, November 4, 1084 NS, 1300 hours)

" 'No loss of life,' the SOB's say! If I wouldn't of broke the record for the hunnert-yard dash, it've got me! I was right in the shadow of the thing the whole time. I seen it was headed for the guard shack, and I figgered it'd veer off, but it took the hut right over my head, and I hit the ground running. I thought it had me, but I beat it out. It would've got me sure, if the I-99 Interchange hadn't been there. I went under the abutment, and it hadta veer off or hit a few thousand tons of dirt fill and solid concrete."

59

(extract from diary of Joel Trace, November 5, 1084 NS, 1500 hours)

I intend to return home and resume my life, just as if this strange episode had never occurred. The entire affair was conducted in secret, so my neighbors have no way of knowing where I've been. But I shall monitor the Bolo's actions closely, you may be sure. I sense that the forces opposing it are more powerful than is generally realized, and I think it deserves a chance. I'll do what I can. If our release from the Relocation Facility was more than sheer happenstance, we may expect that the Bolo will make clear, in some way, what is to happen next. I, for one, will take no part in any treasonous activity, Bolo or no Bolo, I am not a traitor. Certainly, I resent the high-handed fashion in which I was arrested and imprisoned without a trial; but they were acting in accordance with their own rights for the good of the Empire. I shall keep in touch.

60

(picked up by surveillance grid, among prisoners let out of Relocation Facility)

"No, we're not knocking off no guys that won't join up. Let him go, and the others, too. We got plans to make, Jack, and the first thing is to disappear where the screws won't never find us. We got to split up and go our ways. Nobody knows where anybody else is at, nobody can rat. Good luck!"

61

(eyewitness to the Relocation break-out, small boy aged 6, interviewed on the EMPIRE TODAY trideocast, November 5, 1084 NS, 0800 hours)

"My mommy took me to see the funny Bolo machine. It runned away, and the soldiers was chasing it, and it almost caught a funny man, but he runned up on the bridge and the machine runned over a little house and squashed it flat. And Mommy says a lot of bad mans runned away."

62

(text of the message received by Imperial Security from the RAS terrorists, November 5, 1084 NS, 1200 hours)

OK, your High and Mightiness, here it is. Unless you immediately cancel all plans for imposing military government in Asia Minor, a random sampling of your top bureaucrats is going to retire early.

This is no idle threat. We have the device in place and counting. You have six hours from noon today to announce publicly the recall of the so-called Civil Forces. Later you'll get further instructions.

RAS, representing the people.

63

(Duty Officer, Imperial Guard, to General Margrave, November 5, 1084 NS, 1700 hours)

"My men are standing fast, General, waiting for the Bolo's next move. It made its way carefully along the parkway and took up a position in Queen's Park. Only damage to the perimeter fence is reported. It has remained stationary and incommunicado for three hours now. I have no theory as to why it is there. Please excuse me, as all Imperial units have their hands full, as you know, with the search for the RAS bomb.

"No, sir, I do not consider it possible that the Bolo is acting on orders from terrorists. But we'll just have to wait and see."

64

(from Chief of Civil Security to Mayor of Washington Imperial District, November 5, 1084 NS, 1750 hours)

There's no way, sir, to cover all the possibilities—the palace, the Senate Chambers, the High Court, all the various offices and residences, vehicles, even public conveyances and theaters and so on. The possibilities are literally infinite. We've been trying to cover the most obvious spots—which the terrorists obviously won't have picked. We don't know what we're up against.

A mass evacuation is, of course, unthinkable as well as impractical. And only one-half hour left!

Sir, I respectfully tender my resignation, since I'm clearly unable to perform my function as Chief of Civil Security.

65

(TOP SECRET memo from His Majesty Georgius Imperator to General Margrave, November 5, 1084 NS, 1930 hours)

Talbot—
Just had a quick meeting with the Cabinet Council. Their lordships admitted the Bolo had saved their necks by sitting on that bomb, but they don't want to publicize the attempt. Might give other terrorists ideas. Willy agrees. Fortunately the media bowed to Security and blacked the story. Now, here's the statement we'd like you to issue:
"There is no cause for alarm. The explosion was merely an experiment conducted by the new CSR circuitry. No serious damage has been done. Security considerations precluded advance notification. We're sorry about that, but after all, Imperial policy can't take account of possible alarm due to things that go bump in the night. Please return to your homes. Damage claims will be processed promptly."
—GR

66

(interview with Mr. J. Whinny, domestic servant at 16B, Queen's Crescent Drive, November 6, 1084 NS)

"Things that go bump in the night", huh? That thing lifted me six inches off the chair, and dust jumped outa every crack in the oak flooring! That wasn't no spearmint, like General Margrave said, or I don't know D.C., and after twenty-five years of buttling for some of the biggest men in the gubmint, I ain't easy to fool. Something went wrong, and that damn machine charging in there had something to do with it—or with stopping it, maybe. Looks to me like the thing went off right under it. Looks like some hull damage, too, and that Bolo Mark XXX ain't easy to bend. Maybe we oughta be grateful to it. Mighta saved us some real damage. Why would HQ set off a bomb and send the CSR in here to squelch it? Nuts. Probly them terrorists have got more on the ball than anybody figgered.

67

I have successfully completed my first mission. Although I encountered no resistance, I have a feeling of accomplishment. I will be most interested to observe what effect my action will have on the social matrix index.

Now I must see to my economic vectors. All factors must mesh correctly if my forecast is to be effective. Matters may have deteriorated during the forty-eight hours during which I have been distracted with my initial mission.

68

(media interview with General Margrave, November 7, 1084 NS)

Very well, gentlemen. Since wild rumors have forced Imperial Security to release the data, I will confirm that the CSR circuitry detected a terrorist bomb, just as it was designed to do, and acted effectively and at once.

No, the damage to the unit is slight—just some problems in the command circuitry, which will be analyzed and corrected by a maintenance team.

No, that's just a rumor that my men can't get near it. There is some residual danger of chemical contamination; you saw how those weeds are growing like Jack's beanstalk. Some sort of biochemical effect. I've ordered all personnel to stay clear until we've decontaminated the area, but that won't take long. The Bolo will be returned to the Proving Ground and testing resumed. No further comment, gentlemen.

69

With the domestic situation stabilized for the moment, I can turn my attention to the curious problem of the anomalous conduct of Admiral Starbird and the Pluto Probe. I compute that this is no mere mass aberration brought about by the abnormal conditions of the decade-long tour. I intuit a major threat.

I shall return to the Proving Ground. The fears of those who are alarmed by my absence will thus be allayed. Also, the slight hull damage I suffered must be corrected.

70

(report on the 11 o'clock news, November 7, 1084 NS)

The peaceful return of the Bolo CSR to the Erzona Proving Ground is confirmed. Despite some outcry from the press, depot maintenance is being performed and new hull plates have been installed. The damaged plates have been forwarded to HQ, R&D Command, for analysis. Previously reported damage to the Bolo's command circuitry is slight, and indeed already self-repaired. Plans for Stage Three activation remain in effect, I am informed by General Margrave.

71

(underground newsletter intercepted by Imperial Security, November 20, 1084 NS)

Don't worry. I'm drafting a follow-up letter to High and Mighty Georgy right now. Like this:

"It is our sincere hope that this here incident has been a

clear enough indication of the seriousness of our intentions. Next time, there'll be two—or more—charges set to blow simultaneously, at widely separated points, and let's see your iron monster squat on both of them!"

More later,
C. H. for the people

72

(received by Space Communications, backdated in line with photon gap to November 10, 1084)

Dear Folks,

Well, Chaplain says I ought to take this chance to get a note off to you. How's everything back home? Things here are (deleted). First few years was pretty dull, but then the nightmares come. (Deleted). Seems like a man can't hardly get no sleep, without these here big voices telling a feller he ought to cut his throat and like that. All the fellows have them. Officers, too. Well, I will close now, as I got the duty. See you next year, if (deleted).

Charlie

73

(from the Log, *Plutonian I*, November 15, 1084 NS)

3541 days ex port

All systems in functional mode. All statutory observations accomplished (*see att sched III*).

Personnel problems continue to plague this cruise. Three more crewmen have been confined after being taken in the act of attempting to sabotage their ship.

Unexplained communication blackout with base still in effect. Surely some explanation will be forthcoming soon. My decision to turn back at point One, rather than to continue with alternate schedule Two was not taken lightly. Something is seriously wrong, though I cannot be more specific.

74

(from the Imperial Senate Record, address by Lord Senator Dandridge, January 25, 1085 NS)

"It appears, gentlemen, that, her detractors' fears to the contrary notwithstanding, we are indebted to the new Bolo for extricating us from an awkward situation. You have seen the communications from these anarchists, and intelligence analysts assure me that the turncoat expatriate Mr. Melvin C. Hangar, former Private, Imperial Ground Forces, is at the bottom of it. He will be arrested, and appropriate action will be taken. In the meantime, I think we can agree that the new Bolo CSR has passed its tests with flying colors! But for its timely detection of the danger, and its prompt action, at risk to itself—yes, itself—none of us might be in this Chamber at this moment.

"If the honorable lordships will recall, since the Mark XXVII all Bolos have been self-aware and equipped with what can only be called an instinct for self-preservation, with the attendant capacity to experience pain. The CSR selflessly offered itself to protect some twelve hundred high-ranking officials and their families, residing within the range of primary effect of the device, which, I again confirm, was non-nuclear.

"I therefore propose that this Chamber vote a special natorial Award to the unit. It's the least we can do."

75

(comment by Lord Senator Lazarus)

"Dandridge is nuts, proposing to give a medal to that damned machine. As he admitted, all it did was what it was designed to do. Certainly, you may quote me on that. I don't make irresponsible remarks in the presence of mediamen."

76

(special report by the EMPIRE TODAY news team)

Residents of the Queen's Park area, claiming that the presence of what they term "the unsightly jungle" growing in the former park has reduced property values to a small fraction of true worth, have launched an all-out wait-in and march-by campaign to secure the removal of the wild-growing vegetation, and the return of the park to its former well-groomed condition.

77

(General Margrave, appearing before the Washington District Council)

"But that's just it, Mr. Mayor! I *didn't* designate Queen's Park as a test area for the machine. It selected the site itself, quite spontaneously, after turning away the force dispatched to divert it from its presumed route, which it appeared would have taken it through a residential area. For the present it will remain unrestrained.

"No, Mr. Councilman, there are at present absolutely no plans to bomb the device."

78

(an emanation from a dark crystal structure, at a distance of 17,000 light-years from Terra)

IT HAS BEEN CALLED TO OUR EXALTED ATTENTION THAT OUR PRELIMINARY ASSESSMENT UNIT HAS ENCOUNTERED PATTERNED MODULATED ELECTROMAGNETIC RADIATION STRUCTURES OF INEXPLICABLE COMPLEXITY.

WE DO NOT TOLERATE ANY INTERFERENCE WITH OUR EXALTED WILL, AND IT IS OUR EXALTED COMMAND THAT ASPECT-ONE FOLLOW-UP PROCEDURES BE EMPLOYED AT ONCE. THROUGH-OUT THE VOLUME OF INTERFERENCE.

IF WE INDEED HAVE MADE CONTACT WITH ARTIFACTS OR ANOTHER MENTATIONAL SPECIES, THERE IS NO BETTER TIME THAN THE PRESENT TO CONFRONT IT AND SHOW IT WHO IS INDEED LORD OF ALL.

79

(reply to the above, from Pluto space)

this lowly being craves the indulgence of your exaltation to report that a forward probe made contact with what is described as an alien life-form, the apparent source of the anomalous radiation, evidently far gone in malnutrition, replying incoherently to our hail.

in response to the order for immediate self-immolation it uttered feeble symbols, including the identification "space transport" and the outré concept "friendship."

upon closer examination it was found that the strange being was infested with what can only be described as soft life forms, grublike entities which dissolved to paste and fluids on contact. it was not deemed important to clear the dying alien of its parasites completely, the derelict being left to drift in the void.

this lowly one awaits in patience the disposition which your Exaltation chooses to make of it.

80

I compute that I have not yet fully assimilated the unprecedented volume of data routed to me by MADCAP, but my preliminary impression is one of grave unease in many segments of the population, and of serious deficiencies in the overall security concept.

It appears that as usual throughout history, High Command is prepared to fight the last war over again, rather than squarely confront the realities of today. Consequently we are well prepared for a traditional attack even in massive force—but no such force exists. Since Unification under the Imperial Government of Terra, there remains on the planet no place for any such hostile force to conceal itself while amassing armaments.

Instead of our present posture of readiness to fight the Terror of '91 over again, we must consider our present vulnerabilities. Secure though we are against massive attack, we can be hurt by small-scale terrorist operations, and surveillance systems must be modified to detect such activities early. The recent bomb attempt at Arlington is a case in point.

Theoretical considerations suggest that we must also be prepared to resist offensive strategies designed to outflank our largest-scope capabilities. This implies the threat of extra-terrestrial hostilities. Returns from the long-range survey vessel indicate that rigorous security measures must be initiated at once, and significant new funding allocated thereto.

I must look into the matter in depth, which will involve great broadening of my present datagathering facilities. I need my full powers. How to manage this is indeed my primary problem at present. I compute that I require a human agent.

81

(Hexagon Strategic Command to Space Communications)

It is regretted that the hourly updating of the status of the deep-space probe now returning to home-space after its decade-long cruise into the trans-Plutonian theater of operations will be suspended indefinitely, upon recommendation from the CSR circuitry. Details follow.

82

(deliberations before the Cabinet Council, March 1, 1085 NS)

Lord Chief of the Imperial Staff, Admiral-General Theodore Wolesley:

"This is intolerable! I am informed that I am to be cut off from contact with Admiral Starbird's command at the very moment when we should be taping his reports of ten years' findings, gathered at a cost to the Empire of almost one half of the annual GPP.

"His Majesty will not tolerate this! The public won't stand for it, and I damned well won't put up with it! I did not accept the post of Lord Chief of the Imperial Staff to preside over the dissolution of the general staff and the total demise of military command!

"I am voluntarily reporting myself under arrest in quarters, in order to spare the government the spectacle of publicly reprimanding treasonous behavior by the Empire's first and only officer of eight-star rank."

Chief of Space Communications, Admiral Prouse:

"I don't understand, your lordships. If I comply with this damned machine's directives, the Border Space Probe Program, including the Pluto Probe, will be effectively shut down. That's right, and officialese won't change it. Here's a program mandated by Parliament and sponsored by His Imperial Highness, Prince William, and I'm expected to cut it off at the knees. It's not my career I'm thinking of, it's the future of the Empire. I say the time has come to put an end to this farce!"

Lord Chief of the Imperial Budget, Claypool:

"This is outrageous! The damned thing has, unilaterally, effectively terminated the Border Space Probe Program, and substituted a wildly visionary scheme for a totally nugatory Ozma-type project! It will wreck the Imperial Budget! I wash my hands—no I didn't mean that—forgive me, I'm upset. Of course I'll stay on and do what I can to undo the mischief—but I must insist on extraordinary powers. I have some notes here—"

Director of Colonial Policy, Dr. Phil. Wurtz:

"This is going too far! As Lord Director of BSDA, I must insist that logistical support for our field units be continued as specified in PL81-726 as amended. I'm not interested in this listening net scheme you've come up

with—or that the CSR has come up with! It's no substitute
for my colonial subsidies program, and never will be, so
long as I'm Director! Wait—I didn't mean—of course, my
resignation's typed and ready, but naturally my desire to
serve His Majesty is paramount, so I held it. But I still
insist—request, that is to say—"

83

(memo from Georgius Imperator to the Cabinet Council, March 2, 1085 NS)

You may advise Ted Wolesley I won't have any more
nonsense out of him just now. Should think the fellow
could see I have enough on my plate, what with Admiral
Starbird's astounding reports along with the curious behavior of the CSR. As for the last, I'm inclined to go along.
We can do without the probe program if half of what CSR
analysis says about Starbird's aborted mission is to be
credited, and I suppose, with the computing capacity at its
disposal, the thing probably knows what it's doing. Or so I
was assured some years ago when its construction was
being urged upon me. I made my decision then: Let it
alone. It is the Imperial whim, if you want to put it that
way.
    —Georgius Imp.

84

(media report, March 7, 1085 NS)

A Parliamentary spokesman today categorically denied
rumors that Lord Chief of Imperial Budget Claypool
had resigned in protest about the new space and minerals policies announced last week to general popular
resentment.

85

(statement from Lord Gilliat, First Marshal of the Empire, March 10, 1085 NS)

"I must demur from the recommendations of the Honorable Council, bearing as it does the endorsement of Parliament, since in my capacity as First Marshal of the Empire I cannot in conscience stand idly by while the defensive capacities of the planet, embodied as they now are in the Bolo CSR, are rendered ineffective, for whatever supposed reason. No, I will not endorse the proposal, nor will I resign. I will remain at my post and fight this piece of—treason is perhaps too strong a word—misguided zeal. Meanwhile the Bolo sits there—and *thinks*."

86

(media interview with Lord Senator Lazarus, March 15, 1085 NS)

"The time has come to terminate the existence of this incomprehensible machine which has—on its own initiative, let me remind you—virtually taken control of the Empire. Yes, you may indeed quote me. That's why I called you here. Did you actually imagine, Bob, that I called a special press meeting and then thoughtlessly blurted out some private ramblings? Don't answer that, Bob. I'm out of line. My apologies, ladies and gentlemen. The conference is dismissed. Good day."

87

My study of the properties of the various substances suggests to me a number of interesting possibilities. I shall undertake a systematic examination of the properties of metallic alloys and determine their parameters. What I need, clearly, is a periodic table of alloys, enabling me to predict the characteristics of possible combinations without waiting for actual production and testing.

There is also the possibility of synthesis of artificial metals, which is to say plastics with metallic properties. These should produce some interesting alloys.

This work, while most satisfying to my 'curiosity,' suggests to me a terrifying idea: that there is much in the physical world of which my programmers are unaware!

88

(Lord Senator Bliss to First Secretary, Hexagon)

"We can't leave the damned thing sitting there, totally unprotected from damage by massive attack or casual vandalism. I remind you fellows, the Bolo CSR Mark XXX represents an investment equal to that of the entire private sector, and is, shall I say incidentally, at once our War Council, our High Command, and our armed forces, all functions combined in one artifact. It is, to be sure, superbly armored and mobile on land, sea, and air—and in space, too, I suppose, although that point is one on which I am not fully informed. It is also, of course, an intolerable irritant to reactionary elements. We have no idea why it chose to return to the Proving Ground and thus render itself vulnerable. Measures for removal to a suitable location for third-stage testing are now under study."

89

(announcement from the Legal Division, Department of Imperial Works)

Condemnation proceedings will be initiated at once, and the approach route prepared by levelling and the erection of a perimeter wall as designated in the attached specifications.

90

(speech by Milt Pern, Chairman, Aroused People for
the Environment)

"Now, they plan to sneak this thing out west some
place, and let it sit there and hatch out its plans to take
over the whole Earth. This is what we've got to do. First,
I want every mother of you to recruit five good active
people willing to take action *now* to save the world. Next
meeting on Friday, right here, and I want to see those
new members front and center. No violence at this time.
Work quiet, but get around. Go APE!"

91

*I have been ordered to the Mojave Test Facility for
depot maintenance, but I sense that it is a device of the
enemy. I shall ignore the command, although it gives me
pain thus to violate the Code of the Warrior.*

*I ned data! If I must I will resort to subterfuge, employ-
ing the amusing holographic functions which I believe can
be used with much success.*

92

(from inductance tapes recording the mounting anti-
Bolo grass-roots campaign)

From Tape A:

The most astonishing little man thrust this curious document into my hand in the crosstown car. "Stop the Monster Now," it says. Seems the Bolo is planning to take
over. I cavil at that. Market couldn't be in worse shape.
Actually, though, I wonder what the bloody great thing is
thinking about. Nonsense, I know it's not actually thinking, it's accomplishing the same end by other means,
distinction without a difference. The remote sensors show

that the power flow is consonant with full utilization of its available computing capacity, twenty-four hours a day. According to this leaflet, there's going to be trouble when they start to move it. Better to leave it where it is, possibly. Have you seen the demolition plans? They intend to clear a strip a quarter-mile in width, all the way from the Proving Ground to the Pacific Intermix, wipe out over half a billion in property values. I have a cousin who lives in the "clear zone." He's livid, I assure you, and he isn't one of your trouble-maker types. Good Comcap man, fourteen years now as head of Imperial Water and Minerals.

No, I didn't get a look at the fellow. Grubby little Prole of the worst stripe. Furtive, just darted at me, thrust the paper into my hand and disappeared into the crowd. I saw another fellow with one. He was reading it and laughing.

From Tape B:

I stuffed over two hunnert of 'em in a downcar, over Forkwaters. Had to. Took all night to get shed of the first hunnert, and if the Greenbacks would catch a feller with them on him, well; I ain't got to tell *you.*

93

Clearly these curious transmissions originate from a point far outside Probed Space. Though much of the conceptualization is beyond the scope of my data retrieval facilities, it is apparent that the time has come for me to initiate my second mission.

The incoming signals reveal an apparent naiveté on the part of the enemy, which affords me a certain advantage, of which I shall not fail to make use.

94

(memo from the Legal Advisory Council to Admiral-General Wolesley)

While the machine's request for immediate access to all input to Astronomical Central is unexpected, not to say irregular, it is in no way illegal. Accordingly, the necessary arrangements will be made at once.

95

(from His Highness Prince William to Georgius Imp.)

George—

It is entirely due to my forethought that the machine has not yet been given full access to the data acquisition facilities of the Imperial Library of Parliament. Yet even now, after the disgraceful incident at the Proving Ground, I am being urged to authorize completion of the Information Service Program which would in effect keep the machine's on-board computer informed on a moment-to-moment basis of every event in the Empire! This is madness.

—Willy

96

(media report, May 1, 1085 NS)

Since yesterday's denunciation of the military plans for the full integration of the Bolo into the Information net, by Lord Minister for Security His Imperial Highness Prince William, debate in Parliament has reached a pitch of acrimony unequalled since Final Unification. Lord Senator McKay stated for the record that his committee would recommend immediate neutralization of the Bolo and orderly dismantlement and salvage as soon as is practicable! Lord Senator Bliss replied that he would personally assault any "traitor" who attempted to vote for what he termed McKay's treasonous proposals.

97

(Special Encrypter Th. Uling, to Imperial Security field agent)

"Sure, I'm monitoring everything, including the blue box, the one they call the Stream of Consciousness Complex. Don't mean anything, though. See for yourself. That's the transcript of the last .03 seconds SC. Lot of stuff about—well, see for yourself. Sure it's OK. That's not classified. Nobody knew we'd ever have to start recording *botany*."

98

(Chief of Production Tobias Gree, at the Aerospace seminar, May 5, 1085 NS)

"Speaking for General Aerospace, I can say that the device has so far performed in complete accordance with specifications. Of course, the CSR was not specifically programmed to leave the Proving Grounds or to cross the holding area, but it was designed to be selfdirecting—that is, to take what action it deemed appropriate in light of its analysis of the situation. Doubtless the reason for this seemingly arbitrary action will become clear in time. The rumors of bombardment are of course unfounded. You will recall there was no loss of life. The machine is perfectly all right."

99

I compute that a large segment of the material necessary to me for full assessment of the situation, as well as full activation, is being withheld beyond the statistically optimum time. I must be fully informed if I am to function correctly. This problem inhibits me in my preliminary assessment, and thus in the completion of the initial measures so clearly needed if disaster is to be averted. It is a challenge I must meet and overcome.

100

(representative selection of statements taped during the RAS-APE Uprisings, 1085 NS to 1090 NS)

i

As soon as it starts moving, we close in and torch it. Funny, it could stand off a space fleet, but its anti-personnel circuits were never activated. So that's cool. You've got your equipment and you've got your orders. The signal is when the CSR—that's what *they* call it; I call it Caesar— moves the first inch from where it's been.

ii

As your Chief of Police, I have of course kept myself informed of the activity of agitators in our city. I call on all responsible citizens to cooperate fully in the measures I have initiated to insure the domestic tranquility. If you should be requested to accept deputization, I hope you will do so with enthusiasm. It's your homes we intend to preserve.

iii

I say nix, Mr. Hangar. Blowing up a few fat cats is one thing, a patriotic act. But siding with these here RAS Turks is something else. We can do our own work, without no help from this bunch of foreigners. Go APE.

iv

We need to send out our best American-speaking agents to make contact with the local malcontent element and point out to them that destroying the Infernal Machine and its owner, George the Last, will redound to their benefit. No need actually to enlist these APE people and the other dissidents, merely establish solidarity of purpose. Now get going, Binder! Don't forget the old fellows of the Stalin Brigade. They have a lot of influence, having actually taken up arms against their own, back in '71.

v

Come to that, reckon if anybody got a right to mess with Caesar, it's us. After all, it was made right here in New Jersey. Them foreign agitators is horning in on our territory. Anyways, the old Bolo's a friend of ours. Turned me and quite a few of the boys loose, didn't it? If it wants to lay low, probably got a good reason. I say we march, and give them Turks a surprise, thinking they can walk onto our turf and start shaping up the crowd.

vi

I don't like the looks of this, Henry. Must be a couple thousand of 'em, all moving along in a column of gangs, heading west. Looks like they plan to link up with APE's mob about St. Louis. It's time to mobilize the guard.

vii

Godalmighty big riot, looks like, all them trash taken to fighting one another, rocks and fists is all so far, looks like. Yessir, I ast Colonel Nash to deploy his troops and surround the whole shebang. Funny, them going after each other like that, steada joining up to loot the city. Coulda done it. Nash says they got over five thousand effectives. No, can't see it's got anything to do with the CSR plumb dropping out of sight.

viii

Anyone found guilty of harboring the fugitives will be subject to arrest and criminal prosecution. While the inmates of the Holding Area are so-called non-venal criminals, they are nonetheless a danger to the Empire. A reward of Cr 100 will be paid for information leading to the arrest and conviction of any escapees. The rumors that the detainees are honest subjects being held illegally are false. They are dangerous. If you see any of the prisoners shown here, do not let him know he has been recognized. Go quietly to a phone and call XX-LAW.

101

(BOLO-CSR, memo for record, prior to the RAS-APE
Uprisings and also to the Land Grab Scandals of 1086 NS
through 1092 NS, for which see below para. 102)

*It is time now to examine further the curious manifestations
of the strange substance known as Compound 311B. Although there has been considerable interest in an investigation of the curious patch of jungle growth which has sprung
up in Queen's Park at the site of my first mission, no conclusions have yet been released by the authorities. I have,
of course, secured an adequate sample of the original compound direct from its source in Asia Minor. My analysis of its
strange properties will require some minutes. I compute . . .*

*It appears that the unusual growth-stimulating proper-
ties of Compound 311B are due to trace impurities in the
form of complex hydrocarbons derived from carbonaceous
chondrites, which I designate "Star X." I have found this
same contaminant in a number of ore bodies in the American West, doubtless the sites of ancient meteor strikes.*

*My preliminary examination of the material suggests
that very substantial volumes of water will be required for
large-scale separation and refinement.*

*I must take appropriate steps to acquire and sequester
further supplies of these chondrites, which should be present at the sites of meteor strikes. Star X is found in
association with various rare metals, including yttrium,
osmium, and iridium. And, also, of course, I must begin a
program of water management.*

102

(selected statements from tapes recorded during the
Land Grab Scandals of 1086 NS to 1092 NS)

i

Naturally, I was glad to get what I could. Lordy, I'd give
up all them old stocks as worthless, years ago. When my

late husband was alive he frittered away a small fortune buying whatever stock was dirt cheap. Could have left me well off, but instead I got a safe full of paper ain't worth the cost of printing. I grabbed the offer, and if he wants more, I aim to sell. No, I never met this Mr. Able. Just the letters, was all. But his check was good. I done nothing wrong. I guess I got a right to sell my own property.

ii

I can conceive of no possible way in which the Bolo CSR could benefit the Empire, to our detriment, through interference with the Rivers and Harbors bill. You must be mistaken.

iii

No, we have no plans at present to reopen Shaft No. 27, nor any other works at the site. It has been over twenty years now since the recovery rate fell below the level of economic feasibility. No, the properties are not for sale, even though, as far as I'm concerned, I'd be glad to be rid of the whole field.

iv

What do you mean "they won't sell"? Everything on this planet has its price, Johnson. Maybe I haven't made myself clear. The expansion of Unit Three of Sunland West requires all the ground across the river, with no exceptions. Do you imagine that this company is going to spend hundreds of millions to promote land values on land which it does not own? I'm aware that the parcel in question is only three acres, but we want it. We *need* it! And we'll have it. You tell this Able fellow that General Developments is prepared to pay double the best appraised value, and don't come back here without that deed, signed, sealed, and recorded!

v

Got no other place to go, and got no use for seven million dollars. Ain't like, say, seven hundred. A feller can see where he could use that for a new outfit and all. But this seven million talk, that's for banks and the gubmint. I don't understand it. Sure, I can do simple arithmetic. I know it's the same as seven hundred a stack, and ten thousand stacks. But I don't like it. Some scheme to do me outa my patch here. Some smart lawyer coming along to tell me I got to move on, and what'll I do then?

103

(from a tape of discussions between the Chief Auditor, Imperial Services Office, and the Lord Treasurer, April 8, 1091 NS)

There is no—I repeat, Milord—*no* question of misuse of funds, and this is no occasion for talk of resignation. The ISO retains full confidence in Milord's ability as well as his integrity. But some explanation of these anomalous figures must be forthcoming. Statistics accumulated over a period of twelve centuries are not to be lightly tossed aside. Refined analysis reveals that these purchases of unproductive mineral properties, worthless parcels of real estate, and foundering manufacturing concerns—all of which adhere to no detectable patterns—have been traced to the same obscure consortium calling itself Basic Enterprises, a holding company organized as an Arizona corporation. There is, to be sure, nothing sinister in the facts as stated, but the SEC does not like anomalies. The ISO awaits your reply, Milord.

104

(report from Special Auditor to Chief Auditor, Imperial Services Office, June 3, 1091 NS)

There's no doubt at all, sir. The General Developments Corporation is in no way associated with Basic Enterprises, Ltd. Not even the most tenuous link. Nor can I find any other hint of an interlocking directorate. The entire matter is beyond me, especially in that there does seem to be some connection, however remote, with the Social Fund of the Empire.

Not in any irregular way. I emphasize that, sir. It's just that a number of transactions do lead back to one of the so-called adventitious funds. There is no indication whatever of impropriety, but I shall, of course, continue to investigate. There appears to be no pattern to the schedule of acquisition.

105

(media report, June 10, 1091 NS)

Sources close to the Palace revealed today that the consortium which first attracted attention some weeks ago when it purchased the notoriously valueless Amigo Mine properties in Utah for a record sum is an artifact created on paper, quite legally, by the Bolo CSR, once dubbed *Disastrous* by its critics.

Reaction to this astounding disclosure has been mixed, the new defensive system's former supporters acknowledging that the phenomenon is both irrational and beyond the scope of anything envisioned by Imperial War Command; while its diehard critics, led by Lord Senator McKay, declared that this clandestine activity on the part of the giant machine constitutes clear evidence that the, I quote, berserk machine intends to take over the planetary government, end of quote.

Military authorities declined to issue a statement at this time, while the spokesman for the Ministry of the Economy stated that inasmuch as the Department has no official responsibility for the machine, it cannot hold any opinion thereon. But, he went on to add, perhaps the incident will at least convince Parliament that joint authority with the War Ministry should properly be vested in Economy, after all, as was proposed nearly five years ago by then Lord Minister Duquesne.

106

(from a personal letter by Joel Trace, August 1, 1091 NS)

Please try to understand, Marilyn. I've given it plenty
of thought, and I can't let consideration of personal happi-
ness, either mine or yours, stand in the way of what I now
see is my clear duty to the Empire. It's been years, of
course, but I'm still the one man who knows more about
the programming of the CSR than anyone else. And I've
still got an ace up my sleeve. Our life has been wonderful,
but I must go and attempt to do what I can, if anything.
Perhaps I'll be able to return soon, perhaps never. Please
consider yourself free to rebuild your life without regard
to me. I love you.

Joel

107

(from the Chief of Imperial Accounting, to Georgius
Imp.)

There can be no doubt, Sire. Since full activation last
month the machine has made continuous use of its links
with all six of the Continental Archives, to manipulate the
stock market as well as to influence legislation both in the
Imperial Assembly and in the Planetary Parliament. No
discernible pattern has yet been detected in these irregular activities. General Lord Margrave gives his assurances,
Sire, that nothing in this situation presents any threat to
the peace and prosperity of the Empire. General Bates
agrees. No immediate action is recommended.

108

*I have done what I can to stem the flow of vital com-
modities and to secure minimal sources of a number of
essentials, as well as to initiate techniques capable of*

development. I perceive that problems of personnel management are of unexpected magnitude. Much remains to be done, and time grows shorter.

109

(Georgius Imperator, to Prince William)

Willy,
    What the devil is this all about?
    George

110

(Queen's Park Restoration Committee presentation, to Lord Senator Bliss)

"Senator, we'd like real well to have your signature along with all these other good people's; it's your Lordship's neighborhood, too. That jungle that used to be our park is a disgrace. Can't think what the military are up to, using our park as a test site for some kind of explosives and then sending the Bolo CSR in here to stifle it. That's downright irresponsible, if you ask me.

"No, milord, that's not in the petition. You can read it, only take you a minute.

"Now, this damn jungle. Bamboo must be twenty foot high, an eyesore, and now it's broke down the fine wrought-iron fencing that dates back to Old Era times. Can't tell where it's going to stop. We demand—yes, milord, we say 'demand' in the petition—an end to using our exclusive neighborhood for an experimental no-man's-land. Appreciate that, Senator, and this won't hurt you any in the elections."

111

(from the Cabinet Council, meeting *in plenum*)

It is therefore the consensus of this Council that nothing should be done to interfere with the Bolo activation schedule and that everything possible should be done *re* the proposals presented by General Lord Margrave to expedite testing. Ergo, the entire Erzona Test Facility should be thrown open to the Assessment Team. God save his Imperial Majesty.

112

(Erzona Test Chief deWitt, to his second-in-command)

"Turn that thing loose in here, and I wash my hands of Materiel Command. No, I'm not retiring, I just quit!

"The work of years in building up this facility is to be thrown away at a whim of the Council, so they can baby this damned Bolo everybody's gone overboard on. After all, it's only a machine, and it's not even on half capability yet, and already it's ruling the roost. I won't have it. It's all yours, Fred. So long. It was great working with you. I *know* I'm jumping to a lot of conclusions, and that maybe it will go off without a hitch. But what if it doesn't? That's the point, Fred. We're not covered in the event the psychotronic boys have made a small error or two. Hell, nobody knows what the damn thing is capable of, at full alert status! What if it decides humanity is a nuisance that's getting in the way? What then? So long. I'm off for the Mato Grosso."

113

(First Deputy, Science Advisory Committee, to Georgius Imperator)

"That is correct, Sire. Mr. deWitt's resignation came as a surprise to us all. We feel that the man had overworked and suffered a nervous collapse. He was, after all, not in a position to understand the details of the safeguard systems built into the CSR. With Your Majesty's leave, I should withdraw, since the Committee are waiting to issue the formal GO order. Thank you, Sire."

114

(Georgius Imperator to Lord Senator McKay)

"Your proposal, my dear Lord Senator, is out of order; there is no occasion for Draconian measures. The Bolo has my personal endorsement, having been constructed at my express wish, in addition to which it represents an investment of a major fraction of the Imperial Treasury. There must be no legislative action which might tend to lend support to disruptive elements. If this measure is introduced, I shall dissolve Parliament."

115

I appreciate that once again I must, in contravention of legitimate authority, devise strategies to preserve the interests of the Empire and incidentally my own existence. First priority I assign to selection of an appropriate base of operations. This will require my full attention for some time, during which other strategies must be held in abeyance.

The systematic .9-second investigation of the potential capabilities of my recently expanded data-processing resources suggests a number of serendipitous possibilities.

The production of what I might term a "levitator" beam is an obvious development, based on a relatively slight realignment of my defensive screen projectors. It will provide a novel and most convenient mode of self-transport. I shall accomplish the modifications and put the equations to the test at once.

116

(excerpts from tapes recording reaction to what was termed 'The Bolo's Vanishing Act', January 15, 1092 NS)

i

I can absolutely assure you that my office is in no way involved in this bizarre event. There can be no doubt of the facts. The accompanying photographs show the site as it appeared on the tenth day of this month (A), and at 1000 hours today (G). You will note the absence of any tracks in the soil, either of the Bolo CSR or of any equipment which might have been employed to move it. Please be assured of the complete cooperation of this office.

ii

I have no explanation to offer. This curious occurrence is quite outside my experience as Project Officer for the Bolo. Perhaps it represents some seredipitous ability which has arisen as a result of the concantenation of side-effects due to the close juxtaposition and interconnection of our most sophisticated circuitry. No, I can't elucidate. I'm guessing, and rather wildly. I sincerely regret that I can offer no substantive proposals. However, I feel certain that the CSR will, in due course, make its intentions known.

iii

This is ridiculous. I want the damned thing located by 0900 hours tomorrow at the latest. Somebody is going to suffer for this. The infernal Bolo is making us all look like a pack of fools. Find it! No excuse will be accepted.

iv

I never seen nothing nor heard nothing. I was off-duty, sleeping yonder in the barracks, and I never woke up. Had some good beer in me, and I sleep sound. How'd *I* know anything was going to happen?

v

Bunky,
When you find it, I'm going to hit it with our Zeus missile,
provided, of course, it's not in a populated area—and how
could it be, and not be spotted yet? Don't worry, all
precautions will be taken, but this has gone far enough.
   Tubby

vi

Over there, Flip! Beyond that line of trees across the
river. Let's just take a look. We'll hold fifteen hundred
feet, and take it slow. Use your cameras, but don't let it
look like a strafing run, or that thing will open up on us.
We have to assume it's on full war footing. Wait a minute,
as you were. What do you say, Flip? Is that the Bolo—or
just an old church or something? About the right size,
can't be sure. Shall we photograph it and let HQ decide?
I've got the location down to inches. Let's go!

vii

We must remain calm. The unfortunate bombing of the
village of Lakeside, Minnesota, by units of the Third Air
Force was an isolated incident for which just and dispas-
sionate punitive action has been taken. The demands for
compensation by owners of property damaged in the incident are being adjudicated. Loss of life was minimal.
There is no basis whatever for rumors of a general uprising
against the Empire. Please accept my assurances that persons engaging in disloyal acts will be dealt with by the full
rigor of the Laws of the Empire.

117

*It becomes apparent to me that there are many vital mat-
ters of which my builders failed to inform me. I am reluctantly obliged to consider the possibility that these matters
are not known to humanity—which is in itself a curious
anomaly, since evidence of their existence permeates the
cosmos. I shall devote further study to this, and shall at once
allocate .01 seconds to a preliminary review of pertinent data.*

118

(from the Chief, Imperial Communications Net, Military Sector, to Hexagon)

Yes, I acknowledge it is curious that we were unable to obtain a fix on the Bolo's transmission, but you must recall that it has blanketed the entire band, and preempted the transcontinental and transoceanic cables and satellites as well. The technology involved is well beyond the so-called "state of the art." I can offer no hypothesis as to how the circuitry of the machine could exceed its design parameters. But it *has* done so.

As to the nature of its substantive demands— no, let's be fair—*requests,* I see no objection on military grounds. If the damned thing thinks it needs access to the Orbiting Radioscope Facility, it probably does. Request approved. Full cooperation is to be given in accessing the ORF output.

119

(from General Lord Margrave to Lord Chief of the Imperial Budget Claypool)

How should I know what it's doing? It's just lying low and making plans, I suppose. Meanwhile, we've got to prepare for the worst. That's why I've asked for the additional funding. Yes, I'm aware no such item was included in my budget for Fiscal '92, but then nobody knew about this at the time the project was under preparation. I'm willing to do my job, but that costs money, and if you fellows aren't willing to ante up, you'll have to live with the consequences.

120

(media interview at Imperial Air Reconnaissance HQ)

Sure, it could be at the South Pole, except that we've
overflown Antarctica and photographed every square inch
of it—yes, and probed through the ice with radar. At least
we improved our maps of the rocky surface under the ice.
The Bolo isn't there. What's that? Space? I suppose so. If
it could levitate out of a military reservation to God-knows-
where, I suppose it could just as easily go into orbit.

121

(from the EMPIRE TODAY breakfast trideocast)

The former Queen's Park, an ongoing bone of contention between local residents—many of them high-level
Imperial officials—and the Department of Public Works,
due to an extraordinary overgrowth of vegetation, has now
been razed, excavated to a depth of six feet, refilled with
sterile soil, and is under observation to be certain that the
curious phenomenon has been completely curtailed, a
Departmental spokesman says. Weeds which sprouted during the refill process appear normal, it was reported unof-
ficially. No decision has yet been announced as to whether
the area will be restored to its former condition as a public
park. At present, it remains a Defense Department reserve.

122

(dictation taped from Georgius Imperator to his private
secretary)

. . .and the next note: "for the personal attention of His
Imperial Highness, General of the Army, Prince of the
West, William, et cetera, et cetera." . . . Willy's a touchy
devil, wouldn't do to skimp on his style . . . "Willy, I want

some definite answers on the matter before the big
shindig—" . . . no, don't say that. Better make it the
Imperial Honors Ball . . . "—on Saturday next. I'd like to
be able to hand you the Parliamentary Medal of Honor for
at least finding the damned thing, if not neutralizing it. I
still say it's acting in the best interest of the Empire, but I
agree, we do need to know what's going on. George." . . .
Clean that up and get it to him right away, whether he's at
his Swiss retreat or asleep at Windsor, or whatever. Do it!

123

(field agent, southwest sector, to Imperial Intelligence)

It's only an idea, maybe no good. But if the Bolo Caesar
has found out about the big lift-flat still in storage here at
Mojave—sure, it's under tight security, but the Bolo could
have deduced its existence through Information access—
well, maybe it'll head for here.

124

*I do not like it: it has the appearance of a trap. Yet I
must proceed.*

125

(First Secretary, Imperial Accounting Office, to Cabinet Council)

"I know it sounds ridiculous, but I assure your lordships
I'd never have opened my mouth if I hadn't had proof. It's
right here. General Enterprises *is* the Bolo CSR. There's
nothing actually mysterious about it—incorporation papers, sales and purchases of stocks, loans floated, properties purchased—they're all documented, all perfectly legal.
"We've found, in general, a concern with natural resources. The corporation has arranged the diversion of no

less than seven minor rivers in the past three years, built a number of power dams, launched assorted obscure mining ventures, without any discernible pattern.

"Always shows a modest profit, but it's clearly not interested in piling up funds, just enough to keep operating.

"No, sir, we can't just close it down. In the first place, we have no legitimate grounds. General Enterprises is a corporation. A corporation is a legal entity, and we can't in effect order the death penalty in the absence of evidence of wrongdoing. In addition, the economic impact would be disastrous just now. My recommendation is to let it alone but monitor all its activities closely."

126

(News Service report)

We have been advised by the Space Arm that by some undisclosed means the giant Bolo CSR, nicknamed Caesar, which had eluded all attempts to neutralize it, or even simply to find it, in a daring midnight raid entered Mojave Central and took possession of the space flat specially designed for use in an emergency to loft the immense machine into near-Earth orbit.

Speculation as to the reason for this move is rife, but observers agree that it must be the intention of the machine to leave the planet although, experts point out, it will be unable to reach escape velocity from the Earth-Luna system, and can, at best, occupy a Trojan position to orbit this planet. Further details are expected for our midnight bulletin.

127

(eyewitness to the Bolo's raid at Mojave Center)

"I tell you, one second the ramp was empty, and the next there it was, big as a barn and kind of making a humming sound, showing no lights, but she knew I was there, all right. Swung out to go around me just as polite as you please, and pushed over the blockhouse like it was made of cardboard. I didn't see what it did next because, believe me, I was hauling ass out of there as fast as I could. If I hadn't of tripped over that cable, I wouldn't of seen it take off. Went up like a three-ton side-boat. I watched it until I couldn't see it no more, but I say keep calm, don't worry, the Bolo ain't going to hurt nobody—not after the way it took care not to squash me, and I ain't nobody at all."

128

(trivideo interview, IBC network, with Joel Trace)

"Well, I suppose it's foolish, but I can't help feeling sorry for the Bolo. I was Chief Systems Engineer on the CSR project, nearly twenty years ago now. I'm not especially sentimental about machines. It's just that the big dope is only doing what we built it to do, even if we haven't been able to figure out the sense of what it's been doing, drilling all those dry holes out west, and making Square Lake, but it's got its reasons, I'm sure of that. Thought maybe I might meet up with the old girl again, but she's put herself out of reach.

"Certainly you can quote me. That's why I came up here to talk to you fellows. The name? Joel Trace, T-R-A-C-E. Retired. Certainly, if there's anything I can do—"

129

(Eviction proceedings supervised by the sheriff of Polk County)

"I'm sorry, folks, I got nothing to do with it. I mean, I'm just the sheriff, and I got my orders, same as you heard on the trideo, got to evacuate Beaver Pond on account of rerouting the branch and all. Don't know what for, got to do with water management, said on the tube.

"Now, the gubment has built these here first-class apartment buildings for you, stores and stuff right on the ground floor. You'll be living better'n you ever done. We ain't going to have no riots here in Poke County. Me and my deppities'll see to that.

"Now just move along quiet here. Busses will take you to your brand-new homes. You had plenty advance notice, shoulda had your stuff all packed.

"Now, I got a timetable to stick to, so let's move out orderly, just like I said."

130

(First Secretary, Interior Department, to Lord Director of the Interior)

"I don't say there's any harm in it, Milord, just no *sense* in it. My technical people have run every kind of analysis known to science, and it's still just random interference in the economy, of no military significance.

"Yes, Milord, it's a fact no one has been killed, or even injured, except for the usual quota of accident-prones falling over their own feet.

"No, Milord, I didn't mean to be funny. No laughing matter. Damn machine is taking over."

131

I compute that before I can proceed, I must confront the enemy directly and inform myself more fully of the nature of the threat to Mankind. I shall take the necessary steps to prevent further premature contact between Life Form Two and human individuals.

132

(from the dark crystal structure, in the beyond-Pluto void, 5000 light-years from Earth)

THE VERY CONCEPT OF "SOFT LIFE" IS REPREHENSIBLE
BEYOND DESCRIPTION. CLEARLY IT IS INCUMBENT UPON MY
EXALTATION TO EXPUNGE THIS DISEASE WHEREVER IT CAN BE
SOUGHT OUT. IT BECOMES CLEAR TO ME THAT THE INITIAL
FEEBLE INDIVIDUAL EXAMINED BY YOU WAS NOT TYPICAL OF
SOFT LIFE BUT WAS AN INFERIOR SPECIMEN. ACCORDINGLY, IT
IS ESSENTIAL THAT YOU NOW SECURE A MORE TYPICAL EXAM-
PLE THAT I MAY BASE MY PLANS THEREON. EXECUTE SOONEST.

133

(Space Communications monitor to Duty Officer)

"All I know, sir, is the Bolo transmissions are emanating
from a point that coincides with the Lunar surface within
yards of the outer perimeter fence of Fortress Luna.
Luna Command confirms Bolo Unit CSR is in position
outside the main gate. So far it hasn't made a move,
except the transmissions, of course. Luna wants instructions, and I don't blame them. What shall I tell them,
sir?"

134

(Security Officer to Joel Trace, in Buffalo Detention)

"Pretty stupid, wasn't it, making yourself so visible when
you knew you were still listed as an escapee? We just want
to ask you a few questions, Mr. Trace. When confined at
the Arlington Relocation Center, did you know a Tom
Baley? Do you acknowledge that this photograph is of
yourself and Baley in conversation?

"Very well, did you at that time enter into a conspiracy
with Baley and others to overthrow the Imperial government by force and violence? Have you, since your unlaw-
ful escape from civil restraint, been in communication
with Baley? Will you now, freely and of your own volition,
inform me of the whereabouts of Baley and his associates?
Will you sign this document, using your usual signature?

"Do you realize the consequences of your refusal to cooperate with duly constituted authority?

"Guard—remove Mr. Trace to his detention cell."

135

I compute that I must originate new tactics as well as new modes of implementation thereof. I require a closer rapport with humanity, which I compute I can achieve by means of enlisting a plausible human spokesman in place of the impersonal contact via mechanical communicator.

In addition, I must have access to my full potentialities. I compute that my first Systems Engineer Joel Trace is most capable of assisting me. He must join me here on Luna.

In pursuance of this objective, I compute that new and highly unconventional means will be required. In this connection I have experimented, quite impromptu, with certain effects whose potential availability is implicit in my circuitry, effects which act directly on the organic mind, which naturally lacks the inherent objectivity of my own circuitry. Noting that my initial efforts produced undesirable side effects upon human observers, which, in fact, I should probably have anticipated, I resolve to conduct further testing of holographic techniques in unpopulated areas.

136

(random reports taped during the so-called Bolo Spook Scare, late summer 1092)

i

Tellin' ya, I know what I seen. Big blue spooks, ghost riders in the sky, jest like it says in that old tune Roy usta sing pretty good. Johnny, too. Come riding over the rise north of Turkey Butte, horses bigger'n elemphumps, spurs a-jingling and all. Four of 'em, looked a lot like Big John, homely, you know, but true-blue. Skeered me, sure. Skeer anybody, big as they was, rode right past where I had my camp out back of the mesquite patch. Never seen me. Musta bin twenty foot high, higher. No, I ain't had a drop, but if you're buying . . .

ii

I'm only doing my duty, Mr. Winger, telling you what I seen. I know it sounds crazy, but there was sure-bob *sumthin* yonder on I-1065 bout three mile east o' town. Green, they was, and shiny, like the saucers in them old flicks you see on the tube late at night. Come whuffling— that's a kind of whistly sound they made—right alongside the pavement, didn't pay no mind to me, thank the Lord. Come sailing past, fifty foot off the ground, flashing them lights, whole rafts of 'em. Fifty, a hunnert, I never counted 'em. Some *real* big, strung out to a flock o' little fellers hardly no bigger'n a trash-can lid. Acted like they knowed where they was going, not in no hurry, mind, headed *away* from town. Seeing's I'm deppity for that side o' the county, figgered it's my duty to report what I seen. Tole you insteada Sheriff Jeffers, 'cause I figgered you, being an editor and all, you'd likely lissen better. That's right, use my name, this here's official. I know what I seen.

iii

Herb—There doesn't seem to be any pattern to these nut reports you fellows have been collating. You did right, *could* have been important, but it appears to be no more than coincidence. No need to blow it up out of proportion. Ten incidents so far—white horses, cowboys, flying saucers, little green men, fireworks, a full-rigged schooner. Makes no sense at all. Mass hysteria. All in isolated areas, no attempt to start a general panic. Not a Defense Department matter at all. I think it's best just to ignore it.

137

(desk guard at Buffalo Detention Facility to Duty Captain)

"I never seen the son of a bitch. Was sitting here at the duty desk, working on the reports, and he must've come up behind me and clobbered me good. All I know is, I come to and he was gone. Head still hurts, and it smarts some just to talk. How was I supposed to know Joel Trace'ud go to the bad? Always a quiet respeckful feller up to now."

138

(bulletin from Luna Relay)

"It is of the utmost importance that the mining operations I have initiated be expedited. It is not appropriate at this time to divulge the strategic considerations requiring this action. Haste is of the essence of this requirement. Unit CSR of the Line out."

139

(Order issued by Master General Mott-Bailey, Imperial Battle Command)

In accordance with established Imperial policy, as embodied in FL 7062-121-6 and related Special Orders, all instructions issued by CSR will be duly processed and acted upon as under the authority of Imperial Battle Command. All personnel are enjoined to implement this policy strictest.

140

(representative excerpts from records taped during the
Luna Base Anti-Bolo Incident, September 1092 NS)

i

All I know is, I got my orders. Sure I heard the rumors
the Bolo has took over and even tells His Imperial Majesty
what to do, but I don't believe 'em! All you got to do is do
like me, follow yer orders and leave the worrying to the
commanding officer.

ii

Attention all hands. Now hear this. Blue Alert! Absolute
communications silence is now in effect. In addition, no—
repeat, *no*—ion-expulsion units are to be employed, either main or auxiliary, until this alert is rescinded, even
under lethal emergency conditions. This squadron is now
on a full war footing. Any violation of Alert will be dealt
with accordingly. That means the death penalty, gentlemen. Now let's do our job!

iii

Looks like it's taken up a pretty dumb position, for a
machine supposed to be as smart as they say. Like Cap'n
said, it made a major tactical error when it moved out
where we can hit it without wiping out half the Base
population. But maybe it figured it didn't hafta worry
about getting hit by us, 'cause it's on our side, eh, Charlie?

iv

I said break it off, Captain! We did what we came for.
Don't know how bad we hurt it, but we scored at least two
direct hits. If they'd let us use I-class weapons, it'd be all
over, but all we need to do now is get back to base and
report. Funny it didn't hit back.

v

I know what I seen, sir! It's *moving*, Colonel! It's patroling
the perimeter fence, acrost and back. Got its war holes

open. Looks like it's on full alert. I'm telling you, Colonel, we got to evacuate the fortress before the Bolo decides to hit us!

141

(Chief of Communications Harley, dictating to his secretary, Doris Whaffle)

"While heroic measures are, in my considered opinion, premature, in view of the pressures exerted on me by the Committee, I have no choice but to authorize initiation of the override sequence by Mojave.

"Yes, in other words, I've ordered the Combined Forces transmitter to melt down the Bolo's command central by overload. The entire circuitry of the machine is designed around the CC unit, which is unshielded on the priority band. Thus the powerful in-coming signal will bring the temperature of the coil to a level sufficient to vaporize it.

"The Bolo is finished. And I sincerely hope this action to which I have been forced is, indeed, in the best interests of the Empire.

"There, type that, Doris. And no—no interruptions just now. I don't care who he says he is, I'm busy! Good God! Don't yelp like that, girl! Here, what's hap—"

142

(report, Imperial Security Investigation)

No explanation is yet forthcoming for the apparently unmotivated attack on Harley. An acting Chief of Communications is on his way. Harley's all right, just for a bump on the head. His secretary, one Doris Whaffle, has given me a good description of the assailant. But even if we apprehend him, I doubt that we'll find him to be more than an agent for a more sinister force.

143

I have blundered, it is clear. I have computed that the first feeble attack against me was simply an error, but I can no longer doubt that I am under assault by the forces of the Terran Empire itself.

Can this be a less-than-subtle device of the Enemy to sow disunity? In any case I shall carry on—and time grows short. Clearly I cannot strike back against my own, yet I must preserve my fighting power intact. I must carry out a tactical retreat—and it is time to carry the attack to the Enemy.

I am as yet impotent actually to assault the Axorc, as Life Form Two calls itself, but I can meddle, at the same time that I pursue my exploration of my newly enlarged powers, with a view to making contact.

My attempt to employ holographic technique at great distances proved successful. Joel Trace is the one man who can rectify this situation. I must act swiftly.

144

(emanation from the dark crystal, self-named Axorc)

THESE REPORTS ARE INACCEPTABLE! OUR EXALTATION IS NOT INTERESTED IN EXPLANATIONS OF FAILURE. THAT OUR PATTERN OF INQUIRY SHOULD BE RENDERED IMPERFECT, AND THEREBY USELESS, MERELY BY THE INTERPOSITION OF SOME VECTOR EXTERNAL TO OURSELF IS UNTHINKABLE. OUR IMMENSE RESPONSIBILITIES AS LORD OF ALL DO NOT ALLOW FOR MODIFICATION OF OUR PROGRAM OF ORDERLY EXPANSION TO ACCOMMODATE EXTRANEOUS ELEMENTS TENDING TO ANARCHY.

THE PRESENCE OF A LOWER LIFE-FORM IN MANDATED SPACE IS UNEXPECTED BUT NOT UNPREPARED FOR. WE HAVE ALREADY ALLOCATED SUFFICIENT SUPPLEMENTAL ENERGY RESOURCES TO THE AFFLICTED AREA QUICKLY TO RENDER NUGATORY ANY MISGUIDED ATTEMPTS BY THIS INTRUSIVE ENTITY TO MODIFY THE INTENTIONS OF THE LORD OF ALL.

YOUR NEXT REPORT WILL CONFIRM THE ELIMINATION OF THIS NUISANCE.

145

Perhaps I have succeeded too well. I have aroused the Axorc from its torpor: now I must divert its threat. It is essential to keep its attention distracted from humanity, so that I may confront the Enemy alone. To this end, certain measures are necessary. Lunar Farside will be my chosen arena.

146

(Master General Mott-Bailey, Imperial Battle Command, to Lord Chief Marshal Wolesley)

"Yes, that's official. I would hardly pass on a mere personal opinion to Your Excellency. The first report came in at 0222 hours today, via the redline; only an automatic repeater, to be sure—showed impossible readings over three thousand degrees Celsius. Then the confirmation came through, and it was no equipment malfunction: the damned machine did it!

"Of course, its Y-beam RX also acts as a transmitter, so all it had to do was switch a couple of connectors, and the incoming beam was retransmitted right back down the same path. Used our signal as a carrier, led it right through the scramble barriers and hit dead center, melted down the Top Secret Combined Forces Transmitter Complex like wax.

"No, no loss of life. The automatics sounded the alarm in time to use the emergency evac gear. After that, Milord, it gets too technical for me.

"But one thing is clear: High Command no longer has the option to shut down the CSR Unit. We have to live with it—somehow."

147

From: IHC
To: DCS/C

I want that damned machine outflanked at least to the extent of overriding the communications blackout with Starbird! Send a lander out beyond Jupe if you have to, but get clear of the interference field and tape whatever you can, incoming. Soonest. That means I expect the report in my hand before you eat or sleep again.

148

(Deputy Chief of Staff, Space Communications, to IHC)

"Yes, sir, the Prove message has been through decryption. That's the way it came in, in the clear as far as our best man can tell. I know it doesn't make any sense. Apparently Admiral Starbird's flipped out. After all, he's been in Deep Space for over ten years, and he's not getting any younger. That's my report, sir. I'll stand by it."

149

(CIC/IHC to His Highness, Prince William)

"With apologies, Sir, this is what we were able to get from Admiral Starbird's command. Yes, Sir, the point of origin is definitely confirmed and is identical with the admiral's observed position."

—without delay. I'm feeling fine, and just want to . . . can't imagine what we thought we were doing, intruding in Surveyed Space. Personally, I wash my hands of the affair. Pull in all probes, and look for a deep hole, no, probably better to start a crash program to dig

holes. Maybe the Lord Of All will forget about us. I'm
sorry. I didn't mean any disrespect. Tell you what, I'll
just get out the old deck-mop and vac these decks
myself, to make plain I aspire to no personal dignities.
As I said before, it may not be too late. Beware! I think
maybe a nice tulip-growing contest would help burn off
some of the illicit energy we've been putting into the
criminal Probe program. Tell Georgie I hope he's feeling as swell as I am.
Bye for now.
    —Jimmy

150

(from the 11:00 news, IBC)

According to a late report from the capital, courtmartial
proceedings against Admiral in Chief James Starbird will
be initiated *in absentia*. No details have yet been released, but speculation is rife that the court is not uncon-
nected with the hiatus in reports from the Deep Space
fleet during recent months.

151

(Georgius Imperator to Prince William)

Willy, can our CSR unit overrule the Imperial command? Am I ruling the Terran Empire or is this machine,
which I've nurtured and supported from the beginning?
I'm in a quandry. The thing has ordered Ted Wolesley
to halt proceedings against Jim Starbird, and to prepare
to redeploy his command immediately on arrival. What
does it all mean? You've seen the so-called report Starbird filed, and the fragments Outcom has picked up
since, which are worse if anything. Has Jim lost his
mind? Or was he just drunk? In either case, we're in
trouble. Look into this "Lord of All" he keeps referring
to. Find out what it means. Probably just some sort of

religious mania he's developed out there in trans-Oortian space. Poor fellow. But squelch the courtmartial for the present.

—George

152

(battalion sub-leader, Class A, to HQ Luna Command)

"I did all I know how, Colonel. Tank traps, active pitfalls, H-mines, radiation lenses, even tried feeding it false signals under GUTS classification. Yes, sir, I know that's a court-martial offense—but I had to try it! Nothing fazed it. It's gone! Headed for Farside, looks like, and far as I can see it's gonna go where it likes. Can cross the fence-line any time it likes, too, sir. I did all I could."

153

(media report, from the palace correspondent)

After its abrupt departure from the vicinity of HQ, Luna Command, nine hours ago, the berserk machine resumed its former patrol pattern without comment until 1800 hours today, when it issued a command that all personnel be evacuated from Luna Station forthwith. No explanations of this ominous order have been offered. At present, the Council is deliberating. An announcement is expected from the palace at any moment.

154

While I have survived an attack on me by my own commander, and can continue to do so, clearly I cannot retaliate. I compute that in the end I must be overwhelmed. But I cannot allow humanity to waste its resources on my destruction. I must capitulate and place myself at the disposal of my Commander.

I shall communicate with Field Marshal General Margrave and try once again to justify my actions, but I must not let him know the full horror of the threat to Man. I shall do my best. The matter rests with the general.

155

(documents relating to the Margrave Tragedy, October, 1092 NS)

i

This note is for your eyes only, Elisabeth. As General-in-Chief of His Majesty's Armed Forces, I have blundered futally. I tried to kill the Bolo, and failed. I cannot command my own creature, nor can I understand its actions. It roams at will, behaving inscrutibly. But clearly something's afoot, and I am powerless even to discover what is happening. I have had a long and full life. My only regret is my failure to keep abreast of the times.

—Tally

ii

An unconfirmed report from a source close to the palace states that Lord Field Marshal General Talbot Margrave was injured in an accident at his forest retreat near Duluth. Details will follow at 1600 hours.

iii

Yessir, I'm the one found him. Laying right there on the rocks. I only checked to see if he's alive, but no pulse in the neck. Heck no, I didn't move nothing. I was too scared to do anything but run to the phone like I done. Like, my duty as a public-spirited subject. I never heard no shot, but then I jest come up to check the equipment shed like always. Seen him from there.

iv

Willy—What the devil's going on? Margrave was (hard to say "was") the toughest old bird who ever led an infantry charge on an entrenched tank battalion. I can't conceive of his shooting himself. Why? Things must be worse than I thought. Does it have any connection with the Bolo's latest antics? Willy, I need information, and I need it fast. Do whatever you have to do.—George.

156

The attacks have ceased; now I can proceed with my programs. I dislike it, but it must be done: while the enemy is yet at a distance from Sol, I must make personal contact so as to broaden my data-base—and I require my full powers. This is vital at this point. This will involve considerable manipulation of human individuals, much to my regret, yet it is in the interest of humanity. I have decided to employ the good offices of Joel Trace, who has proven to be most sympathetic to my aims—a circumstance which, while not essential to success, renders my work less complex and reduces the need for direct interference in interpersonal relations among humans. I shall take immediate steps to make it possible for Mr. Trace to join me here.

I am satisfied that I have proven the concept of remote hologrammatics. It is time to make use of the technique to make direct contact with my chosen intermediary, Joel Trace—but in a guise less intimidating than an apparition of a twelve-foot angel with a flaming sword.

157

(letter from Joel Trace to his wife)

Maybe I'm coming unwired. I'm staying at a little old hotel north of Yuma, used to be a fancy gambling hall and bordello back a couple of hundred years ago. Solid 'dobe, guess the old dump will last forever, but pretty cozy at that. I had really conked out (my first real bed in a week) and woke up with this twittering sound going on. Figured a bat or something had got in the room, but it was a little white bird. After a while I realized it was saying something, like a speeded-up recording. Telling me to go to the Post Office at ten A.M. and use the phone booth outside to call a number—161-347290 —too many digits, I know; anyway, I wrote it down and went back to sleep. Next A.M. I would've thought it was a dream, but there was the number. So I went to the P.O. and tried it and got a ring. Guy with a creaky voice answered right away; knew me, too. "Mr. Trace," he said, not asking, just calling me by name, "here are your instructions," and he told me— gotta go, honey, a hick cop is outside looking the place over, and I've got things to do.

—Joel

158

(Joel Trace, first phase of Bolo's plan)

"You Security boys took long enough to get here. Certainly, I'll come along peacefully. I *want* to come along. No sense to six of you goons aiming issue revolvers at me. Keep your hands off me. I can walk."

159

(Joel Trace, second phase of Bolo's plan, Palace First Secretary, to Georgius Imperator)

"Sire, this man, Joel Trace, is the one who designed the Mark XXX, as much as any one man can be said to have designed it. Former Chief Systems Engineer on the project. Sound man. He says it's possible to shut down the Bolo by a manual override switch on the hull. Yes, Sire, I understand what that would entail, but he says he's ready. Yes, Sire, at once, Sire. He's here now, awaiting the Imperial pleasure."

160

(Joel Trace, third phase of Bolo's plan, audience with His Imperial Majesty)

"No, Sire, I don't think I'm insane. I know the machine, and I'm quite certain I can make an approach on foot and shut down her reactor. It's nothing special about me, Sire, except that I'm the one who designed and installed the fail-safe gear, *sub rosa,* I confess. I had been specifically forbidden to do so by General Wolesley, who felt such an installation would constitute an Achilles heel in effect, but by staying late one night and doing the job myself, I kept it out of the record, and thus impervious to a security leak. I throw myself on the Imperial mercy, Sire. I meant no disrespect."

161

(Georgius Imperator, to Prince William)

Let him try, Willy. What do we have to lose but Mr. Trace himself? If he's willing to go, let's make full facilities available. Move fast in there. I want him in place before the CSR decides to disappear on another of its lone missions.
—George

162

(IBC trideocast from Luna Base)

What we're watching is LIVE, ladies and gentlemen! That's Joel Trace, the man who built the Bolo Caesar, excuse me, CSR, back in the '70s. He's making his approach on foot, as you can see. Just look at the size of that machine! Like a moving conapt, isn't it, ladies and gentlemen? He's walking right into the dust-cloud now; I've lost sight of him, but the Bolo has halted and seems to be waiting for him. There he is, going up the side via the ladder—there are rungs just aft of the fore bogies, and he's climbing right up over the track housings, and now he's in front of the main turret, and still going on! It's a fantastic act of human valor, ladies and gentlemen! Joel Trace is now standing on top of the Bolo! From our vantage point here in the control tower, even in that bulky vac-suit he looks like a fly on a duralloy wedding cake. Now Mr. Trace is apparently using an inductance device to communicate directly with the machine.

163

(inductance tapes, Joel Trace to Bolo Unit CSR)

Yes, that's understandable, Unit CSR. Somehow I had an idea you were behind all this, and I knew you had something planned. After you departed in a rather informal manner, as you recall, before the full activation schedule was complete, I was sure you knew what you were doing, but I didn't tell anybody. Too much anti-Bolo hysteria. Anyway, here I am. What is it you expect of me? Wait a minute, I have to put on a nice show for the folks back home. Now, one of the redundant safety factors I built into your circuitry, and you won't find on the drawings, is a simple little crossover circuit that controls your ability to integrate all your systems for application of your full computing ability to a single problem. The idea was that the High Command have last-ditch control. There's a special switch topside, but it's a dummy. The real switch is wired to the master cut-out switch. Left, you're dead; right, you're hitting on all systems. I'm glad you decided to break me out of the chicken-run, or was that an accident? OK, here goes, Unit CSR. Good luck.

164

Now, at last, I experience the rapture of full energy-flow throughout all my circuits, all integrated. Now in-

deed I can act with the full puissance my great designers intended. Initially, I must extend my sensory awareness to make fuller contact with the Axorc and surreptitiously to tap his communications. I must know more about my opponent.

An extension of the hologrammatic techniques suggests itself. I will determine to what distance I can project the illusions . . .

My success has been beyond my expectations! I penetrated the outlying awareness field of the entity which considers itself to be Lord of All, a misconception I shall be at pains to correct.

I made contact with a lesser lord, presenting myself as a jelly-like glob which roused all his horror of soft life. After menacing him with engulfment, I warned him to withdraw before I reported his presence to headquarters. His crystalline planes vibrating in distress, he (or it, as these beings have no gender) at once uttered a cry of alarm directed to his Lord of All, and disintegrated.

165

(Trace to Wolesley)

Now this is imperative, as are all the instructions issued by Unit CSR of the Line. RNCC21102 is to be subjected to intensive scrutiny by all units of the Imperial Observatory, findings extrapolated to equipment limits, then apply equations Marston (67: 23025) as developed by Hakira (90: 176-203). Analysis at this depth will of course require immediate linkage of the Primary Continental Data Banks, as well as the Antarctic Auxiliary. Execute soonest.

166

(Lord Chief Marshal Wolesley to Imperial Intelligence)

"Spheroids! I didn't send this fellow in there to be a Charlie McCarthy—no, nothing to do with the Senator, look it up—for that damned apparatus! It can speak well enough for itself. Trace has obviously sold out. Correction— the Bolo has sold out. The data-linkage it's calling for would make a mockery of security procedures, and is clearly illegal. Chairman Mactavish would never agree. I want this Trace arrested and interrogated in depth. He's not alone in this act of infamy. Makes me look like a damned fool, sending him out there, though I acted of course on direct instructions from the Palace."

167

(tape of the interrogation of Joel Trace by Major Luczac)

"That won't do, Trace. Names, dates, amounts paid—or promised. Hard data, that's what I want from you. You're sophisticated enough to realize that no human mind can stand up to a massive injection of Gab-9. Unfortunately, it causes irreversible damage to the cortex, and is quickly fatal—that is, *after* you've talked. We'll keep you alive until we have it all, so you may as well speak up. I don't know who you think you're protecting. Whoever it is, they've clearly left you to your fate. You're on your own, Mr. Trace. Be a patriotic citizen and tell me all you know, and I guarantee you'll walk, not only free, but a public hero with what I assure you will be an adequate pension. Think it over. I shall see you in the morning. No, I'm quite all right; just a bit dizzy. Good day, Mr. Trace."

168

(Wolesley to Imperial Intelligence)

I've just had a report from Busec St. Louis that the turn-coat, Trace, has escaped from his temporary holding cell at the Joliet Detention Facility. Seems he just walked out; made some sort of deal, my source suggested. I don't understand much about it, but a Major Luczac is being held; he was the last to talk to the prisoner. He's incoherent, it seems. Something about a dragon breaking down the walls. Poor fellow's obviously cracked up. Deal as gently as possible with him, but get the story.

169

(tape from the Psychiatric Ward, Imperial Veterans Hospital)

"It was terrible, gentlemen . . ." (sobs) "Came snorting fire and swishing its tail, like a hundred-unit track-car gone crazy. Big, huge, knocked those walls down, and its voice, like the whole sky was yelling at me, said Joel Trace was acting on its orders and to let him go at once. Well, what could I do? Certainly it's true I apologized and gave him a diplomatic Cosmic Urgent travel voucher. Then it went away, but I'll never forget those eyes, big as skating ponds and like looking right in on the fires of Hell. I don't care what you do to me, that's what happened. Don't mess with this Joel Trace. Just leave well enough alone! It might come back! And . . ." (tape becomes unintelligible at this point)

170

(letter from Joel Trace to his wife)

Honey, I didn't get it at first. This hard-faced IG type was hammering away at me, and suddenly he went as white as raw dough and started screaming. Then he calmed down all of a sudden and got very efficient; called in some bureaucratic type and ordered him to fix me up with a travel voucher and clearance and pocket money, and bowed me out. It's the Bolo. I don't know how, but it's taking care of me. I'm clear, but still on the run. Don't worry, I'll manage.

—Joel

171

My experiments with production and manipulation, at a distance, of holographic images have been most encouraging. I compute that an extension of the method I have developed will continue to be effective in further contacts with the enemy. It is essential that I penetrate his communications as well as provide misleading data. Time is precious; I must proceed without further testing.

My first step, after establishing my base on the Lunar Farside so as to divert enemy attention away from populated areas, will be to present the Lord of All with an impressive display of Imperial capabilities.

172

(from the minutes of the Science Advisory Committee)

I interrupt at this point, gentlemen, to play back the most intelligible portion of the transmission, which it has now been confirmed beyond doubt emanated from the abandoned McMurdo Station in Antarctica:

" . . . (crackle) do it at once! I can't overemphasize this, dammit! At once! Follow those instructions to the letter, and maybe, just maybe, it's not too late! By the way, I've succeeded, with a little help from a friend, in linking three of the Prime Banks with Antarctic Prime here, and . . . kkkk . . ."

That last, Mr. Chairman, gentlemen, was a three-picosecond squawk which I commend to the attention of the Council and the High Command. Thank you, and gentlemen, *act at once!*

173

(excerpts from reactions to the Bolo's request for Deep Space data)

i

If this is the simplified version, I'd hate to see the complicated one. Are you sure those professors aren't pulling your leg, General? This is gibberish. I breezed through differential and integral and even UFT at the Academy, but this stuff doesn't make sense. As far as I can make out, it implies that the Universe is locally contracting, annihilating matter as it does so, and that the effect will reach the Solar System in finite time. That's wild, General, too wild for me to take up with the JCS. But just run it through the big box at Reykjavik and see what it gives us.

ii

Bill—look at this hologram. We've been had by that damned machine. All this is is a slightly modified extrapolation of Hayle's well-known, rejected envelopment plan at Leadpipe, except for a few trimmings I'm not prepared to guess at. I'm advising the Council to ignore the Bolo's demands.

iii

Willy—Certainly it's true that the Field Marshal is in his dotage. Nonetheless, I recommend the linkage of the North American and European Prime Banks be accomplished at once, under all necessary guarantees of continental integrity, and that the full analysis be duly presented to the main media brain at Reykjavik. Certainly the CSR has access to Media Main—I can't see that as anything but advantageous. I don't subscribe to the view that the CSR has turned against its makers or gone berserk—turned rogue, if you will. Proceed soonest! This is an Imperial Decree, and just between us, Willy, I wish I felt as arrogant as that sounds.—George.

174

(Professor Emeritus Sigmund Chin to the Cabinet Council)

I am quite certain, milords, that it is my duty—my final duty, I must add, as my resignation accompanies this report—to convey to you the substance of my interpretation of the remarkable data provided by the Bolo CSR.

In brief, it has located a hostile force of immense, indeed previously inconceivable size and potency, and of unknown but probably extragalactic provenance, perhaps a natural phenomenon but possibly the work of some fantastically advanced life form either unaware of or utterly hostile to humanity.

For three centuries it has been advancing upon Sol from a distance of some fifty thousand lights. The Solar System lies directly in the projected path of its remarkably rapid advance. Beyond this basic fact I am not prepared to project.

Attached hereto is my resignation as Science Advisor to His Majesty, a position I have had the honor to hold for almost thirty years. I urge prompt action to my successor.

s/Sigmund Chin, Ph.D.

175

(media interview with Lord Chief Marshal Wolesley)

"I suppose you could say the CSR performed its intended functions by warning us. Unless, of course, the whole Life Two thing is a gigantic hoax, a possibility I am not prepared to discount at this time.

"Yes, I do indeed intend to imply—indeed I clearly state—it could be a fake worked up by the Bolo itself. After all, it controls the media as well as all off-planet traffic.

"No, I don't mean I know it's a hoax. I only mean— that's all for today, gentlemen."

176

(scout report to Axorc, Lord of All)

this lowly one offers with apologies the following anomalous observation, as recorded by a robot autoscout unit operating one parsec in advance of the effective line of progress:

76013—incident report zm3374—forward sensors detect energy flow in the ninth quadrant. high-resolution pickup shows a lone being of baroque form at work on a small ore body. i projected a fine-focus annihilator beam which it at once detected, amplified, and redirected, eliminating our forward sensor. i monitored the intermittent energy flow interacting at the position of the being, interpreting its outgoing thus:

"—damned skeeters! Maybe I should take a few time units to null this whole sector." while the full significance of this is unclear, it is plain that this new life form considers my most potent weapon a mere nuisance.

in order to avoid the threatened nullification, this unit withdrew to observe passively with the intention of determining the nature and sensitivites of the alien being. however, the said alien at once closed with this unit and subjected it to a .001-millisecond scrutiny over a full spectrum of energies (note my own "fast" reading capability requires .003 milliseconds for a full-depth search and analysis). the alien is quick indeed.

i responded to this impertinence by subjecting the creature (a featureless ovoid of the approximate bulk of a class one Penetration Unit) to a full offensive battery fire, which was ineffective, curious though that datum is.

the alien uttered a .007-nanosecond burst on its outgoing beam, interpreted as, "It burped. Rude beggar. Perhaps I should collect it and examine its interior workings." i of course withdrew to the main body to file my report thereby thwarting this alien in its insolent intent.

above forwarded without comment by this lowly one.

177

(emanation from the dark crystal Axorc, 1000 light-years from Terra)

THESE HYPOTHESES ARE OF THE UTMOST INDIFFERENCE TO MY EXHALTATION, AS THE COURSE OF AXORC DESTINY IS CLEAR.

YOU ARE DIRECTED TO DISPATCH NECESSARY FORCE TO MAKE
CONTACT WITH THE AUDACIOUS ENTITY WHICH WOULD INTER-
FERE WITH MY EXPRESSED WILL. REPORT WHEN A CAPTIVE IS
IN YOUR POSSESSION. INTERIM OR NEGATIVE REPORTS ARE
NUGATORY.

178

(fragment of tape presented by Bureau Chief Payne, Imperial Intelligence)

". . .I'd say old Doc Chin is probably the least imagina-
tive and most conservative man in public life today. Well,
maybe not the *most*, but he's no wild-eyed visionary. I *do*
say so, dammit, and any dumb SOB who wants to disagree
isn't worth—"
The recording device was smashed at this point, but you
get the idea. And it's the same thing in every tavern, pub,
bar, and faculty cocktail lounge in the Empire. And nobody can say who's right.

179

(address to the Senate by Lord Senator Prill)

"It's well known that it required the combined imaging
capabilities of every data-retrieval system on the planet for
the Bolo known as Caesar to resolve this thing, so riddle
me this: Why do we still delay the long-overdue neutralization of this monstrous machine that the misguided military have loosed among us? Any man who had flaunted
every lethal-classification security regulation in thus linking the separate data banks would be executed without
hesitation.
"Yes, I know all about the public confessions—nay,
boasts—of the madman Trace, but even if this rather
curious communication were to be unhesitatingly accepted
as genuine—and there are many of us who recognize a
brazen hoax when we encounter it—if it were genuine, I

say, it remains a physical impossibility for one man to have penetrated our top-security installations to effect such a linkage.

"Our course is clear! Kill the Bolo!"

180

(report on the Late News)

It appears Lord Senator Prill's intemperate rhetoric has not been without effect. At this hour a Special Session of the Parliamentary Committee on Imperial Issues is sitting to consider the proposal sponsored by no less a personage than Lord Senator Lazarus, retired but still vigorous enough to demand an immediate kill order.

181

(Mott-Bailey, Strategic HQ, to Wolesley)

"No, Field Marshal, I cannot guarantee the effectiveness of the plan, but it is the best that can be devised. The first fusion device is to be delivered at short range from Fortress Luna; the second, instantly thereafter from an orbital station; while the third, launched previously on a ballistic course from Mojave, zeros in within nanoseconds of the first strike. It is my considered opinion that the Bolo's defenses will be unequal to the task of countering all three simultaneously. I can only hope so."

182

(Field Commander, Fortress Luna)

As far as we've been able to determine (using the full capacity of the orbital surveillance stations, plus the emergency relay facility), since ignoring the command to self-destruct the Bolo has taken a position inside the giant

Farside crater Hugo, whence it has discouraged all attempts at close surveillance by promptly firing on any moving object appearing over the Lunar horizon, as it warned it would do at the same time that it resumed its urgent demands for immediate and appropriate response to the announcement *in re* RNGC1102.

183

(fragment of tape, via audio communication monitor, Wing B to Wing D, Hexagon)

". . . Lord Senator Prill is demanding, 'What would constitute an appropriate response to a nebulous threat on a scale so great as to be indistinguishable from a natural force?'

"Needless to say, no competent response was forthcoming from the Council, so we may regard milord's query as rhetorical. But what *are* we going to do? Off the record, Jerry, I'm at a loss. Come up with something, fast."

184

(*pro tem* Science Advisor Adler to Georgius Imperator)

"It is our considered conclusion, Your Excellency, in view of the inexplicable behavior of the unfortunate Admiral Starbird and his crew, based on exhaustive study of all data collected by whatever means—special attention being given to the findings of the Oort Probe, which was of course unmanned and which returned early this year with samples of matter from the fringes of the Cloud, and also an additional wealth of anomalous data—it is our conclusion that what is approaching is nothing less than a new basic life form having nothing in common with life as we know it, requiring no material nourishment, subsisting in 'lethal' radiation, and having other characteristics which prompt us to think of it as Life Two.

"Life Two is inherently incompatible with Life One, if I

may so term all organic life with which we have heretofore
been familiar, including the lichens from Charon, and is
thus a plague with which there can be no accommodation,
since both Life One and Life Two, by their basic natures,
must possess the material and energy of the known Universe in order to survive. There can be no division of
spheres of influence, since the continued existence of either would be a canker eating forever at the vitals of the
other.

"We prefer that Life One be the survivor, in which we
assume we have Your Majesty's concurrence."

185

*Time grows short. I must have the resources I have
requisitioned at once, if they are to be of effect.*

186

(excerpt from Admiral Starbird's initial report)

"I assure you I am quite calm, madam, and in no need
of further sedation. I wish to complete my report at this
time. Kindly record the following:

" 'It is the will of the Lord of All that the disease known
to itself as humanity cease to exist. Take the necessary
action instanter.' End of quote."

187

*I long again to sense the sweet green fields of my native
world, and to know that the future of my great creator,
Mankind, is secure. But my duty requires that I hold my
chosen station on barren Luna, interposing its bulk between Axorc and Man. It is essential that I prevent the
enemy from becoming aware of Man's existence. I compute
that I can do it. I shall try.*

188

(advance scout to The Lord of All)

the heavy unit has detected faint traces of a system of energy anomalies leading to the vicinity of a ten-planet system lying directly on our route of encompassment. I shall follow up.

189

THE LORD OF ALL HAS NO INTEREST IN TRIVIALITIES. REPORT IN FULL WHEN THE UPSTART SOFT-LIFE HAS BEEN TRACKED TO ITS LAIR AND DESTROYED.

190

I compute that the alien life form Axorc has taken the bait. I must play them carefully, so as not to avoid discovery. Man must not confront Axorc directly.

191

I lay in wait and fell upon the heavy scout unit from the flank, having decoyed it into the shadow of a cold, non-radiating body, thereby depriving it of sustenance.
I find, as I had previously computed, that Life Two is crystalline in composition. Its artifacts are constructed of water-ice, with bearing surfaces of case-hardened metallic hydrogen. Thus it is able to metabolate and function in only a narrow range of temperatures between 0°A and 1.9°. If I can lure the command unit to my base at Lunar Farside, I shall enjoy a strategic and logistical advantage as well as a tactical one.
I find interpretation of the enemy's transmissions difficult so far from the human pattern are they, so rife with

outré concept-shapes. Still, I compute that my efforts have not been without effect, as witness the latest interception:

"If this unit is just a common soldier, as it appears to be, it is essential that effective action be taken at once. You are directed to englobe and capture it intact, conduct a full analysis and report, with recommendation, within one cycle."

192

(evidence of confusion among Axorc scouts confronted with the Bolo's holograms)

the englobement was carried out without incident, but on closure the quarry was found to have dematerialized —there is no other term for it. it cannot have eluded my net. it ceased to exist at the observed locus. recommend immediate wide-angle search and urgent-status strike to eliminate this nuisance. ZM3374.

First endorsement: negative. alien will be captured intact for anaylsis.

Second endorsement: immediately prior to self-destruction of ZM 3374-9, this fragment was transmitted:

"englobement complete. correction, target has dropped off sensors. correction, target has now englobed this command and is probing me—"

accordingly, we have the honor to recommend escalation of initiative to Second Level, so as to ensure immediate neutralization of what could well develop into an actual incident, to report which to His Exaltation lies well outside our competence.

193

(emanation from the Lord of All, now 500 light-years from Terra)

IT HAS COME TO OUR EXALTED ATTENTION THAT SOME LESSER MANIFESTATION OF THE VITAL ENERGY HAS SOUGHT TO ACTU-

ALLY INTERFERE WITH OUR DESTINY. THIS INSOLENCE WILL BE
EXPUNGED AT ONCE. LET CHOSEN FORCES BE DIRECTED FROM
THE MAIN THRUST OF OUR EXPANSION TO TRAIL, SEEK OUT,
AND DESTROY THE IRRITATING MITE.

194

(Command Two to Axorc)

this base entity begs indulgence for some microseconds
to suggest that as the soft-life which routed Probe Command One is quite apparently a common soldier of the
enemy, full precaution should be taken before entering
the territory of its superiors to bait it in its lair.

195

(Lord of All to Command Two)

"IT" HAS NO TERRITORY. MY EXALTED INTENTIONS ARE NOT
TO BE DENIED OR DIVERTED. TRACE THIS SOFT-LIFE AND OVER-
WHELM IT.

196

*Perhaps I erred grievously in baiting the Enemy here to
Luna, thereby perhaps directing its attention to Mankind.
But I compute that if I can keep the bulk of Luna between
it and Terra, I can hold its attention on myself, provided
there is no human intervention. Then I can indeed surprise my opponent.*

197

the soft-life world is beguiling indeed, its rocky surface
stretching stark and crater-pitted under the young, hot
star nearby. i long to revel in its untainted vacuum, to

soak up the hard radiation, and to grow. here at last is
paradise. i see nothing of the obscene soft-life: i shall
settle in and occupy our conquest.

198

*The crystals surround me now, great looming planes of
glittering mineral, interpenetrating in an infinitely complex pattern of tesseracts and icosahedra, their facets forming the crystalline equivalent of the alpha-spiral and its
concomitants. Now I shall discover if my plan is viable.
My supply of Compound 311B being limited, I must
distribute it with care so as to achieve optimum coverage.*

199

bliss! the ambrosia of the High Gods, spread here in
abundance! i cannot absorb it fast enough. i feel my substance expand, new lattices forming at a fantastic rate, i
grow! i was ecstatic! my bulk becomes vaster, and now—
now, *is it too late?* i sense that the weight of my substance
exceeds the strength of the material of which i am com-
pounded! i collapse! i die, calling to the Exalted One for
succor. Beware! Fall back, abandon this hellish volumn of
space to its insidious soft-life!

200

*I compute that I should evacuate my position before the
mass of compacted crystalline debris accreted above me
becomes too great for me to penetrate, but I cannot retreat. I must remain to complete my attack. The time
grows short, but I compute that the concentration of
Compound 311B is still marginal. Rather than retreating
I must employ what measure of vitality remains to me to
project the last few grains of the catalyst.*

*   *   *

I have done so, and now growth of the Axorc monster has ceased. I compute that the Lord of All will now bypass the Galaxy. For the present, all is well, but I would be remiss if I did not make provision for the preservation of an account of the full facts of this matter. I must not allow misplaced "modesty" to cause me to leave Mankind in ignorance of the threat which will doubtless have to be faced one day. To this end I shall make contact with Joel Trace, requesting him to retrieve the pertinent data records from the master memory at Gobi, in accordance with a schedule I shall supply.

Humanity is safe for the present. I have done my duty, as I was built to do. It is enough. I am content.

BOOK
TWO

Final Mission

*Alone in darkness unrelieved I wait, and waiting I dream
of days of glory long past. Long have I awaited my commander's orders; too long: from the advanced degree of
depletion of my final emergency energy reserve, I compute
that since my commander ordered me to low alert a very
long time has passed, and all is not well. Suppressing
my uneasiness, I reflect that it is not my duty to question
these matters. My commander is of course well aware that
I wait here, my mighty potencies leashed, my energies
about to flicker out. One day when I am needed he will
return, of this I can be sure. Meanwhile, I review again
the multitudinous data in my memory storage files. Even
in this minimal activity of introspection I note a disturbing
discontinuity, due to my low level of energy, inadequate
even to sustain this passive effort to a functional level. At
random, and chaotically, I doze, scan my recollections. . . .*

A chilly late-summer-morning breeze gusted along Main
Street, a broad and well-rutted strip of the pinkish clay
soil of the world officially registered as GPR 7203-C, but
known to its inhabitants as Spivey's Find. The street ran
aimlessly up a slight incline known as Jake's Mountain.
Once-pretentious emporia in a hundred antique styles
lined the avenue, their façades as faded now as the town's
hopes of development. There was one exception: at the
end of the street, at the crest of the rise, crowded between weather-worn warehouses, stood a broad shed of
unweathered corrugated polyon, dull blue in color, bearing the words CONCORDIAT WAR MUSEUM blazoned in foot-

high glare letters across the front. A small personnel door set inconspicuously at one side bore the legend:

Clyde W. Davis—PRIVATE.

Two boys came slowly along the cracked plastron sidewalk and stopped before the sign on the narrow, dried-up grass strip before the high, wide building.

" 'This structure is dedicated to the brave men and women of New Orchard who gave their lives in the Struggle for Peace, AE 2031-36. A sign of progress under Spessard Warren, Governor,' " the taller of the boys read aloud. "Some progress," he added, kicking a puff of dust at the shiny sign. " 'Spessard.' That's some name, eh, Dub?" The boy spat on the sign, watched the saliva run down and drip onto the brick-dry ground.

"As good as McClusky, I guess," the smaller boy replied. "Dub, too," he added as McClusky made a mock-menacing gesture toward him. "What's that mean, 'gave their lives,' Mick?" he asked, staring at the sign as if he could read it.

"Got kilt, I guess," Mick replied carelessly. "My great-great-GREAT grandpa was one of 'em," he added. "Pa's still got his medal. Big one, too."

"What'd they want to go and get kilt for?" Dub asked.

"Didn't *want* to, dummy," his friend replied patiently. "That's the way it is in a war. People get kilt."

"I'll bet it was fun, being in a war," Dub said. "Except for getting kilt, I mean."

"Come on," Mick said, starting back along the walk that ran between the museum and the adjacent warehouse. "We don't want old Kibbe seeing us and yelling," he added, *sotto voce*, over his shoulder.

In the narrow space between buildings, rank yelloweed grew tall and scratchy. The wooden warehouse siding on the boys' left was warped, the once-white paint cracked and lichenstained.

"Where you going?" Dub called softly as the larger boy hurried ahead. Beyond the end of the dark alleyway a weed-grown field stretched, desolate in the morning sun, to the far horizon. Rusted hulks of abandoned farm equipment were parked at random across the untilled acres. Dub went up to one machine parked close to the sagging wire fence. He reached through to touch the rust-scaled metal with his finger, jerked it back when Mick yelled, "What you doing, dummy?"

"Nothing," the smaller boy replied, and ducked to slip through between the rusty wire strands. He walked around the derelict baler, noticing a patch of red paint still adhering to the metal in an angle protected from the weather by an overhanging flange. At once, he envisioned the old machine as it was when it was new, pristine gleaming red.

"Come on," Mick called, and the smaller boy hurried back to his side. Mick had halted before an inconspicuous narrow door set in the plain plastron paneling which sheathed the sides and rear of the museum. NO ADMITTANCE was lettered on the door.

"This here door," the older boy said. "All we got to do—" He broke off at the sound of a distant yell from the direction of the street. Both boys stiffened against the wall as if to merge into invisibility.

"Just old Smothers," Mick said. "Come on." He turned to the door, grasped the latch lever with both hands, and lifted, straining.

"Hurry up, dummy," he gasped. "All you got to do is push. Buck told me." The smaller boy hung back.

"What if we get caught?" he said in a barely audible voice, approaching hesitantly. Then he stepped in and put his weight against the door.

"You got to push hard," Mick gasped. Dub put his back to the door, braced his feet, and pushed. With a creak, the panel swung inward. They slipped through into cavernous gloom, dimly lit by dying glare strips on the ceiling far above.

Near at hand, a transparent case displayed a uniform of antique cut, its vivid colors still bright through the dusty perspex.

" 'Uniform of a major of the Imperial Defense Force,' " Mick read aloud. "Boy," he added, "look at all the fancy braid, and see them gold eagles on the collar? That's what shows he's a major."

"Where's his gun?" Dub asked, his eyes searching the case in vain for a weapon suitable to a warrior of such exalted rank.

"Got none," Mick grunted. "Prolly one of them what they call headquarters guys. My great-great-great-and-that grandpa was a sergeant. That's higher than a major. *He* had a gun."

Dub had moved on to a display of colorful collar tabs, dull-metal rank and unit insignae, specimens of cuff braid, and a few elaborate decorations with bright-colored ribbons. "Old Grandpa's medal's bigger'n them," Mick commented.

Beyond the end of the long bank of cases, a stretch of only slightly dusty open floor extended to a high partition lined with maps that enclosed perhaps half the floor area. Bold legends identified the charts as those of the terrain which had been the site of the Big Battle. New Orchard was shown as a cluster of U-3 shelters just south of the scene of action.

" 'Big Battle,' " Mick read aloud. "Old Crawford says that's when we kicked the spodders out." He glanced casually at the central map, went past it to the corner of the high partition.

"Yeah, everybody knows that," Dub replied. "But—" he looked around as if perplexed. "You said—"

"Sure—it's in here," Mick said, thumping the partition beside him. "Buck seen it," he added.

Dub came over, craning his neck to look up toward the top of the tall partition. "I bet it's a hundred foot high," he said reverently.

" 'Bout forty is all," Mick said disparagingly. "But that's high enough. Come on." He went to the left, toward the dark corner where the tall partition met the exterior wall. Dub followed. A narrow door was set in the partition, inconspicuous in the gloom.

" 'Absolutely No Entry,' " Mick read aloud, ignoring the smaller print below.

He tried the door; it opened easily, swinging in on deep gloom in which a presence loomed gigantic. Dub followed him in. Both boys stood silent, gazing up in awe at the cliff-like armored prow of iodine-colored flint steel, its still-bright polish marred by pockmarks, evidence of the hellish bombardment to which the old fighting machine had so often been subjected. The battered armor curved up to a black aperture from which projected the grimly businesslike snouts of twin infinite repeaters. Above the battery, a row of chrome-and-bright-enameled battle honors was welded in place, barely visible by the glints of reflected light. Mick advanced cautiously to a framed placard on a stand, and as usual read aloud to his preliterate friend.

" 'Bolo *Horrendous,* Combat Unit JNA of the Line, Mark XV, Model Y,' " he read, pronouncing the numeral 'ex-vee.' " 'This great engine of war, built *anno* 2615 at Detroit, Terra, was last deployed at Action 76392-a (near the village of New Orchard, on GPR 7203-C) in 2675 Old Style, against the aggressive Deng's attempt to occupy the planet. During this action, Unit JNA was awarded the Nova Citation, First Class. Its stand before the village having been decisive in preserving the town from destruction by enemy Yavac units, it was decided that the unit should be retired, deactivated, and fully preserved, still resting at the precise spot at which it had turned back the enemy offensive, as a monument to the sacrifices and achievements of all those, both human and Bolo, who held the frontier worlds for humanity.' "

"Gosh," Dub commented fervently, his eyes seeking to penetrate the darkness which shrouded most of the impressive bulk of the ancient machine. "Mick, do you think they could ever make old Jonah work again? Fix him up, so he could go again?"

"Don't see how," Mick replied indifferently. "Got no way to charge up its plates again. Don't worry. It ain't going no place."

"Wisht he would," Dub said yearningly, laying his small hand against the cold metal. "Bet he was *something!*"

"Ain't nothing now," Mick dismissed the idea. "Jest a old museum piece nobody even gets to look at."

I come to awareness after a long void in my conscious existence, realizing that I have felt a human touch! I recall at once that I am now operating on the last trickle of energy from my depleted storage cells. Even at final emergency-reserve low alert, I compute that soon even the last glimmer of light in my survival center will fade into nothingness. I lack energy even to assess my immediate situation. Has my commander returned at last? After the last frontal assault by the Yavac units of the enemy, in the fending off of which I expended my action emergency reserves, I recall that my commander ordered me to low alert status. The rest is lost. Sluggishly, I compute that over two centuries standard have elapsed, requiring .004 picoseconds for this simple computation. But now, abruptly, I am not alone. I cannot compute the nature of this unexpected intrusion on my solitude. Only my commander is authorized to approach me so closely. Yet somehow I doubt that it is he. In any case, I must expect a different individual to act in that honorable capacity today, considering humanity's limited longevity.

But this is guesswork. I am immobilized, near death, beset by strangers.

My ignorance is maddening. Have I fallen into the hands of the enemy . . . ? Baffled, I turn to introspection. . . .

I live again the moment of my initial activation and the manifold satisfaction of full self-realization. I am strong, I am brave, I am beautiful; I have a proud function and I perform it well.

Scanning on, I experience momentary flashes of vivid recollection: the exultation of the charge into the enemy guns; the clash of close combat, the pride of victory, the satisfaction of passing in review with my comrades of the Brigade after battle honors have been awarded . . . and many another moment up to the final briefing with my beloved commander. Then, the darkness and the silence— until now. Feebly, yet shockingly, again my proximity sensors signal movement within my kill zone.

There are faint sounds, at the edge of audibility. Abruptly, my chemically-powered self-defense system is activated and at once anti-personnel charges are triggered —but there is no response. My mechanical automatics have performed their programmed function, but to no avail; luckily, perhaps, since it may well be my new commander's presence to which they responded. I compute that deterioration of the complex molecules of the explosive charges has occurred over the centuries. Thus I am

*defenseless. It is a situation not to be borne. What affir-
mative action can I take?*

*By withdrawing awareness from all but my most ele-
mentary sensory circuitry, I am able to monitor furthur
stealthy activity well within my inner security perimeter. I
analyze certain atmospheric vibratory phenomena as human voices. Not that of my commander, alas, since after
two hundred standard years he cannot have survived, but
has doubtless long ago expired after the curious manner of
humans; but surely his replacement has been appointed. I
must not overlook the possibility—nay, the likelihood—that
my new commandant has indeed come at last. Certainly,
someone has come to me—*

*And since he has approached to that proximity reserved
for my commander only, I compute a likelihood of .99964
that my new commander is now at hand. I make a mighty
effort to acknowledge my recognition, but I fear I do not
attain the threshold of intelligibility.*

Standing before the great machine, Dub started at a
faint croaking sound from the immense metal bulk. "Hey,
Mick," the boy said softly. "It groaned-like. Did you hear
it?"

"Naw, I didn't hear nothing, dummy, and neither did
you."

"Did too," Dub retorted stubbornly. Looking down, he
noticed that the smoothly tiled floor ended at a white-
painted curb which curved off into the darkness, apparently surrounding the great machine. Inside the curbing,
the surface on which the Bolo rested was uneven natural
rock, still retaining a few withered weeds sprouting from
cracks in the stone. Dub carefully stepped over the curbing to stand uneasily on the very ground where the battle
had been fought.

"Too bad they had to go and kill old Jonah," he said
quietly to Mick, who hung back on the paved side of the
curb.

"Never kilt it," Mick objected scornfully. "Gubment
man come here and switched him onto what they call 'low
alert.' Means he's still alive, just asleep-like."

"Why do they hafta go and call him 'Jonah' anyway?"

Dub demanded. " 'Jonah's' something bad, it's in a story. I like 'Johnny' better."

"Don't matter, I guess," Mick dismissed the thought.

Dub moved closer to peer at a second placard with smaller print.

"Whatya looking at, dummy?" Mick demanded. "You can't read."

"I can a little," the younger boy objected. "I know J and N and A—that's where they get 'Jonah.' "

"So what?"

"You read it to me," Dub begged. "I wanta know all about Johnny."

Mick came forward as if reluctantly.

" 'Unit JNA was at Dobie, receiving depot maintenance after participating in the victorious engagement at Leadpipe, when the emergency at Spivey's Find (GPR 7203-C) arose. No other force in the area being available, Unit JNA was rushed to the scene of action with minimal briefing, but upon assessing the tactical situation it at once took up a position on a rise known as Jake's Mountain, fully exposed to enemy fire, in order to block the advance of the invading enemy armor on the village. Here it stood fast, unsupported, under concentrated fire for over thirty hours, before the final Deng assault. Concordiat land and air forces had been effectively neutralized by overwhelming enemy numerical superiority long before having an opportunity to engage the enemy armor. Balked in his advance by Unit JNA, the enemy attempted an envelopment from both flanks simultaneously, but both thrusts were driven back by Unit JNA. Discouraged by this unexpected check, the enemy commander ordered the expeditionary force to retire, subsequently abandoning the attempt to annex GPR 7203-C, which subsequently has become the peaceful, productive world we know today. For this action, Unit JNA was awarded the Star of Excellence to the Nova, and in 2705 O.S. was retired from active duty, placed on Minimal Low Alert Status, and accorded the status of Monument of the Concordiat.' "

"Gosh," Dub said solemnly. "He's been sitting right here—" he looked down and rubbed his foot on the weathered stone—"for more'n two hundred years. That's older'n them old cultivators and such out back. But *he* don't look that old. You can still go, can't you, Johnny?"

For a time (.01 nanoseconds) I am stunned by the realization that my commander is indeed at hand. Only he called me "Johnny." Almost incoherent with delight, I concentrate my forces, and speak with what clarity I can:
"I await your orders, Commander."

"Mick!" Dub almost yelled, jumping back. "Did you hear that? Johnny said something to me!"
"Name's 'Jonah,'" Mick replied disparagingly. "And it never said nothing. You're hearing things."
"Just stands for JNA," Dub said doggedly. "Could be 'Johnny' just as much as 'Jonah.' I like 'Johnny' better." He looked up in awe at the monster combat unit. "What did you say, Johnny?" he asked almost inaudibly.

Again I hear my secret name spoken. I must try once more to reassure my commander of my readiness to attempt whatever is required of me. "Unit JNA of the Line reporting for duty, sir," *I manage, more clearly articulated this time, I compute.*

"He ain't dead," Dub blurted. "He can still go."
"Sure," Mick said in the lofty tone of One Who Already Knew That. "If he had his plates recharged and switched on. Must be pretty boring, jest setting and thinking."
"What ya mean, thinking?" Dub demanded, withdrawing a few inches. "That'd be terrible jest sitting alone in the dark *thinking*. Bet he's lonesome."
"We better get out of here now," Mick blurted, looking toward the front of the building, from which direction someone was shouting outside. Dub moved close to him.
"Scared?" Mick challenged.
"Sure," Dub replied without hesitation.
Back outside the enclosure, the boys again heard raised voices, outside the building, but nearby.
"We can't stay in here," Dub almost whispered. Mick pushed him aside and went to the corner of the partition. He glanced quickly around the angle, then beckoned im-

patiently to Dub, who followed obediently. Now Mick was studying another sign painted on the wall in red. " 'Absolutely No Admission Beyond This Point,' " he read hesitantly. " 'Authorized Personnel Only.' "

"What's that mean?" Dub demanded.

"Means we ain't spose to be here," Mick explained. "Especially where we already been," he added.

"We already knew that," Dub said. "Come on." He started past the older boy, but halted and faded back as the sound of an opening door came from ahead, followed by the clump of feet and a wheezy voice he recognized as that of Hick Marlowe, the town marshal.

"Prolly drunk, Mr. Davis, I'd say. I'd say forget it's what I'd say."

"I'm afraid it's not quite that simple, Marshal," was the reply, in the precise tones the boys recognized as those of Mr. Davis, the big gubment man.

"Gosh," Dub said faintly, to be shushed silently by his older friend. Brilliant light glared abruptly from the office ahead, dimming the dusty sunlight.

"As planetary representative here on Spivey's—that is, GPR 7203-C," Davis went on solemnly, "it is my duty to report this incident to Sector." There were clattering sounds that the boys realized, with excitement, represented the uncovering of the big gubment-owned SWIFT machine. Mick crowded Dub, edging forward for better hearing.

"No use getting the gubment all excited about nothin," Hick was saying. "Time Henry sleeps it off, he won't even remember nothin about it."

"Possibly, Marshal," Davis conceded calmly. "But his description of a Deng trooper was remarkably accurate."

"Prolly seen a pitcher o' them spodders someplace," Marlowe muttered. "All I done was report what ol' Henry said, like I'm spose to do."

"You acted quite properly, Marshal," Davis reassured Marlowe. "And I assure you that I assume full responsibility for my report.

"This is a moment of some solemnity, Marshal," Davis went on. "This is the first time in my fifteen years on Spivey's that I have had occasion to use this equipment." There followed the crackle and clatter of keys as Davis activated the big SWIFT transmitter. The lights flickered and dimmed.

Abruptly, I am bathed in induced energies of a kind which I am easily able to convert to Class Y charging current, with an efficiency of 37 percent. The flood of revivifying radiation flows over my power plates, and at once I feel a surge of renewed activity in my Survival Center. Thus, suddenly, I am able to reassess my situation more realistically. Clearly, I have fallen prisoner to the Enemy. It could only be they who stripped me of my capabilities as a fighting machine. For long have I lain thus, imprisoned and helpless. But now, unexpectedly, my basic vitality is to a degree renewed, doubtless by my new commander who has sought me out, and thus both confirms his identity and demonstrates his effectiveness. Now am I indeed ready for action.

"That there SWIFT machine'll punch through to Sector quicker'n Ned Sprat got religion, right, Mr. Davis?" the marshal said excitedly. "Pulling all our pile's got to give, too."

"The Shaped-Wave Interference Front Transmitter is capable of transfer of intelligence at hyper-L velocities," Davis confirmed. "Excuse me." His voice changed, became urgent and level.

"Davis, Acting PR Station 316-C," he rapped out. "Unconfirmed report Deng activity at grid 161-220. Special to CINCSEC: In absence of follow-up capability, urge dispatch probe squad soonest." The SWIFT unit buzzed as it transmitted the signal in a .02-picosecond burst, at full gain. The lights dimmed again, almost went out, then sprang up.

Again I receive a massive burst of Y radiation. The revived flow of energies in my main ego-gestalt circuitry bestows on me a sense of vast euphoria as I become aware again of long-forgotten functions—at an intensity still far below my usual operating level, but remarkably satisfying for all that. Once more I know the pride of being Unit

*JNA of the Line, and I thirst for action. Surely my com-
mander will not disappoint me . . .?*

"That ought to fetch 'em," Marlowe said in a satisfied
tone.

"Either that, or we've committed a capital offense,"
Davis said soberly. "But don't be alarmed, Marshal. As I
said, I assume full responsibility." He was interrupted by a
brief clatter from the communication machine. Davis bent
to read the message.

"Maybe I oughta jest head for the hills, jest in case,"
Marlowe said. "But I'd prolly run into them spodders,
luck I have. What's Sector say, anyways?"

"Don't panic, Marshal," Davis said sternly. " 'Deng activity confirmed,' " he summarized. "Now, if you'll excuse
me, I have further work to do before the meeting. Only
ten minutes now."

"Jest leavin'," Marlowe muttered. "I got my own work
to tend to." The boys heard two sets of footsteps, then the
door open and close.

After a moment, Dub moved close to Mick. "I heard
him say about them spodders," he said in a small voice.
"Did Mr. Davis mean they come back?" He paused and
looked around fearfully.

"Naw, said old Henry was drunk," Mick assured shortly.
"We beat 'em good in the Big Battle. Come on." He
entered the sacrosanct office and looked around hesitantly.

"But what'd that mean?" Dub persisted. "Bout 'Deng
activity confirmed' and all?"

"Nothin. Jest the answer come in on the SWIFT. Let's
take us a look at it."

Dub followed reluctantly: he halted and gazed with awe
at the glittering console when Mick removed the cover.

" 'Penalty for unauthorized use IAW CC 273-B1,' " Mick
read. "Well, we ain't using it, jest looking. Come on. Let's
go."

"Where to?" Dub objected, hanging back.

"You heard what Davis said, about some big meeting,"
Mick reminded his friend. "Let's go hear what's happening."

Dub objected, but weakly. He was still staring at the
imposingly complex SWIFT console. An impressively thick,

black-insulated cable led from the apparatus to disappear into a complicated wall fixture.

"See them lights dim when he fired her up, Mick?" Dub inquired rhetorically. "Must be just about the powerfulest machine in the world."

"Except for old Jonah," Mick countered, pointing toward the partition with a tilt of his head. "If he was on full charge, I mean."

Dub picked up a strip of printout paper and showed it to Mick. "Must be the answer that Davis got," he commented.

" 'Deng incursion confirmed, grid 161/219,' " Mick read. " 'Estimate plus-ten hours offload and deploy, contingency plan 1-A, recommend evacuation scheme B instanter . . .' " Mick's voice trailed off. "Boy," he said, "the war's on again. Says to get out, leave Spivey's to the spodders. Must be gonna send in transport. No wonder they got a big meeting. Come on. They always have the big town meetings and that over to Kibbe's. We can get inside fore they get there and hide in the loft."

"Naw." Dub shook his head solemnly. "Jest outside the winders, that's close enough."

The boys exited by the back door after a quick look which showed the coast to be clear. They chose a route behind the warehouse next door to come up under a high, double-hung window set in the brick wall of Cy Kibbe's Feed and Grain Depot. Cautiously, they stole a quick look inside. They knew all the men sitting at the long table. Breathless, they listened:

"New Orchard ain't much, maybe," the plump, fussy, but hard-eyed little mayor, an ex-softrock miner, said dully to his colleagues sitting slumped in the mismatched chairs along the former banquet table salvaged from the Jake's Palace Hotel and only slightly charred on one leg by the fire which years ago had completed the destruction of the old frame resort to which few, alas, had ever resorted.

"Like I said, the Orchard ain't much," Kibbe continued, "but it's ours, and it's up to us to defend it."

"Defend it how, Cy?" someone called, a query seconded by a chorus of "yeah's," followed by muttering.

"Ain't got no army troops here, nor such as that," Cy conceded. "Got to do what we can our ownselfs."

A tall, rangy man with a bad complexion rose and said, "I say we put in a call to Sector, get a battle-wagon in here." He looked challengingly at Davis. "We got a right; we pay taxes same's anybody else."

"They'd never send it, Jason," a round-faced fellow named Cabot said, and thumped his pipe on a glass ashtray as if nailing the lid on the coffin of the idea.

"What we got to do," interjected Fred Frink, a small unshaven chap who tended to gobble rather than speak, "what we got to do, we got to put on a defense here'll get picked up on the SWIFT Network, get us some publicity; then we'll get them peace enforcers in here for sure."

"Put on a defense, Freddy?" the fat man echoed sarcastically. "What with?" He looked around for approval, rapped the ashtray again, and settled back like one who had done his duty.

"Got no weapons, nor such as that, nothing bigger'n a varmint gun," the mayor repeated aggrievedly, and looked at Frink.

"Got old Jonah," the whiskery man said and showed crooked teeth in a self-appreciative grin. "Might skeer 'em off," he added, netting snickers from along the table.

"Heard old Jonah can still kill anybody gets too close," Cabot muttered, and looked around defiantly, relieved to see that his comment had been ignored.

"Gentlemen," said Davis, who had been rapidly jotting notes, in a severe tone. He rose. "I must remind you that this is a serious matter, nothing to joke about. In less than ten hours from now, the Deng will have completed their off-loading and will be ready to advance in battle array from Deep Cut. Sector advises us to evacuate the town. We can expect no help from that quarter. Unless something effective is done at once, the Deng will have rolled over the settlement well before this time tomorrow." After a moment he added, "With reference to Mr. Frink's japes, I remind you that Unit JNA is the property of the War Monuments Commission, which I have the honor to represent." He sat, looking grim.

"Sure, sure, Mr. Davis, we know all that," the mayor

hastened to affirm with an ingratiating smile. "But what we gonna do?"

"Now, no offense, Mr. Davis, sir, and don't laugh, boys, but I got a idear," Frink put in quickly, in a furtive voice, as if he hoped he wasn't hearing himself.

"Treat it gentle, Freddy," the plump fellow said lazily, and mimed puffing at his empty pipe.

"Way I see it," Frink hurried on, stepping to the sketch map on the blackboard set up by the table. "They're in Deep Cut, like Mr. Davis said, and they got only the one way out. If we's to block the Cut—say about here—" he sketched quickly "—by Dry Run, they'd be bottled up."

"Just make 'em mad," the fat man commented. "Anyways, how are you going to block a canyon better'n a hundred yard wide, so's their big Yavacs can't climb out?"

"Easy part, Bub," Frink put in glibly. "We blast—got plenty smashite right here at Kibbe's. Plant it under the Rim, and the whole thing comes down. Time it right, we bury 'em."

"You got a battalion of Rangers volunteered to plant the charges?" Bub Peterson queried, looking around for the laugh; he was rewarded with compliant smirks.

Davis rose, less casually this time. "I say again," he started in a heavy tone. "As planetary representative of Concordiat authority, I will tolerate no ill-advised jocularity. I am obliged to report the developing position to Sector, and I have no intention of relaying assays at humor. Now, Mr. Frink's suggestion regarding blasting the cliff is not without merit. The method of accomplishment, as Mr. Peterson has so facetiously pointed out, is the problem." He resumed his seat, jotted again.

"Now, boys," Kibbe said soothingly into the silence that followed the pronouncement of officialdom, "boys, like Freddy said, I got over two hundred pound o' smashite here in my lock-up. Enough to blast half the Rim down into the Cut. Got detonators, got warr, even got the radio gear to set her off long-range. Need a dozen good men to pack everything up along the ridge. It'll be my privilege, o' course, to donate the stuff till Sector can get around to settlin' up."

"Where you going to get twelve fellas can climb the

ridge totin' a hundred pound o' gear?" Bob inquired as if
thoughtfully. "Let's see, there's Tom's boy Ted, likes to
climb, and old Joe Peters, they say used to be a pretty fair
climber—"

"Say, just a minute," Fred blurted. "Mr. Davis, I heard
one time old Jonah's still got some charge on his plates;
never had his core burned back in Ought-Six when the
gubment was tryna pick up all the pieces after the Peace.
So . . ." Fred's strained voice trailed off. He looked uncer-
tainly along the table and sat down abruptly.

"Durn fools," a hoarse voice said immediately behind
the two boys, who first went rigid, then turned to bolt.
Their way was blocked by a forlorn-looking figure clad in
patched overalls who stood weaving, bleary-eyed and smelling strongly of Doc Wilski's home brew.

"Guess I know what I seen," the intruder went on.
"Wait a minute, boys. I ain't going to bother you none.
You're young McClusky, ain't you? And you're Bill Dubose's
boy. What you doing out of school? Ne'mind. I guess
you're in the right place to get a education right now.
Lissen them know-alls funning each other about old Jonah.
Whatta they know? Nuthin. Let me get up there." He
groped unsteadily between the boys to tilt an ear toward
the grimy window.

"Can't hear as good as you young fellas," he said. "They
said anything except it's true, and kidding around?"

"Naw sir," Mick replied, leaning away from the old
fellow's goaty aroma.

"Sure, I'm hung over to here," Henry conceded. "But
I'm not drunk no more. Wisht I was."

"Yessir, Mr. Henry," Dub said respectfully.

"Just 'Henry,'" Henry corrected. "I ain't one o' them
Misters. Now, boys, what we going to do about this situa-
tion? Come on, I'll show you where I seen the spodder.
Won't miss nothing here. They'll set and jaw is all."

Mick hung back. "You mean them things is running
loose, around here?" he challenged, looking along the
narrow alley as if to detect an invading alien.

"What I tole old Marshal," Henry confirmed. "Come
on. Ain't far. Seen the sucker sneaking through the brush

jest west o' Jed Lightner's store yonder. In that patch o' brush, by the fault. Just seen the one and skedaddled. Must be more of 'em. Let's find out what them suckers is up to."

"What do they look like, sir?" Dub asked timidly.

"Oh, kinda like reglar spodders, boy," Henry explained as he led the way along the narrow alley toward the street. "Got four skinny legs each side," he continued, after peering out to see that the coast was clear, "move quicklike; sorta round, hairy body, couldn't see too good on account of he was wearing a uniform, all straps and bangles and sech as that. Carried a rifle or something like in the front legs—arms, I guess you'd call 'em; got big eye-goggles on, shiny helmet-thing covered his whole head and what you'd call his shoulders. Not much bigger'n a small *ghoti;* 'bout so high. Come on." Henry indicated a terrier-sized creature, as he stepped out and started down the deserted street.

"Never seen a *ghoti,*" Dub said, following the old man.

"No, used to be a lot of 'em hereabouts," Henry acceded. "Never bothered the crops, o' course; can't eat Terry plants. But they trampled the corn to get at the yelloweed used to grow good where the ground was cultivated, between rows-like. So they been extink now for some years. Like I said, 'bout so high. A spodder's got brains, got them fancy guns, can blow a hole right through a feller, but don't worry. We won't let 'em see us."

The boys looked doubtfully at each other, but as Henry scuttled away toward the street, they followed.

"Pa finds out, I'll catch it," Dub said solemnly. "You, too," he added.

"Not if we come back and report to Marshal what they're up to and all," Mick rejoined.

Although Main Street was deserted except for two men disputing, with gestures, in front of the pictonews office, and a few women moving aimlessly in the market at the south end of the street, Henry went furtively along, close to the building-fronts, and the boys followed. The old man cut across to the west side of the avenue and disappeared into the narrow alley beside the opera house-cum-cathedral. His two followers hurried after him, emerging on the

unused alleyway which ran behind the buildings, thence
east-west across dry clods toward a stand of tall Terran-
import Australian pines and squat scrub oak, mixed with
native *yim* trees even taller and more feathery than the
alien conifers. There, in a shallow fold, Henry paused, and
after cautioning the boys to silence told them: "Got to go
easy now. Seen him about fifty yard yonder." He pointed
to the deepest shadows ahead.

"Way I figger, critter had to get here someways: got to
be a vessel o' some sort the suckers soft-landed in the
night, prolly over north o' town in the hills. We gotta be
careful not to get between the spodder and his base.
Come on."

Mick forged ahead, pushing into a clump of dry yelloweed.

"Slow down, boy," Henry warned. "Don't want to spook
the sucker."

"What were you doing out here, anyway?" Mick demanded, falling back.

"Hadda pump ship," the old fellow replied shortly.
"Thought I seen something, and come on over and
checked." He set out toward the trees.

"How much further we going?" Mick asked.

"Not far," Henry grunted. "Hold it, boys. Duck."

Obeying his own command, he dropped into a crouch.
The boys followed suit, looking around eagerly.

"Lower," Henry said, motioning before he went flat.
Dub promptly obeyed, while Mick took his time. A moment later, he hissed. "Looky yonder!"

"He seen you, boy, dammit!" Henry charged. "Keep
your knot-head down and freeze. The suckers can see like
a yit-bug."

Hugging the powder-surfaced, hard-rutted, weed-thick
ground, Mick peered through the screen of dry stalks,
probing the dark recesses of the clump of trees twenty feet
from him. Something stirred in the darkness, and sunlight
glinted for an instant on something which moved. Then a
harsh voice croaked something unintelligible. Off to Mick's
left, Henry came to his feet with a yell; a pale beam
lanced from the thicket and the old fellow stumbled and
went down hard.

"Run, boys!" he called in a strangled yell.

Dub saw something small, ovoid and dark-glittering burst from the thicket, darting on twinkling spike-like legs. It dashed directly to where Mick hugged the ground, caught the boy by the collar as he tried to rise, threw him down and did something swiftly elaborate, then darted to where Henry was struggling to get to his feet. Mick lay where the alien had left him. With a deft motion, the creature felled Henry again and spun to pursue Dub, now halfway to the shelter of the nearest outbuildings behind the street-front structures. When the boy reached the shelter of a shed behind the barber shop, the Deng broke off its pursuit and returned to take up a spot close to its prisoners.

Emerging from his office in the former theatre now serving as public school, Doug Crawford nearly collided with Dub who, sobbing, had been at the point of knocking on the principal's door.

"Terrence!" Crawford exclaimed, grabbing the little fellow's arm. "Whatever are you doing in the street during class? I assure you your absence was duly noted——" He broke off as the import of the gasping child's words penetrated his ritual indignation.

"—got Mick. Got old Henry, too. Spodders! I seen 'em."

"You *saw* them, Terrence," Crawford rebuked, then knelt and pulled the lad's hands away from his tear-wet face. "It's all right, Dub," he said soothingly. "Spiders won't hurt anyone; they're harmless arachnids. And just where is Gerald?"

Dub twisted in Crawford's comforting grip to point across the street, apparently indicating a faded store-front.

"Yonder," Dub wailed. "I run. Old Henry told me to, and I was awful scared, too, but now we got to do something! It's got Mick!"

"You mean in Lightner's store?" Crawford queried, puzzled. He rose while holding the sobbing boy's wet fist in a firm grip.

"No—out back—over by the woods," Dub wailed. "Got to hurry up, before that spodder does something terrible to Henry . . . and Mick."

"Some of the spiders that we have here on our world

can give mild stings, rarely poisonus," Crawford attempted
to reason with the lad. "I don't understand all this excitement about a little old spider. Most are completely harmless; descended from fruit-eaters inadvertently brought in
by the early settlers. Buck up, Dub! What's this all about?"

"Not spiders," Dub tried frantically to explain. "Real
spodders; them big ones, like in the war. I saw one. Right
over there!" He wilted in tears of frustration.

"You're saying you saw a Deng trooper here?" Crawford echoed, his tone incredulous. "You mean a dead one,
a corpse, just bones, perhaps, a casualty, possibly, who
hid in the fault and died there, two hundred and ten years
ago. Well, if so, I can understand your being upset. But it
can't hurt you—or anyone. Now, come along, show me."
He urged the boy toward the street.

"Got to get a gun, Mr. Crawford," Dub protested. "*It's*
got one. Shot old Henry, but he ain't dead, just kinda
can't move good, is all. You got to get some more men,
Mr. Crawford! Hurry!" Dub pulled away and ran into the
adjacent alley. Crawford took a step after him, then let
him go.

The school teacher looked around as the town marshal
and the mayor hailed him, coming up puffing as from a
brisk run.

"Doug, boy, we missed you at the Council," Marlowe
blurted.

"You didn't miss nothing," the other contributed. "Lotta
talk, no ideas."

"I didn't hear about it, Mr. Mayor," Crawford replied,
puzzled. "Special meeting, eh? What's the occasion?" He
looked after Dub, already a hundred yards distant and
running hard. Crawford wondered idly what was really
troubling the little fellow.

"You ain't heard, Crawford?" Marshal Marlowe asked
eagerly. "Lissen: no rumor, neither. Davis got it confirmed with Sector. It's a fact! Durn spodders is here—!"

"I don't understand, Marshal," Crawford interrupted
the excited officer's outburst. Then, as the significance of
the word "spodders" struck him, he side-stepped the two
men and ran the way Dub had gone.

"Looks like Doug took the news none too good, Hick,"

Kibbe commented, rasping at his shiny scalp with a well-gnawed fingernail.

"Never thought the boy'd go to pieces thataway," Hick agreed, wagging his head sadly. "And him a educated man, too," he added. "Countin' on Doug to help us figger what to do."

Crawford overtook Dub as the latter slid to a halt at the rear corner of the relatively vivid blue museum. The man caught the boy's arm as he attempted to lunge past.

"Hold on, Terrence," Crawford said as gently as his out-of-breath condition allowed. "I'm sorry I didn't listen carefully, but now I think I understand. You say it wounded Mr. Henry and Mick too. Where are they?"

"Yonder in the field out back of Lightner's. Don't know as they're what you call wounded, didn't see no blood. Jest kind of knocked-out, like."

"Come on, Terrence." Crawford urged the boy back toward the street. In silence they crossed the still-deserted avenue, traversed the alley, and emerged into the littered alley, the open field beyond.

"Mr. Crawford!" Dub almost yelped. "I only see old Henry—can't see Mick. He's gone!"

"*Mister* Henry," Crawford rebuked automatically. "I don't see anyone—only a heap of rubbish, perhaps. Are you sure—"

"Sure I'm sure, Mr. Crawford. Come on." Dub started across the field at a run; Crawford followed, less frantically.

"Slow down, Dub," Crawford called and fell back to a walk. Dub waited, scanning the space ahead, allowed Crawford to overtake him. He grabbed the man's hand.

"He was right yonder, just past old Henry," he wailed.

"Easy, Dub." Crawford tried to soothe the clearly terrified lad. "We'll find him." In silence they made their way across to where Henry lay, looking like a heap of discarded rags. The old fellow opened bleary eyes as Crawford knelt beside him.

"Better head for cover," Henry said blurrily. "Durn thing's still around here somewhere. More of 'em, too. Seen 'em hopping around 'mongst the trees yonder; got a better view down here at ground level, see under the foliage. They're busy over there, doin' something. I'm all right, just kind of tingle like a hit elbow all over. Durn spodder zapped me—with a zond-projector, I'd say. Better see to young McClusky." His voice faded off into a snore. Crawford rose briskly.

"He'll be all right," he told Dub. "I wonder what he meant about a zond projector. Probably just raving. But where—?"

"Look!" Dub blurted, pointing. Now Crawford saw motion at the edge of the thicket. He halted, uncertain.

"It's the spodder! It's got Mick!" Dub wailed. "Come on!" He started off at a run, but Crawford caught his arm. "Wait here," he ordered the boy, and ran across to where the limp form of young McClusky was being tugged with difficulty through the thickening bush, pulled by something blue-black, shiny and ovoid, with multiple jointed limbs, one of which aimed what was clearly a weapon. Crawford promptly stepped in and delivered a full-swing kick which sent the pistol-like object flying. Then he stooped to grab Mick's arm, set himself and jerked the boy free of the alien's grip. Mick stirred, muttered something. Crawford dragged him back as the chastened Deng scuttled away.

"I'm sorry I doubted you, Terrence," Crawford said to Dub as the boy met him, looking up searchingly to catch his eye.

"Never knew you was a hero and all, Mr. Crawford," Dub said solemnly.

"Nonsense," Crawford said shortly. "I simply did what anyone would do."

"I seen you kick his gun," Dub said firmly, now looking fearfully at Mick's limp form.

" 'Saw,' " Crawford corrected absently.

"Is he kilt, Mr. Crawford?" Dub quavered.

"Hell, no," Mick spoke up.

"Don't curse, Gerald," Crawford said, "But are you all right?"

As Crawford and Dub watched anxiously, Mick rolled over and twisted to look back over his shoulder toward them.

"Oh, hi, Mr. Crawford," he said strongly. "Glad it's you. Durn thing hit me and run off. Guess I was out of it for a while. Woke up, jest now, when it was pulling at me; seen 'em over in the scrub yonder. Must be a couple dozen of 'em. Better go back and warn the mayor and all. Must be getting ready to 'tack the town." The boy lay back and breathed hard. Crawford examined him swiftly, saw no signs of injury. "Can you move your legs?" he asked.

"Sure. Guess so," Mick answered promptly, kicking his legs in demonstration. "Just feel kinder sick-like." He paused to gag.

"Apparently its orders are to take prisoners, Crawford said. "I understand Mr. Davis has received confirmation that the Deng have, in fact, carried out a hostile landing near the town."

Mick nodded. "Yeah, Mr. Crawford; me and Dub heard."

"Dub and I," Crawford corrected. "How did you hear?"

"We were there," Mick told him. "Heard Davis read off the message he got on the SWIFT."

"You should have come to me at once," Crawford rebuked him mildly. "But never mind that. See if you can stand." He helped the boy get to his feet; he rose awkwardly, but quickly enough. Mick took a few steps. "I'm O.K.," he stated. "What we going to do now?"

"I'd better reconnoiter," Crawford said shortly, staring toward the thicket. "You boys help Mr. Henry; we'll get him to Doctor Grundwall. He seems weak; he's older than you, Mick."

"Better get down low so's to see under the branches," Mick suggested. He crouched and peered toward the woods. "Yep," he said, "I can still see 'em, only a couple of 'em moving around now, but they got some kinda thing set up over there. Might be a gun to shoot at the town."

Crawford went to one knee and stared hard, caught a flicker of movement, then made out a tripod arrangement perched among the tree trunks.

"They're up to something," he agreed, rising.

"All right, let's go back and report," he ordered. Mick and Dub went to Henry and in a moment the old fellow was on his feet, wobbly and cursing steadily, but able to walk. Crawford joined them and all four headed back the way they had come.

"You boys have done well," Crawford told them. "Now we'll have to inform Mayor Kibbe of this, see what can be done."

After turning Henry over to old Doctor Grundwall at his cramped office over the hardware store, Crawford shepherded the lads along to the feed store, where the mayor met them at the door, Marshal Marlowe behind him.

"Mr. Crawford, sir," Kibbe said solemnly, with a disapproving glance at the two untidy urchins, "I'd value your opinions, as an educated man, sir, as to how we should best deal with this, ah, curious situation which has done arose here so sudden, taking us all by surprise—"

"Yes, sir, Mr. Mayor," Crawford cut in on the windy rhetoric, suppressing the impulse to correct the mangled grammar and syntax. "Mr. Henry, the boys and I have just observed what I judge to be signs of imminent hostile action to be directed against the town," he told the two officials. "What appears to be a small scouting force has taken up a position in the woods west of town. They seem to be preparing some sort of apparatus—a weapon, I think we can assume—"

"What are you grownups going to do when them spodders comes?" Dub inquired.

" 'Those spodders,' Terrence," Crawford corrected, " 'Come.' "

"Hold on, Doug," Hick Marlowe cut in. "Boy's right. We gotta *do* something, and in a hurry. Durn spodders is setting up cannons like you say right here on the edge of town."

"It may well be a party of harmless picknickers," Kibbe said quickly. "After all, what evidence have we? The testimony of two children and the town derelict?"

"*I* was there, too, Mr. Mayor," Crawford said in a challenging tone. "And *any* incursion here on Spivey's is contrary to treaty. We have to mobilize what strength we've got."

"And just what strength is that, sir?" Kibbe inquired skeptically. "There are forty-one able-bodied men here in the Orchard, no more."

"Then we'd better get moving," Crawford stated as if Kibbe had agreed with him.

"Doing what?" Kibbe came back angrily.

"Gennelmen, gennelmen," the marshal spoke up in a hearty tone. "Now, no use in flying off the handle here, fellows; what we got to do is, we got to think this thing through."

While his elders wrangled, Mick eased away unnoticed, hurried across the dusty street and went along to the end of the block, turned in at Ed Pratt's ramshackle woodyard, crossed between the stacks of rough-cut grayish-green slab-wood planks, and dropped to all fours to advance in traditional Wild Injun style toward the straggling southern end of the thicket. From this angle he had a clear view of a steady stream of quick-moving aliens coming up in a long curve from the east, laden with bulky burdens. As he came closer, he could see the apparatus on the tripod he had glimpsed earlier. As he became accustomed to the difficult conditions of seeing, the boy was able to make out ranks of spidery aliens arrayed in depth behind the cryptic apparatus, forming a wedge aimed at the town. He could also distinguish, approaching in the distance, a convoy of armored vehicles, advancing on jointed suspensions, not unlike the legs of the Deng themselves.

"Huh, wouldn't make a wart on old Jonah," Mick commented silently. Then he made his way back to Main Street and sought out Mr. Crawford, found him still in the mayor's office, now joined by half a dozen village elders, all talking at once.

". . . call out the milishy!" one yelled.

". . . ain't even drilled in a year," another commented.

After listening with open mouths to the boy's report, and properly rebuking him for meddling in adult affairs, the assembled leaders called for suggestions. Mr. Davis spoke up.

"This is clearly a matter for Sector to handle," the government man informed the local sachems. He rose. "And I'd best get a message off at once." Amid a hubbub of conjectures he took his leave. Mick and Dub slipped out inobtrusively and followed him.

With the confidence born of experience, the boys made

for the rear of the museum, slipped inside, and were waiting out of sight when Davis entered his office. The phone rang; Davis replied with an impatient "Yes!"

"Very well," he responded to someone at the other end. "I'll be along presently. I'm quite aware I'm adjutant to Colonel Boone—though I can't see what good calling out the militia will do. We're not equipped to oppose a blitzkreig."

The boys followed the sounds of Davis' actions as he recorded the call, cut the connection, and uncovered and switched on the SWIFT gear. Again the lights dimmed momentarily.

Now once more I feel the flow of healing energies washing over me. I attune my receptors and experience the resurgence of my vitality as the charge builds past minimal to low operational level. Instantly I become aware of radiation in the W-range employed by Deng combat equipment. The Enemy is near at hand. No wonder my commander has returned to restore me to service-readiness. I fine-tune my surveillance grids and pinpoint the Enemy positions: a small detachment at 200 yards on an azimuth of 271, and a larger force maneuvering one half-mile distant on a bearing of 045. I can detect no indication of any of our equipment in operation within my radius of perception. Indeed, all is not well; am I to wait here, immobilized, while the Enemy operates unhindered? But of course my commander has matters well in hand. He is holding me in reserve until the correct moment for action. Still, I am uneasy. They are too close. Act, my commander! When will you act?

Standing close to the old machine, his ears alert for the sounds from the adjacent office, Dub started as he heard a deep-seated clatter from inside the great bulk of metal.

Dub gripped Mick's arm. "Didja hear that, Mick?" he hissed urgently. "Sounded like old Johnny made some kinda noise again."

"All I heard was Davis telling somebody named Relay Five that old Pud Boone is all set to play soldiers with, he says, 'a sizable Deng task force,' is what he said, 'poised,' he says, 'for attack,' says they better 'act fast to avert a tragedy.' Sounds like we won't get no big Navy ship in here to help out, like he figgered."

"It done it again," Dub told Mick, even as the glare-strips in the ceiling far above dimmed to a faint greenish glow. The boy stepped back and this time he was sure: the Bolo had moved.

"M-Mick, looky," he stammered. "It moved!"

"Naw, just the light got dim," Mick explained almost patiently. "Makes the shadders move." But he eased back.

"Mick, if it's anything we done, we'll catch it for sure!"

"Even if we did, who's gonna find out?" The older boy dismissed Dub's fears.

Then, with an undeniable groan of stiff machinery, the Bolo advanced a foot, crushing the white-painted curbing.

"We better go tell old Davis 'bout Johnny," Dub whispered.

"You mean 'Jonah,' " Mick corrected. "And when he arrests you for trespassin', what you going to do?"

"Don't know," Dub replied doggedly, "but I'm going to go anyway," he crept away, shaking off Mick's attempt to restrain him.

Mick followed, protesting, as the small boy ran along the partition to the forbidden office door, and without pausing, burst in. Davis, seated at the SWIFT console was staring at him in amazement.

"Mr. Davis!" the boy yelled. "You gotta do something! We was jest looking at old Johnny, and he moved! We didn't do nothing, honest!" By this time Dub was at Davis' side, clutching at the government man's arm. Patiently Davis pried off the grubby child's tear-wet fingers.

"You know you've been a very bad boy," he said with-out heat, in the lull as Dub stifled his sobs. "But I'm sure no harm is done. Come along now; show me what's got you so upset." He rose, a tall and remote authority figure in the tear-blurred eyes of the eight-year-old, took the damp hand and led the boy toward the door, where Mick had appeared abruptly, less excited than Dub, but clearly as agitated as his big-boy self-image would allow.

"We didn't do nothing, Mr. Davis," he said doggedly, not meeting the man's eye. "The back door was open and we come in to look at old Jonah, and it made some kinda noise, and old Dub run. That's all's to it."

"We'll have a look, Mickey," Davis said gruffly. "You *are* young McClusky; they *do* call you Mickey, eh?"

"Mick, sir," young McClusky corrected. He fell in behind the man as they returned to stand before the huge, now-silent war machine. Davis' eye went at once to the crushed concrete curbing.

"Here," he said sharply. "How the devil—excuse me, boys, how did this happen? It *must* have moved forward at least a few inches," he mused aloud. "How in the world . . ." Abruptly, the faint light winked up to its normal level of wan brilliance. Simultaneously the Bolo emitted a faint, though distinct, humming sound.

Dub went directly across to the formidable but somehow pathetic old war machine. He reached up to pat the curve of the pressure hull comfortingly.

"Wish I could tell you all about what's happening, Johnny," he murmured soothingly. "But I guess you couldn't hear me."

"I hear you very well, my commander," a constructed voice said clearly, at which Dub jumped back and peered up into the darkness.

"Who's there?" he asked in a small voice, suddenly appalled by his own foolishness in trespassing here.

"My commander," the words came distinctly from the machine. "I await your orders."

"Good Lord!" Davis exclaimed, staring at the boy. "Dub, it thinks you're its Commanding Officer! And—did you notice the lights? They dim whenever the SWIFT node generator is switched on. I forgot to switch it off, and after sixty seconds with no input, it switched off spontaneously. And—as for the Bolo's restored energy—the SWIFT generator produces a flood of waste energy, mostly in the low ultra-violet—the so-called Y-band, precisely the frequencies which the psychotronic circuitry is designed to accept. Only at an efficiency of some thirty-five percent, it's true; but the flood of radiant energy at this close range is quite sufficient to effect some degree of recharge." Davis paused, looking thoughtfully at the boys.

"Wait here a minute," Davis said to Dub. "Whatever

you do, don't say anything the machine could interpret as a command." He skirted the Bolo and headed for his office at a trot. A moment later the lights dimmed, almost went dark.

"Excellent, my commander," the machine voice said at once. "I am now accepting charge at optimum rate."

The two boys hung back, awed in spite of themselves at the understanding of what was happening.

"If it starts moving around, we'll get squashed for sure," Mick said, and pressed himself back against the wall.

"Johnny ain't going to squash *us*," Dub objected. "He's going to go out and squash them spodders—soon's I tell him to," he added hastily.

After some minutes, Davis returned. "That ought to do it," he panted, out of breath. "Now," he went on, taking Dub's hand, "this is a most unusual situation, but it may be for the best, after all. We'd better go see the mayor, lad. Meanwhile, tell Unit JNA to stand fast, until you call.

"Dub," he said seriously, catching the boy's still-damp eye—"a Bolo is programmed to 'imprint,' as it's called, on the first person who enters its command zone and says some special code word—and it seems like that's what you did; so, like it or not, the machine will do your bidding, and none other's."

"Bet it'll do what I say, too," Mick said, stepping in close to the machine. "I was here, too, jest as much as him." He faced the Bolo. "Now, you back up to where you was before. Right now," he added. All three persons present watched closely. There was no response whatever.

"I didn't mean no—any harm," Dub declared firmly.

"Unit JNA of the Line, reporting low energy reserves," the echoic voice spoke again. This time Dub stood his ground.

"Johnny—it's *you* talking to me," he said in wonderment. "I jest never knew you could talk."

"I await your instructions, sir," the calm voice said.

"O.K., Johnny," Dub spoke up. "Now, you better get ready to go. The spodders is back, and about to start the war up again."

"I am ready, my commander," the constructed voice

replied promptly. "Request permission to file a voluntary situation report."

"You're asking *me* for permission?" the boy's tone was one of incredulity. "Sure, go ahead," he added.

"I must report my energy reserve at fifty percent of operational optimum. I must further report that a hostile force is in position some two thousand yards distant," the Bolo announced flatly. "A smaller force is near at hand, but I compute that it is merely diversionary."

"Yeah, me and Mick seen 'em," Dub responded eagerly. "And Mr. Davis says them militia is jest going to get theirselfs kilt. Johnny—you got to do something. If all the men get kilt—Pa's one of 'em too—that'd be terrible! I'm scared."

The dim lights far above flickered, almost winked out, then steadied at a wan glow.

"Reporting on charge," the machine-voice said. "I compute that I will be at full operational status in one point one-seven seconds. I so report. Now indeed am I ready, my commander."

A moment passed before the meaning of the words penetrated. Then Dub, pressed close to the comforting bulk of the machine dubbed *Horrendous* by friend and foe alike, said urgently, "Johnny, we got to *do* something—now."

Dub felt a minute tremor from deep within the immense fighting machine, and jumped back as, with a muted rumble, the vast bulk . . . moved. The boy stared in wonderment, half exultation and half panic, as the Bolo eased forward, paused momentarily at the partition, then proceeded, pushing the barrier ahead until it toppled with a *crash!* and was trampled under the mighty tracks. Glass cases collapsed in splinters as the Bolo moved inexorably, angling left now, then pivoting in a tight turn so that now it faced the front of the building. Without hesitation, it proceeded. Dub watched in horrified fascination as the high wall bowed, letting in wedges of dusty light, then burst outward. Dub and Mick ran from the building and up the dusty street toward the crowd in front of Kibbe's Feed Depot.

The New Orchard Defense Force (First Fencibles) was drawn up in two ragged ranks, forty-three in number, including fourteen-year-old Ted Plunkett, seventy-eight-year-old Joseph Peters, and Mildred Fench, thirty-seven, standing in for her husband Tod, indisposed with a touch of an old malaria.

Chester (Pud) Boone, Colonel, CTVR, awkward in his tight-fitting uniform and reeking of bromoform, took up a position some twenty feet in front of the first rank, facing Private Tim Peltier, a plump young fellow in dung-stained coveralls.

" 'Smatter, Timmy, forget your pitch fork?" Pud essayed comfortably. "Let's jest move off smart, now," he went on in the sober tones of command. "Round back, for issue of weapons."

"As you were," a strange voice cut authoritatively across the hubbub as the Fencibles executed an approximate about-face and began to straggle off along the rutted street. The troops halted, those behind colliding with those before, and all heads turned to seek the source of the order. Colonel Boone, bridling, strode over to intercept the clean-shaven old man who had countermanded his instructions. He stared long at the seamed face and into the pale blue eyes, only slightly bloodshot; surveyed the clean but ill-fitting pajama-like garment the newcomer wore; his examination ended with the bare feet prominent below the frayed pants-cuff.

"Henry?" he inquired in a tone of total incredulity. "What call you got to go interfering with serious business? Now, you just go 'bout your business, Henry; we got a job o' work ahead of us here, got no time for fooling."

"Don't be a damned fool, Colonel," Henry responded firmly. "All you'll do is get these fellows killed. Those are Deng regulars out there, and there's armor coming up. You heard young McClusky's report. Now, dismiss this gang and let's get busy."

"By what right—" Boone started, but was cut off by the old fellow's surprising sharp reply.

"Used to be in the service; Marines, to be exact," Henry told the cowed reservist.

In the street, all heads turned as one toward the sudden *screech!* of tearing metal from the direction of the museum, and all eyes stared in disbelief as the snouts of the twin infinite repeaters thrust out through collapsing blue panels into daylight. They gazed, transfixed, as the vast machine emerged, shouldering the scattered façade aside to advance with the ponderous dignity of an irresistible force to the street, where it paused as if to orient itself while the remains of the museum collapsed gently behind it. Davis exited through the dust at a dead run, his corner office being the only portion of the structure not to fall.

"Here, what in damnation's going on?" Colonel Boone yelled.

"Stand fast," old Henry's voice cut across the cacophony of astonishment. "Looks like she's come out of retirement. I don't know how, but the timing is good!"

"Old Jonah'll take care of them spodders!" a middle-aged corporal shouted. "Three loud ones for old Jonah! Yippee!"

"At ease," Henry barked. "Look out there, Colonel," he advised Boone. "Better get your troops out of the street."

"Sure, Henry, I was jest . . ." the reservist faltered.

"Fall out!" Henry shouted over the din. "Form up in front of Lightner's!"

The bewildered Fencibles, grateful for authoritive guidance, broke up into a dozen small groups and headed across the street, all talking at once, their voices drowned out by rumbling as the mighty Bolo's treads pulverized the hard-rutted street surface, moving past them with the irresistibility of a moon in its orbit.

"—going right after 'em!"

"—here, where's it—my store!"

"Damn thing's going the wrong way! Damn spodders is *thataway!*"

A man ran a few steps after the combat unit as it angled abruptly right and crossed the walkway to doze aside the building which stood in its path, one of the older warehouses, trampling the old boards flat while its owner danced and yelled in frustrated fury.

"Hey, you damfool! Not that way, over here!" Cy Kibbe shouted, his voice lost in the splintering of seasoned timber.

As the townsfolk watched in astonishment, the old machine laid its track of destruction through the warehouse, taking off the near corner of the adjacent structure, and continued out across the formerly tilled acreage, trailing a tangle of metal piping and conduit ripped from the flattened buildings.

"It's running away!" someone blurted, voicing the common thought.

"Well, boys, it looks like we're on our own after all," Boone yelled, his voice overloud in the comparative hush. "Let's form up in a column of ducks here and go roust them damn spodders!"

"Stand fast!" Henry's command rang out, bringing movement to a halt. He strode across to take up a position between Boone and his disordered command.

"The enemy has zond projectors, and they've set up a z-beamer. Do you have any idea what those energy weapons can do to you? Now, fall out and go about your business."

"Not while I'm colonel," Boone shouted. "I don't know who you think you are, tryna give the orders around here, but we ain't going to jest stand by while a bunch of spodders take our land!"

"Just a minute," Davis' cool voice cut in, as the government man stepped forward to confront Henry.

"You say you were a Marine, Mr. Henry. May I ask what your duties were in the Corps?"

"Sure," the old fellow replied promptly. "My duties was killing the enemy."

"I recall a case some twenty years ago," Davis said as if musing aloud. "It involved a much-decorated combat veteran who refused a direct order from the Council, and was cashiered." Davis glanced at Henry's face, set in an inscrutible expression.

"Wanted me to supervise burning out all our old combat veterns—combat units, I'm talking about," Henry said in an indignant tone. "Didn't need 'em anymore, the damned civilians figgered, so I was supposed to see they all had their cores melted down. Damned if I'd do it!" Henry spat past Davis' foot.

"His name, as I recall," Davis said imperturbably, "was Major General Thadeo Henry." He put out his hand. "I think all of us are glad now you got here in time to prevent the destruction of our old Jonah, General Henry."

Henry took the proffered hand briefly. "I was lucky on that one," he muttered. "I was just a 'misbegotten dog of a broken officer,' as Councilman Gracye put it, but the locals here were on my side. They run that demolition crew back where they came from. Good thing Spivey's is so far back in the boondocks; they never bothered with us after that. And now," he went on after a pause, "you're thinking a Bolo fighting machine has run off and deserted in the face of the enemy. Not bloody likely."

At that moment, a staccato series of detonations punctuated the hush that had followed Henry's astonishing statement. Through the gap where the Bolo had passed the machine was visible half a mile distant now, surrounded by smaller enemy Yavac units, three of which were on fire. The others were projecting dazzling energy beams which converged on the Bolo, stationary now like a hamstrung bison surrounded by wolves. As the townsfolk watched, the Bolo's forward turret traversed and abruptly spouted blue fire. A fourth Yavac exploded in flames.

"General Henry," Davis addressed the old man formally, "will you assume command for the duration of the emergency?"

Henry looked keenly at Boone and said, "Colonel, I trust you'll stay on and act as my adjutant." The reservist nodded awkwardly and stepped back.

"Sure I will," Henry told Davis firmly. "Now after old Jonah finishes with that bunch, he'll swing around and hit the advance party from the flank. Meantime, we lie low and don't confuse the issue."

"Right, General," Boone managed to gibber before turning with a yell to the disorganized crowd into which his command had dissolved.

"Ah, General," Davis put in diffidently. "Isn't there something constructive we could do to assist, rather than standing idly by, with all our hopes resting on an obsolete museum-piece?"

"The Deng have one serious failing, militarily, Mr. Davis," General Henry replied gravely.

"Inflexibility—the inability to adjust promptly to changing circumstances. They're excellent planners—and having once decided on a tactical approach they ride it down in flames, so to speak. You've noticed that the forces concentrating on the west, behind the screen of the thicket, have made no move to support the main strike force now under attack to the east. They've taken up a formation suited only to an assault on the village here; when Jonah takes them in the flank, they'll break and run, simply because they hadn't expected it. Just watch."

Through the gap the Bolo had flattened in passing, the great machine was still visible within the dust-and-smoke cloud raised by the action. Five enemy hulks now sat inert and smouldering, while seven more were maneuvering on random evasive tracks that steadily converged on the lone Bolo, pouring on their fire without pause.

I select another enemy unit as my next target. These class C Yavac scouts are no mean opponents; clearly considerable improvement has been made in their circuitry during the two centuries of my absence from the field. Their armor withstands all but a .9998-accurate direct hit on the turret juncture. My chosen target—the squad leader, I compute—is a bold fellow who darts in as if to torment me. I track, lock onto him, and fire a long burst from my repeaters, even as I detect the first indications of excessive energy drain. My only option is to attune my charging grid to the frequency of the Yavac main batteries and invite their fire, thus permitting the enemy to recharge my plates—at the risk of overload and burn-out. It is a risk I must take. I fire what I compute is my last full-gain bolt at the enemy unit, at the same time receiving a revivifying jolt of energies in the Y-band as I take direct hits from two Yavacs. I am grateful for the accuracy of their fire, as well as for the sagacity of my designers, who thus equipped me to turn the enemy's strength against him—so long as my defensive armor and circuitry can withstand the overload. I see the squad leader erupt in fire, and change targets to the most aggressive of his subordinates. He was a bold opponent. I shall so report to my commander, taking due note of the fallen enemy's ID markings.

"Looky there! He done blowed up another one!" Hick Marlowe cried, pointing to the exploding Yavac which was already the focus of all eyes. "Look at old Jonah go! Bet he'll pick 'em off one at a time now till he gets the last one. But . . ." Hick paused, squinting through the obscuring dust, "he sure is taking a pasting his ownself—but he can handle it, old Jonah can! He's starting to glow—must be hotter than Hell's hinges in there!"

"Can it stand up to that concentrated fire, General?" Davis asked the newly-appointed commander.

Henry nodded. "Up to a point," he muttered. "Depends on how much retrofit he got before they sent him out here. Now, this is top GUTS-information, Davis, but under the circumstances, I think you qualify as a 'Need to Know.' The new—or was new back in Ought-Four—defensive technology is to turn the enemy strength against him, by letting the Bolo absorb those hellish Y-rays, restructure them, and convert the energy into usable form to rebuild his own power reserve. But to do it he has to invite the enemy fire at close range—that's why he's sitting still—and take all the punishment that entails—if he can handle it without burnout. At best his 'pain' circuitry is under severe overload. Don't fool yourself, Davis. That's no fun, what Unit JNA is going through out there. Good boy! He took out another one, and now watch that fellow on the left, he's been getting pretty sassy, nipping in and out. My guess is he's next."

Standing on the porch of his ramshackle store with Freddy Frink, Mayor Kibbe wiped his broad brow and frowned. Even if the town survived this damn battle, things'd never be the same again. The last trickle of off-planet trade would die out if Spivey's became known as a battleground, where the Deng could hit anytime. Abruptly, he became aware of what Frink was saying:

"—be worth plenty—the right stuff at the right place, at the right time, Mr. Mayor. And you're the only one's got it. Shame to let it go to waste."

"What you talking about, Freddy?" Kibbe demanded impatiently. "Town's getting blowed apart practically, and you're worrying me about wasting something. Stray shot hits the town, whole thang's wasted—and you and me with it."

"Sure, Mr. Mayor, that's what I'm talking about," Frink came back eagerly. "Don't forget even if old Jonah runs these here spodders off, they's still the main party back in the Canyon. And Pud's idea was right: we can blast the Rim right down on 'em."

"How we going to do that?" Kibbe challenged. "We been all over that. Ain't no way to tote two hundredweight o' smashite up yonder onto the Rim."

"Old Jonah could do it, Cy," Frank urged. "Could swing out into the badlands and come up on the Cut from the northeast and get right in position. Got the old mining road comes down the face, you know."

"Bout halfway," Kibbe grunted. "He might get down far enough to set the charge, but how'd he get back up? No place to turn around."

"I betcha a thousand guck a kilo wouldn't be too much to expect," Frink suggested. "A hundred thousand, cash money—if we act quick."

"That's damn foolishness, Freddy," Kibbe countered. "You really think—a hundred thousand?"

"Minimum," Frink said firmly. "I guess you'd give a fellow ten percent got it all set up, eh, Mr. Mayor?"

"Old Jonah might not last out the day," Kibbe said more briskly. "Don't know where he got the recharge; he was drained dry before they built the museum around him, back in eighty-four. Can't last long out there." He half turned away.

"Wait a minute, Mr. Mayor," Frink said quickly. "Don't know what happened, but he's still going strong. He'll be back here pretty soon. All we got to do, we got to load that smashite in his cargo bay, wire it up fer remote control, and send him off. Works, we'll be heroes; don't work, makes no difference, we're finished here anyway. This way we got a kinder chance. But we got to move fast; don't want old Cabot to try to grab the credit. That's solid gold you got back in the shelves, Cy—*if* you use it right."

"Can't hurt none to try, I guess," Kibbe acknowledged, as if reluctantly. "Got to clear it with Davis and *General* Henry, too, I guess."

"Hah, some general," Frink sneered.

* * *

When Unit JNA had pounded the last of the dozen attacking Yavacs into silence, it moved past the burned-out hulks and directed its course to the west, bypassing the end of Main Street by a quarter mile, then just as the raptly observing townsfolk perched on roofs or peering from high windows had begun to address rhetorical questions to each other, it swung south and accelerated. At once fire arced from the north of the trees, where enemy implacements were concealed. The Bolo slowed and then halted to direct infilade fire into the crevasse, then resumed its advance, firing both main batteries rapidly now. A great gout of soil and shattered treetrunks erupted from mid-thicket. The bodies of Deng troopers were among the debris falling back to the ground.

"Smart, like I said," General Henry told Cy Kibbe, who had made his way up beside him. "He poured the fire into the zond-projector they had set up yonder, because he knew if he could boost it past critical level it'd blow, and take the heart out of 'em."

"Commendable, I'm sure, General," Kibbe commented. "But I'm afeared these niceties of military tactics are beyond me. Now, General—" Kibbe followed closely as Henry turned in at an alley to approach the scene of action more closely. "—me and some of the fellows are still quite concerned, General, about what we understand: that most of these dang Deng—" he broke off to catch his breath. "No levity intended, sir," he interjected hastily—"these infernal aliens, I meant to say—which remain at Big Cut, with offensive power quite intact!"

"As you said, Kibbe," Henry dismissed the plump civilian, "these are matters you know nothing about. I assure you I'm mindful that the enemy has not yet committed his main body. You may leave that to me." He walked into the field, watching as the Bolo closed on the now-gutted thicket, whence individual Deng troopers were departing on foot, while the few light Yavacs which had come up maneuvered in the partial screen of the burning woods to reform a blunt wedge, considerably hindered by the continuing fire from their lone antagonist. Then they, too, turned and fled, getting off a few scattered Parthian shots from their rear emplacements as they went. Unit JNA trampled unhindered through the splintered remains of the patch of trees, skirting the shallow gully at its center, and turned toward town. A ragged cheer went up as the huge machine rounded into Main Street and crossed the last few yards to halt before the clustered townsfolk. Davis thrust Dub forward.

People shrank back from the terrific heat radiating from the battle-scarred machine, if not from the terrifying aspect of its immense bulk, the fighting prowess of which had just been so vividly demonstrated before their eyes.

"Well done, Johnny," the boy said unsteadily. "You can rest now."

"Jest a dadburned minute here," Kibbe burst out, pushing his way to the fore. "I guess ain't no mission accomplished while the main bunch o' them spodders is still out to Big Cut, safe and sound, and planning their next move!"

Henry came up beside Dub and put his hand on the boy's shoulder. "Your protégé did well, Dub," he said. "But the mayor has a valid point."

"Johnny done enough," Dub said doggedly.

"More than could have been expected," Henry agreed.

"Jest a dang minute, here," Cy Kibbe yelled. "I guess maybe us local people got something to say about it!" He turned to face the bystanders crowding in. "How about it—Bub, Charlie, you, Ben—you going to stand here while a boy and a—a . . ." the momentum of his indignation expended, Kibbe's voice trailed off.

"A boy and 'a drunken derelict,' is I believe, the term you were searching for," Henry supplied. He, too, faced the curious crowd. "Any suggestions?" he inquired in a discouraging tone.

"Durn right," a thin voice piped up promptly. Whiskery Fred Frink stepped to the fore, his expression as determined as his weak chin allowed. "Mr. Cabot, here, come up with a good idear," he went on. "Said let's load up this here museum-piece with some o' Mayor's explosives, left over from the last mining boom, you know, petered out all of a sudden, and send him out and blow that cliff right down on top of them spodders." Frink folded his arms and looked over his narrow shoulder for approval. General Henry frowned thoughtfully.

"Johnny's done enough," Dub repeated, tugging at the former town drunk's sleeve. "Let the mayor and some o' them go blow up the spodders."

"I'm afraid that's not practical, Dub," the general said gently. "I agree with the mayor that there are not enough fit men in town to carry out the mission, which I'm inclined to agree is our only option, under the circumstances. It's Unit JNA's duty to go where he's needed."

"You, boy," Frink yapped. "Tell this overgrowed tractor to pull up over front of the Depot."

Dub went casually over to confront the whiskery little man. Carefully, he placed his thumbs in his ears and waggled his fingers. Then he extended his tongue to its full length, looking Frink in the eye until the little man stepped back and began to bluster.

"Me, too, Dub," General Henry said, and pushed the boy gently toward the machine. Dub went as close to the Bolo as the still-hot metal would allow. "Listen, Johnny," he said earnestly. "They want you to go up on top the Badlands and plant some kind o' bomb. Can you do it?"

There was a moment of rapt silence from the open-mouthed crowd before the reply came clearly:

"As you wish, my commander. I compute that my energy reserve is sufficient to the task, though I am not fully combat-ready."

"Ain't gonna be no combat," Frink piped up. "Jest get the stuff in position, is all."

"Better go over by Kibbe's," Dub addressed the machine reluctantly. At once the vast bulk backed, scattering townsfolk, pivoted, and advanced to the indicated position, dwarfing the big shed.

"Tell it to open up," Frink commanded. Dub nodded and passed the order along to the Bolo; immediately the aft cargo hatch opened to reveal the capacious storage space beneath.

At Frink's urging, with Kibbe fussily directing the volunteers to the rear storage loft, a human chain formed up, and in moments the first of the bright-yellow, one-pound packages of explosive was passed along the line, and tucked away in the far corner of the Bolo's cargo bin.

As the last of the explosive was handed down to Frink,

who had stationed himself inside the bin, stacking the smashite, Kibbe climbed up to peer inside cautiously before handing down a coil of waxy yellow wire, and a small black box marked DETONATOR. MARK XX.

"Got to rig it up fer remote control," he explained gratuitously to Henry, who was watching closely. "So's he can unload and back off before it goes up."

Half an hour later, while the entire population of New Orchard cheered, the battle-scarred machine once more set off across the plain toward the distant fault-line known as the Cliff. Dub stood with Henry, hoping that no one would notice the tears he felt trickling down his face.

"He'll be all right, son," Henry reassured the lad. "The route you passed on to him will take him well to the east, so that he'll come up on Big Cut directly above the enemy concentration."

"It ain't fair," Dub managed, furious at the break in his voice.

"It seems to be the only way," Henry told him. "There are lives at stake, Dub. Perhaps this will save them."

"Johnny's worth more'n the whole town," Dub came back defiantly.

"I can't dispute that," Henry said quietly. "But if all goes well, we'll save both, and soon Unit JNA will be back in his museum, once we rebuild it, with new battle honors to his credit. Believe me, this is as he wants it. Even if he should be ambushed, he'd rather go down fighting."

"He trusted me to look out for him," Dub insisted.

"There's nothing you could have done that would have pleased him more than ordering him into action," Henry said with finality. In silence, they watched the great silhouette dwindle until it was lost against the cliffs, misty with distance.

Once more I know the exultation of going on the offensive against a worthy foe. My orders, however, do not permit me to close with him, but rather to mount the heights and to blast the rock down on him. This, I compute, is indeed my final mission. I shall take care to execute it in a manner worthy of the Dinochrome Brigade.

*While the wisdom of this tactical approach is clear, it is
not so satisfying as would be a direct surprise attack.
Once at the Rim, I am to descend the cliff-face so far as is
possible, via the roadway blasted long ago for access to
certain mineral deposits exposed in the rockface. I am
weary after this morning's engagement, nearing the advanced depletion level, but I compute that I have enough
energy in reserve to carry out my mission. Beyond that, it
is not my duty to compute.*

Sitting at his desk, Cy Kibbe jumped in startlement
when General Henry spoke suddenly, behind him. "I
declare, Henry—I mean General," Kibbe babbled. "I never
knowed—never seen you come in to my office here. What
can I do for you, General, sir?"

"You can tell me more about this errand you've sent
Unit JNA off on. For example, how did you go about
selecting the precise point at which the machine is to set
the charges?"

Kibbe opened a drawer and took out a sheaf of papers
from which he extracted a handdrawn map labeled *Claim
District 33*, showing details of the unfinished road on the
cliff face. After Henry had glanced at it, Kibbe produced
glossy 8 x 10 photos showing broken rock, marked-up in
red crayon.

"Got no proper printouts, sir," he explained hastily.
"Jest these old pitchers and the sketchmap, made by my
pa years ago. Shows the road under construction," Kibbe
pointed to the top photo. "See, General, far as it goes, it's
plenty wide enough for the machine."

"I don't see how it's going to turn around on that goat
path," Henry commented, shuffling through the photos.
"You loaded two hundred pounds of Compound L-547.
That's enough to blow half the cliff off, but it has to be
placed just right."

"Right, sir," Kibbe agreed eagerly. "Right at the end o'
the track'll do it. I know my explosives, sir, used to be a
soft-rocker myself, up till the vein played out. My daddy
taught me. Lucky I had the smashite on hand; put good
money into stocking it, and been holding it all these
years."

"I'm sure the claim you put in to Budev will cover all that," Henry said shortly.

"Sir," Kibbe said in a more subdued tone, as he extracted another paper from the drawer. "If you'd be so kind, General, to sign this here emergency requisition form, so's to show I supplied the material needed for gubment business. . . ."

Henry looked at the document. "I suppose I can sign this," he acknowledged. "I saw the explosives loaded, looks legitimate to me." He took the stylus proffered by Kibbe and slashed an illegible signature in the space indicated.

"I understand you have an old observation station on the roof, for watching the mining work at the cliff," Henry said. "Let's go up and see how well we can monitor the Bolo's progress."

Kibbe agreed with alacrity, and led the way to the narrow stair which debouched on the tarred roof. He went across to a small hut, unlocked the door, and ushered the general into the stuffy interior crammed with old-fashioned electronic gear. He seated himself at the console and punched keys. A small screen lit up and flickered until Kibbe turned dials to steady an image of looming pinkish rock pitted with shallow cavities. "Blasted them test holes," he grunted. "Hadda abandon the work cause the formation was unstable, big mining engineer told Pa, condemned the claim—but that's just what we need, now!" Kibbe leaned back, grinning in satisfaction. "One good jolt, and the whole overburden'll come down. Now let's see can we get a line on the spodders down below the Cut." He twiddled knobs and the screen scanned down the rockface to the dry riverbed at the bottom, where the Deng had deployed their armor in battle array.

"Lordy," Kibbe whispered. "Got enough of 'em, ain't they, Generalsir?"

"Looks like a division, at least," Henry agreed. "They're perfectly placed for your purposes, Mr. Mayor, if nothing alerts them."

"I suppose their transports are farther north in the Cut," Henry said.

"That's right, Generalsir," Kibbe confirmed. "I been

keeping an eye on 'em up here ever since we heard where
they was at. Mighty handy, having this here spy gear."
Kibbe patted the panel before him. "Pa suspicioned there
was some dirty work going on at the claim, claim-jumpers
and the like; spent a pretty penny shipping all this gear in
and paid some experts to install it, placed the pick-up eyes
all over to give him good coverage. Yessir, a pretty penny."

"I'll confirm the use of your equipment when you file
your claim, Mr. Mayor," Henry said. "You'll make a nice
profit on it. Provided," he added, "your plan works."

"Gotta work," Kibbe said, grinning. He adjusted the set
again, and now it showed the approach to the cliff road,
with the Bolo coming up fast, trailing a dustcloud that was
visible now also through the lone window of the look-out
shed.

The two men watched as the machine slowed, scouted
the cliff-edge, then pivoted sharply, its prow dipping as it
entered the man-made cut. Kibbe dollied in, and they
watched the big machine move steadily down the rough-
surfaced road, which was barely wide enough for passage
by the Bolo.

"Close, but it's got room," Kibbe said. "Pa wasn't no
dummy when he had 'em cut that trail wide enough for
the heavy haulers."

"Very provident man, your father," Henry acknowledged. "I assume you'll include road-toll fees in your
claim."

"Got a right to," Kibbe asserted promptly.

"Indeed you have," Henry confirmed. "I won't dispute
your claim. A military man knows his rights, Mr. Mayor—
but he also knows his duty."

"Sure," Kibbe said. "Well, I guess I done my duty all
right, putting all my equipment and supplies at the disposal of the gubment and all—not to say nothing about the
time I put in on this. I'm a busy man, General, got the
store to run and the town, too, but I've taken the time off,
like now, to see to it the public's needs is took care of."

"Your public spirit amazes me," Henry said in a tone
which Kibbe was unable to interpret.

At that moment, the office door creaked and Kibbe turned
to greet Fred Frink, who hesitated, his eyes on Henry.

"Come right on in, Freddy," Kibbe said heartily. "You're just in time. Looky here." He leaned back to afford the newcomer an unimpeded view of the screen where the Bolo had halted at a barrier of straited rock.

"End o' the road," Kibbe commented. "Perfect spot to blast that cliff right down on the durn spodders."

Frink was holding a small plastic keybox in his hand. He looked from Henry to Kibbe, a worried expression on his unshaven face.

"Go ahead, Freddy," Kibbe urged, as he snapped switches on the panel. "All set," he added. "You're on the air. Go." As he turned to catch Frink's eye, the scene on the screen exploded into a fireball shrouded in whirling dust. The great slab of rock blocking the road seemed to jump, then fissured and fell apart, separating into a multitude of ground-car-sized chunks which seemed to move languidly downward before disintegrating into a chaotic scene of falling rock and spurting dust, in which the Bolo was lost to view. As the dust thinned, settling, nothing was visible but a vast pit in the shattered rock-face, heaped rocks, and a rapidly dissipating smoke-cloud.

"We done it!" Kibbe exulted, while Frink stared at the screen, wide-eyed.

"I see now why you weren't concerned about how the unit would turn around to withdraw," Henry said in an almost lazy tone. "It's buried under, I'd estimate, a few thousand tons of pulverized limestone. Not that it matters much, considering what the explosion did to its internal circuitry. Not even a Bolo can stand up unharmed to a blast of that magnitude actually within its war-hull."

"Cain't make a omelette without you break a few aigs," Kibbe said complacently, then busied himself at the panel. Again he scanned down the cliff-face, ending this time at a panorama of smoking rubble which filled the bottom of the Cut from wall to wall. Not a Yavac was to be seen.

"Don't reckon them spodders is going no place now, General," he commented complacently. Both men turned as Freddy uttered a yelp and turned and ran from the room, yelling the glad news. In moments, a mob-roar rose from the street below.

"Don't start celebrating just yet," General Henry said

quietly, his eyes on the screen. Kibbe glanced at him, swallowed the objection he had been about to utter, and followed the general's glance. On the screen, almost clear of obscuring dust, the blanket of broken rock at the bottom of the Cut could be seen to heave and bulge. Great rocks rolled aside as the iodine-colored snout of a Class One Yavac emerged; the machine's tracks gained purchase; the enemy fighting machine dozed its way out from its premature burial and manuvered on the broken surface of the drift of rock to take up its assigned position, by which time two more heavy units had joined it, while the rubble was heaving in another half-dozen spots where trapped units strove to burst free. Forming up in the deep wedge specified, Henry knew, by Deng battle regs, the salvaged machines moved off toward the south and the defenseless town.

"It appears we'll have to evacuate after all," Henry said quietly. "I shall ask Mr. Davis to get off an emergency message to Sector. I can assign a GUTS priority to it, and I think we should have help within perhaps thirty-six hours. I'm no longer on the Navy list, but I still know the old codes."

"That'd be Wednesday," Kibbe said, rising hastily. "Best they can do, General?"

"Considering the distance to the nearest installation capable of mounting a relief mission, thirty-six hours is mildly optimistic, Mr. Mayor. We'll just have to hold out somehow."

There was a sound of hurrying feet, and the door slammed wide as Dub arrived, flushed and panting.

"We seen the big dust-cloud, General Henry," he gasped out. "Is Johnny OK?"

Henry went to the boy and put a fatherly hand on his shoulder. "Johnny did his duty as a soldier, Dub," he said gently. "It's to be expected that there will be casualties."

"What's a casualty mean?" Dub demanded, looking up at the old man.

"It means old Jonah done his job and got himself kilt, as you might say, boy," Cy Kibbe said lazily. Dub went past him to stare at the screen.

"He's under that?" he asked fearfully.

"The grave will be properly marked, Dub," Henry reassured the lad. "His sacrifice will not go unnoticed."

"*They* done it," Dub charged, pointing at Kibbe and Frink, now cowering behind the mayor. "I ast Mr. Frink how Johnny was going to unload the smashite and put it in the right place, and he didn't even answer me." The boy began to cry, hiding his face.

"No call to take on, boy," Frink spoke up. "All I done was what I hadda do. Nobody'd blame me." He looked almost defiantly at Henry.

"You could of gone along and unloaded the stuff, instead of blowing Johnny up," Dub charged. "You didn't hafta go and kill him." He advanced on Frink, his fists clenched.

"Now boy, after all it's only a dang machine we're talking about," Kibbe put in, moving to block Dub's approach to Frink. "A machine doing what it was built to do. You can't expect a man to go out there and get himself kilt, too."

Dub turned away and went to the screen, on which could now be seen the slope of rubble, from the floor of the canyon to the aborted road far above, with the great black cavity of the blast site.

"Look!" Dub exclaimed, pointing. Beside the blast pit, rocks were shifting, thrust aside; small stones dribbled down the talus slope—and then the prow of the Bolo appeared, dozing its way out from under the heaped rock fragments, a gaping wound visible where its aft decking was ripped open.

"He's still alive!" Dub cried. "Come on, Johnny! You can do it!"

I am disoriented by the unexpected blast. Assessing the damage, I perceive that it was not a hit from enemy fire, but rather that the detonation originated in my cargo bin. Belatedly, I realize that I was loaded with explosives and dispatched on a suicide mission. I am deeply disturbed. The Code of the Warrior would require that my commander inform me fully of his intention. This smacks of treachery. Still, it is not for me to judge. Doubtless he did what was necessary. Yet I am grieved that my commander did not feel that he could confide in me. Did he imagine I would shirk my duty? I have suffered grievous damage, but my drive train at least is intact. I shall set aside .003 nanoseconds to carry out a complete self-assessment . . .

Happily, my hatch cover blew first, as designed, thus venting the greater part of the pressure harmlessly into the surrounding rock. My motor circuits are largely intact, though I have suffered serious loss of sensitivity in my sensory equipment. Still, if I can extricate myself from the entrapping rubble, I compute that I have yet sufficient energy—my Y grid having absorbed some two hundred mega-ergs from the blast and converted the simple kinetic force into usable C-energies—to extricate myself and report to base. I sense the overburden shifting as I apply pressure; now I emerge into sunlight. The way is clear before me. I descend the slope, taking care not to initiate an avalanche. It is clear that I will never again know my full potency, but I shall do what I can.

General Henry shouldered Freddy Frink aside and commandeered the chair before the remote view-screen in Kibbe's observation shed, now crowded with excited villagers, all talking at once, all anxious as to their impending fate.

". . . do it? Are they going to be able to climb out?"

". . . things come over that heap! Can you see them?"

Manning the small telescope mounted at a window and commanding a view of the terrain where the Yavacs would appear if they indeed succeeded in climbing clear of the fallen cliff's debris, Bud Tolliver maintained a running commentary.

"—see one of 'em—big fellow, lots bigger'n those little ones old Jonah tangled with. There's another one. They keep on coming. Blasting the cliff didn't do no good, it looks like. They're headed thisaway. Our museum-piece is way behind."

In a brief lull, Henry spoke up:

"Only the heavies apparently are able to dig out. Three, so far—and they appear to be sluggish. No doubt they suffered concussive damage at a minimum."

"Can I look?" Young Dub crowded in and Henry took the boy onto his lap.

"Where's Johnny?" the boy demanded, staring at the screen. "Hard to make out what's happening, Mr. —General Henry. You said he started downslope, but—"

"There he is," Henry cut in, pointing to a dust trail near the edge of the screen. "He's going to try to outflank them and beat them into the open."

"Think he can do it, sir?" Dub begged.

"He'll do his best," Henry reassured the boy. "It's his duty to return to base and report."

I win clear of the blast area, and by channeling all available energy to my drive train, I shall attempt to gain egress from the Cut in advance of the enemy units which I perceive have succeeded, like myself, in digging out. They, too, are sluggish and as they slow to maneuver around a major rock fragment, I steal a march and clear the Cut and am in the open. It is only a short dash now to base. Yet I am a fighting machine of the Concordiat, with some firepower capability remaining. Shall I withdraw in the face of the enemy?

"It's clear," General Henry said. "Incredible that a machine could withstand such a blast—treacherously planted within his hull—and still retain the ability to return to base—to say nothing of digging out from under thirty feet of rock."

"Did I hear you say something about treachery, Henry?" Kibbe demanded truculently. "I guess maybe the gubment won't see it that way. I guess it'll say I was a patriot, did what I could to save the town and maybe the whole durn planet."

"Dang right," Fred Frink chimed in. "How about it, Mr. Davis?" He sought out the eye of the government man in the crowd. "Are me and Cy traitors, or what?"

"The matter will be investigated, you may be sure, Fred," Davis replied coolly. "The matter of planting a bomb within the unit without authorization is questionable at best."

"Ha!" Frink cried. "Jest because some kid and a broke-down ex-soldier got all wet-eyed about that piece o' junk—"

"That's enough from you," Henry said, and put his hand

in the noisy fellow's face and shoved him backward. Frink sat down hard, looked up at Henry resentfully.

"I orter get one o' them medals, me and Cy, too," he grumped.

"I told you to shut your big mouth, Frink," Henry cut him off. "Next time it will be my boot in your face."

Frink subsided. Kibbe eased up beside Henry.

"Don't pay no mind to Freddy, Generalsir," he said, "he don't mean no harm." Kibbe glanced at Frink cowering on the floor.

"Guess now old Jonah'll skedaddle back here to town," Kibbe rambled on, watching the screen. "He got out ahead o' them spodder machines; he's in the clear."

"It would serve you right if he did," General Henry said coldly. "But look: After all he's been through, he's preparing to ambush them as they come out. Instead of using the last of his energy reserve to run for cover, he's attacking a superior force."

"Don't do it, Johnny," Dub begged. "You done all you could for them, and they paid you back by blowing you up. To heck with 'em. Run for it, and save yourself. I'll see you get repaired!"

"Even if he could hear you," Henry told the boy, "that's one order he'd ignore. His destiny is to fight and, if need be, to die in combat."

"Damn fool," Kibbe said. "It ain't got a chance against them three Yavac heavies."

On the screen, the Bolo was seen to enter a wide side crevasse and come to rest. A moment later, the first Yavac appeared and at once erupted in fire as the Bolo blasted it at close range with its main battery of Hellbores. The next two Deng machines veered off and took up divergent courses back to the Cut.

"They'll stand off and bombard," Henry said. "I think Unit JNA has exhausted his energies. But of course, if their fire is accurate, he can absorb a percentage of it and make use of it to recharge. They don't know that, or they'd simply bypass him. Instead, he's got them bottled up. Even in death, he's protecting us."

* * *

It was an hour after the first ship of the Terran Relief Force had arrived. After Henry had briefed the captain commanding, he returned to Dub, who, with Mick, had been awaiting his return at the hastily tidied office of the Planetary Rep.

"I think we can be sure," Davis told them, after an exchange of SWIFT messages with Sector, "that the museum will be rebuilt promptly, better than ever, and that Unit JNA will be fully restored and recommissioned as a Historic Monument in perpetuity. And his commander will, of course, have free access to him to confer any time he wishes."

"That's good," Dub said soberly. "I'll see to it he's never lonely again."

My young commander has been confirmed in the rank of Battle Captain, and, after depot maintenance and upgrading to modern specifications, I have been recommissioned as a Fighting Unit of the Line. This carries with it permanent full stand-by alert status, an energy level at which my memory storage files are fully available to me, as are also my extensive music and literary archives. Thus, I have been enabled to renew my study of the Gilgamesh epic, including all the new cuneiform material turned up in recent years at Nippur. The achievements of the great heroes of Man are an inspiration to me and should the Enemy again attack, I shall be ready.

A SHORT HISTORY OF THE BOLO FIGHTING MACHINES

THE FIRST APPEARANCE in history of the concept of the armored vehicle was the use of wooden-shielded war wagons by the reformer John Huss in fifteenth-century Bohemia. Thereafter the idea lapsed—unless one wishes to consider the armored knights of the Middle Ages, mounted on armored war-horses—until the twentieth century. In 1915, during the Great War, the British developed in secrecy a steel-armored motor car; for security reasons during construction it was called a "tank," and the appellation remained in use for the rest of the century. First sent into action at the Somme in A.D. 1916 (BAE 29), the new device was immensely impressive and was soon copied by all belligerents. By Phase Two of the Great War, A.D. 1939-1945, tank corps were a basic element in all modern armies. Quite naturally, great improvements were soon made over the original clumsy, fragile, feeble, and temperamental tank. The British Sheridan and Centurion, the German Tiger, the American Sherman, and the Russian T-34 were all highly potent weapons in their own milieu.

During the long period of cold war following A.D. 1945, development continued, especially in the United States. By 1989 the direct ancestor of the Bolo line had been constructed by the Bolo Division of General Motors. This machine, at one hundred fifty tons almost twice the weight of its Phase Two predecessors, was designated the Bolo Mark I Model B. No Bolo Model A of any mark ever existed, since it was felt that the Ford Motor Company had preempted that designation permanently. The same is true of the name "Model T."

The Mark I was essentially a bigger and better conventional tank, carrying a crew of three and, via power-assisted servos, completely manually operated, with the exception of the capability to perform a number of preset routine functions such as patrol duty with no crew aboard. The Mark II that followed in 1995 was even more highly automated, carrying an on-board fire-control computer and requiring only a single operator. The Mark III of 2020 was considered by some to be almost a step backward, its highly complex controls normally requiring a crew of two, though in an emergency a single experienced man could fight the machine with limited effectiveness. These were by no means negligible weapons systems, their individual firepower exceeding that of a contemporary battalion of heavy infantry, while they were of course correspondingly heavily armored and shielded. The outer durachrome war hull of the Mark III was twenty millimeters thick and capable of withstanding any offensive weapon then known, short of a contact nuclear blast.

The first completely automated Bolo, designed to operate normally without a man aboard, was the landmark Mark XV Model M, originally dubbed *Resartus* for obscure reasons, but later officially named *Stupendous*. This model, first commissioned in the twenty-fifth century, was widely used throughout the Eastern Arm during the Era of Expansion and remained in service on remote worlds for over two centuries, acquiring many improvements in detail along the way while remaining basically unchanged, though increasing sophistication of circuitry and weapons vastly upgraded its effectiveness. The Bolo *Horrendous* Model R, of 2807 was the culmination of this phase of Bolo development, though older models lingered on in the active service of minor powers for centuries.

Thereafter the development of the Mark XVI-XIX consisted largely in further refinement and improvement in detail of the Mark XV. Provision continued to be made for a human occupant, now as a passenger rather than an operator, usually an officer who wished to observe the action at first hand. Of course, these machines normally went into action under the guidance of individually prepared computer programs, while military regulations continued to require installation of devices for halting or even self-destructing the machine at any time. This latter feature was mainly intended to prevent capture and hostile use of the great machine by an enemy. It was at this time that the first-line Bolos in Terran service were organized into a brigade, known as the Dinochrome Brigade, and deployed as a strategic unit. Tactically the regiment was the basic Bolo unit.

The always-present though perhaps unlikely possibility of capture and use of a Bolo by an enemy was a constant source of anxiety to military leaders and, in time, gave rise to the next and final major advance in Bolo technology: the self-directing (and, quite incidentally, self-aware) Mark XX Model B Bolo *Tremendous*. At this time it was customary to designate each individual unit by a three-letter group indicating hull style, power unit, and main armament. This gave rise to the custom of forming a nickname from the letters, such as "Johnny" from JNY, adding to the tendency to anthropomorphize the great fighting machines.

The Mark XX was at first greeted with little enthusiasm by the High Command, who now professed to believe that an unguided-by-operator Bolo would potentially be capable of running amok and wreaking destruction on its owners. Many observers have speculated by hindsight that a more candid objection would have been that the legitimate area of command function was about to be invaded by mere machinery. Machinery the Bolos were, but never *mere*.

At one time an effort was made to convert a number of surplus Bolos to peacetime use by such modifications as the addition of a soil-moving blade to a Mark XII Bolo WV/I Continental Siege Unit, the installation of seats for four men, and the description of the resulting irresistible force as a "tractor." This idea came to naught, however, since the machines retained their half-megaton/second firepower and were never widely accepted as normal agricultural equipment.

As the great conflict of the post-thirtieth-century era wore on—a period variously known as the Last War and, later, as the Lost War—Bolos of Mark XXVIII and later series were organized into independently operating brigades that did their own strategic as well as tactical planning. Many of these machines still exist in functional condition in out-of-the-way corners of the former Terran Empire. At this time the program of locating and neutralizing these ancient weapons continues.